S0-BBE-304

SO BY KAYVION LEWIS

The Half-Class

KAYVION LEWIS

THIEVES' GAMBIT

 NANCY PAULSEN BOOKS

NANCY PAULSEN BOOKS

An imprint of Penguin Random House LLC, New York

First published in the United States of America by Nancy Paulsen Books,
an imprint of Penguin Random House LLC, 2023

Copyright © 2023 by Kayvion Lewis

Penguin supports copyright. Copyright fuels creativity, encourages diverse voices,
promotes free speech, and creates a vibrant culture. Thank you for buying an authorized
edition of this book and for complying with copyright laws by not reproducing, scanning,
or distributing any part of it in any form without permission. You are supporting writers
and allowing Penguin to continue to publish books for every reader.

Nancy Paulsen Books & colophon are trademarks of Penguin Random House LLC.
The Penguin colophon is a registered trademark of Penguin Books Limited.

Visit us online at PenguinRandomHouse.com.

Library of Congress Cataloging-in-Publication Data
Names: Lewis, Kayvion, author.
Title: Thieves' gambit / Kayvion Lewis.
Description: New York: Nancy Paulsen Books, 2023. | Summary:
Seventeen-year-old Ross Quest, a master thief, enters the Thieves' Gambit,
a competition consisting of dangerous international heists,
in order to save her mother's life.
Identifiers: LCCN 2023019090 (print) | LCCN 2023019091 (ebook) | ISBN 9780593625361 (hardcover) |
ISBN 9780593625378 (ebook)
Subjects: CYAC: Robbers and outlaws—Fiction. | Contests—Fiction. | Mothers and daughters—Fiction. |
LCGFT: Thrillers (Fiction) | Novels.
Classification: LCC PZ7.1.L519 Th 2023 (print) | LCC PZ7.1.L519 (ebook) | DDC [Fic]—dc23
LC record available at https://lccn.loc.gov/2023019090
LC ebook record available at https://lccn.loc.gov/2023019091

Printed in the United States of America

ISBN 9780593625361 (hardcover)

ISBN 9780593698051 (international edition)

1st Printing
LSCH

Edited by Stacey Barney
Design by Suki Boynton · Text set in Mundo Serif

This book is a work of fiction. Any references to historical events, real people,
or real places are used fictitiously. Other names, characters, places, and events are
products of the author's imagination, and any resemblance to actual events
or places or persons, living or dead, is entirely coincidental.

The publisher does not have any control over and does not assume any
responsibility for author or third-party websites or their content.

THIEVES' GAMBIT

ONE

A **QUEST CAN'T** trust anyone in this world—except for a Quest.

So when a Quest, particularly Mama Quest, tells me to curl up like a Twizzler twisted into a pretzel inside a cabinet so small it would be illegal to keep your dog in a cage the same size, I *trust* she has a good reason for it. Or at least, whatever I'm stealing is gonna be worth it.

If I were a normal person, my legs would be in a coma right now. But I guess Mom's intense flexibility training comes in handy for jobs like this.

I'd been crammed in here, on the secluded side of the mansion, for about three hours, scrolling through my dummy Insta. Over the last few months, stalking accounts about dorm life had become more addictive than K-dramas on Netflix.

When my battery dipped to 20 percent at midnight, I had to stop. Mom warned me not to use it up on irrelevant stuff—if I missed her text, I'd be screwed. So instead, I thrummed my gloved fingers impatiently until my screen lit up.

ATTN: Rosalyn Quest, Gambit Invitation

Not Mom's text, though—an email? Did one of the summer gymnastics programs finally get back to me? Or that competitive cheer one? I'd emailed a lot of college summer programs for high schoolers in the middle of the night a few days ago, when our house felt the loneliest and the thought of spending weeks on a bustling college campus with other kids my age was the most refreshing. None had hit me back until now. I was starting to worry they'd seen through the transcripts I frantically forged for the applications.

A text notification dropped down before I could unlock the screen. This time it *was* from Mom. Almost like she sensed what I was about to look at and virtually slapped my hand away.

Your turn.

The email would have to wait.

I cracked open the cabinet door, slipping my fingers under to take the weight off the hinges so they wouldn't creak. A simple trick, but one I'd known since before I could write my name. I took a quick peek out.

The hallway was deserted. According to Mom's recon, this wing was typically empty; she and the other maids spent most of their time polishing vases in the private gallery in the other wing. Here there was less security.

I crept past the mansion's rooms with untouched four-poster beds, sparse bookcases, and bare end tables. The still quiet should have been unsettling, but I was no stranger to lonely houses. If I blinked for too long, I might have thought I was back in our family's home on Andros.

The blueprints I'd memorized took me through a living area on the first floor, where an accent dresser covered with picture frames caught my eye. None of the other rooms had anything so . . . personal.

I picked up the farthest frame. A beaming group of college kids posed on the steps of a redbrick building. In the bottom corner, in neat, black script: *Freshman Year*.

Memories. Relationships. I could steal the picture, but I couldn't take those. If I wanted them, I'd have to earn them myself. Away from home. Away from Mom.

A soft sound made me freeze.

I put down the photo and ducked behind a sofa. Crouching, I unrolled my weapon of choice. The Quest fam isn't fond of guns—they're not stealthy. Mom carries a knife, and according to her, Granny once had a collection of syringes with fast-acting sedatives that she could dish out like spices by a five-star chef.

I suspected I didn't have the stomach to sink a blade—or needle—into someone's flesh, so instead, I adopted the meteor bracelet. The length of links is easy to wrap around my wrist, and the heavy cherry-sized metal weight at the end pops snugly into a magnetized ring on my middle finger. It's less difficult to smuggle past checkpoints than blades, and in my hands, just as effective, if not as final, as a knife.

The pit-pat drew closer.

So much for no security.

Rearing back to snap my chain around someone's neck, I choked out a laugh. The prettiest cat popped onto the top of the sofa. A Siamese with sandy fur that looked like she'd dipped her paws and rubbed her face in ash. She blinked at me with vibrant blue eyes, then jumped to the carpet and purred, rubbing herself between my feet.

I rewrapped the bracelet around my wrist and scratched her behind the ears. She mewed and rolled onto her back. I'd just made her month.

When I was a kid, I binged vlogs on pet adoption while Mom was gone on long jobs. That was before I realized that nothing without Quest blood was ever setting foot in our house—animals included.

Siamese cats are popular because they're gorgeous, but they also get lonely easily. Without companions, they tend to die early. I had a feeling the owner of this isolated house hadn't thought too much about getting their cat a friend.

When I continued on, the cat followed, tail flicking happily. I nudged her away. Cute as she was, picking up a feline sidekick wasn't in the game plan. Turning, I broke into a run. French doors divided the next hallway from the last. I clicked them shut before the cat could get through. She mewed in a voice just low enough to break my heart, before darting off.

With her gone, I reopened the doors in case security passed through and noticed a change.

My mental map led me to a room with the curtains pulled wide. The Kenyan stars and moon lent just enough light to see how stock-standard the room was. Tidy furniture. Tasteful wall art. A bed no one had ever slept in. Another room for ghosts.

A lone vase sat on the nightstand.

Qianlong period porcelain, circa 1740. Estimated value: irrelevant. The only price that mattered was the sum our client offered to get it out of their rival's collection and into theirs. A week ago, this vase had been on display in the private gallery on the other side of the mansion.

Until Mom started working here as a maid.

She called this a Jigsaw Job. Piece by piece, she smuggled in shards of a replica and assembled it. For someone as skilled as Mom, switching the real one with the fake was child's play. Unfortunately, the owner was—rightfully—concerned about theft. Security searched the staff each day when they left. Mom could move the vase around inside the house, but she wasn't gonna get it out.

That was my job.

I dragged out the case Mom had left under the bed. The cushioned interior was perfect for shock absorption. Pro tip: If you don't have a way of getting your product out undamaged, don't bother at all.

Something rattled inside the vase as I picked it up. When I tipped it, a string of diamonds poured into my palm. I rolled my eyes. Mom has so many tennis bracelets you could see her from Mars if she wore them all. If I asked why, she'd just respond, *Why not?*

A laser pointer was tucked in the side of the case. I angled the beam into the motion sensor on one side of the window. Fun fact about motion sensors: You can trip most up with a five-dollar laser pointer off Amazon. They only detect motion when something disrupts the beam connecting them, so I made sure they thought that beam was always there, keeping my laser pointed directly at the sensor while I slipped out. Simple things work best. I would have had a harder time if they'd bolted the window shut with nails. A *little* harder.

In about sixty seconds, I was out and on the windowsill like

Spider-Girl. I squeezed the case between my thighs and was about to slide the window closed when something burst into the room.

Something desperate to get out.

The cat vaulted past me and straight onto the lawn. Landing, well, like a cat. Thank Jesus I still had the laser pointed at the sensor, or that would've been not so great for me.

She mewed endlessly, begging me to come down and play with her. She was persistent, that was for sure.

With the window shut, I scaled the brick wall to the camera facing the lawn. I had ten seconds to stop it from swinging toward me. No time for finesse. I ripped out the larger of the two cords feeding into the wall. The camera stopped midturn, stuck until someone came to fix it. Hopefully not until long after I was gone.

The cat was still screaming her head off.

"Okay, I'm coming," I said.

And now I was talking to cats. But it wasn't like the video-only camera—Mom had gotten the serial numbers off the cams so we could look up their specs ahead of time—was going to hear me.

I leapt down. The cat rubbed herself again all over my legs. How could I resist? I swooped her into my arm that wasn't holding the case and let her melt into my chest.

I made my way quickly to the industrial lawn mowers waiting in a line, ready for the morning. The little four-by-two storage compartment under the driver's bench, right above the engine and behind the bags of fertilizer, was going to be my suite for the next few hours.

I looked out over the horizon, where waves of savannah grass and bushwillow trees met the star-speckled sky. In moments like this, I understood why my family had been in love with this globe-trotting profession for three generations.

But it wasn't always starry nights and cool breezes.

"You know I can't take you with me." The cat made a soft clicking sound as I tickled above her tail. "At least you've got a pretty view, yeah?"

She meowed, and maybe I was losing it, but it sounded like cat for "Are you serious?" I set her down and pushed aside fertilizer bags before folding myself into the space, keeping the case snug to my chest. Everything smelled like gasoline and mildew. But so be it. Mom would tell me to think about a new laptop. Five-hundred-dollar braids. Custom kicks that no one but she and Auntie would ever see me wearing.

I pulled the fertilizer bags back into place, but the cat wiggled through a tiny opening between two of the bags. She settled atop the case on my chest, still purring and mewing.

"You want me to steal you too, is that it?"

She licked my cheek. Okay, she could stay. For a while. I wondered how long it would take her owner to notice if I *did* steal her.

From my hiding place I caught a flicker of light. No, two lights? Somebody was patrolling the lawn. They were early . . . Had something triggered an alarm? Had they noticed the camera?

The cat's purring sounded like an electric fan. I wanted to shush her, but how do you quiet a cat?

I reached to unwrap my bracelet. It sounded like they were coming my way. How the hell was I going to pounce out of this spot fast enough to get the jump on them?

Crap.

"Nala . . ." A man clicked his tongue. Kibble rattled in a jar. "Where are you, you little brat?"

Double crap.

I tried to push Nala out, but she kept springing onto the case, purring relentlessly and *mewing*.

Then I remembered something else about Siamese cats. They're also the most vocal cat breed.

"I can hear her," another man's voice said. "How did she get outside?"

The other guy scoffed. "No clue. This stupid cat's always trying to run away. We'll put her in a closet until Boss returns."

With everything in me, I willed Nala to be quiet. Why hadn't she just run away when she escaped from the window? She could've been long gone by now. The thought of her panicking in a closet for days or weeks twisted my conscience. If she would just be quiet, I'd take her with me. Screw what Mom wanted.

But she wouldn't be quiet.

And they were getting nearer.

I'm sorry, Nala. My arm twisted around to grab the laser pointer from my back pocket. I shined the little red dot over the case, instantly making her eyes dilate and her muscles stiffen. Cat reflexes: activated. The flashlight beams shifted away from the mowers for a split second, and feeling crappier than I expected to, I shined the laser onto the mansion's wall. Nala darted out, tearing across the grass toward the pinprick of light and right into the sights of her pursuers.

"I got her!" Nala's desperate hissing filled up the night. She was putting up a hell of a fight, but she'd already lost.

The flashlights faded. Everything did, except for my own quiet breathing.

I hated what I did to that cat. But she should know, you can't really trust anyone.

TWO

THE FIRST WORDS out of Mom's mouth after a job are never "Are you okay, Ross?" Instead, it's "You have it?"

I rolled out of the mower, landing right at Mom's feet. Never mind the fact that I'd been about to die of heat exhaustion and had been nearly suffocated by fumes for the last half hour since the mower started moving. I was fine. If I was alive and with her, then I was fine. The target was the important thing.

"Look at my baby, being exemplary and all," Mom said, clicking the case open and examining the prize. She looked completely unlike herself disguised in landscaper overalls. Very different from her typical polished island baddie look, even when she fished the tennis bracelet out and slipped it onto her wrist.

Mom sighed, watching the way the bracelet's diamonds danced in the morning sunlight. I had to admit, diamonds suited Mom. She was a glamorous sort of beauty. Long weave and tasteful eyelash extensions. Thick hips and a pinched waist she loved to accentuate—the complete opposite of my more slender build. Her style was dramatic, not fur coat and stilettos level, but enough that whenever we went someplace where she could really flex herself, she was always drawing double takes.

Hence her love for diamonds. Anything that could make her sparkle more.

Mom pressed a quick kiss to my forehead. She smelled like cut grass and gasoline, but I probably smelled worse.

"Exemplary like my mama," I said, because I knew she'd love to hear it, and hopped up onto the driver's bench, leaving room for her too. With a contented smile, probably more about the compliment than the successful job, she cranked the mower on, and we headed toward the edge of the property, where an off-road Jeep, water, and air-conditioning cold enough to make me cry with gratitude waited.

I pressed my forehead to the car's air vent.

"We can go somewhere cooler next." Mom eyed my worship of the cold air filtering through from behind the wheel of the Jeep. "Maybe southern Argentina. Or the Alps, eh?"

"We literally just got off a job. Not to mention, the Boscherts." I'd heard they hadn't appreciated our last jobs in Denmark and Italy, breaking their unofficial claim on the high-end thieving market in Europe. In the world of family-run thieving empires, there could only be one top dog, or at least one per continent.

Forcing myself to sit back, I swiped the charger and plugged in my dead phone. The side-eye from Mom told me she didn't approve. We were having a conversation, so I should be paying attention to her.

"Good thing we'd sooner be caught stealing costume jewelry than caring about what the Boscherts want." She cocked a perfectly threaded brow at me, so I gave her the nod she wanted.

The spark of an idea kindled in my mind. "I mean, if you want us to pick up more jobs in Europe, it'd make sense for someone to network over there. Maybe if I went to school for a while, as a cover, it'd be a good opportunity?"

I held my breath. There were probably smoother ways for me to bring up the leaving thing again. All my life I'd never been anywhere without Mom, or Auntie, and I'd been a lot of places. I thought when I'd turned seventeen a few months ago, when other Bahamian kids graduate high school, she'd start being less . . . you know.

"Hm . . . maybe not." Mom looked straight ahead into the empty stretch of road and savannah grasses. I waited for an elaboration. A reason, something. Instead, she said, "Once we're back, we'll lounge and watch something low-budget for a whole week, huh, baby?"

I forced a smile. "That sounds cool."

Satisfied, she picked a playlist on her phone and turned the volume up. My screen glowed. An email. From one of the summer programs.

I angled it away from Mom as I read.

Dear Rosalyn,

Thank you for applying for our High-Performance Gymnastics Summer Camp. We are pleased to invite you to our second session (July 1–July 28), or if it's not too late notice, we have one spot remaining in our first session (June 2–June 29). As a nationally renowned program, we are excited to attract dozens of talented young athletes every summer who are passionate about befriending peers in their field. We hope you'll choose to join us for this unique experience.

The email went on with housing and fees and contact info. The more I read, the harder it was to school my expression. My bullshit transcripts and fake competition scores actually worked. I could be there . . . in a week if I wanted to be. Today was May 26.

Nala should've outrun the guards when she had the chance. Now she was stuck. I wasn't going to make the same mistake.

I typed back. **I'd love to come!**

Mom rapped along with the lyrics blaring from the speakers, nudging my shoulder to jump in with her. As usual, I pursed my lips and put up a fake fight before joining in. She used a verse about ice on her wrist to flick her new bracelet, and I laughed. On the outside, everything was the same. Same post-job high. Same me and her. But it couldn't be like that forever. I felt like I'd just shifted the wheel of my life off its axis, right under her nose, and she hadn't noticed.

I scrolled through my inbox. Where was that message I got before Mom texted? Weird. Unless it wasn't in my personal email . . .

The black box email account. How our family accepted jobs. Accessible only through the deep web, and 100 percent hack-proof and untraceable—that was the way Mom explained it to eight-year-old me. You needed a passcode just to get an email sent to it. I *never* got notifications from the black box email. It should have been impossible.

I punched in the five consecutive passcodes for the black box's account.

The message was there. Still unopened. Mom must not have checked it yet.

My heart caught in my throat. Someone was emailing the black box just for me?

Hello Rosalyn Quest,

Congratulations on earning our interest. You are invited to participate in this year's Thieves' Gambit.

The competition will begin in one week. We anticipate a two-week run time. Please contact us to make arrangements.

—The Organizers

THREE

THIEVES' **GAMBIT. A** competition. Days later, back home in the Bahamas, while I should have been overwhelmed with thoughts about my summer camp escape, the invitation's words rattled in my brain like dice in a Yahtzee cup.

I assumed—I'd never played Yahtzee. Family game night lost its charm when Mom refused to stop cheating.

It was enough to distract me from my agility practice. I'd been in the training room for over an hour—makes for good stress relief—trying to ace the leap from one square-foot-wide box to another seven feet away. Last month I set a personal best at six and a half feet. Afterward, Mom told me she could jump seven and a half when she was my age.

Balancing, I bent my knees and tried again. The second my feet left the box, I knew I'd screwed up. Not enough momentum. The ball of my foot scraped the edge, and gravity caught me before I could catch myself. I crashed into the mats.

I huffed, blowing one of my braids away from my face. A shadow crossed over me. Auntie Jaya stared down, hands on her flared hips. For being seven years younger, she sure as hell looked just like Mom. If I squinted, I might have thought it was Mom frowning at me with those trademark Quest pinched lips.

"What's wrong with you?" She didn't offer me a hand. No one offered hands up in the Quest family. "It's your goofy shoes. They're tripping you up."

I glanced down at my kicks for the day. Custom-embroidered white Chucks with hundreds of tiny gold leaves painstakingly sewn into the canvas, painted along the rubber seams, and cut into the soles, with sparkling gold laces to match. My shoes were gorgeous. Auntie must have been selectively tasteless.

"I take personal offense to that, Auntie. And even more offense to the thought that I would buy anything I couldn't move in." It wasn't like I collected pumps and platform boots. My custom Chucks were perfectly practical for training.

"Then what's causing this? Come on, tell Auntie what's distracting you." Auntie made it sound like she was annoyed to have to ask, but seeming too cool for every conversation was just her MO. She always came when I needed her, speaking Rosalyn fluently enough to know a message saying **What's up with you** 👀 really meant there was something I wanted to talk about. And in this house on an island so rural convenience stores were in people's living rooms, where you could sit on the gravel road all day and see more wild boars than cars, people to talk to who weren't my mom were few and far between.

Auntie was already here waiting when our private plane dropped us back home.

"Have you ever heard of something called the Thieves' Gambit?" It was the first time I'd said the words aloud, and they sounded as bizarre as they had in my head. *Thieves'*, plural possessive? It was an oxymoron. Thieves don't just get together.

Auntie tensed like she was waiting to get punched in the stomach.

So she had heard of it.

I sat up, leaning back on my palms.

"The organization sent you an invitation?"

"A week ago. Who said they were an organization? Do you know who they are?"

"What'd you say? Did you respond?" Auntie completely ignored my questions.

My nose scrunched. "I know better than to answer weird messages in the black box. I deleted the email as soon as I saw it."

She relaxed. That jab to the stomach didn't land. "Good."

"My turn. Who the hell is the organization, and why do you know about them and I don't?"

I kip-upped to my feet. Auntie, Mom, and I were all about the same height, so I could look her in the eye. If I was curious before, now I had to know. There weren't supposed to be any secrets in this family.

Auntie clicked her tongue, drawing out the moment. "They're just a bunch of rich schmucks with a power complex who run the Gambit once every year or so. That's all *I* know about them."

All *she* knew. Did she mean Mom might know more?

The way she avoided eye contact made me think this all had intentionally not been brought up before, and therefore prying out more information about this organization was going to be a chore. I redirected.

"And the Gambit is . . . ?"

For a second, I thought she really wasn't going to tell me.

"It's a competition, a thieving competition. Kinda like a private . . . illegal game show." She moved her braids over her shoulder and sauntered away, fishing a pair of handcuffs out of a supply box packed with a variety of practice locks.

I followed her. "You were holding your breath about me entering an illegal game show run by a secret one-percenter club?"

"I said *like* a game show. Don't get it twisted, this isn't *The Price Is Right: Heist Edition*." She whipped a bobby pin out of her hair and started picking the handcuffs. "From what I've heard, somebody always leaves bloody. If they get to leave at all." The cuffs popped open. She gestured for my hands. Mindlessly, I gave them over, and she closed one of the cuffs on my wrist.

"Why would anyone play, then? Killer money, yeah?" Thieves never do anything for free.

"More like killer reward." Auntie turned me around and slapped on the other cuff, locking my hands behind my back. On instinct, I double-Dutch jumped the cuffs and fished my own bobby out of my braids. I had enough in there to build a little castle. "They say the winner . . ." Auntie continued. "Gets a wish."

I cocked my head at her. "A wish? Like, there's a shooting star, look, make one?"

"Shooting stars don't grant wishes. Money does." She snapped her fingers in front of my face. "Don't get distracted."

Right. The cuffs. I slipped the head of the pin inside and felt for the locking mechanism.

Auntie frowned. "You could have gotten out easier without the pin . . ."

"I'm not letting you break my thumb, Auntie." The first cuff clicked open—no bone breaking required. She'd been trying to get me on the bone-out-of-socket training for years. It was a line I preferred not to cross.

"It only hurts the first few times," Auntie insisted. I got the other lock open and dropped the cuffs back on the table. She studied me. "You didn't tell your mama about your invitation, did you?"

There was an unsaid *why* behind her words. Trying to ignore it, I moved to reset the boxes for another jump.

"She's busy," I said. "Planning the next heist and all. You know."

And I'm planning on dipping out in a few days . . . Curious as a thieving game was, I didn't need to risk getting distracted by it or anything else Mom might want to drag me into. An underground game wasn't going to help me make friends, especially one that involved a bunch of deceptive con artists.

"Mm-hmm." Auntie may speak fluent Rosalyn, but I spoke fluent Auntie Jaya too. Translation: *Try again.*

I sighed and, instead of jumping back up on the box, sat down. The training room around us was littered with all sorts of practice material. Safes, dartboards, dummies for arm bars and headlocks, boxes of ropes with different knots to unravel. This wasn't the only room that hinted at my family's business.

All over the house there were trophies from jobs spanning con-tinents and decades. I knew all their stories by the time I was five. Grand-Papa swiped that book off a shelf in the US Library of Congress. That still life? It was in storage under the Louvre until Great-Aunt Sara got there. The coins in the bowl where we kept the keys? Auntie pocketed them off the president of Uganda's chief of staff. The house is full of little mementos, lots of them left over from the days the rest of my family lived here too. Back before Mom had the infamous falling-out I still hadn't gotten an explanation for, when even her parents decided they didn't want anything to do with her outside of making sure jobs didn't overlap. I'd say the trophies were hidden in plain sight if there were anyone around to hide them from.

My whole damn house was a thief's paradise. A reminder of what I was born for. The job, the family, those should be the only thing I ever lived for.

But it wasn't all memories and trophies.

There were fresh locks to crack on the fridge and cabinets every week. Car keys would go missing, so you'd have to hot-wire one if you wanted to go anywhere. Let's not forget the many times Mom locked me out of all my devices and the only way I could get the new code was by pickpocketing it off her. Living without a device on this island was its own form of hell. Mom said our family lived this life because it was liberating. Bound-less. Fun. Sure, the jobs could be. But the rest of the time . . .

I couldn't spend another year by myself, isolated like this. Trusting people in the industry, outside of the family, was out of the question. The options were stay locked up here or give up the life and make normal friends. I would give up the exhilara-tion of weekly heists for that.

Auntie's question still hung in the air. *Why didn't I tell Mom about it?*

I only shrugged, fiddling with the end of a braid. "What if I want to take a break from all the thieving stuff for a while?"

"Maybe there's something else you want to do on this break." She said it softly. Like if she spoke at just the right volume with just the right tone, she'd probe the truth out of me.

I crossed my arms. Obvious tactic or not, it was working. Something about Auntie, maybe because she was younger than Mom, was less intimidating. Maybe I could tell her about my getaway plan. I could frame it like there was something for the family I wanted to learn on campus. Something that made it seem less like I was ungratefully tossing aside the cushy, high-octane family I was lucky enough to be born into. She could help me broach the topic with Mom.

The sound of sandals clacking down the hall cut through my thoughts. A reminder—Mom was always listening. At least, as long as I was in the same house as her. I blurted out the best response I could think of. "I don't want anything besides my family. What would I be without us?"

"Boring? Poor? Not living in paradise on one of the most beautiful islands in the world?" Mom strode inside, looking absolutely Caribbean chic in high-waisted jeans and a vibrant off-the-shoulder red top. She finished tapping something out on her phone before gracing us with her full attention. "What're my babies talking about? Nightmares?"

I held my breath. Luckily, it didn't seem like Auntie was going to tattle about my Gambit invitation. I could tell by the way she punched one fist on her hip and narrowed her eyes at Mom that her mind wasn't on snitching me out at all. "Stop calling me your baby! You only have one daughter, and I'm not her."

"Oh . . ." Mom cooed at her. "My dolly is throwing a fit." She pinched Auntie's cheeks before getting her hands slapped away. Apparently, Mom used to think of Auntie as her real-life baby doll when they were kids. When Auntie was five and Mom was twelve, Mom convinced her for a whole month that she wasn't a real girl, just a doll. Twenty-seven years later, and Mom's still messing with her.

Auntie's jaw tightened. She stormed out.

"You shouldn't tease her like that," I said. "It bothers her, for real."

Mom scoffed and flicked some dirt from under her nail. "You don't have a sister. You don't understand."

That stung. No friends, no dad, *and* no siblings. At least two of those were her fault.

I smothered the instant guilt that came with that last thought. It wasn't fair of me to resent Mom for the whole dad situation. She was never into relationships—that was as deep a description as she ever gave me when it came to her sexuality—so she went the sperm donor route. Of all the men in the world, she just had to pick a donor who'd died a couple weeks after turning in his first, uh, sample. Someone who would never be around for me to hunt down or to come looking for any kids that might have popped up from his donation. Mom swore she didn't find out he was deceased until she was in her third trimester, and I knew she wouldn't lie about something like that. But still, it was the kind of thing that was always in the back of my head when I needed a reason to be mad at her.

Mom eyed the boxes behind me. "Seven feet?"

I squirmed. "Almost."

She nodded, then stood in front of me. Though we were the same height now, she still felt taller. Big enough to wrap me in one of those pick-you-up-and-spin-you-around bear hugs she did when I was younger. Coconut lotion wafted off her, and for a second, I really did feel like I was little again. Maybe it was a Pavlov-type training, but smelling her, letting her tuck one of the braids behind my ear, it filled me with comfort. Confidence. This was Mom. If I really wanted something, I should be able to just . . . ask her, right?

My tongue felt dry. But I spoke anyway. "You know . . . Louisiana State University has one of the best gymnastics programs in the US? I bet those students could make a seven-foot jump, easy."

Mom tensed. She drew away, slowly.

That warm Mummy-loves-you look was gone.

I shouldn't have said anything.

"Come on, Rossie?" She groaned, sounding more annoyed than anything else.

"I don't know what the big deal is!" I insisted. "I'm seventeen. All the other seventeen-year-olds on the island are going to start college soon."

"And how would you know that?"

"You're right, I don't know that, because I don't know anybody!" Years of the same thing being drilled into me repeated in my head. *No, you can't walk down to the neighbors. No, you can't go to Central Andros High. Other families can't be trusted.*

Sure, I got it. Revealing the whole thief-family thing and even getting friendly with people on the island weren't stellar moves, and I'd learned a long time ago to never, ever trust someone else in the same profession as us. But if I was away, if I was pretending to be a sheep around other sheep in a whole different country, if I was keeping my guard up, would it really be that dangerous . . . to meet other people?

"You know lots of people," Mom insisted. "Me and Jaya, and Granny and Papa are always a phone call away. And my auntie Sara."

Did she realize how few people that actually was? Not to mention the fact that I was the only one of those people under thirty. I folded my arms in on myself. "They don't count. That's just family. That's not enough—"

I tried to stop myself, but it slipped out before I realized what I was saying. My eyes shot to Mom. The curl of her lips told me the exact translation she'd heard. *You're not enough.*

"I didn't mean—"

She pressed a finger to her lips. I shut up. "Rosalyn," she started, "family doesn't leave you. Family doesn't lie to you. Family you can trust. Look at what we do for a living. Everyone wants something—a lot of the times things that belong to other people. People will play you like a violin to get whatever they need from you. People you think are your friends, people you think you can trust, they'll snap your heart in half and leave you to die. You're smarter than that, baby girl. If you're not yet, then I'm smart enough to make that choice for you. Because I love you. So no, you're not going anywhere. Not without me. Final. Decision."

It was final. The word was on the stone, and the verdict was rendered. No cross-examination. No testimony from me. I clenched my jaw painfully. Heat bubbled in my chest. But there was nothing to do with my anger—it wasn't like I was going to start throwing things.

And if I was going to go route B with this, route *screw what she wants, I'm doing it anyway*, then I needed to keep my calm. No letting anything slip.

Mom and I locked eyes. She was waiting for a response. I forced a nod, and she brightened, clapping her hands under her chin and smiling like what she'd just shot down was no big deal.

"Good girl. Now, where's that pretty black backpack with the gold zippers I got you?"

I froze. That was the bag I'd started stashing things for the summer camp in. Was she already onto me?

"I dunno, somewhere. Why?"

She hesitated. "Don't hate me, but you should pack it. I need you on a last-minute job. Leaving tonight."

"Tonight! We just got back!" It was great that she hadn't found my getaway bag, and but this was pretty bad too. Getting dragged into another job did *not* vibe with my plan.

"Relax, baby girl, I'm not whisking you to another continent. It's just over on Paradise Island. Two days max, we'll be in and out. I'll AirDrop you the details, 'kay?" Mom had started walking away, as if I'd already said yes.

"But I—" She glanced back at me. "What if I have something to do?"

Mom's expression darkened. "What do you have to do that's more important than your family, Ross?"

New experiences?

Friendship?

The chance to figure out if there *was* something more important?

None of those was the correct answer. She'd already told me how it was. My family, my mom, was all I could count on. Nothing else mattered.

I understood why Auntie hated being called Mom's little dolly. Sometimes, it didn't seem like Mom was joking. She was always treating us like her toys, always playing knowing she would win.

If I was going to leave, maybe it was my turn to toy with her. An idea was forming in my head. If I had to show up for this job, what if I disappeared in the middle of it? Wouldn't that be the last thing she was expecting?

I smiled, a real, genuine beam, and wrapped my arms around Mom's waist.

"Nothing's more important than us." I squeezed her side.

She eyed me for a second before possessively snuggling me back. "Good girl." She squeezed a little tighter. "Remember, there's nothing and no one else out there. No one you can really trust, anyway."

FOUR

MAPPED AND PLOTTED." I rotated the iPad for Mom to see on the other side of the table. She turned her attention from her fresh manicure, compliments of the in-resort spa.

We were on Paradise Island—the one most people think of when picturing the Bahamas. Tall coral towers, white sand beaches dotted with shacks selling conch fritters, and a range of marinas hosting sleek and elegant yachts worth more money than most of the tourists flittering around the island would see in a dozen lifetimes. Belowdecks on one of those lavish yachts was our target, and our tenth-floor hotel room had a perfect bird's-eye view.

Mom had tasked me with working out the entrance-exit strategy. Not that she couldn't do it herself. She started having me do it for some of our jobs when I was fourteen. Stress testing my training or whatever. I liked to think she knew I was the best at it. If there's one person who can figure out how to twist out of a tight spot, it's Ross mother-hugging Quest.

Little did she know this was a two-part plan. She was looking at the route she was going to take on and off this yacht, not the separate one I was going to use to hightail it back to shore on a one-way trip to Nassau International Airport and a plane toward something new.

It was hard not to let anything smug slip on my face. Mom had dragged me here for my exit-planning genius, and I was using it to run off. Maybe one day, when she got over my leaving, she'd look back and be proud of the finesse I was about to make.

"The yacht's ninety-five meters from stern to bow. It's got four decks, not including the engine room."

Mom cut in. "Logs say there's five guests and fifteen crew members aboard, so let's assume it's actually double that, right, baby girl?"

"Yeah, course." As if I wouldn't have already figured that into my calculations. One of the Quest rules: Whatever you think you're up against, double it. "I mapped the best route avoiding cabin quarters and guest spaces. There's a small port for detachable speedboats at the back. We'll buoy our Zodiac between that area and the starboard side of the bow, since there aren't any portholes nearby, then follow the map I routed through a manhole on the first deck, through the engine room, and into the hold. It's a pretty efficient route, so we should be able to transfer everything from there back to our boat in less than thirty minutes."

It really was a flawless route . . . almost.

Mom pursed her lips. "What about a backup plan? You couldn't find any other routes for emergencies?"

I tried not to let my increased heart rate show. Leaning over, I swiped to another pair of blueprints, these showing a much more convoluted emergency route tangling through crew cabins around to the bow of the ship. "There's this too, but it's messy. My first route should be fine," I said.

"You're sure there's no other way out?" Mom scanned the blueprints for an exit that wasn't there. Not on the blueprints, at least.

"I'm never wrong about exits."

She couldn't argue with that.

"Perfect." Mom stood, and it felt like she was looking down on me again. "We leave at sunset."

THE WATER WAS inky black.

Speeding over it felt like gliding over a shadow, heading straight for the starry horizon.

Well, it felt like *I* was headed for the horizon, but first I had to get past this job.

The yacht was nearly invisible, a sleek black vessel frozen in a setting just as dark. I reran everything in my head as our Zodiac bobbed over the waves. With any luck, everyone on board would be asleep. Mom would carry the target in duffel bags back while I loaded up the next delivery. Not the most sophisticated job, but this was last-minute, and not everything needs to be a whole event, as Auntie would say.

This was easy money, for real. What was going to be a bit harder was my addendum.

I was so high on anticipation my hands were tingling. My sneakers, a palette of ocean blues with abstract waves and foam and coral-green laces, jumped against the boat floor. I clenched and stretched my fingers. Mom noticed, pulling her eyes from the water.

"Don't tell me you're nervous, baby girl," she teased. Even in all black and with her hair tugged back into a practical ponytail, half-hidden by the night, she managed to look ten times more dazzling than I ever could.

I smiled. "Excited."

She matched my grin and squeezed my thigh. "Winning is exciting."

She had no idea.

A hundred feet or so out, Mom turned off the engine. We paddled the rest of the way to the back of the yacht, away from any windows, portholes, or lights. Most of the ship was unlit. Asleep.

Mom climbed up to the first deck, with me right after. I took the lead, following an invisible path. I stayed on guard, ready to unwrap my meteor bracelet at a moment's notice. But the ship was almost supernaturally silent. It felt empty, even though I knew that wasn't the case.

A silent hop and a skip later, and we were belowdecks in the cargo hold. Moonlight from a tiny porthole illuminated wooden crates. Mom popped off one of the tops. Inside were centuries-old treasures dredged up from meters under the ocean. Gold doubloons, pieces of a wheel from an ancient ship, shards of pottery, silverware, bracelets, a rusted dagger. Our unfortunate hosts tonight were from another subsection of our business. Treasure hunters. Raiding shipwrecks for every piece of antiquity they could get their hands on, sometimes only days after its discovery. Never mind that those treasures technically belonged to whoever originally found the wreck, or the government, depending on where and how close to shore you were. It was a lucrative business, obvious by this fancy yacht, and just as illegal as what we were doing.

Unfortunately for them, there was another team of rival treasure hunters who weren't too happy they'd been beaten to the punch on this find. They hired us last-minute to steal the already stolen treasure and deliver it to them. After my family's fee and the trouble of selling all this on the black market, I couldn't imagine they were going to make that much of a profit, but I figured it was more about pissing off their enemies than the money.

Mom pressed her hands together, then pointed behind her, our silent signal for "pack and go." I nodded and started delicately stacking silverware and doubloons into one of the padded duffels we'd carried in. We worked together to fill it up, before Mom slid the strap over her shoulder and headed out. I started on the second bag. With me packing while she was transporting, we'd be out in half the time with half as much noise.

My heart beat faster with each full bag. The closer we got to the end, the closer I got to my escape. The realness of it tingled across my skin. My fingers itched the way they always did when I was about to steal something. But they weren't itching for treasure this time; I was stealing my own future back.

Soon we were down to the last crate. Three bags, that's how many I guessed it would take to clear out this one.

The time was now.

Mom returned for the umpteenth time, and I traded the latest stuffed pack for an empty one. When she took the full bag, I tried not to give anything away, but I couldn't help but take her in one final time. This would be nothing but a betrayal to her. Even if I came back a week later, a day later, an hour later, even if she tried to drag me back, this would always be between us. Ross ran away. Ross left the family. Ross didn't think we were enough for her. I was about to snap my life into two halves, before and after. Which would I look back on as the better?

Mom locked eyes with me, and I jerked my gaze away. Did she see it? Could she actually read my mind? Would she stop me?

She didn't. Like all of the other times, she took the bag and left unceremoniously. There went her last chance to catch me.

The second she was out of sight, I burst into action. I set a pre-saved message in my email to send in fifteen minutes, approximately when Mom would return, then turned my phone all the way off. The message was simple: **Need a break. I'll come back in a few months, promise.** Short, but nothing she'd let me say to her face. Then I followed the blueprints in my head through the shadows of the hold to a small nook flanked with bolted shelves and dinghies. In the middle of a collection of neatly stacked life-jackets, first aid kits, and emergency provisions, I found it, just like the online yacht-crew message board said. Emergency inflatable life raft, battery-operated engine included.

An airtight door—deemed too narrow and unsafe for evacuation by the International Maritime Safety Committee, and therefore removed from all emergency-exit-planning blueprints—sat closed with a metal wheel smack in its center. I tugged the raft bundle out of place, then spun the wheel to release the door. It creaked open. Outside, dark water lapped at the side of the ship about six feet below. My heart was absolutely thundering by now. It was a straight shot from here. The emergency engine would have enough juice to carry me back to shore. This hidden door opened out of the view of Mom's speed-boat. Ten minutes from now, once she realized I was gone, I'd be gobbled up by the darkness.

I tossed the emergency raft. All I had to do was leap.

A gunshot cut through the quiet. I froze, just a second away from plunging into the water. The sound of pounding footsteps raced through the decks. Outside, the gleam of lights burned to life over the waves. People were awake, and they were shooting.

Mom. Had someone found her?

I raced back into the main cargo hold, toward the rush of footsteps and danger, just in time to see Mom scrambling down a ladder leading into the lowest deck.

No! What the hell was she doing? There was no way out below, she was wandering into a dead end. Instead, she should come this way—

She wouldn't know.

I told her there wasn't another exit on this level.

I opened my mouth to call after her, but my training instantly stopped me. That would tell the pursuers where we were, where she was. On the tiny chance they didn't already know.

Instead, I made a beeline after her. I'd get her to come back the right way with me.

But the second I burst into the cargo hold, two very pissed men skidded in, them and their guns. They didn't bother with questions. One look at the obviously empty treasure crates was enough.

One of them raised a pistol. I turned and sprinted. A gunshot rang out behind me. They were boxing me in. Back at the open emergency door, I did the only thing I could do: I jumped.

The water sucked me in. I held my breath and kicked toward

the back of the yacht. Muffled gunshots cut through the water. The emergency raft, still uninflated, bobbed above me. I kept swimming, a meter under the surface, for as long as I could without air. When I came up for a desperate breath, salt water stung my eyes. I could barely make out the edge of the Zodiac before a wave overtook my sight. Another deep breath and few meters of breaststroke, and I was able to make it to the side. I was just starting to pull myself in when a beam of light shone over the side of the ship. It hit the water first. Two guys were pointing a searchlight and guns over the edge of the yacht. The ball of light was coming toward the speeder. Fast. Getting caught in this boat under the light would be . . . not good for me.

Before I could think of any other options, I let go of my grip and slipped back into the water. I kicked away from the boat, coming back up meters away against the side of the yacht, just in time to see the searchlight centered on the Zodiac, treasure and all. "I see it!" the voice from above said. Pressed against the side of the boat, fighting waves, I strained to look up at the railing, where two guys were scrambling down the steps, eager to get their hands on what they thought they'd lost. Someone above grunted, a woman's voice. I didn't need to see to know it was Mom.

"You carried all of this out yourself?" another voice asked.

Mom didn't answer. Or if she did, I couldn't hear her over the growing drone in my ears. I clung to the side of the yacht, struggling to stay afloat and in the shadows. It was taking all my strength not to cough up water and reveal my position. But Mom . . . I had to do something about Mom.

The two guys, with the defined but slender muscles of frequent swimmers and sunburnt sailor's skin, had the speedboat locked into the yacht's accessory port in no time. It happened so fast. I'd lost my chance to get back on board undetected before I realized it.

"Who hired you, huh?" some guy above asked, his voice like gravel.

"Your wife," I heard Mom say, a laugh in her voice. "Said she deserves a fortune for putting up with you."

A slap. Metal on skin.

The guy asked again.

There was no answer.

"Get her out of my sight. She'll talk soon enough."

No, she wouldn't. I knew she wouldn't. Because once she talked, these people wouldn't have any reason not to kill her.

I needed to rescue Mom before that. Maybe if I could circle back around to the emergency door or—

The yacht's engine roared to life. A massive arc of water blew up, creating a suction that swallowed me. I sputtered under the waves—*don't breathe the water, you can't breathe the water*—fighting my way through the darkness and back up to the surface.

Finally, I broke through, spitting up water and gagging. Everything was a salty, burning blur. I blinked and blinked until the world came back. And when it did, the yacht was speeding away. Disappearing into the night. Along with my mom.

FIVE

I **PANICKED.**

For a few seconds, it wasn't about Mom. It was for me. I was far offshore, alone in dark waters. I could very easily have gotten picked up by a current and swept under for good, but a blinking light was my salvation.

The emergency raft bobbed in the water meters away. I swam for it frantically, until I was close enough to yank the rip cord. The raft swelled to life. I climbed inside and landed on the thick plastic with a defeated squelch. The little motor sat at the back of the raft, ready to be cranked up alongside a glow-in-the-dark warning. *This engine will only run for half an hour. Use wisely.*

Throwing this inflatable out may have saved my life. And all it cost me was my mom's.

She was gone. Captive on a yacht headed to . . . I had no clue where. How long were those people going to keep her alive? What were they going to do to try and get the information out of her?

Even if the lights of the yacht hadn't disappeared, I didn't have enough juice in this emergency raft engine to chase them across a literal ocean.

So I just sat there. Bobbing hopelessly in the dark while everything closed in around me. Mom was gone.

And it was my fault.

My phone buzzed. Sniffling, I pulled it out of my back pocket, a knee-jerk reaction. My waterproof case was worth the money. Despite the dunking it had taken, there was a little notification—my prescheduled email had been sent. It was such salt in the wound, it rivaled all the salt water sitting on my tongue. Even in the middle of all this, I hoped Mom wouldn't see it. Her kidnappers probably had her phone anyway—

I hit call on Mom's contact. The current had pulled me close enough to shore to give me one bar. As expected, no one answered. So I sent a message, all caps.

I'M AN ASSOCIATE OF YOUR CAPTIVE. ANSWER.

This time, they called me. The same male voice I'd heard from before, questioning, then striking Mom, was quick to speak.

"Don't suppose you're still on my yacht. If so, you can make my life a lot easier by telling me what deck you're on." American accent. Southern American. Not that I could do much with that information at the moment.

"Give me my associate back."

"Sure. Do you want an ice cream sundae with that?" There was some shuffling. I imagined he was sitting down somewhere.

"Why don't you tell me who hired you? And we'll leave her body somewhere easy to find, eh?"

My heart cinched. "If you kill her, I swear to god you'll wish you'd offed yourself instead."

"I'm terrified." He chuckled. "You sound young. What are you, twenty or something? I don't scare easy, especially when threatened by overgrown teenagers. Why don't you go fetch your mama, ask her to threaten me instead?"

I sucked in an audible breath and immediately regretted it.

He paused. "Oh, I see. This *is* your mama. Oh, that's real unfortunate for you, isn't it. Look, I feel for you, kid . . . Well, I actually don't. Here's a life lesson, since you won't be getting any more of those from Mommy. Sometimes things just don't work out for you."

My blood was pulsing a million miles an hour. He could hang up any second now. Toss her phone over the railing. Then she'd be gone.

These people weren't just going to give me Mom back. No duh, Ross. But he hadn't hit end call yet. There was still a chance. They were treasure hunters. I just needed to offer them something they wanted.

"What do you want?"

Now I was speaking his language. "About half an hour ago, all I wanted was my treasure back. I've already got that, so you tell me. What do you have for me?"

"One million." *Take it.* I could get that easy. Mom had more than that in her personal savings.

He laughed. Like, a from-the-pit-of-his-belly, funniest-thing-he'd-heard-in-years *laugh*. "Did you see my boat, kid?

Got two more just like it. I've gotten crappy birthday gifts worth more than that."

My stomach twisted. "Ten million." It would be more of a stretch. I'd have to get Granny and Papa to help. But they'd do it. No matter what kind of beef they had with Mom, they'd do it. She was their daughter.

"Come on, does Mommy really mean that little to you?"

I hesitated. How far could I raise it? Twenty? Thirty? I could get that . . . somehow. With some extremely well picked jobs, getting the whole family's help. Selling some valuable mementos. I could do it. Maybe, just maybe—

"I'm getting bored of this slow tick up," the man on the other end said. "So I'll pick my number." More rustling over the line. It sounded like he was talking to someone. Deciding just how much Mom's life was worth.

He returned. "I've got it. One billion."

I shook my head so hard my braids slapped my shoulders. "You're out of your mind! I can't get you one *billion* dollars! It's impossible!"

"Oh, I think you can, Little Miss Quest."

I froze. No way Mom gave up our name. She would never.

"It was an easy peg." The man answered my question without even my asking. "I heard you guys were based somewhere in the Caribbean. That and the whole Black thing. So I'm guessing I'm holding one of the legendary Quests. Am I right?"

I didn't have to reply. He wasn't expecting me to.

"Thought so," he said, self-satisfied. "So, knowing that, I think you *can* get me one billion dollars. If anyone can do it, it should be a Quest."

This was happening. He wasn't going to budge on this number. One billion dollars for Mom's life.

"Okay," I said. Even if I had a whole year, I didn't think I could steal one billion dollars' worth of anything. But hell, maybe I didn't know what I was capable of. For Mom, I could do anything, if I had enough time. "How long?" I croaked the words out.

"Hm . . . I'm a pretty patient man. How about a week?"

"A year."

"No."

I fisted my hand into my braids. "A week isn't realistic. You can barely get an international bank transfer in a week, that's not happening."

He paused. "You can have a month. Not a second longer."

Once I got Mom back, I was adding it to my bucket list to break this guy's jaw.

"I want proof-of-life calls too."

"Whatever. But if they start to annoy me, I'm ending this. All of it. Understand?"

His tone didn't leave any question about what *ending this* meant. I'd have to be frugal with these. Still, I couldn't help it. "I want one now."

He hesitated. "She's not conscious. Guess you'll have to call back later. Don't worry, we'll take excellent care of Mommy in the meantime." He laughed again, and the call ended.

Slowly, I lowered the phone from my ear. Water lapped over the edges of my raft. I had hope. Mom was going to be alive for at least another month.

But after that, they were going to kill her. Because I had no idea how I was going to get one billion dollars before then.

THERE WASN'T ANYONE around when I dragged the inflatable raft into the tiny cove on Paradise Island. Just like I planned. My go-bag waited behind a closed cabana, exactly where I'd left it. I'd been so worried about snags in my runaway plan. Someone would see me speeding onto the island and call border control. My backpack would be missing. The inflatable raft wouldn't expand right. But everything went flawlessly. It was like the universe was laughing at me.

My phone had died after my call with Mom's . . . captor. All I needed was a quick charge from my battery pack, and I was dialing the emergency phone back home. The one whose number I knew by heart and we were only supposed to call when everything had gone to crap.

She picked up in one ring.

"What's wrong?"

I crumpled into the sand and sniffled. "I messed up, Auntie. I really, really messed up."

PAOLO, OUR PRIVATE pilot, met me with the Cessna at Nassau's private airport. In less than an hour I was touching down in Andros, driving Mom's Jeep from the airport to Love Hill, and dragging my feet up into the house in the morning light. Everything happened like a dream. A nightmare. I was sleepwalking through the last hours, my mind replaying everything from last night. The gunshots, the water, the yacht speeding away into the darkness.

How clever and sneaky I'd felt, thinking I was going to disappear from right under her nose.

Alone. If she was killed, if she never came back . . . I was going to be really alone. Auntie would go back to her other home on Nassau eventually, wouldn't she? I barely knew my grandparents and estranged great-aunt. Mom was never invited to any family reunions, so I assumed I wasn't either. What would I have?

No. I could fix this. I *would* fix this.

Auntie was in the kitchen, frantically making her way down a list of contacts. She didn't hug or comfort me. No time. The best she could do was a pitying glance as she slid me a tablet with a list of names. Crying isn't the Quest way. Work and practicality first, always. And the most practical thing to do right now was hit up anyone we knew who knew anything about getting kidnapped moms back, or where to get one billion dollars.

No one could help us.

We spent the whole day trying. We called everyone. Granny and Papa. Auntie Sara. Associates who specialized in extraction. Less-than-legal loan sources. Everyone who owed our family a favor. No one *would* help us.

At some point, Auntie started pacing during her calls. I hadn't even noticed she'd disappeared to her room until I ran through all the names on the list she'd given me, hours later.

I froze by Auntie's door, fresh off the phone with Granny reporting another dead end.

When I heard the desperate tremble in Auntie's voice, my

feet refused to go farther. If that's what she *sounded* like, what would I *see* when I pushed open that door?

"I know what I'm giving you isn't a lot," Auntie said. "Isn't this what you do? Bring people back when no one else can?"

"Calm yourself, Ms. Quest." Whoever Auntie had on speaker sounded painfully disinterested. Like this was a customer service hotline and she was ready to hang it up and go home for the day. Like this wasn't my mom's life on the line. "We're extractionists, not magicians. Finding someone on land is one thing, finding a yacht that could be headed to anywhere in the world is another. Not only does your lack of information not align with how we operate, but given what you have managed to tell us, the captors are highly capable, and there's a high probability the target may be executed before we can get to them."

A lightning bolt struck my chest. *Execution?*

The woman went on: "I'll also note that it was recently suggested we not answer any calls from your family, so *you're welcome* for the time I have spent discussing the situation with you. I recommend you start coming to terms with your loss. Good evening." The call ended.

Something crashed against the wall. Auntie's phone? Quiet sobs trickled into the hallway. I couldn't take it.

I flew into my room, dropped to my knees, and jammed my fingers into my braids. Choking panic swirled around me. My chest heaved. For an awful second, I let everything consume me. The reality of a world without Mom. I couldn't get this money, and she was going to be shot and thrown overboard—I'd never even get to see her body.

My fault. For the rest of my life, it would always be my fault.

Would she figure it out before then? That her only daughter did this to her . . . that I'd been planning to leave? Was this the universe giving me what I wanted, in a messed-up, careful-what-you-wish-for sort of way?

A wish.

I'd deleted the invitation, but I remembered the email address.

My backpack was already packed—a bag I'd packed for a whole different life. With my meteor bracelet still wrapped around my wrist. I swiped a jacket out of the closet and stuffed my feet into my quietest kicks, deep blue embroidered with silver stars and van Gogh's *The Starry Night* painted on the soles.

Auntie didn't hear me leave. I made sure she didn't. What would she think when she realized I was gone? I'd thought she'd be the one person happily waiting for me, resentment free, when I eventually got back from my college excursion, but the world was suddenly so much different than what I'd thought today was going to be. What if I didn't see her again?

I made a detour for the notepad on the fridge.

Making a wish. Promise I'll be back.

Then I continued on as a shadow until I was in Mom's Jeep. Praying for a fast response, I emailed the address my number.

My phone rang less than ten seconds later.

"Hello, Rosalyn Quest," a woman's voice answered. Her accent bounced between English and American and Australian in only three words. That took practice. "You've called to register, I presume?"

I swallowed. "If I win, I get a wish?"

"Yes, that is the prize."

"And you can do *anything*?"

She paused, and I could feel her smiling. "Aside from bringing back the dead or changing the laws of physics, yes. Anything."

"I'm in."

"Excellent." My phone vibrated. "Check your email. Your personal one."

My brow furrowed as I saw a new notification. A digital plane ticket with my name on it. They had this ready?

"Your flight leaves from Andros Town International in one hour. That should give you plenty of time to get there, correct?"

They knew where I lived? Or they knew exactly where I was right now? "Yeah," I forced out.

"We'll see you when you arrive," she said. "Oh, and welcome to the competition, Ms. Quest."

A heaviness sunk into my stomach. Whoever these people were, they were the real deal. They wanted me to know this was *their* game, and I had no choice but to play along. But whatever the challenge was, I'd win.

I put the key in the ignition and started the car. Looking in the rearview, I locked eyes with myself.

The girl looking back at me was not here to play.

SIX

ANDROS TOWN INTERNATIONAL Airport was no bigger than my house and never open after dark. But tonight, despite the empty gravel parking lot, all the lights were on. It was waiting for a single passenger to arrive. Waiting for me.

As I entered, the ceiling fans clicked above. Fluorescent lights buzzed. I eyed the ticketing desk on the other side of the chipped plastic chairs. A blond man, a stranger to me, with a pressed baby-blue jacket totally unlike the tan shades the airport workers usually wore, had his hands folded behind his back. He hovered behind the counter like standing sentinel there had always been his life's dream.

"Where's Elise?" I asked. There were only two gate attendants at Andros Town International. Elise works on Fridays.

"She's off."

I glanced at the customs office, also vacant. Then the flight board. No departures or arrivals listed.

I flashed the attendant my virtual ticket, and he nodded. No penciling in a departure and arrivals sheet. I offered him my passport, but he waved it away and pushed open the glass door leading to the runway instead.

"Have a peaceful flight, Ms. Quest."

No passport scan or security check. It was like getting invited to Willy Wonka's; all I needed was the golden ticket. If I'd known they weren't going to check my bag, I would have brought more weapons than just my meteor bracelet, which I'd worked extra hard to style as a harmless accessory. What were my competitors bringing to the game?

A single jet sat on the runway, all glowing windows and sleek edges. Another white flight attendant, in the same baby-blue uniform, greeted me as I climbed the stairs.

"Welcome aboard." Her teeth sparkled behind cherry-red lips. She had a strange accent. It halfway reminded me of posh English accents, but with hints of Eastern European.

The plane's engines hummed under my soles. A strange smell lingered in the air. A stiff, subtle sweetness. I'd have assumed it was something dangerous if the woman in front of me hadn't been breathing it too.

"May I take your bag?"

I twisted it away from her offering hands. "No, thank you."

She looked pleased at my refusal.

"All right." She swept her hand toward the aisle. "Take whichever seat you like."

I kept my eye on the woman as I sidestepped her into the

aisle. It wouldn't hurt to be extra cautious about everyone from here on out.

The plane was larger than I was expecting, but closer to a private jet than a commercial airliner. Instantly, I scoped for exits. One up front, one in the back. No over-wing exits; the plane wasn't large enough to require them.

Each of the creamy-white leather seats was larger than what you would find in first class on an average commercial jet. A few of them faced each other, sharing a small table between them.

I wasn't the only passenger.

There were two teens who looked about my age already in their seats. A Hispanic girl with her face smushed into her arms, resting on the table between her and the opposite seat. Her long black hair draped over her like a curtain. I was pretty sure she was passed out. It didn't look like a very comfortable angle to sleep in. The other was a white boy who had taken a seat in the far back. One side of his head was shaved, and the other had brown hair long enough that it tickled the arms crossed over his chest. His mouth hung halfway open, and he was slumped against the window.

Why were they asleep? Who the hell sleeps on the plane ride to . . . I didn't even know where.

I settled into a rear-facing seat in the front row. From here, I'd have a good view of all the other passengers. My competitors.

I heard the cabin door shut and latch. I bit my finger, but quickly pulled it back down. I thought Mom had trained that anxious tic out of me years ago. I needed to pull myself together.

The flight attendant brought me a tray with a glass of water and packaged cookies. I waved them away, but she pulled out the tray table and placed them down anyway.

"Complimentary." Was it possible for her to say anything without a cheerful bounce in her voice?

My attention slipped down to her name pin. *Suvetlana.* What a strange way to spell that name. And it was even more curious that she didn't seem to have a Russian accent.

"Uh, thanks." Looking at the water and cookies, my stomach pinched. When was the last time I ate? Maybe the stress of Mom's situation had burned all the calories I'd eaten today. My tongue felt dry. I hadn't been this thirsty before, had I?

I froze after my hand wrapped around the glass. No, I was sure I hadn't felt this thirsty before. This felt wrong. As wrong as this strange smell.

The flight attendant hadn't moved. I peeked around her. The girl had a glass in front of her too. It was empty now, but identical to mine. I couldn't see what was in front of the boy, but I swore that the tray for his seat was pulled down as well.

I let myself feel the dryness of my mouth for a moment. My senses sharpened as I looked back to the attendant, still standing there.

I tapped the glass. "This is gonna put me to sleep?"

Her eyes narrowed. "How very smart you are, Ms. Quest. Yes, yes, it will."

"And I assume this strange smell is making me want to drink it?"

"Perhaps."

"Did the other two passengers figure that out too?"

"One of them."

"Will you tell me which one?"

"No."

The plane hadn't started to taxi. It wasn't like we were waiting on any other planes to get out of our way.

I held the glass at eye level. It looked like water, and probably tasted like it too. "How long am I gonna be out, then?"

"No longer than necessary," she promised. "We have a couple more passengers to pick up. We'd like to help everyone maintain their anonymity. I'm sure you can understand that."

Was I just supposed to let myself stay unconscious while more strangers boarded this plane?

"We promise nothing will happen to you until you awake."

She still didn't move, only waited. This wasn't a request. I had a feeling it was the first test to see if I would play by their rules.

I didn't have a choice. Mom was on borrowed time. And I was awfully, awfully thirsty.

I downed the entire glass. It was the most delicious water I'd ever tasted. Cool, crisp, and strangely sweet. The woman left the tray and my empty glass where they were—a clue for whoever was coming next.

I settled back into my seat and closed my eyes. The engines revved to life. I didn't even know what continent I'd wake up on. *If* I would wake up.

I swallowed, feeling my head start to loll. These people put in a lot of work to get me here—I was going to wake up. And when I did, I was going to win.

SEVEN

I WOKE IN a small, windowless room.

The walls and ceiling were lined in black velvet—same as the plush settee I was lying on. A fog-like substance danced over the floor, but it was swirling out through a grate. A gas to wake me?

I scanned the room and checked under the sofa. Nothing here but me. Where was my backpack? I thought *I* was supposed to be doing the stealing. A glass dome camera winked at me from the corner.

Guess it wouldn't be fun if they couldn't watch.

A metal door like you might find on a submarine was on the opposite wall.

At least thirty different locks bolted it shut. Combination locks, key locks, number locks, directional locks, and even a lettered keypad at the very bottom. Another test. Whoever was watching wanted to see if I could get out.

Easy work.

I found one of the multiuse lockpicks I'd sewn into my jacket pockets. Fiddling open the key locks with the pin was second nature. For the combination and number locks, I pressed my ear to them and listened to the machinery tick and turn until I had them down. Before I knew it, I had a little mound of locks by my feet.

Only one left—the keypad.

I stretched my fingers. They needed a rest, and I needed a second to breathe. This last lock was going to be tricky. Not to mention, I didn't know what was behind this door.

Mystery doors are not my favorite things in the world.

I tried to peek between the edge of the door and the wall. What kind of lock was connected to the keypad? If it was magnetic, maybe I didn't need to try the keypad at all.

Scratch that. They took my backpack. No backpack, no credit card.

I dragged my fingers over the buttons. Which keys were the worse for wear? Looked like this was going to be a math thing—

The screen at the top lit up. A question scrolled across.

What was your flight attendant's name?

A smile swept across my lips.

S-U-V-E-T-L-A-N-A

The door clicked ajar. Cautiously, I slipped through, not knowing what to expect. More doors to get through, this time with a hundred locks? Maybe a good old-fashioned dungeon?

Not a dungeon. Or a very nice dungeon if it was. I squinted while my eyes adjusted to the light. The windowless room was round, with at least a dozen doors. A random collection of plush antique armchairs and velvet sofas were positioned in a circle, facing each other. They gave off a musty smell, like mildew and wood chippings.

And . . . her.

She sat at the edge of her sofa with her ankles elegantly crossed. Her pale hands were clasped over her skirt, which, paired with her blazer and boots, gave her an I-just-got-home-from-boarding-school look. She tilted her head, shifting her shoulder-length blond hair, and then narrowed her blue eyes at me. I glared back at her from the depths of my soul.

Noelia Boschert. As if things couldn't get any worse.

Her lip curled for a second, the twin freckles at the corner of her mouth shifting. But one glance at the door behind me turned her scowl into a smug smile. "Always one step behind, hmm, Quest? Or five. Or ten."

"Ten? Is that how many jobs I beat you to this last year?" At this, her grin faltered.

Noelia Boschert was the one person on the planet I would have paid money to never see again. So of course, because the universe is just like that, she was the only person my age I had relatively frequent interactions with. The Boscherts were the biggest family-run thieving operation in Europe. As far as I knew, my family's enterprise was the most well-renowned in North America. You'd have thought we'd be destined to be perfect friends, right?

Wrong.

Tried that. One winter Mom left me at a ski camp where I first met nine-year-old Noelia. Just a coincidence that we met at all. We stole pink friendship bracelets from the girls in the dorm next to ours. I taught her to do the splits, and she showed me my first wristlock. We made a game of seeing who could steal the most Starbursts from the other.

Then she set me up for swiping fine jewelry from four of our ski instructors on the last day of camp and left me to be hand-cuffed in the office and nearly sent to Swiss juvenile detention at the age of nine. Mom saved me just in time, and I spent the entire ride down the mountain sobbing while she reminded me over and over, *This is why we don't trust people. A Quest can only trust another Quest, baby girl.*

Noelia Boschert had been a recurring cockroach that kept crawling into the corners of my life ever since. Catching glimpses of her on miscellaneous jobs, her sending the police my way at common rendezvous points or spreading slander about me to some client so they'd request I didn't join my mom on a job. After that incident, which really pissed me off, I went through a phase in which I went out of my way to push Mom to snatch all the available jobs we could around Switzerland for three months, anything that would have been convenient, easy money for Noelia and her fam. It all culminated when I received a rather threatening email in the black box telling me to back off. I made it my screen saver for a week.

"Those clients must not have paid well," Noelia said, try-ing to dismiss my last comment, "if all you can afford are worn jeans and ratty T-shirts." She looked down to my shoes, paus-ing like she was going to add that to the list of disappointing clothing choices, but actually stopped herself when she saw my kicks. I braced for a snicker, or something like *goofy* or *silly*, Auntie's favorite terms for my shoes, but Noelia said nothing. She squirmed in her seat a touch.

Mimicking her, I glanced down at her riding boots. They looked like your average dime-a-dozen designer boots at first glance, but under, on the sole that I could just barely see with her crossed ankles, was something colorful. The design was understated and impressionist from what I could tell, but it was definitely there.

She recrossed her ankles, hiding the soles, like that was gonna spare either of us the embarrassment of knowing that we apparently had the same shoe quirk.

"I guess even the dingiest broken clocks are right twice a day," Noelia murmured.

I hopped over the back of the sofa farthest from her and settled into a seat, ignoring the whole situation.

A small screen above the door behind Noelia was a nice distraction. In fact, there was a screen above every door but one. Twelve screens, each counting up by the tenth of a second. My screen showed a final time of 11 minutes, 30.3 seconds. Noelia's time was 9 minutes, 44 seconds even.

My teeth ground. She'd beaten me . . . for now.

Another door clicked open. The white boy from my plane flipped his hair back and turned to see the screen above him. I hadn't noticed before, but he was wearing dark eyeliner. Unstrapped suspenders swung over his pant legs. It was a casual look. Maybe he was *trying* to appear casual. Casual people are more approachable.

He looked back to us and raised his hands, as if to ask, *What the hell?* "Where's the next test?" The guy's accent was standard American. Noelia and I both cocked a brow at him. "The next *thing?*" he reiterated. "Like those locks? I thought I was gonna be walking into a series of increasingly difficult tasks or something." Deciding that there really was nothing of interest, he claimed the nearest armchair with a defeated huff. He ripped a phone out of his pocket, put it facedown on his lap, and fished a deck of cards out of the other pocket. He started doing arch shuffles, but I noticed the close eye he was keeping on Noelia and me.

You know, I'd never seen someone so disappointed not to find themselves in immediate danger. He almost seemed annoyed. Noelia opened her mouth, but after looking him up and down, she shut it. If I knew her, she was already prowling for her newest expendable but useful best friend. Guess he didn't make the cut.

A minute later, out came a thin girl who looked like she might be Indian. I did a double take when I saw her. She might have walked straight off a runway. Tall, slender, and with a black high ponytail, flawless makeup, and strikingly long lashes around intimidating brown eyes. She had a gold-trimmed-and-embroidered jacket, which was a meld between what I assumed was traditional Indian style and Western high fashion, with complementary leggings, slippers, and a scarf. If Noelia was posh, she was chic. She wore a ridiculous number of sparkling rings—at least one on each finger. Very sharp rings.

Noelia gasped in awe, clasping her hands under her chin. She said something to the girl in what I was pretty sure was Hindi—which I didn't even know Noelia spoke. The girl smiled smugly, gesturing to her jacket, then Noelia's.

And just like that, they were cool with each other. Well, as close as you could get after two minutes in a room with your competition. I'd call this new girl naïve for falling for it, but that'd make me a hypocrite. Once upon a time, I fell for it too, when a much younger Noelia started gushing over my barrettes.

At least I knew her MO this time. I wasn't falling for any other thief's bull.

Still, when she and Ring Girl laughed about something, I fought the urge to punch a pillow.

Another door opened, and a boy in a cream sweater exited. He had the most perfect, sculpted black hair—a side part with not a strand out of place. He was East Asian, with a focused gaze behind some pretty vogue glasses.

"The specs are sharp, man." The white boy gave him a chin-up nod, like they were classmates passing in the hall.

Perfect Hair pushed the glasses up. "I know." He didn't sit until he made a full turn around the room, analyzing everything he could in it with slow precision, us included. The boy with the cards leaned back a little and smirked when Perfect Hair studied him, still playing with his deck.

"The last time a guy looked that closely at me, I got laid," he said with a saucy smile.

Perfect Hair didn't seem amused or flustered. He took out his phone and started taking notes, I assumed. "Don't get your hopes up."

The next person out was a girl, also East Asian. Her hair was wavy with a frizz and copper colored. Around her neck, bunching her hair, was a pair of retro-sized gold headphones. Even from the other side of the room, I could hear the buzz of music coming from them. She sunk into an armchair next to Card Boy, curling into the cushions. Her gaze was affixed to the arch of cards Card Boy was shuffling.

"Can I try?" She held out her hands. Card Boy was down for it and started telling her something about shuffling.

Two more contestants escaped their rooms, almost simultaneously. One was the Hispanic girl from my plane. Her hair was in a braid now—curious use of her time—which she flicked over her jean-jacketed shoulder. She walked with an angelic grace, airy and light on her feet. *Dancer*, I considered. *Or maybe acrobat?* I didn't have much of a chance to think—the guy who had come out then too demanded all our attention.

The first thing I heard was his boots. Like in movies, when they zoom in on bikers' boots hitting the floor in slow, measured steps and everyone in the bar shuts up. The room was quiet for a second. In walked a tall white guy. Crew cut. Bomber jacket. He cracked his knuckles. I shivered. Something wasn't right about this guy. He was too aggressive when he cracked his knuckles. He walked too slowly. Even without the years of training telling me when I needed to be on edge, and when I *really* needed to be on edge, I would've known that this was a guy you'd see on the sidewalk and immediately cross to the other side.

At least he was on the other side of the room. I sure as hell didn't want him sitting next to me. Everyone seemed to be of the same opinion.

Everyone except for Card Boy. The same one who was disappointed that he'd walked into a sitting room and not a torture chamber.

As the new fellow crossed in front of him, Card Boy kicked his foot out. Scary Guy's foot caught his, and he tumbled forward a couple steps.

Noelia sucked in a breath. Honestly, ditto.

"Oh, sorry, pal." Card Boy clucked his tongue. "Gotta watch where you're going."

Scary Guy's face cracked. There was bloodlust in his eyes. He spun around with a hand headed straight for Card Boy's neck.

"Ack!" The cards Headphones was shuffling shot out into a fluttering rain, scattering everywhere. Lucky Card Boy. It gave him just enough time to scramble away from Scary Guy's outstretched hand.

"So *that's* why you said to keep your thumb on the corner." Headphones shrugged, like that was all just an accident. Had she been trying to save Card Boy? She was so nonchalant about it, I couldn't tell. If that was her game plan, it worked. Playing cards shooting all over is a dampener on a brawl, I guess. Scary Guy clenched his fists and settled into an armchair, arms resting on the sides, fingers flexing and unflexing like some movie sociopath thinking about the hostages in his basement. It immediately gave me Buffalo Bill serial killer vibes, and there was no way I was the only one thinking it, right?

"It places the lotion in the basket . . ." Noelia whispered in French. I couldn't help my smirk. Noelia was hiding one herself, but after seeing that Ring Girl didn't get the movie reference, she dropped it.

Headphones started swiping up the cards. "Help?" she asked, glancing at us.

The sociopath was an obvious no. Perfect Hair mindlessly kicked a few her way between his note-typing. Noelia and her new BFF, Ring Girl, looked more annoyed than anything. The only person who went all in was the dancer girl with the braid. She'd caught a few while they were still fluttering, and I watched as she bent her arm at a near inhuman angle to reach a pair that had slipped under a sofa.

I glanced over the side of my cozy sofa, not necessarily intending on helping—maybe Headphones was trying to weed out the weaker links with this stunt—but I saw a single card facedown. Flicking one back to them wouldn't hurt, and maybe it would throw them off about just how generous I was actually planning to be.

I leaned over to pick it up, but another hand reached at the same time, warm fingers brushing over mine.

My head shot up, and I was breathlessly face-to-face with a new boy. My heart skipped. Another Black person, finally. I hadn't even heard his door open.

With a sly smile, he swiped up the card, turning it over. "Queen of Hearts." His British accent took me aback for a second. It was so smooth. He whispered, and we were still so close it felt like he was talking only to me. "Maybe it's a sign."

I sat back before my stomach started flip-flopping and let him return the card to Headphones.

The new boy was the sharpest dressed of all, wearing a button-down vest with a tie tucked in. He sleeves were folded to his elbows, showing off his Rolex. His hair, though coarse and sponged to perfection, was just textured enough to make me think he had a little something else mixed in him besides Black. That, and his eyes, which were just brown enough that I could tell they weren't fully coal.

He was beyond handsome, and judging by the way he stood, and that first line he dropped on me, he knew it. And used it to his advantage whenever he could.

I mentally chided myself. Ross Quest was *not* going to be that girl who started swooning over the hot guy after five minutes. On the to-do list of life, the top priority was winning and rescuing Mom, not falling for some guy who probably flirted with anything that walked as long as it could do him a favor.

No, I was definitely *not* interested.

"Guess I'm late to the fun," Handsome Brit said, and somehow he made that sound sexy too. He approached the sofa I was sitting on. "May I?"

I didn't object, and he sat with his ankle crossed over his knee like a talk show host. He twisted a gold tie pin between his fingers—perfect for lock-picking—then slipped it onto his tie.

"Did I miss the part where we all introduce ourselves?" Handsome Brit asked.

"Who says anyone wants to do that?" Noelia said, her first words to anyone else since her new supermodel BFF walked in.

"I would like introductions." The dancer girl sat next to me, tickling the tail of her braid as she spoke.

"Like on a reality show?" asked Headphones.

Perfect Hair snorted. "This isn't a reality show."

Another domed camera in the corner of the room caught my attention. I gave it a meaningful look. "Sure about that?"

"I'm down." Card Boy's leg was bouncing. He'd gone back to quietly shuffling his own cards.

Handsome Brit smiled. "We're going to learn each other's names sooner or later. And I'm sure most of us could find out on our own if we wanted." He stood and pressed a hand over his heart. "Devroe Kenzie. England."

"Countries too?" I asked.

"Why not?" Devroe sat back down. "It'll save us the trouble of guessing each other's accents."

"Okay." Headphones spoke up next, her upbeat music still playing. "I'm Kyung-soon Shin. I'm from Korea. South, obviously." Her oversized shirt had an image of some K-pop band

I wasn't familiar with printed across it in pastel-pink Korean lettering. Damn, I should have noticed that before.

Kyung-soon passed the metaphorical mic to Card Boy. He ran a hand over the unshaved side of his head. "Right. The name's Mylo Michaelson. Some people call me M-squared. Most people don't. If you hate on the eyeliner, we can't be friends. Oh, and I'm from Vegas. That's in Nevada, USA."

"We're aware," Perfect Hair said.

Kyung-soon giggled.

"A gambler, then?" Devroe asked.

Mylo sat back, looking scandalized. "I'm not old enough to gamble, sir."

I cracked a smile. If he was faking the nice-guy thing, he was doing a really good job.

Next in line was the brawler buff dude. He seemed like he was debating with himself whether to say anything, then ground out, "Lucus Taylor. Aussie. Next."

On to Perfect Hair. He planted his elbows onto his knees and steepled his fingers under his chin.

"You may call me Taiyō. I will not tell you my last name unless the organizers ask me to. I'm from Japan."

"You're not going to tell us your last name?" Ring Girl flipped her ponytail while her rings twinkled; it was honestly one of the most effortlessly glam things I'd ever seen. "Come on, we won't tell anybody. Or are you scared?" She flashed a wicked smile.

Taiyō didn't even flinch. He started typing again on his phone, which seemed to irritate Ring Girl.

"What the hell are you writing?" she demanded.

Taiyō didn't answer. Ring Girl might have pounced on him, but Noelia stopped her with a delicate hand on her shoulder.

She cleared her throat and stood. "My name is Noelia Sophia Boschert. I'm from Zurich, Switzerland." She brushed the wrinkles out of her skirt. "Let's see, I prefer rubies to emeralds, enjoy moonlit walks, and I hope none of you take it personally when Adra or I beat you."

With that, she sat back down as the room collectively rolled their eyes. Except for Ring Girl, Adra, who looked smug to be included. All part of Noelia's playbook. Make it seem like it was you and her against everyone else.

"The Boscherts are one of the oldest families in the industry, right?" Adra announced, and I wondered if Noelia asked her to say that.

"That's true." Noelia blushed. Somebody strangle me, please.

Ring Girl gestured to herself. "Like Noelia said, I'm Adra. India."

Kyung-soon's mouth fell open. "Didn't you just call out Taiyō for not revealing his last name? Tell us yours!"

She shrugged, but her eyes sparked with mischief. Adra clearly couldn't help but mess with people. "I changed my mind." She pointed at the lithe dancer girl from the plane. "You're next."

She held herself with perfect posture, and I thought she looked something like a swan. "Yeriel," she said. Her accent was thick and luscious, but her voice wobbled. Was that nervousness? "Yeriel Antuñez. Nicaragua."

She didn't add anything else.

And that left me.

"Last but not least?" Devroe offered.

Sighing, I flipped back my braids. "Ross Quest. The Bahamas."

"Quest?" Mylo almost fell out of his chair. "Your family is legendary! I didn't even think you guys were real! Is it true someone in your family swiped a necklace from the crown jewels and the royal family's been trying to keep it a secret ever since?"

Everyone was watching me, but it wasn't all warm attention. Noelia in particular looked furious that my last name had gotten more fanfare than hers.

"I assume Granny exaggerated that," I said.

He nodded and stroked his chin. "Still a hell of a bedtime story."

He wasn't wrong there.

A dozen alarms chimed. The remaining three timers stopped counting, frozen at twenty-two minutes. Time was up, but their doors remained shut. The door without a countdown clock swung open instead.

From a dark hall, a white woman entered carrying a tablet in the crook of her arm like it was a clipboard. Her pixie-cut hair was a dark red like her pantsuit. If hell had a concierge, this woman worked at the front desk.

"Good to see you've already gotten acquainted." The door shut behind her. There was an empty sofa between Kyung-soon and Lucus. I expected her to sit, but she remained standing. Looking down on all of us.

"Was that your way of saying you've been spectating?" Lucus asked. "How many people have front-row seats to this game?"

"You should assume we're always watching." She smiled. "You may call me Count. I'll be your contact for this year's competition. You've each been selected because you've caught the attention of our organization."

"What about the people in the remaining three rooms?" Taiyō asked.

"That was a pretest. A competency exam, if you will. They

failed," Count said. "Don't worry about them, they're no longer in the competition."

Twelve to start, and three down already. They weren't playing around.

Count continued. "Let me clarify the rules. The Thieves' Gambit is divided into three phases, with various tests in each phase. Any of you may be eliminated at a moment's notice if our judges deem your performance to be . . . underwhelming."

"So even if we pass a phase, we can still be eliminated for not doing it well enough." Noelia said it more than asked. Not that she sounded worried or anything.

"Correct," Count said. "In addition, if you're injured to the point of incapacity, you will be disqualified."

I shifted in my seat. Auntie told me this thing could get bloody. Who was doing the injuring, though?

"I should add"—Count's face twisted into something stronger and more serious—"you cannot win the Gambit by killing your competitors. Violence outside of the phases is prohibited."

"And *during* the phases?" Lucus asked.

"If your paths should cross, and force—even deadly—is required, then that's acceptable. But attacking your fellow competitors for no reason isn't looked upon favorably. This is a thieving competition. Outclass your opponents with your mind and skills, not your fists. Our contracted victor should be sharp of mind and—"

"Contracted?" The word fell out of my mouth.

Count turned to me. "I suppose that brings me to the next point. In addition to your wish, whichever of you is victorious will have the honor of becoming our organization's primary thief for the year. You'll do any job we ask of you, and you'll be paid well for it." She smiled deviously. "Better than you're used to, I assure you."

A year as a contracted thief. I didn't know this was part of the deal. Was it such a bad thing, though? I'd wanted to leave . . . before. But I had a feeling this wouldn't be anything close to the freedom I'd imagined. "You mean *if* we want that job."

"The position is mandatory," Count said. "You *will* work if you win. If you have a problem with that, you may leave."

She paused, challenging us. No one moved. Not even me.

There was no future without Mom. This was the only way.

Mylo sighed dramatically. "Let's get to work. No one's backing out. When does the first phase start?"

"It already has."

Everyone tensed. Next to me, Devroe looked hyperfocused as he leaned onto his knees.

Count swiped across her tablet. An image appeared on the table in the middle.

"Whoa . . ." Kyung-soon studied the lit-up table. She had a greedy luster in her eyes that made me think she was imagining she could steal this too. Schematics of a building oscillated on the screen. Three floors, few windows. At least four exits that I could see at first glance.

"We're sitting in the basement storage of the privately owned Museum of Historical Fashions just outside of—"

"Cannes, France," Adra finished for her. She gave Noelia a pleased look. Guess this wasn't her first time at this museum.

"Correct," Count went on. "There are fifteen items you should note."

A series of objects blinked quickly across the screen. A miniature portrait of a well-made-up French aristocrat, a gilded music box, a sculpture of a Roman emperor in full regalia. Most of the targets looked small enough to fit under an arm. I flagged the centurion as a possibility. People don't tend to display sculptures behind glass. Once all fifteen items had been shown, they organized themselves in three rows of five.

"Your task is to bring one of these items to the Graphe Hotel in Marseille by ten this evening. Tell the receptionist you're with the Spaggiari party."

Spaggiari party? As in—

"The *Albert* Spaggiari party?" Taiyō asked. No one else got the reference. At least I wasn't the only one who knew Albert Spaggiari was the mastermind behind the famous Nice bank heist. He was a personal icon of mine, partially because his determination was hardcore enough to spend months burrowing a tunnel through a sewer under a bank vault, but also, there was something charming about a thief who undertook his first job to afford a diamond for his girlfriend.

Count only nodded in response. "The current time is 4:02 p.m. The museum closes to the public at seven on Saturdays. You'll find a staircase to the first floor behind the door to my left." With that, Count stood, leaving the items up on the screen. "Only eight of you will move on to the second phase."

"Excuse me—" Kyung-soon jumped up. "What about my stuff? I brought some bags with me on the plane. The flight attendant told me I'd get them back."

At least I wasn't the only one who'd had her stuff snatched.

"We're well aware of what you're all missing," Count said. "Consider the lack of your belongings a test of your ingenuity. They will be returned at a later time. Any other concerns?" She scanned the room. Nothing. "Good. Happy hunting. Oh, and one more thing." She stopped just before crossing through the doorway. "They say the wife of a Mafia boss owns this gallery. The security is . . . tight. Best of luck."

My fingers twitched.

The first phase had begun.

EIGHT

MUSEUMS ROBBED BY Rosalyn Quest in her seventeen years of life: 30.

Museums robbed by Rosalyn Quest without the help of anyone else named Quest: 0.

First time for everything?

Yeriel twisted the end of her braid. "They're just trying to scare us out about the security, right?"

"Hope not," Lucus said, cracking his knuckles. He was probably hoping he'd get to snap some poor guard's neck during this.

"I don't see how that approach would benefit them," Taiyō said. He took a pic of the schematics. Had he not already memorized them?

"You should go ask. Get a copy of their security rotations while you're at it," Adra said, circling around the couches.

Noelia laughed. She winked at Yeriel and pulled Adra aside. Yeriel opened her mouth, like she was genuinely concerned no one else was worried, but just sighed.

I prowled the room. The schematics Count left didn't include this basement. The room we were in was an unmapped mystery, and I hated not knowing everything about my location.

There were our nine doors, each a bit ajar, and then four more, including the one Count came and went through. Aside from Count's door, all the doors had screens above. I peered into some of the other rooms, and then the one I'd woken up in. All identical. Black walls, sparsely furnished. A litter of locks left on the floor. Though, while I noticed Mylo and Adra had left their locks in a sloppy pile like me, Lucus seemed to have kicked all of them under his settee, Noelia's were in a neat line, and Kyung-soon's were arranged in a smiley face.

Curiosity got the better of me. What about Devroe and Taiyō? Yeriel?

I was about to peek into Taiyō's room, but I froze in front of one of the still-closed doors. This one sat a touch off level. While the bottoms of the others dug into the carpet, this one floated noticeably a couple millimeters off the ground.

Or at least, noticeable to me.

After a quick moment of hesitation, I reached for the door's lock. This door was different. Who, or what, was inside?

My phone vibrated, my fingers just inches from the knob. Not just mine; everyone's went off.

A message from a number I didn't recognize:

> The rooms holding your former
> competitors are off-limits. Attempt
> to open one of them and you will
> be disqualified. ☺

"I think that's Count's way of saying don't touch her stuff."
Mylo gave me a lazy smile. "Trying to pickpocket the defense-
less. That's cold." His tone told me that was the total opposite of
what he thought.

"It's no crime to steal from a thief," Taiyō noted, heading out
the way Count left.

"Is that from a movie or something?" I heard Adra ask.

"It's a proverb," I answered, not really sure why I bothered.

I'd been wasting my time. There weren't any exits down here.

I followed after Taiyō, barely managing to weave around
Noelia and Adra. A tiny part of me felt bad for Adra—disposable
bestie number who-knows-what.

Mylo had slipped into the corridor right before me. It was a
one-way shot to an elevator, one of those older types with the
accordion door you have to pull open and shut yourself.

Neat, but I needed to stop getting distracted by doors. I had
limited time to explore the museum, analyze its security, make
a short list of optimal targets, and plan an escape route.

Mylo glanced over his shoulder. "You followin' me?"

I nodded toward Taiyō. "Only if you're following him."

Mylo straightened and rubbed his chin, trying to look wise,
I guess. "The thief who follows another thief is . . . um . . . not
lacking in direction?"

I bit back a chuckle. "Was that supposed to sound like another proverb?"

"Guess I'm not as well-versed as the rest of you all," he answered. "But come on, when has a quote ever helped someone jimmy a safe, ya know?" Mylo glanced at his phone. His home screen was empty. His hand twitched, and he reluctantly put his phone back away. He'd been doing that since I first saw him, checking his phone or trying very hard not to check it.

"Expecting a message or something?" I probed.

Mylo didn't look at me. "Course not."

Taiyō yanked back the elevator's grate. If he'd heard Mylo talking noise about his proverb thing, and he probably had, he wasn't taking the bait.

Mylo stepped in after him. I stayed back. Riding snug elevators with other people is a really great way to get pickpocketed. At least, that's what I'm always thinking about in elevators.

Taiyō pressed a button inside the elevator, and a warning buzz rattled the car. He tried again. Same result.

Had Count trapped us down here with a broken ride? Was shimmying up an elevator cable the next mini test?

"Huh." Mylo tapped a sign drilled into the back of the car. "One person at a time. They actually *mean* that."

Taiyō dragged the door back open and shoved Mylo out.

"Hey!" He stumbled and spun around just in time to see Taiyō snapping the door shut. This time, the elevator rose easily. "We could've played rock, paper, scissors for it!"

"I choose scissors." Taiyō held up two fingers, then dropped one so just his middle finger was left.

"Whatever," Mylo said as Taiyō and the elevator disappeared. "I always pick paper, anyway."

AFTER MYLO, I took the elevator and found that it opened up into a storeroom. The elevator door was hidden behind fake shelves. From there, I slipped into a wide hallway and was immediately engulfed by the buzz of the museum. Two steps out, I collided with a white woman wearing an obnoxiously large ladybug brooch. She nearly jumped out of her skin when I bumped into her.

My fingers warmed—her hideous brooch would make Auntie chuckle. Mom would chuck something that atrocious into the ocean.

My breath caught, thinking of Mom, wherever she was. Unreachable.

Focus.

I started in the west wing of the museum, since that was where the storeroom the elevator was connected to let out, and decided to work my way across from there. I'd scan for the exits and size up all the targets. There were fifteen items and nine of us. The odds of me picking a target that no one else was angling for weren't perfect, but they weren't awful either.

I entered the sparkling white sunlit Hall of Sculpted Styles. The room, with a cathedral ceiling, was a forest of marble and porcelain. At least a hundred different sculptures from different eras of history sat on pedestals. Silver information panels named each piece and provided a QR code inviting visitors to read more about the fashion depicted. It took me a minute or so to find the right figure, but as soon as I did, the idea of this phase being easy evaporated.

In the center of the gallery, basking under a downpour of

sun from a skylight, was the first item from Count's list. The marble sculpture of the emperor. When I saw it on her screen, I was picturing something as tall as my forearm. Maybe knee high, at most.

My head didn't even come up to its waist.

I tried not to grit my teeth as I craned my head up to meet the centurion's milky gaze. Marble is 160 pounds per cubic foot, and this thing was a lot of cubic feet. Moving him was impossible. It was a joke.

Striding out of the hall, I twisted my hands in my jacket pockets. Item number one was a no go. How many of the targets on the list were there just to mess with us? I spent the next hour pacing through galleries and showrooms, getting a good look at each and every item on Count's list.

Out of the fifteen targets, only eight were viable.

Without a month to plan, there was no way I was carrying a fifty-foot-wide oil painting out of here, or the commemorative plaque that was drilled into the lobby floor. Oh, and I doubted any of us were going to swipe the fountain from outside.

It made me want to bury my face in a pillow and scream. I could imagine the organizers snickering at our expressions as we came across their "gag" targets.

I'd been keeping an eye out for the competition as I hunted, and judging by the way I saw Kyung-soon shuffling out of the sculpture hall and Lucus storming out of the gallery with the oil paintings, I wasn't the only one wanting to rip their hair out. Scouting these bogus targets had wasted valuable time.

My phone vibrated. Frustrated, I fished it out of my back pocket and winced. Auntie.

Honestly, it was a wonder she hadn't already called.

Slipping into one of the smaller display areas where one of the targets was, a cozy showroom with low lights, I took a breath before answering.

I cleared my throat. "Yeah?"

"*Yeah?* You leave in the middle of the night to join Satan's favorite game show, and the first thing you say when I can finally get through to you is *yeah?*"

My knee-jerk response was another *yeah*, but I stopped myself. "I don't know what else to say besides sorry, but we both know I'm not sorry for leaving, so *yeah*."

Sighing, I leaned against the glass of a display shelf. Inside was the easiest attainable target from Count's list. A small portrait inside an oval frame, with a red ribbon tethered to it. There were about twenty just like it on the same shelf. *Boîtes à portrait*, according to an info panel. Seventeenth-century Europe's version of carrying a selfie of your girlfriend around. I was sure there'd be at least one other person going for this—maybe all of them. Was that the real point? Were we *supposed* to come in conflict with each other?

I could hear Auntie sucking her teeth.

"Don't tell me to come home, Auntie. We both know that's not an option. Unless a billion dollars washed up on the beach after I left."

"I know. I know, Rossie." She paused. "What's happened so far? Where are you?"

"France. We're in a museum."

"We?"

"Nine of us. I haven't had to strangle anyone with my bracelet yet, and besides being drugged and locked in a basement, I guess no one's messed with me either . . . so that's a plus. Noelia Boschert is here."

"Oh, lord help us." I could almost see Auntie roll her eyes. There wasn't anyone who understood my beef with Noelia better than her. "Don't let her distract you. If you're gonna win this, you can't afford that, Rossie."

"Yeah, no duh," I snipped, and stepped away from a couple who came to admire the boîtes à portrait. "I might have bigger problems than her. There's nine of us, Auntie. But there's only eight targets. I feel like I'm pulling straws."

Auntie hummed. "Maybe . . . you should partner with someone."

Did my phone just break up or something? "I don't get the joke."

"I'm for real!"

"Auntie." My voice dropped to a whisper. "Rule one, I can't trust these people."

"Obviously. Don't trust them, use them. Maybe you partner up with someone, double up your chances of getting what you need. Pick someone pliable. Then, if it comes down to it and you both only get one target, you make sure you leave with it and not them."

My stomach twisted. That was a tactic I was too familiar with, just from the other side.

That wasn't how I wanted to play this.

"Mom wouldn't do it that way," I said. "Mom'd figure it out herself."

"Don't be so sure."

The couple glided out of the cozy gallery hand in hand, and

a familiar dapper figure replaced them. Devroe flashed me a flawlessly debonair smile. I told myself that it made my heart skip only because he'd probably perfected it, likely in a bathroom mirror.

"I gotta go. Text you later." I ended the call. Devroe glanced at my phone as I returned it to my pocket.

"Boyfriend?" he asked.

"No." Why did I answer so fast?

"Hm. *Girl*friend?"

"Why do you ask?"

"So that's a no too. Good to know."

He really was infuriating. I pushed past him, not because I felt myself flushing again or anything, and settled back in front of the case with Count's target inside. He followed.

"The little portrait, huh? The easiest, yet most difficult target in this museum."

I scoffed. "I think the fountain might be a little more complicated."

"Yes, but you'd have no competition. This, though . . ." He nodded toward the glass. "I saw Mylo and Lucus skulking by here at least twice. Not to mention that girl Yeriel." He focused on the glass and then stepped aside a bit. It took a second, but I caught the reflection of Yeriel and her lengthy braid behind us, pretending to observe another display. She'd ditched her jean jacket, leaving a soft blouse that made her look much more upper-class. Neat trick.

I glanced back at Devroe, then walked away. He kept up, matching my stride.

"Is that what you're up to?" I asked. "Seeing what everyone

else is going after?" I'd been keeping notes on where I'd seen everyone throughout my scouting, but with limited time, I knew better than to burn too much of it playing guess who. Making my own plan was the priority.

"Sort of," Devroe answered. "I prefer to think of it as curious observation rather than spying."

I led us into one of the corridors lined with benches between galleries. What did he want? He was entertaining and handsome and all, but neither of us had time for chitchat.

"Go away." I stopped to face him, careful to keep my voice cheerful. People remember things like "couples" arguing. You don't want to be remembered when you're scouting a place.

"No, thank you," he said in a smug way that really made me want to punch him. He leaned against the wall next to me. Too close. We truly did look like a couple.

His vivid brown eyes gazed at me. I tried to focus. He was probably used to using his looks to disarm people.

"What do you want?" I asked.

"Work with me," he said, surprising me. "Some of the targets are easier than others, but all of them would be easier with two people rather than one. How about a little alliance?"

Auntie's suggestion repeated in my mind. This was a perfect in for that . . .

"You do realize we both have to bring an item to the rendezvous point. One item between the two of us isn't gonna cut it."

"That's not what I meant, and you know it," he said. "We'll acquire two items together. One for each of us."

"And whose item will we go after first? Yours?"

"We'll work that out later."

Don't trust them. Use them. If that was the plan Auntie wanted for me, didn't it make sense that was the way Devroe was looking at the situation too?

Did he think I was the most pliable? Easiest to manipulate?

Devroe's gaze sharpened on me. "What do you say?"

I pursed my lips. "Why are you asking *me*? Or did everyone else already reject you?"

"Perish the thought. You were my first choice."

"Why me, then?"

He cut a smile. "Would you believe me if I said it's because I think you're beautiful?"

"No. And I'd be insulted if that was the actual reason too."

"Fair enough." He leaned back a bit. "From where you were seated, I assume it was you who had the second-fastest time escaping the room and Noelia who had the first. I would've gone for her, but she's chosen her ally already. I didn't want to waste my time on a lost cause."

"And you assumed you'd have better luck with me?"

"I'm pretty good at reading people."

I studied him for a moment.

His offer almost sounded genuine. I almost wanted to take it . . .

A phantom chill breathed down my neck. A memory of cold metal cuffs biting my wrists at a ski school in the mountains flooded back to me. The girl who set me up was in this museum right now. I let foolish emotions get in the way back then. I couldn't again. Not when the stakes were this high.

Rule one: If they're not a Quest, they can't be trusted. Today was not the day to be stress testing that.

"Not gonna happen," I said. "I don't need your help. If you need mine, then you probably shouldn't be here."

His face fell, but it wasn't anger I saw; it was disappointment.

"Too bad." He sighed and pushed himself off the wall. "I hope you don't regret it."

I hope so too, I thought as he strolled away.

NINE

I'D BE LYING if I said I wasn't a little excited, waiting in the vents above the thirty-foot drop into the gallery. My fingers itched, ready to get my hands on something hot.

I spent the last of the museum's open minutes redrawing my mental map, running through all the exits. Two main entrances, four emergency doors. Two staff entrances around back. Then there was the ventilation system. I traced the pattern of them over my palm, thinking of the seventeen different entrance and exit points I'd noted. Keeping quiet in the vents until the museum closed wasn't my first idea. It'd have been better if I could've left and then slid back inside through one of the emergency exits, but I didn't know what the guards' rotations looked like, and risking coming face-to-face with a flashlight beam was not smart.

I'd watched the patrons drain out, security do their first check, and the lights darken, leaving only the low lights rimming the display cases. The museum was closed.

Security was doing walk-throughs in twenty-minute intervals. I had twenty minutes to get my target and dip. Fifteen to be safe. Always assume you have less time than you think.

It'd take two hours to get from Cannes to Marseille, with the help of a hijacked car. That left sixty minutes for me to get a target and get the hell out.

Below, behind a waist-high glass case, was Plan A. A mask that curved into a crescent moon under the eye from a nineteenth-century Parisian opera. As far as I knew, I was the only one of us going for it.

I'd spent the last hour before shimmying into the ventilation system scouting out the competition. Mylo was going for a pearl-beaded neck ruff, allegedly worn by Elizabeth I. Interestingly, he was using some sort of laser pen, making little incisions in the metal locks around the glass. For a while, I thought he might be bold enough to try and swipe the ruff while the museum was open, but once he got a good idea that his tool could cut through the metal, he seemed to leave it alone. For the moment.

Lucus had somehow gotten his hands on one of the guards' uniforms, and when I first saw him in it, I imagined some half-dressed guy hog-tied and left behind a dumpster somewhere. Last I saw, he was pretending to do a walk-through of the gallery that held the lipstick set used by Vivien Leigh. Lucky prick—blending with the guards was probably the easiest way to get your hands on something, but since I wasn't a six-foot intimidating white guy, that plan wasn't going to work for me.

Kyung-soon took way too many selfies with a certain diamond-encrusted music box. For Noelia, I knew she wanted Marie Antoinette's slippers. I might have gone for them too if she weren't here. She even waved at me when we passed in the Treasures of Versailles gallery. Adra had been floating around that area as well. Fingers crossed Adra would catch on to the fact that she was being used and betray Noelia first, knocking her out of the game for me.

Unfortunately, I couldn't peg what *everyone* was going for. Devroe went completely MIA after our chat. And Taiyō? I hadn't seen him for hours. That was fine. As long as I knew what someone *wasn't* going after.

Plan A—the mask below. This gallery was locked with a keypad, so the only viable entrance was this drop from the ceiling. There weren't any flight attendants around to sneak codes to us, so I doubted anyone would be getting through that lock faster than I could make my landing, grab the mask, and be out through the emergency door down the hall.

Plan B—the Empress's Ring. A million-dollar cluster of rubies and gold only a couple of galleries away. If I went back through the ventilation system, it would lead me right above the display case, sitting in the middle of crisscrossing red-beamed heat sensors. I have no problem flexing and twisting through a grid of sensors, but they were annoying enough to make this Plan B.

And finally, Plan C. If all else failed, I was shimmying all the way through these vents to the lobby and making my way into the heart of the museum to swipe a pair of ivory fans. Going deeper into the museum on foot was a risk, so hopefully it wouldn't have to come to that.

My pulse quickened as I kept my attention below, waiting

for a flicker of movement and the perfect time: 7:20. It would take twenty minutes for security do another walk-through.

Now. I moved the grate aside and lowered my legs through the opening first, keeping a good grip on the inside of the vent. I swung lower until only my forearms were supporting me. Then my hands.

Common knowledge for traversing high spaces is *don't look down*, but that's advice for people who are trying not to fall. No time to be afraid. Mom wouldn't be hesitating. Mom would've already jumped.

Something across the room clicked. I regripped just before I fell, barely managing to keep hold of the vent. Was security coming back early? No way could I get into the ceiling quick enough to hide.

The lock on the door clicked again. A beep, then a scratching sound and another beep.

My meteor bracelet sat heavy on my wrist, reminding me that, if worse came to worst, I could fight.

I took a shaky breath, getting ready to let go. *Okay, bring it.*

The door slid back, but the light of a guard's flashlight didn't follow. A shadow slipped inside instead.

The figure, casual and confident, kept close to the wall as they crept into the gallery and headed straight toward the case with my mask. I knew that stride.

Devroe.

I made out Kyung-soon, too, peeking inside. She held a small, blue-lit screen with thin wires connecting it to the keypad outside. Her too? I thought she was going for the music box.

My blood was pulsing, and not in the thrilling way I was used to feeling on heists. I glared down, hoping he could feel my fury.

As he reached the mask, Devroe glanced up.

We locked eyes. His brows rose. My fingers gripped even tighter. Here I was, dangling from the ceiling like Mardi Gras beads stuck on a power line. As if this was the most entertaining thing ever, Devroe waved.

I could die, right here.

My face was on fire. So much for Plan A. Getting into a hand-to-hand fight with Devroe was not on my to-do list. Even if it was, what were the odds his new partner, Kyung-soon, was just going to watch?

Still absolutely delighted, and like he'd read my mind, Devroe reached into his vest pocket, leaving some type of small multitask tool atop the glass case, then took a few steps over so he was standing right under me. And in the most frustrating, look-I'm such-a-gentleman display I'd ever seen, he held his arms out to catch me.

I really hated him.

I heaved myself back into the vent, thinking way too much about how I looked as I was doing it.

Despite an urge to scream, I kept my calm like a professional. So he got the mask. Whatever. That was why I had Plan B.

On to the ring.

TEN

RED BEAMS ZIGZAGGED across the ring's gallery. Thankfully, they were visible. I had no red-light glasses.

It was only a ten-foot drop from the ceiling. I could land right in front of the case, then use a case to climb back into the vents.

But nothing could be easy, apparently.

For the second time that night, a figure moved at the edge of the room. I froze. Fresh panic dug into my chest. This was *not* happening again.

The lithe figure flipped and rolled, maneuvering around the sensors like it was a dance.

Noelia.

I'd done my due diligence scoping everyone out. She'd made it pretty clear she was going for the Marie Antoinette shoes. Had it been a setup?

Frozen in fury for the second time in half an hour, I remained silent as she reached the case underneath me. Something gray nestled in her ear. Earbuds? The little blue light on the side was on. Someone was talking to her. I couldn't make out what they were saying.

"No, I'm here now," Noelia said in that whisper-quiet yet perfectly clear voice only a proper thief could master.

From her blazer pocket, she retrieved what looked like a thin silver credit card with an edge so sharp I might cut my eyes just looking at it. I frowned. Was she going to do a shave job? It was safer than the shatter job I was planning—cutting a clean line through the top of the case let you put the box back together, no one the wiser—but it also took too long.

Why did I get the feeling it wasn't going to take her that long?

She slid her blade along the glass like a hot knife through butter. Plan B—gone too. On to Plan C?

And if Plan C was gone? What then?

If Noelia didn't go for the shoes . . .

I glanced back down. Noelia had gained a pale brown messenger bag, hung across her torso. Something dainty and pink poked out of the corner of the bag.

No way, were those . . . ?

She shifted, leaning forward to trim away the other side of the glass, and the toes poking up from the corner of the bag became clear.

The Marie Antoinette shoes.

My mind raced as I watched her. She already had one target; why was she going after this one? For Adra? Why hadn't Noelia dumped her the second she got what she wanted?

That little voice murmured inside her earpiece again. I suspected I knew who was on the other end, which annoyed me even more.

Not moving her gaze from her work, Noelia answered. "I figured it would be. If you're in the area, you should go for the music box too."

My heart stopped. The music box—another target from Count's list? How many targets had they gotten already?

I dug my hands into my braids. This was a disaster.

Why was everyone so quick to team up?

I should've accepted Devroe's offer.

The sweep of a flashlight shone in from the corridor. Noelia swooped back, twisting through the sensors and pressing herself against the wall. The guard passed with only a flick of his flashlight inside, sparing the room only a glance to make sure the sensors were still in place.

His footsteps faded, and Noelia said, "All clear. Yeah, better him than Quest, though."

It clicked. She didn't want *me* to get past this phase.

My blood boiled. Was she really that pissed about me stealing her jobs? It was her fault; she was the one that started this beef all that time ago. This wasn't just a game, and this wasn't me getting arrested on the line. Mom's life depended on this.

Noelia wasn't going to take her from me.

Screw it.

I jumped from the vent.

Noelia startled, instinctively stumbling back through the laser grid. Perfect. A few seconds to get ahead is all a good thief needs.

I slid the top of the glass aside and plucked the ring out of the case. Noelia reached for me, but I twisted through the lasers toward the other wall. She might have chased, but a light returned at the end of the hall. With a silent huff, she stumbled back, pressing herself into her wall just as I pressed into mine. We watched each other, holding our breaths while the light neared.

The guard shined the flashlight inside again. My heart raced. Exactly what was going to happen if this dude strolled in here and saw us, I didn't know.

A long-lost memory bubbled to the surface. A mirror of right now, but with a much younger me and a younger Noelia too, in pajamas, in the kitchen at ski camp, looking for butter cookies when we were supposed to be in bed. We hadn't gotten caught then.

I watched Noelia. Was she remembering that too? She had to be, something in me felt it.

Her expression dug into a grimace. Guess it wasn't a happy memory for her. Why would it be? It was all an act back then.

Satisfied, the guard carried on. I pinched the ring between my fingers. Did she hate every memory she had with me? Maybe I could find one I *knew* she hated.

I suddenly remembered a game we used to play, seeing who could slap their hand over a Starburst on the table first. She always lost, and every time she'd fume. The winner got to flick the loser in the forehead.

As the guard was leaving, I flaunted the ring at her, then angled my fingers and flicked the air, as if she was right in front of me.

Just like back then, she turned ten different shades of red. I grinned.

Noelia, however, was not amused.

She slipped her hand back into her blazer, retrieving the blade she'd used to trim through the glass case. Game on.

ELEVEN

NOELIA DOVE INTO the web of lasers first. I flipped in after her, ducking and weaving through the beams. It was a deadly dance, but I was a touch faster.

I snapped my bracelet toward her. She ducked, but managed to snap-kick my hand with the ring at the same time. It tumbled from my grasp. I swooped in to retrieve it. She kicked my hand away.

I ground my teeth in frustration.

Noelia slashed at me; I tried to snap my bracelet into her soft spots. We both dipped and weaved around the lasers, playing the deadliest game of limbo trying not to set off any sensors.

Her blade swiped inches from my eye—too close. I needed to disarm her. On my next attack, instead of going for the ring, I snapped my bracelet around her wrist and yanked it between two of the beams. My foot slammed into her torso, then into her hand. Her blade flew up and across the room. No more slicing and dicing for her.

A grimace twisted her face. Too bad, so sad. My weapon wasn't so easily lost, and I managed to swipe up the ring too.

My meteor bracelet was still wrapped around her wrist. Before I could release her, she grabbed the links and used them to wrench me toward her. She strained for the ring, but I yanked my arm away.

In the back of my head, seconds were counting down. When was that guard going to come back? We couldn't do this forever. I needed to get her attention off me, just for a second.

My gaze dropped to the frilly tips of the Marie Antionette shoes peeking out of her messenger bag. I grabbed one and kicked it into the back of the gallery. Noelia instantly loosened her grip on my bracelet. What was she going to do, keep scrapping with me or go after her actual target?

I knew what the smart option was, and so did she.

With a little growl, she let go and hopped back in the direction of the slipper. I darted off the other way, rolling out of the web of lasers just as a flashlight beam rounded an adjacent corridor. Looked like Noelia was going to be stuck there for a while.

Before the guard turned into the hallway, I dipped into the Treasured Fashions gallery. Past a runway of centuries-old corsets and satin gowns, there was a main hall leading to the lobby. From there I could get to an emergency exit. As long as I steered clear of heavy footsteps and flashlights, it would be a breeze from here to Marseille and the next phase.

Right as I turned the corner into the main hall, a hand gripped my arm. I froze, feeling a sharp point sink into my neck.

I drew a quick breath as my attacker pressed harder. My heart jumped. My brain screamed to use my meteor bracelet, but I knew one wrong move and my throat would be slit.

Slowly, I put my hands up. This wasn't a guard, and it wasn't Noelia. Who?

Keeping a hand on my arm and the sharp blade tight to my neck, the figure moved out of the shadows. A blue blinking earpiece caught my eye.

Adra.

TWELVE

CLENCHED MY jaw so hard it might snap. The pain almost made me forget what was pressed against my neck.

I risked a glance down. It was one of her rings. I wasn't the only one making practical use of my jewelry. They were hella sharp, and she knew exactly how to use them.

I swallowed. "Am I the only one who didn't opt to be codependent for this phase?"

"Probably why you're the only one who's going to fail." Adra's dark brown eyes glimmered with delight. "The ring. Give."

"Don't you have enough rings?"

She shoved me back into the wall. I winced as a warm drip of blood slipped down toward my shirt.

"Try again."

Everything in me wanted to slap her hand away. But she

watched me with the precision of a tiger. Any movement, and that ring was sinking into my jugular. I remembered Count's words. *During the phases, force—even deadly—is acceptable.*

I had no opening, but I couldn't just give her the ring. I'd worked too hard for it.

"Your partner's got moves," I said carefully. Quietly. "Noelia has it. I was just trying to get away."

"Oh my god, it's like you want me to cut you—"

A figure flinched behind Adra. I caught the movement out of the corner of my eye.

Another thief was scouting the corridor. She'd donned her jean jacket once again.

Better Yeriel than a guard. But that still didn't help me.

Adra pressed the ring deeper into my skin. "Last chance."

My heart pounded. I needed a distraction.

Maybe I could give her the ring, then jump her the second she lowered her hand?

What was my most probable chance of success?

"Okay, okay," I whispered. The second she looked away, I'd slap her wrist, swipe the ring back, and bolt. Hopefully. "My pocket." I used my eyes to gesture down to my jacket, waiting for that precious moment she dropped her gaze. I'd have half a second, if that. I wouldn't waste it.

But before Adra could move, Noelia popped into the hallway, slightly out of breath, with her blond hair falling in a mess around her face. Her elastic headband was pulled back like a slingshot, with a projectile I couldn't make out. What happened with that guard? Did she take him out *with a headband*?

Adra turned to catch her partner entering the gallery. Before she could speak, I shoved my palm into her shoulder, then slammed my other hand into her chin. Momentum shot her back. A sliver of a scream slipped out of her. Impressive control, but screw waiting around to commend her for keeping quiet.

I bolted down the main corridor.

Yeriel's shadow tensed. She was probably wondering what the hell was going on. That emergency exit was only a couple turns away.

Someone grabbed my jacket, yanking me to the floor. Gripping my legs, Adra dragged me back. Annoying. Before she could pin me, I twisted, bucked my hips, and bridged her off me. She barely caught herself, and on impulse, I rolled on top of her.

I caught her wrist and stopped her hand only a couple inches from slapping my face; the edges of her rings danced right next to my pupils.

I might as well take away her edge. With one hand gripping her wrist, I used the other to tear the rings off her fingers.

Noelia's footsteps approached. My head snapped around as she slowed. She raised her weapon. Something dark and metal glinted.

I ducked. The projectile licked the air above me.

The silence broke.

A storm of glass crashed only meters away. One of the display cases had shattered.

"Hey! Freeze!" a guard's voice echoed distantly. Yeriel was nearest to the broken exhibit, caught right at the mouth of the hallway. She didn't even have time to run.

A gunshot rang out. Yeriel screamed.

Oh my god.

I was frozen, my gaze stuck on Yeriel and the red seeping through her jacket.

Adra shoved me off her. I stumbled, my palms pressing into the floor for a second. Move. I needed to move.

There was a subtle tug at my side. She was pickpocketing me.

Life snapped back into me.

"No—"

Adra's hand clenched. She was on her feet in an instant.

"Thanks for the new ring." Adra winked.

She and Noelia had what they wanted, and they were ready to bolt in the other direction. Noelia stared at Yeriel for a moment, her expression torn, haunted, and it almost looked like she was going to race to her aid. But instead, she turned and ran.

I jumped up. Adrenaline pumped through me like fire. I could catch them—

A moan escaped behind me.

I could hear the guard sprinting closer. Adra and Noelia were slipping away. My heart pounded. I had no target.

I bit my lip, turning back to Yeriel.

The ring or her? Mom's life or hers?

Mom would tell me to pick her, pick family, obviously. Any smart thief would leave me behind if it was the other way around.

But it wasn't the other way around.

I hated myself, but I raced toward Yeriel.

THIRTEEN

STOPPED BY the hall corner, listening, waiting for the guard to get close enough. Yeriel's breathing was already an agonizing sound. I wondered if she saw me. If she did, I prayed she wouldn't look my direction.

I saw the barrel of his gun first. He crept closer, keeping his attention on Yeriel, like she could attack at any second. Like he would need to shoot her again.

More guards were undoubtedly on the way.

While his back was still to me, I jumped him. With a choke I'd practiced a hundred times, I squeezed with one arm and pressed a hand over his mouth with the other. He thrashed, trying to buck me off, but I kept my grip. Mom was the only one who could ever break my hold. A half a minute at most, and he was out cold.

"Can you walk?" I hoisted Yeriel up before I got an answer. Blood poured from the fresh hole under her ribs. She groaned out a low moan. Trying to get her to stand by herself was like trying to get the training dummy at home to balance on its beanbag legs.

So that was a no.

A smeared pool of blood sat where she'd been on the floor. I threw one of her arms around my shoulder and gripped her wounded side, keeping pressure on it. My hand was slick and slippery and warm. We took two steps, and little droplets of her blood trailed behind us. This was really bad.

"Come on, I need you to walk with me," I told her in Spanish. The smaller galleries had crimson carpet. If we were going to leave a trail, that was the place.

Yeriel's weight pulled down on me. I practically dragged her back into the Treasured Fashions hall. Lights, jingling keys, and anxious voices followed us. I tugged her behind one of the mannequins with a wide antebellum skirt, barely managing to hide us both under the fabric before a gaggle of guards passed through. Even with barely any light, the strain on Yeriel's face as she tried not to breathe too loudly was clear.

Once they were gone, we sat under the satin petticoat for a few seconds in silence. I swallowed, trying not to show just how screwed we were. A blood trail, a knocked-out guard, and Yeriel could barely stand.

"They're going to find us," she whispered. The first thing she'd said since being shot, and it was no help at all.

I shook my head, even though I couldn't have agreed more. But that's what people do, right? "We'll get past them."

She sniffled. I'd probably be crying too if I'd been shot. "All the exits will be covered now. Even the emergency ones. How will we get out?"

She was right. All the exits I'd mapped out were useless now. In my head I ran through each of them, now adding in a pair of trigger-happy guards standing sentinel at each.

Except for the one we entered in. I couldn't imagine any guards waiting by that inconspicuous storeroom door.

"Up." I took a quick peek out from under the skirts before heaving Yeriel back on her feet. Her face twisted in pain.

"Where—" She cut herself off, like she didn't trust herself to go on without screaming.

"Back to the elevator. The one we came in through," I whispered. "Now shut up."

She shook her head vehemently. "No . . . exit . . . down there . . ."

Even if there was no exit, being down there was better than being up here, waiting to be shot again. At least, that was my initial thinking. But there was something else. Something I couldn't quite figure out.

The elevator was only one person. It literally wouldn't function with both of us.

So how had we gotten down there in the first place?

We were all unconscious, someone had to have carried us in. What was the other option—we were hauled in through the museum while knocked out, no questions asked?

The elevator wasn't just inconvenient. It was a clue. There was another exit down there. I was sure of it.

Yeriel's jacket was drenched dark red. I held her tight to me and kept to the shadows. The once-silent museum was like an echoing cave now. Voices bounced around every corner. Lights in distant galleries were starting to come on. They were search-ing room by room, and it was only a matter of time before they found us.

I followed my mental map, hiding between pillars and show-cases until we reached the storeroom. It was locked from the outside, but a quick fiddle with a bobby pin got it open just as the lights in the hallway flickered on.

I dragged Yeriel inside and leaned her against the wall while I ran my fingers over the shelves, looking for something that would open the hidden elevator door. Between two cans of paint, I found it, a little switch. The wall beside Yeriel popped out. Behind it, the grated door of the elevator.

I sent Yeriel down first, reiterating how important it was that she somehow get out of the elevator so I could call it back up. She nodded, but I still hesitated as I helped her inside. I was sending someone else down first, going on faith alone that she'd send it back up for me.

My stomach sunk. Trust. If I insisted on not leaving her, the trade-off was trusting her.

I shut the grate of the elevator. After it disappeared below, I watched the light above desperately, waiting for it to turn green.

And waited.

And waited.

Voices grew louder outside. Blood, someone was mention-ing blood. Were they following the trail?

They were getting closer.

I shouldn't have let her go down first. She was going to leave me up here. Of *course* I was going to get screwed over trying to help her.

The light switched to green. I could've fainted with relief if I wasn't so hopped up on adrenaline. The elevator arrived, and I eagerly got in and pressed the down button.

It looked like Yeriel had literally crawled out of the elevator, judging by the way her blood had smeared across the elevator floor and into the hallway. She moaned weakly as I hoisted her back up. We hustled into the same room we'd started in, musty sofas, fancy screens, and all. Finally, we were back in front of that door I'd wanted to open earlier. The door just a few millimeters off angle. A door that couldn't possibly be airtight and so couldn't have held one of our would-have-been competitors behind it.

I pushed the door, and it opened with ease.

The rooms holding your former competitors are off-limits.

I bet Count thought she was quite the wordsmith, didn't she?

Inside, a staircase climbed into the darkness. The secret exit.

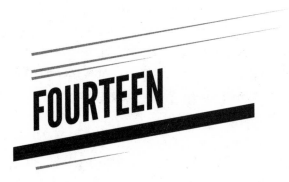

FOURTEEN

YERIEL WAS CORPSE pale under the moonlight, but she'd used everything in her to make it up a dark staircase in her state; I'd give her an Olympic medal if I could.

A new pool of blood was already gathering under her. Even her grip on her wound was weakening.

Ahead of us was a long courtyard separating us from the main streets. Yeriel hummed with pain as I slung her arm around my shoulder again and started trekking. If we could just make it to the street, I was sure none of the guards from that particular gallery were going to come guns blazing after us. But the way Yeriel was deteriorating, we weren't going to make it that far.

A selfish voice echoed in my head. A voice that sounded a lot like Mom's. *I* could make it. If I left her behind.

"Thank . . . you . . ." Yeriel wheezed. Her voice was so weak. So desperate. I swear she decided to speak at that moment on purpose. I was a lot of things, but I never wanted to be a murderer. And if I left her behind, I'd be something of that kind.

My ears stayed trained for the sound of one of the emergency doors opening. If the guards came outside, what would we do? Was there anywhere to hide where they wouldn't find us?

Headlights flashed to the left of us.

"Is that yours?" I asked Yeriel.

She managed to shake her head.

The car accelerated, stopping a few meters in front of us. The driver's window rolled down.

Devroe.

I should have taken his help earlier. I wouldn't make the same mistake now.

"Move," I told Yeriel. I'd been dragging her along, but that wouldn't do anymore. She needed to get her feet moving.

We hustled to the car—a European model, with round headlights and boxy doors.

As I reached for the door handle, the car jerked forward. What was he doing?

Devroe held my gaze. "You get in, you owe me."

I hesitated. There's always a catch.

"Open it for me."

He pushed the door open from the inside. I threw Yeriel in. She scream-yelped as she landed against the seating. Only when I jumped inside did I notice that Devroe wasn't alone. Kyungsoon watched with panic from the passenger seat.

Devroe hit the gas before my door was even closed. I looked

out the back window just in time to see the guards flooding the museum's courtyard. They were too late; we were already skidding away, into the streets of Cannes.

"What happened to her?" Kyung-soon twisted around so she was sitting on her knees in the passenger seat. A backpack, probably with her and Devroe's targets in it, slid to the floor.

"I think it's pretty obvious what happened, Kyung-soon." Devroe clicked his tongue at her as he swerved into the street, blending into nighttime traffic. He acted as if driving like this was an everyday thing for him.

"It's Noelia's fault." I took off my jacket and pressed the fabric into Yeriel's wound. The hole was somewhere between the abdomen and chest. She screamed, but I couldn't just let her keep bleeding. "We need to take her to a hospital."

Kyung-soon grabbed a phone that was sliding back and forth in the cup holder. "It's already seven fifty. Marseille is one hundred and sixty kilometers away. Maybe we could call an ambulance and drop her—"

A painful, screaming moan from Yeriel cut her off. Her blood was starting to seep through my jacket. She was really, truly dying. A human being was dying right in front of me.

"I—" Kyung-soon sucked in air through her teeth, conflicted. "The plan. I don't like veering from the plan."

"Take us to the damn hospital!" I ordered, glaring at Devroe, since he was the one driving.

He frowned at me via the rearview. A dozen different thoughts flipped through my mind like pages in a book. Why did he help me? Noelia and Adra had no problem leaving us to die, why did these two give a damn? Why wasn't he taking this dying girl to the hospital? And at the very back of my mind, behind all those concerns, one other thought gnawed at me. I had left the museum with nothing. I was out.

Devroe continued to hesitate. I wanted to throttle him.

"It's not as if we can simply walk her into a hospital," he said. "People will have questions that we don't want to answer."

"Then we'll leave her on the curb," I offered. "Put the nearest hospital in your GPS. It'll add ten minutes max. You'll see."

Kyung-soon swallowed hard, looking at Yeriel, who was struggling to breathe beside me. "Do it, Devroe."

He swerved to make the next turn. I braced myself against the back of his seat.

"If you insist."

Devroe weaved through the streets toward the nearest hospital. I kept mumbling something to Yeriel about how she was going to be okay. I had to press my anger down. Not just for the fact that she'd been shot and could very well die, but that all of this was completely avoidable. There wouldn't have been any guards if Noelia hadn't yeeted a projectile at me.

The hospital finally showed itself. A large building nestled within a private plot of land. Devroe snaked past other cars, honking and shouting at them to move, before hitting the brakes and skidding to a stop at the front doors. My heart cracked just a little as I dragged Yeriel out of the car. We really were just going to leave her here.

"What the—" A pair of nurses smoking outside the entrance rushed to us. Without thinking, I transferred Yeriel to their arms.

"She needs help," I said in French.

Help like Mom needed help. Help I couldn't get her any-more. Phase one, and I was already out of the Gambit. This was her best hope, and I failed saving a stranger. I was practically an orphan already.

Yeriel grabbed my hand one last time. "Wait." She fumbled, twisting her hand into her back pocket. I twitched, ready to get the hell out of there. Until a flash of gold stopped me in my tracks.

The mini portrait.

She dropped it into my hand, giving me a little nod. I gripped the warm metal as I stumbled back toward the car.

I was still in the game.

FIFTEEN

WE'RE HERE WITH the Spaggiari party." Devroe gave the hotel receptionist his most charming smile. Her cheeks turned pink as she rang up a bellman to take us wherever we needed to go.

I had my hands folded into my jacket. Thankfully, my dark clothes hid Yeriel's blood, but there wasn't anything in the car for me to scrub it off my hands. The remainder of the ride to Marseille had given me too much time to sink back into reality. I'd been this close to failing the first phase. Even now, Devroe, Kyung-soon, and I were only twenty minutes from being late. If not for luck, I'd have been screwed. No moving on. No wish. No ransom money. No saving Mom.

The phases were probably only going to get harder from here.

I had to step up my game.

Or stop worrying about strangers and focus on my own problems, as Mom would probably say.

Our bellhop stopped in front of gold-trimmed double doors. With his white-gloved hands, he pushed them open, then bowed his head and hurried back to the entrance. Devroe motioned toward Kyung-soon. She swung the bag off her shoulder and passed him the opera mask. Devroe glanced back at me as if to say, *This could have been so much easier if you'd said yes.* Whatever. I couldn't—or rather shouldn't—be pissy with him or Kyung-soon right now. As embarrassing as it was, they'd really saved me.

We entered a sitting room. An assortment of sweet and savory scents swirled around me. At least six service carts waited along the back wall covered with silver-domed platters, porcelain cups resting on saucers, plates, and silver pitchers of (hopefully not drugged) drinks. Count, still in her red suit, was standing with her tablet behind a table, like the maître d' at a restaurant where everything might be poisoned. Lucus was playing paper football with himself in the corner. Taiyō was settled in an armchair, pointedly trying to ignore Adra, who was obviously pestering him with questions, and the gleeful look on her face told me she knew exactly what she was doing.

Noelia stood against the wall as she stirred her drink with a little spoon. She stared into the cup like it held the answer to all her problems.

"Hey!" Adra slapped Taiyō's shoulder. He looked at the spot she hit like he wanted to sanitize it. "You owe me a hundred euros."

"I said it was *improbable* they would return before the deadline, not impossible." He checked his smartwatch. "And I never agreed to that bet."

Mylo, with a plate piled high with finger sandwiches, spoke through a stuffed mouth. "There was a bet? Why didn't anyone tell me?"

Noelia looked up. For a second there was only me and her, and the sound of her spoon against the porcelain.

Did she feel anything? Would she ask what had happened to Yeriel?

She made a show of taking a casual sip and then looked away.

I marched across the room.

"Ladies . . ." Count warned. My face must've shown what I was thinking.

Noelia lowered her cup to the floor and shifted into a fighting stance. She'd gained a silky white scarf since I last saw her, probably to cover any wear and tear from our altercation at the museum. It was so easy to toss a scarf over something and pretend it didn't happen, wasn't it?

"Ross, don't be reckless," Devroe called behind me.

I flexed the hand where my meteor bracelet was, paused, and then unraveled the scarf from around her neck in one smooth motion. I stared into Noelia's wide eyes as I used it to scrub Yeriel's blood off my hands. The dried red flakes smeared against it, startling against the bright-white fabric.

When I was done, I tossed the scarf at her chest.

"She's alive for now," I said, then turned on my heel to stand by the door.

Noelia dropped the scarf as if it burned. The room sat in silence for a few agonizingly long seconds.

Then Mylo stage-whispered to Kyung-soon, "Feels like I'm missing some context here . . ."

"Count." Noelia picked up her teacup and returned to her seat. "Why is Quest still here? You're going to disqualify her, correct?"

I scoffed. "Excuse me?"

"Count said no weapons during the first phase. The whole point was to show our ingenuity. You've been walking around with that garrote around your wrist since the Gambit started."

"Says the girl who tried to decapitate me."

"That was a glass cutting tool—"

"Then this is a glass *breaking* tool."

"Count never told us we weren't allowed to have weapons," Devroe jumped in. "She said we had to use what we started with. Ross started with that on, just like Adra started with her rings and like Taiyō started with those lock-picking glasses."

At the mention of them, Adra wiggled the remaining rings on her fingers. Taiyō glared at Devroe. Clearly, he took it personally that the secret of his spectacles had been exposed. Exactly what that secret was I felt a little itch to find out for myself.

Devroe twirled the mask in his hand, looking past me to Noelia. "Don't be petty because she was better prepared than you."

Noelia's knuckles went white. She squeezed her cup so tightly I thought it might break. Devroe gave me a tiny nod. He was defending me or, even better, pressing her buttons on my behalf. I . . . didn't know how to feel about that, so I just ducked my head.

"Mr. Kenzie is correct," Count said. "We were also interested in seeing how prepared each of you would be." My jaw clenched.

She continued. "Those of you who just arrived, please bring

your targets up." She pulled back the cloth from the table in front of her. A handful of items from her list sat atop it, including the Marie Antoinette slippers.

Kyung-soon bopped over and left a jewel-encrusted music box on the table. Devroe was right behind her. He gently laid the opera mask next to Kyung-soon's target. A feeling of pure failure drenched me as I dug the mini portrait—Yeriel's target—out of my pocket and set it on the table as well. Count tapped something into her tablet, and a curious thought hit me.

"Who's keeping all the things we steal during this competition?" I asked. "The organizers?"

Count didn't respond.

"Day one, and I've done my best work and made no money." Mylo sunk back into an armchair and popped a macaron in his mouth. "At least it was fun." His gaze found its way to me. "I mean, minus the bloody stuff, of course."

"Hm," Lucus said from his spot at the back of the room. The way he was looking at the little specks of blood on his own cuffs made me think that the blood was what made it fun to him.

I was in a room with multiple literal psychopaths.

Rubbing the bridge of my nose, I returned to leaning up against the wall. Count seemed to be waiting for some sort of message on her tablet, and she smiled when she received it. "The judges have agreed that you've all passed phase one. Congratulations. We'll discuss phase two tomorrow morning. Do check your phones."

A second later, mine buzzed. It was a miracle I had any battery left. A message from the hotel topped my notifications.

"You'll find your room number and an electronic key. All

your belongings are in your rooms as well. Rendezvous back here at six tomorrow morning. Get some rest . . . or don't. It doesn't really matter to us." Without so much as a good night, Count disappeared into an adjoining room.

MY FEET FELT like bricks as I carried myself into the elevator. According to my digital key, my room was on the tenth floor. I pressed the button and shot Auntie a text. **Passed phase one. It was . . . complicated.** What would phase two be? Another poorly planned heist? Should I have taken Auntie's advice and partnered up from the start?

Is that really what Mom would've done? Jesus, what would Mom think if she knew I'd almost lost this saving a stranger?

But . . . that stranger had saved me. Yeriel put her life in my hands, though to be fair, she didn't have much of a choice, but still. She trusted me, and it worked out. Just this once.

A hand snuck through the closing elevator doors and they reluctantly parted. Devroe stepped inside. Wonderful.

"Good, I caught it just in time." He gave me one of his charming smiles and pressed the close door button. I wasn't much in the mood to be charmed. Mylo and Kyung-soon were also approaching the elevator, but it didn't look like they were going to make it now.

I cocked an eyebrow.

"I hate crowded elevators," he said.

"Then maybe you should've waited for one of your own."

He pressed a hand to his heart. "You sound like you don't want to be around me. I'll remember that the next time you need a ride."

Auntie texted back. **Found a partner? Guessing they're out now?**

Of course, if I had a partner, she'd assume I swindled them. Because that's what people like us do. That's what everyone does eventually. Yeriel was a fluke.

So what the hell was Devroe thinking?

I swung around to face him. "I don't understand why you did it. You could've left us there, why help?"

"I didn't do it for free," he said. "You owe me a favor now, remember?"

I laughed. "Yeah but—" Let's be real. He didn't have any leverage on me. Who said I was going to honor that favor? "Why do you think I'm going to hold up my end? What's making me, huh?"

He gave me a measured smile. The same kind that made the receptionist flush on a dime. "I have faith you'll make good on it."

He had faith. He was just . . . trusting me?

I laughed. Partially because it was funny, and also because of how close we were, and the way he knew just how to inflect his voice to make it feel like everything he was saying was a whispered, dirty little secret just for us.

"You're a fool," I said.

"A fool in love?"

"Don't play." This time, there was a laugh on his lips, and it was hard for me not to smile with him. But if I did that, then we'd be laughing together, and then it would be a moment and we'd have a rapport with each other and then I'd be trying not to think about said moment in the elevator the next time I saw him. "You don't even know me."

His grin fell. "Maybe I just didn't want to leave someone to die."

It got quiet. Something in me cracked, just a smidge. Maybe the same part of me that cracked and helped Yeriel instead of getting myself out of that museum.

"I'll hold up my end," I said. His eyes lit up. "But if you think I owe you something . . . excessive, you're wrong."

"Don't worry, I don't want anything too wild." He placed a hand on his chest. "Cross my heart, dearest."

I rolled my eyes.

The elevator bell dinged, and the door opened onto the tenth-floor hallway. I walked out, and Devroe followed.

"I'm tired. Stop following me."

"This is my floor too." He turned so he was walking backward in front of me. "Our rooms might be next to each other. Maybe with adjoining doors. Perfect for a date. We can have dinner in one of our rooms, and no one would ever even know. Wouldn't want to make the other competitors jealous."

Date? Was it just me, or did he jump a dozen different steps in our conversation? I will admit, hearing that word come out of his lips, *date*, sent a little flutter through my stomach.

"Excuse me?"

"You just said you'd hold up your end of the bargain. You owe me a favor, and I want a date with you."

"A *professional* favor," I clarified.

"Well, that's no fun."

"Devroe—" I huffed, almost having to shake my head to get my thoughts straight. "Let's get this outta the way now. There's no world in which this Ross Quest is ever going on a date with you or indulging . . . whatever this is. Let's save each other both the distraction and the time."

Any other human would have gotten the point. But Devroe

latched on to everything I didn't say instead. Some part of me knew it just by the way his eyes narrowed. "Interesting. You didn't deny that you want to." He tilted his head, and damn was it like being eye to eye with a celebrity heartthrob.

Yet another slight little movement I bet he'd practiced a billion times. Little tricks from his own personal playbook, probably.

Maybe, maybe, some tiny bit of me wanted to. And maybe he was astute enough to tell. But that was part of the reason I had to nip this now. He could trust me for a favor, sure, but I wasn't putting any more of myself at risk with this boy. With *anyone* for that matter.

I pressed my hand against his chest, pushing him against the wall. Shocked, he let himself be pressed, looking excited at the touch.

"Devroe . . ." I said in a slow, seductive way.

His chest rose under my palm. The fabric of his vest was crisp but soft. I leaned in until we were only centimeters away. "Leave. Me. Alone."

I pulled away from him and resumed the journey to my room. A strange twinge of disappointment licked at me when he didn't follow. I held my phone against the lock of my door. The little light blinked red, then green. "You'll need this to get back into your room." I tossed his phone back to him, glancing behind just long enough to see Devroe catch it against his chest.

The corner of his mouth twitched, like he couldn't decide whether to be irritated or impressed. With something of both, he tipped an invisible hat to me.

I entered my room, taking a long minute to just breathe after

I flopped onto the bed. My phone buzzed. Right, Auntie. She'd been texting back.

??

Sitting up, I replied.

Tldr: no partner. Got into a fistfight with Noelia B. A girl got shot. Barely passed. I'm fine tho.

And I got asked on a date for the first time . . . I deleted that part before I hit send.

Instead of a text back, Auntie rang me with a FaceTime request within seconds.

"Are you good? Oh, god, are you bleeding?" Auntie, as much of a mess as when I'd left her, shook inside the camera frame.

"I wasn't the one who was shot, Auntie. That would've been something worth mentioning."

"I wasn't talking about that, I was talking about your brawl with the witch bitch. Did you whup her?"

"Auntie!" I actually smiled. She was good at doing that to me. "I—kinda?" I rolled my lips, feeling a little bit of tension drop from my shoulders. It was good to talk to a little piece of home. Almost like talking to Mom . . .

I sucked in a breath. "How are things going back over there?"

Auntie stilled. "No better than yesterday. All our leads are dry, and you know nothing that big has come into the black box. You're the only . . ."

She wouldn't say it, since she didn't have to. I was still the only hope. And I'd almost fumbled it on try one.

"I'm going to call her," I said, surprising even myself.

"The kidnappers?" Auntie scoffed. "Give 'em my best wishes. But then . . . get some sleep, girly world. You need to be on your game for whatever comes next."

Auntie gave me a reassuring smile and ended the call.

Then I dialed Mom's contact.

It rang and rang. I was sure it was about to go to voicemail when my new archenemy number one picked up.

"Ah, Little Miss Quest. Calling to ask for my routing number?"

My hand shook with anger. "I'm working on it."

"Eh? How's that? Am I gonna hear about the *Mona Lisa* being lifted on the news tomorrow?" He laughed.

The *Mona Lisa*, the highest valued work of art in the world and 100 percent unstealable, is only valued at $870 million. I wondered if this prick even knew that.

"Things are in the works," I reiterated. "I wanna talk to my mother on the phone."

"But I was so enjoying our conversation. All good things, I guess." The line went dead silent, but he hadn't hung up, so I must have been on hold. My nails dug into my palm, waiting.

What if they hung up? What if they'd messed up and already killed her? What if—

"Baby girl?"

I let out a sob. *"Mom."*

Jesus, I didn't even know I was on the verge of tears. It was like they'd been summoned out of nowhere. I slid to the floor by the foot of the bed, clutching the comforter, bawling like I hadn't since I was nine and had been betrayed by my only friend.

"I'm . . . sorry . . ." For everything. For letting that boat take her away. For lying about the other exit. For trying to run away in the first place. I'd turn back time and undo it all if I could. Talking to her, hearing her voice when I thought I might never again, I knew I'd do anything to have my momma back.

"Don't be sorry. We all do things we don't mean sometimes. It's okay." She hushed me, as if I was the one being held against my will, who needed consoling. I calmed my sobs into sniffles and wiped my face on the comforter. "Are you good? Did you get hurt?"

"I'm fine, I'm perfectly fine. Don't worry about me." I blinked back the last of my tears. "I'm getting you out of there. There's this thing called the Gambit, and I didn't tell you about it, but it can help you—"

"I know what the Gambit is."

Right. Auntie had known about the organization and the Gambit. No duh Mom had too.

"I didn't know they asked you to enter." Mom paused. "Look, if you're playing that game, you have to play to win. No matter what. Do you understand?"

I nodded, like she was there to see it. "I know. I mean, I know that now."

"*Now?*"

My voice got stuck in my throat. There was no reason to tell her the details. About Yeriel. About how I promised a favor to a boy who had no leverage. "I won't let anything get in the way," I said, finally finding my voice.

I imagined Mom nodding, or tilting her chin up and looking down at me in that protective, challenging way she sometimes did. "Rule one, baby girl."

I'd already been starting to break it. Not anymore.

"Trust no one."

SIXTEEN

TAIYŌ WAS THE last person I expected to come knocking on my door the next morning. Well, maybe not the last person, but it was curious nonetheless.

"Um, good morning?" I said cautiously, slipping into the hall. He was in a freshly ironed sweater and snug slacks, again with the perfectly molded hair. Honestly, if the thief thing fell through, he could pivot to making millions as a salon model. His look was made for an upper-class hotel like this, and it reminded me just how underdressed I must be in my black tee, jeans, and overnight-dry-cleaned jacket. But hey, I was working with my getaway gymnastics camp bag, which didn't have much, since training attire was supposed to be provided and the only things I just had to bring with me were my favorite pairs of shoes. (RIP yesterday's *Starry Night* kicks, the soles now permanently stained red.) At least my braids were still fresh and looking pretty fly, I thought, in an efficient half-up, half-down do.

I started toward the elevator, since it was about twenty minutes to rendezvous time and I'd been preparing to head there anyway. Taiyō fell into step with me instantly. "How did you escape the museum?" His eyes were trained closely on me. It felt like this was a question that had kept him up all night.

"Who cares?" I shrugged. "First phase is over now."

"Why does anyone care about the United California Bank heist? Or the Dresden Green Vault robbery? It's frustrating but fascinating when someone breaks through in a way you couldn't have predicted."

I frowned at him. "Are you saying you're fascinated by other thieves? Kind of like being mesmerized by your own reflection, don't you think?"

"How much to get you to tell me?"

We stopped by a little alcove between two pointless end tables. I crossed my arms, eyes narrowed. My curiosity was piqued, but if anyone asked, I'd say it was just me trying to understand my competition better.

"Don't need your money," I said. I mean, not unless he had a billion bucks. "But I'll tell you if you explain why you really care. And don't just say you think it's interesting." I cocked a brow at him. He side-eyed me for a second before pushing up his glasses, which I took as a sign of resignation.

"I do genuinely find thievery to be engrossing," he insisted. "However, my family are not thieves like yours. No one's ever showed me the ropes. The only way I've been able to teach myself is by examining others. If I'm going to become the perfect thief, then that means understanding what I missed."

"'Perfect' is a pretty high bar. I'm sure you're doing well enough if you made it into the Gambit."

"'Well enough' isn't good enough." He paused. "The Boscherts run the European thieving market. Your family has North America. There's no major operation that dominates the Asian market right now, just a collection of small syndicates and families."

"Not yet, huh?" The spark of a dream was in his eye.

"I need to understand what makes all the best thieves tick. How are the most talented similar to one another? How do they differ? It's the only way I'll be able to boil down a checklist for creating other brilliant thieves out of ordinary people."

It was an intriguing idea. An ingenious one if he could pull it off. If he could come up with a streamlined curriculum for training ordinary people into stellar thieves and enlist them into an agency of his own, he might just be able to take over a whole continent's market. Maybe in just a few years, if he had enough thieves with talent.

A dozen other questions bubbled up. Like how young would you need to be to start training, and where exactly do you find candidates for that sort of thing? But I'd leave Taiyō to that and tell him what he wanted.

TAIYŌ, WANTING TO write something down, rushed back to his room after our conversation. I went down to the rendezvous room alone.

Devroe and Kyung-soon were already there, sitting together at one of the two oak tables that had appeared since last night. Devroe glanced up at me when I entered, offering one of his charming smiles. I could read between the lines, there was an ask in his eyes—which, fair, since the more I thought about it, the more . . . teasing I might have seemed last night. Maybe that was intentional—at the time. But after my call with Mom, there wasn't any room for being wibbly-wobbly with him. Anything between us, anything between me and any of these people, was a hard no.

And I made sure to say so, with the stone glare I returned his glance with. His smile faded. His jaw clenched, and he leaned back, jamming his hands in his pockets. Obviously, I was turning down someone who wasn't used to being rejected. Or at least really didn't like it.

I was so attuned to the silent exchange between me and Devroe, I didn't notice until it was too late that a certain blond girl was approaching the breakfast cart I'd stopped behind.

For a second, I thought about just walking away, but then it'd seem like I was the one running, and we couldn't have that, could we?

I picked up a plate, even though I wasn't actually very hungry. Noelia took a glass and a started pouring from a pitcher of orange juice. She was subtle about it, but I noticed her glance down at my shoes. Against my will, it made me wiggle my toes, and I struggled not to squirm. I was wearing different shoes from yesterday, all black with black embroidered stars that you couldn't really make out unless you were looking hard. The real showstopper was the soles, which had an elaborately painted constellation landscape underfoot. In a different world, a very different world, I might have kicked up my heel to show her. But that reality was at least two hundred jumps away from this one. Noelia was wearing a new pair of tasteful ankle boots today. Did she have a scene under her feet too? What was it?

"I used to have a pair like that, the booties edition," Noelia said, taking a sip of her orange juice. "My papa made me throw them out. I don't remember why. Such a shame."

I just looked at her for a long second. She was here, starting a conversation with me about shoes? After all of . . . everything?

"Is that supposed to be your pivot to keep me from bringing up Yeriel?" I countered.

Noelia winced. She twisted the glass in her hands, her voice dropping. "I *was* going to ask about her. You didn't give me the chance."

I scoffed. "I'll be sure to let you state your case the next time you attempt manslaughter."

Adra announced her arrival with a grand "morning, losers" to the room before Noelia could reply. She was carrying a little wooden box, which she settled on the vacant table before reeling Noelia over with a finger. Noelia put on a smile and headed her way, shoving my shoulder with hers as she left. It was far too early in the morning for a brawl, so I let it be.

I peeked at the bottom of her shoes as she was leaving, though. It was a scene of abstract swirls and zigzags today.

Who the hell was Noelia Boschert?

A shadow passed over the cart as a figure stepped between me and my view of Noelia and Adra's table. Lucus. He grabbed a plate and then stood glaring straight at me. It felt something like seeing a semi coming directly at you on a one-way, and it took me a second to realize he wanted me to move. I was in the way of . . . whatever he wanted.

It's too bad I was so not in the mood to be intimidated today. If he wanted me to move, he could say so.

"Something to ask me?" I tested, holding my ground.

He slid an all-black switchblade out from his sleeve. He flicked it open. I tensed, my brain immediately going to all the knife defenses I knew.

But damn, Lucus was fast. He reached past me, his knife a blur, and pierced one of the sausages on the tray. "I don't ask," he said. Despite myself, I let out a little breath when he put the knife away.

A sinister smirk crossed his lips. "Chill out, Quest. Violence is prohibited . . ." He grabbed a bottled water. I could see inside his jacket just enough to spot a holster and the curve of a gun's handle. Lucus leaned in to whisper to me. "Until the next phase, at least."

It felt like a drizzle of ice had run down my back. I needed to sit down. But that meant I had to pick a table. There were only four chairs at each. All the other seating had mysteriously disappeared since last night.

Lucus had gone off to eat standing, stationed against the wall like last night, so that left Kyung-soon and Devroe, plus the other table, where Noelia was currently comparing rings from Adra's box to see what best fit Adra's outfit. A long-lost memory came flooding back to me. She used to help me pick out my barrettes like that.

Devroe and Kyung-soon it was.

Devroe, with only a mug in front of him, watched me take the seat opposite with an annoyed look on his face.

Kyung-soon pulled off her headphones. "Huh?"

"I didn't say—"

"She said she likes your music," Devroe lied. His expression was flat. What was he doing now?

I was going to tell Kyung-soon that I definitely hadn't said that, but she perked up before I could say anything. "Really? It's DKB. The K-pop group? Do you listen to them?"

"Um . . . no. But they sound cool."

"I met them once, you know. They do concerts in Seoul, like, all the time. They're usually sold out but obviously I'm still able to get my hands on tickets whenever I want to go. During one concert last spring, I finessed my way backstage and pretended to be one of their makeup artists." She sighed, reliving the memory. "My bias, E-chan, was even sweeter in person."

I smiled. "Just E-chan? What about the rest of them?"

"Eh." She shrugged. "They were kind of dicks. I swiped a few of their shoes and sold them online."

"I'm more of a J-pop man myself." Mylo sat down, taking the final seat. He was carrying a full plate, piled with pancakes and toast and crepes and a dozen other things. All drenched in syrup. "Unfortunately, J-pop's not that popular in Vegas, though. Not yet at least." Mylo kicked the leg of his chair. "You guys don't mind, do you? I don't like the vibes everywhere else." He nudged his shoulder Noelia and Adra's way, before casting a glance back to Lucus with a shiver.

"That's a polite way of putting it," I said.

Mylo scanned the table, patting the white tablecloth. "Who took the silverware?"

I hadn't noticed, but even though the table napkins were in place, there wasn't a piece of cutlery in sight, except for the spoon in Kyung-soon's hand.

"Don't look at me, I just got here," I said, though I doubted Mylo believed me.

"I'm too hungry for this." Mylo fished out his wallet and

pressed a twenty-dollar American bill in the center of the table. Kyung-soon swiped the bill and dropped a fork in its place.

And I thought I had sticky fingers.

"So," Mylo continued on, like that was a totally normal breakfast event, "I've been trying to fill in the blanks from last night." His voice dropped, and for the first time in my life, I felt like I was in some kind of school clique, talking noise about the populars. "Did she really shoot Yeriel?"

Kyung-soon tapped her spoon. "Yeah, also . . . look, I'm sorry for not saying yes to taking her to the hospital, like, pronto last night." She dragged the spoon across her bowl, dredging up a shrill sound. "I've been told I can be indecisive sometimes. Trying to fix it."

That didn't feel like an apology that was for me to accept, and I also didn't really know how to take it without agreeing that what Kyung-soon had just said about her being indecisive was a fault, so I only nodded. Thankfully, Mylo broke in by reiterating with a gesture that he wanted to know all the deets about how it was Noelia's fault that someone almost bled out in the back of a car a few hours ago.

"She didn't *literally* shoot her," I admitted. "But it's her fault. One second she's shattering a display case and the next a guard has put a bullet in Yeriel's abdomen."

Mylo shook his head and pushed his hair behind his ear. "That's messed up."

"That's the competition," Devroe said. He looked dead at me as he spoke. "If you're not making friends, you're making enemies."

Subtle.

Mylo dug into his stack of pancakes and pastries. Back when

everyone was accusing one another of bringing tools with us last night, there was one that didn't get mentioned.

"What was that pen you had?" I asked.

He laughed nervously. "Uh, you mean like a writing pen?"

"I saw you cutting through metal with it yesterday. Too late to lie."

Mylo sighed. "All right, you got me." He tugged his sleeve up until a slender and unassuming silver pen slipped into his palm.

Kyung-soon gawked. "You can cut through metal with that? Like a *lightsaber*?"

If I'd been drinking something, I might have choked. Never had I heard the word *lightsaber* used so seriously. "He's a Jedi thief," I couldn't help but say.

Mylo, riffing off of the Star Wars reference, wiggled his fingers. "This is not the wallet you're looking for."

Devroe, even in his pissy mood, couldn't help but crack a smile and study the tool too.

"It cuts through most metals." Mylo flipped the pen so the other end pointed toward us. "The other side welds. You have no idea how many times I've welded door hinges together when people were on my trail. Saved my butt at least ten times."

I leaned forward, getting a look at his magical pen from a new angle. "How does it work?"

He slipped it back into his sleeve. "Hell if I know. I'm no scientist. I used to run with a guy who was really tool oriented. When he dipped, he left me this." Mylo paused. "Well, he ripped me over for ten grand and then left me this as a consolation prize. But whatever."

When Taiyō finally did show up, it was with the kind of on-the-dot punctuality that I assumed was part of his perfect thief thing too. He had a book open in his hand, littered with sticky notes and bookmarks. Barely peering up from the pages, he picked up two pieces of dry toast and looked between our table and Noelia's. I kinda wanted to wave him over, but there weren't any other seats at our table, so he migrated over to Noelia's.

Count, equally punctual, entered through the same door she'd left through last night.

"Glad to see you've all made it in time." Instead of solid red, her pantsuit today was gray with red trim. "We trust you all slept well."

"Get to the point," Lucus said from the back. "Phase two. Is it like yesterday? Don't tell me we're already here and you want us to steal the lobby furniture or something."

"No. The second phase *will* begin today, but last time you were given fifteen targets to choose from to pass the phase. This time, it's a little more complicated than that." Count switched on a TV behind her and swiped an image from her tablet onto the screen.

My jaw nearly dropped.

An elaborately carved golden face. Age had worn down some of the details, but the fragile high cheekbones, vibrant teal eyeliner, and popping white eyes made it seem like a man was looking out at us from behind a sheen of gold and less like an artifact from a time long, long ago.

"The burial sarcophagus of an unidentified Egyptian pharaoh," Count said. "Made of pure gold and approximately a hundred and ten kilograms, or around two hundred fifty pounds in the Imperial system. Estimated value is upward of twenty million euros, though it will probably be auctioned for much more than that." She paused, like even she was taken aback by the stunning treasure. "This is what you'll be going after for phase two."

A small panic was starting to settle over me. Competing against each other at the museum was—I couldn't believe I was admitting this—*reasonable* compared to this.

I can steal things, I'm *good* at stealing things, but trying to fight off seven other people trying to steal the same thing?

Breathe, Ross.

"Let me get this straight," I said, leaning forward. "Does that mean only one person is gonna pass this phase? That doesn't make phase three sound very challenging."

"Of course not," Count said. "Four of you will be passing this phase."

Mylo leaned back in his seat, scratching his head. "Um . . . so there are four sarcophaguses?"

Noelia crossed her arms. "Ms. Count, please continue before you're interrupted again."

Ugh.

Count obliged: "This next phase will be a team challenge. We're dividing you into two groups of four."

"Oh my *godddd* . . ." Adra dropped her head back and moaned. "What is this, kindergarten? At least tell me we get to pick our own teams."

I turned back around to my tablemates. Devroe tried to stifle his smirk with a sip of coffee. Kyung-soon and Mylo watched Count intently. They hadn't figured it out yet.

Everyone on Team Noelia looked as stiff as a board as Lucus made his way up to the final seat at Noelia, Adra, and Taiyō's table. As he sat, Count spoke again. "Consider the people at your table your teammates."

The four of us exchanged glances. Kyung-soon looked skeptical. Mylo looked decently content. And Devroe, well, he looked pretty damn smug. I must have looked beyond ridiculous for trashing on his idea to team up yesterday. Now it was a mandatory part of the game.

I pressed my lips together and folded my arms.

"Secure the sarcophagus with our teammates' assistance." Taiyō nodded slowly, clearly already thinking at least a dozen tactics through. He opened his book and started scanning for something. "Is that all?"

"Not entirely. There may be some . . . side tasks from us along the way, but I won't be elaborating about those now." The screen clicked off. "I hope you were paying attention during my presentation. I won't be repeating myself. You have three days to acquire your target. I'll contact you with a rendezvous location once you have the target in possession."

My pocket buzzed with a new notification. An e-ticket. Time for a train ride to Paris.

SEVENTEEN

I **THINK WE** should offer them a truce."

I paused jamming things into my backpack, gaze snapping toward Kyung-soon. Did she really just say that?

Exactly how we all ended up in *my* room was anyone's guess. But we needed somewhere to start working on our game plan, and when I'd headed back to pack, the group just followed.

"A truce?" Mylo asked. "With Team Enemy? Kinda defeats the purpose of the phase, don't ya think?"

"Not for forever, just for the train ride to the airport." Kyung-soon was lying with her head dangling off the foot of my bed. She'd been in a handstand for about a minute before flopping onto her back. With how loud her headphones were blaring, I hadn't been sure if she was even paying attention until now.

"Wouldn't it make everyone happy if we agreed not to mess with each other for a few hours?"

"They won't agree to that," I said. "If they do, they're lying. Count is probably putting us on the train together *so* we can screw with each other. I don't see anything wrong with that." I ripped my charger out of the lamp socket by my bed. Okay, maybe I didn't have any specific plans to derail Team Noelia during our three-hour trip together, but just the idea of playing nice with any of them except Taiyō was enough to boil my blood.

"Let's calm down." Devroe stood by the window with his hands in his pockets. "I agree we can't trust them, but that doesn't mean asking for a cease-fire wouldn't hurt. Not everyone is out to get you all the time, you know." He shot a meaningful look my way, a testing one, not entirely unlike our silent conversation this morning. I ignored it.

Mylo started pacing, clearly not on board yet.

"You know, I thought you all piled into my room so we could discuss . . . I don't know . . . exactly how we're going to get our hands on the sarcophagus before them? Some sort of way to put them off their game during this phase? Now suddenly, it's a let's-give-them-a-break session." I pulled my backpack's zipper a little too roughly, almost catching my finger.

"What's your problem with Noelia?" Kyung-soon asked, nodding along with the music from her headphones and threading fingers through her hair. "I don't like what happened to Yeriel either, but she's just playing to win. We all knew what we were getting into. You can't take it so personally."

Personally. Why is that everyone's excuse? Sorry I shot you, don't take it personally. Sorry I left you to be arrested at age nine, don't take it personally. Sorry I betrayed you, don't take it personally.

Some things are personal.

"I understand the game, but maybe I did take it a little *personally* when she went out of her way to steal my target and get me eliminated," I said.

Mylo stifled a laugh. "Wait, that's why you guys were beefing? That's hilarious."

I gave him a death glare. Mylo cleared his throat. "I mean, hilariously cruel."

At least someone was on my side . . . sort of.

"We should take into consideration that there's probably some other factor here we don't know about yet. Marseille has an international airport. Why would they have us take a train to Paris to catch a flight out of the country?" Devroe rubbed his temple.

I'd been so hung up on the Noelia stuff I hadn't thought about that. The organizers weren't trying to save money on transportation, so there could only be one reason we were taking part of our trip by rail. "Something's gonna happen on that train," I said.

"Agreed," Devroe said. "Which means, it would be easier to stay on our feet if we weren't worried about petty rivalries."

Another tally in the deal-with-the-devil column. Because that never backfired on anyone.

"Why don't we just ask them?" Kyung-soon proposed. "Isn't it objectively in everyone's best interest if we cooperate with each other? I don't see the harm in asking, even if they lie to us."

"They *will* lie to us," Mylo said.

Devroe nodded. "Then it's settled. I'll go make the proposal. Face-to-face. Either they'll work with us or they won't, but either way, I'll get a read on them. Anyone coming with me?"

He was already heading for the door.

The hell? Was he about to just leave like we'd actually made a decision?

"Wait, we didn't agree to that yet!" Mylo called after him. He muttered, "He's very Hans Gruber, even down to the tie."

Kyung-soon sat up. "Who?"

Mylo gawked. "How have you not seen *Die Hard*?"

"I'll go with him," I said, feeling us getting distracted. "Stay here."

I rushed to catch up with Devroe. "Great teamwork. I really see what I was missing the last time around."

He waved away my comment as we headed to the elevator. "I don't have time for pointless debates."

"Or just the word no." I twisted my fingers into my palms. "I don't feel comfortable with this."

"Then you should step out of your comfort zone. I'm not asking you to actually work with them, but at the very least, I think I can get a vibe for if they're planning anything during our trip. Trust me."

"I don't."

"Well, you could." He stepped closer to me, cutting a sly smile. "And, oh, the fun we could have even if you just pretended you did."

I caught a whiff of his autumn-spiced cologne, and my stomach somersaulted. That was the real reason he stepped closer to me, wasn't it? Oh, he was good, and he was quickly spinning this detour into something I didn't need it to be. Thankfully, the elevator was there to save me. We entered, and I hesitated, looking at the floor numbers.

Devroe pressed the eighth-floor button. I frowned. "How do you know where to go?"

"I know where all our rooms are. Seemed like something useful to know."

So I wasn't the only person he was keeping a close eye on last night. For some reason, that disappointed me. "Are we going to knock on all their doors until we find the right one?"

"They'll be in Taiyō's room."

"Taiyō's?" If anything, I was expecting it to be Noelia's. In my mind she was their de facto team leader.

"He's the most controlling out of the four of them, so they'd end up in his room."

I thought back to how we ended up in my room. Was that the same conclusion he'd come to about me?

He really must have been a mind reader, because he answered my question. "We only went to your room because you started heading there without asking. Take from that what you will."

The elevator bell dinged, and the doors pulled apart to reveal exactly who we were looking for. Half of them at least.

Noelia was carrying a chic leather duffel by her side, and Taiyō had a boxy backpack balanced on his shoulders. Their conversation—in Japanese, which I unfortunately didn't speak— cut off midsentence when they saw us.

"Perfect, we were just coming to see you," Devroe said. He blocked the doorway with his body and held the elevator door open with one hand.

Noelia was skeptical. "Don't tell me you're here to harass me about the past again."

Me harass *her?*

"Don't worry," Devroe said charmingly. "I've talked Ross out of fighting you, physically or verbally, for the day. We've come to ask a question."

"We don't have any answers," Taiyō snipped, not meeting my eye. We were enemies now, and I guess being friendly with the adversaries was not proper thief behavior. "Excuse you." He moved to twist around Devroe, but Noelia grabbed his shoulder.

"Wait." She looked to Devroe. "I wanna hear what they have to say. But make it quick, we're on a schedule."

Taiyō looked like he wanted to squirm at the prospect of being late.

Devroe raised a finger. "Just one question. Are you planning anything against us during the train ride?"

A hint of a smile touched Noelia's lips.

"Don't answer that," Taiyō told her.

"Why not? We have nothing to lose by telling them the truth. No, Devroe. We have better things to do than taunt you for three hours."

Devroe studied her. "So you'll agree to a temporary truce, then?"

Noelia tapped her chin. "Sure. If Quest asks me."

It was like she *wanted* me to snap, and like she knew exactly what to ask to make me too. "Take the truce or leave it. I honestly couldn't care less either way." Making sure she could see it, I touched the links of my bracelet, ever present on my wrist.

Her almost-smile faded. "*Fine.* We'll leave you alone, since you both asked so nicely." Noelia slipped past Devroe into the elevator, and Taiyō followed. We stepped out.

"But don't expect it to continue after we set foot in Paris." She glanced at a domed camera in the corner of the elevator. "Wouldn't want to keep the show dull for too long." The doors closed, and then they were gone.

I folded my arms. "Well?"

"They weren't lying."

"You're sure?"

Devroe pressed the up button to call the elevator again. "Think about it. They probably want to chill before things get messy again too."

I should have paid more attention to Mom's psychological reading techniques. "And if you're wrong," I said, "and they try to throw us off the moving train?"

"Then we'll throw them off first."

EIGHTEEN

THIEVES LIKE TRAINS—less security than airports. The last time I was on a train, Mom and I were in a private car. She was appraising a pile of loose diamonds, while I was trying to think of an excuse to go search for the cute attendant boy who'd taken our luggage. By the time she let me leave, we'd made two stops, and he was nowhere to be found.

Now I stared outside as the French countryside whipped past us, like a peaceful oil painting wrapping around the train windows. How unfair that I got to see something so serene while Mom was trapped in a nightmare. She was caught Thursday night; it was Sunday now. When did three days become a lifetime?

I was hit with the urge to ask for another proof-of-life call, but testing her captor's patience with two in less than twenty-four hours wasn't very bright. Instead, I let my attention get gobbled up by my new teammates.

My crew was seated around a small table closer to the front of the train car.

Team Noelia had migrated a few seats back, a little more dispersed than us. When we first boarded, they'd been chatting in whispers, even though the white noise of the jostling train drowned out a lot of their voices, but now everyone seemed to be doing their own thing.

Not our team. Kyung-soon pouted as she flung her cards onto the table. This was our third game of Texas Hold'em, and Mylo's third win. Devroe, Kyung-soon, and I had already had to cash-app him over a thousand dollars each. Those were *baby stakes*, according to Mylo.

"He's cheating," Devroe said, flicking his cards at Mylo.

We probably shouldn't have been letting him shuffle, but he did it in such a waterfall-of-cards, cool-to-watch way that it was almost worth playing with a rigged deck just to see him do it.

"*No duh* I'm cheating." Mylo shuffled a rainbow arch with the cards. Watching them settle effortlessly into his other palm was like watching a really satisfying ASMR video. "Wait, you guys *haven't* been cheating? No wonder this has been so easy."

Kyung-soon kicked Devroe, who was sitting across from her. "Ouch!"

"How dare you not say something sooner!"

"I don't know how he's doing it. I can't call him out if I don't know how."

"Give me the cards." I held out my hand.

Mylo cradled them to his chest like they were the most precious thing he owned, but a glare from Kyung-soon made him give them up. "My mom is always cheating at games," I said. "Sorry, Candy Land, Connect Four—"

"Connect Four?" Mylo snorted a laugh. "How do you cheat at Connect Four?"

"I kid you not, my mom once went out of her way to order these digital pieces that you could hook up to a device and flip the colors. Then she'd get me to look over my shoulder, and when I turned back, she'd have four in a row. Hundreds of dollars spent just to beat an eight-year-old." I bridged the cards a little harder than I intended to. "I stopped playing games with her after that, except for BS."

"Ah, the game where you have to cheat." Devroe smiled.

"Double or nothing. If anyone but Mylo wins, he gives us our money back. Mylo, if you win, we'll each double down on what we already paid you. Cool?"

Devroe shrugged. Kyung-soon nodded. Mylo's eyes lit up at the challenge.

I started dealing out the deck, after making sure everyone knew the rules and that all fifty-two cards were in fact there. Taiyō left the car with only a glance our way as I started dealing. I breathed a sigh of relief when he returned just as I finished flicking the last card out. "Player with the ace of spades starts."

"Wonder what he's up to." Mylo frowned and threw the first card onto the pile between us. "One ace."

Devroe didn't even try to hide how carefully he was studying Mylo. I think it was bothering him more than Kyung-soon or me that Mylo was managing to beat us.

"He probably wanted to see what we were up to," Devroe said. "Just because we've agreed to a cease-fire doesn't mean they're not spying."

I suppose I should have been glad about them abiding by our little truce. An hour in, and they hadn't tried to throw any of us out a window.

"One two." Kyung-soon put a card on the pile. BS is an easy game—the goal is to get rid of all your cards. When it's your turn, you must put down the next card or cards in the sequence. Or at least you're supposed to. The cards go facedown, so really, you could put down any card you want. If someone calls your bluff and you put down a five when you were supposed to put down a king or you put down four cards instead of three, the entire pile goes to you. If you were telling the truth, the pile goes to them. First one to get rid of all their cards wins.

"I feel like we should be doing something. Planning?" Kyung-soon said.

Devroe scanned his cards. "We're not talking about anything while we're in the same car as them, no matter how many seats away they are." He picked a card from the edge of his collection and threw it down carelessly. Too carelessly. "One three."

I narrowed my eyes at him. "BS."

He grumbled, pulling the small pile toward him.

"You're pretty good at this game, Ross," Mylo said.

"I told you, it's all I play with my mom anymore."

"Yeah, but don't you play games with your friends too?"

Friends? "No." I fumbled and put down a card without thinking. "Four."

Mylo didn't even say BS. He just flipped the card over. Lucky me, it actually was a four of diamonds. His lips pinched and he picked it up, before putting down two others. "Two fives." He tapped their backs, baiting one of us to call him, which is why none of us did.

"Three sixes." Kyung-soon put her cards down one by one. I wasn't going to call her out, but I noticed Devroe watching to see if I would, so I decided to try something. I opened my mouth like I was going to say BS, and he rushed in before me.

"BS."

Kyung-soon giddily flipped the cards. Three sixes. I bit back a grin.

"That won't happen again," Devroe promised me.

Mylo leaned nearer to me. "Since you're pretty good at this, after everything is over, you should come visit me in Vegas. I've been looking for a new partner to help me with a casino sting."

"What happened to the old partner?" Kyung-soon asked.

"Pro tip: If I say, 'We gotta dip, the police are here,' I'm not joking, even if it is April Fool's Day."

"I thought your partner skipped town," I said.

"Different guy."

Devroe slapped down a seven. I didn't have an eight to follow, so I put down a jack and cocked an eyebrow, daring him to call me.

Mylo caught what I was doing and slid the card back to me without even flipping it over.

I shrugged and put the pile in my hand. "If you want me to be your new partner, then you must think we're both going to lose the Gambit."

Mylo laid down two nines. "We're not gonna disappear if we win. I mean, I hope not."

Kyung-soon poked his forehead. "She's talking about the

year-long contract, silly." Kyung-soon put down three of her own cards. "Three tens."

Devroe hesitated for a second, but didn't call her BS either.

Mylo made it sound like I was being ridiculous. "Come on, it's not like we'll be working for the organizers the entire year. Even criminals deserve vacation time."

Devroe's expression sunk a bit. "Don't get your hopes up."

He slapped down three "jacks." But I noticed his flinch.

I smirked. "About having free time or about winning? BS."

"Both. Ouch." Devroe pulled in the pile of cards.

"How are you going to win the Gambit if you can't win a card game?" Mylo added insult to injury.

Devroe scoffed as he flipped through the pile. "Kyung-soon, do you ever put down what you're supposed to?"

She was in her own world—or at least avoided the question by acting like it—twisting the tips of her hair and gazing up. "I wonder where I could get some digitally changing cards, like the Connect Four pieces Ross's mom has."

"Aaaanyways," Mylo went on. "Who said I'm going to work for the organizers at all if I win?"

"One queen. Um, *they* do," I told him, putting down an actual queen.

Mylo threw down a card, not bothering to call it. "Oh, really?"

"Don't kid, Mylo," Devroe said, his voice serious. "If the organizers want the winner to work for them, they will."

"They shouldn't be so anal," Mylo said. "And who said anything about breaking the rules? What if I won the Gambit and my wish was not to take the contract for the year? What would they say then, huh?"

"Maybe they'd ask what you were on," I said. "Seems a little circular to go through all of this just to reestablish your status quo." I licked my teeth. Wasn't that exactly what I was doing? But that was different.

"Maybe Mylo's just in it for the hunt," Kyung-soon teased. "But I don't intend on wasting my wish."

I could feel where the conversation was turning.

"Threes." I threw down three random cards, trying to divert attention back to the game. But no one, not even Devroe, called me out.

"Then enlighten us." Mylo waved toward Kyung-soon. "What's your grand, worth-every-bead-of-sweat wish?"

Kyung-soon pressed her lips together. "Well, um . . ." She shrugged and fumbled with her cards. "I think . . . I want . . . or maybe . . . you know." She closed her mouth, opened it, and then shut it just as fast.

Mylo and I exchanged frowns. "Do you want to try that again?" I asked.

"She doesn't know!" Mylo laughed. "And she trashed on me for playing for fun—"

"I'm not playing for fun. I want my wish." Kyung-soon's face soured at Mylo. "I just . . . need more time to make a decision like that." She traced the edge of her cards and shrugged. "I don't know. I can't wish for one thing then realize two days later there was something smarter or more impressive I could've gotten. Or more practical? Right now, I think I'd just wish . . . to make my wish later."

"That was the most self-sabotaging overthinking I've ever heard," Mylo tsked. He wagged a finger in her face. "Indecisive people never get anything done, you know. You're not going to come up with a perfect wish just because you sat on it for a few months."

Kyung-soon crumpled a little, which dampened the mood, and from the way his face twisted, I guess Mylo wasn't expecting her to take it like that.

"Are you allowed to do that?" I asked. "Stash a wish for later?"

"I assume so," Kyung-soon said. "They did say anything, right?"

Devroe set his jaw.

"How do you guys know about the organization?" I asked. "I thought I knew everything about this industry, but I didn't know about them . . . or the Gambit at all until a week ago."

"You didn't?" Kyung-soon blinked at me. "But I thought this would be, like, a Quest bedtime story."

Apparently not.

I shrugged and tried to make it look like I wasn't the only one out of the loop.

"Could be for the best you hadn't heard about them," Devroe said. "For all you know, your family didn't want you to."

That much was obvious. The question was why.

"Well, *I've* known about the Gambit for at least three years now," Kyung-soon boasted. "My mentor told me about it. I thought she was screwing with me for a while. She would be like, 'Don't mess with those people, Kyung. I think they're connected with the Gambit.' Or 'If you do this job well enough, maybe word will get back to the people who organize the Gambit.'" Kyung-soon dropped her shoulders. "All that ordering me around and stuff got old, so I didn't think about it for that long after I left her. But then I got that invite two weeks ago. No one in the world gets into my phone with an unknown number. That's how I knew they were legit. They really must be able to make wishes come true. And to do that, they must have some powerful people in their circle."

"Sounds like you're taking your mentor's word on a lot of things." I tried not to flinch, remembering I was doing pretty much the same thing with Auntie. But she was Auntie. She had no reason not to tell me the truth. We were both Quests.

"*I* haven't taken anyone's word on anything," Mylo said. "I actually met one of the organizers."

All of us slacked our cards. "Don't screw with us, Mylo," I warned.

"I'm for real!" he insisted. He put his cards facedown in front of him and leaned forward. "About eleven months ago, I got hired for this gig back home. Easy money—raiding a couple hotel rooms at some bigwig places on the strip. Had no idea who the people who hired me were. It was a no-contact thing.

"So I do the job, crack the safes in the hotel rooms and take everything inside. And it was a lot. Killer watches and laptops and all that. They told me to take *everything* in the safes, so I did. That included a bunch of folders and flash drives."

"Mylo," Kyung-soon snapped. "Get to the point."

"Right." He tucked his hair behind his ear. "So I finished the job, met at the rendezvous point, and turned in all the stuff. It was a parking garage under some business tower. Very James Bond. No other cars around. I met my contact and got ready to head off, but then the guy called me back to his car. He said his boss wanted to meet me. Curiosity is my greatest weakness, so I went with it. I didn't recognize the lady, but I could tell she was the type of person who's always chauffeured around. She invited me to sit with her and asked if I'd ever heard about the Thieves' Gambit."

"She told you about it herself?" Kyung-soon asked.

"And you believed her?" I added.

Mylo shifted. "Well, it was kinda fifty-fifty at the time. You know, maybe the lady was messing with me, maybe she wasn't? When I was leaving, she grabbed the files and flash drives, then handed everything else back to me like it was trash. Said she had no use for secondhand jewelry and then paid me triple what we'd agreed on." Mylo's eyes widened with dramatic effect. "I barely had time to say anything before she said *they'd* be in touch and pulled away. Not that I was gonna follow and try to give her the money back."

Triple? No way. You should never *ever* accept more than what a client offered you from the start. Extra always has strings attached. Guess in Mylo's case the strings were entering the Gambit.

"Your story doesn't make sense," Devroe said. He was the only one still holding his cards, even though the game had been all but completely abandoned. "None of that proves that woman was one of the organizers."

Kyung-soon waved a hand at Mylo. "The lady said *they'd* be in touch. And here he is. Sounds legit to me."

"Who said that was the end of the story, though?" Mylo cracked back. "I didn't tell you about the people I was targeting."

"Yes, you did," Devroe said. "You said you knew nothing about them. Changing your story now?"

"I said I didn't know when I was doing the job," Mylo clarified. "I learned who they were *afterward*. Call it more of my intense curiosity, but I did some digging. Apparently, the people I jacked were back channels for some facet of the Chinese government."

"Back channels?" Kyung-soon's brows knitted together.

"Back channelers are kind of like off-the-books employees," I said. "People who aren't technically the government but still negotiate for them?"

"Uh-huh . . ." Kyung-soon nodded slowly.

"But that's not the real point, is it?" Mylo continued. "What was on those flash drives and files? And what did the person I gave them to do with them?"

My throat felt tight. I was no conspiracy theorist. The amount of time I'd devoted to pondering the Illuminati or any other underground group of shadowy figures controlling things from behind the curtains would be less than an hour.

But I'd be lying if I said the thought wasn't pinballing through my mind now.

Who are the organizers? And do I really want to do their bidding for a year?

"I'm either starting to get why my family didn't tell me about the Gambit or really struggling to get why they didn't," I said quietly, throwing all my embarrassment about being out of the loop before out the window.

Devroe squirmed next to me.

Mylo sighed. "Guess all families keep secrets. That's what they do." He reached for his phone, in the same barely conscious way I'd noticed him doing before, but hadn't since we started playing our game. Was it because . . . we weren't distracting him anymore?

Family. Or was that the word that triggered him to think about whatever he was waiting for on his phone again?

For some reason, I found my gaze going to Devroe. He was the only one of us that hadn't laid anything about their history with the organization on the table yet. If now was the time that we were swapping tales . . .

Devroe threw down his cards. It was so fast, it made me jump. "Since we're not going to finish this game, I'm going to get some air." Without another word, he left, striding away to one of the adjacent cars in a stiffer way than I'd ever seen from him before.

I grimaced watching him leave. He knew what I was going to ask, didn't he? With his self-proclaimed people-reading skills.

Why was he running away from the question?

Why did I want to go after him?

"Let him go. He'll think a little and then come back," Kyung-soon said. "Probably."

She put her cards down too, and that was the end of that.

With the game abandoned, Mylo started gathering the cards. He held up Devroe's thick stack. "Well, we know one thing. Either Devroe left because he didn't want to answer any questions or it was an excuse, since he knew he was going to lose."

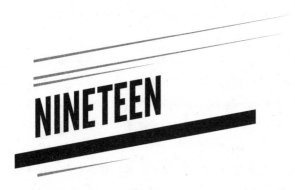

NINETEEN

Hi Rosalyn,

This is Coach Mutter from LSU's High-Performance camp. You didn't check in today. Are you still planning on attending? Please note that your fees are nonrefundable if you choose not to, and there is no room remaining in the second session.

I stared at the email for way too long before deleting it. Sour guilt racked through me. It had been a silly idea, selfish. I was going to leave Mom alone . . . for what? To try and make friends with a bunch of high schoolers who could also hit the splits?

I hugged my arms to my chest, imagining the smell of Mom's cocoa butter skin. Even just in my memory, it felt like comfort.

Wasn't I happy with her? I'd been fine my whole life with her and Auntie. Things would've been okay if I'd listened to her. Screw friends. Screw trying new things. Everything would've been okay if I had my mama.

I had to win, and after that, I'd make up for trying to run away and causing all of this . . . somehow.

Steeling my thoughts, I went back to tracing an invisible outline of the train over the tabletop, along with all my possible exit routes to match. Studying specs for this train model I found online and plotting hypothetical escape routes was calming. Or it would have been. After the escape plan for my own life failed, maybe I wasn't as talented at exit plans as I'd thought.

On the other side of the car, Taiyō was annotating a different book from before. Curious, I used my phone's camera to zoom in on the title, *Confessions of a Master Jewel Thief* by Bill Mason. I'd watched a couple YouTube documentaries about the guy myself, but judging by all the sticky notes, Taiyō probably knew more about him than I ever would.

Taiyō's concentration broke when Adra flicked a peanut into one of his lenses. Her back was to me, so all I could see of her was her snickering shoulders under her oh-so-posh jacket as she sent another his way. Taiyō took a deep breath and polished his glasses with a cloth before putting them back on. Adra flicked another one, but he caught it and dropped it into a cup next to him. I had a feeling he was keeping track of how many she flicked so he could do something twice as irritating to her later, and just as strong a feeling that Adra was only doing it because she was curious to see what he would do about it. It was a shame he ended up stuck with Team Archenemy.

Devroe settled himself into the seat across from me.

"You've returned from your sudden sabbatical?" I asked, then chided myself. Why didn't I shoo him away immediately? He was probably coming over here to flirt again. I knew better.

"Indeed I have. But don't worry, I brought you something back."

"Oh?"

"Myself. You're welcome." He cut me a smoldering smile to top that horrible joke off, but damn it, it made me laugh nonetheless. I averted eye contact, as if that would keep him from hearing me chuckle. When I looked back, he had a softer, much more satisfied expression on.

I folded my arms over the table between us, narrowing my eyes at him. "So what's the success rate for this tease-and-smile tactic? Twenty percent? Thirty percent?"

"Oh, it's at least sixty when well-executed." He leaned in, dropping his voice to a sultry whisper. "And it's not really the smile that gets people. It's the eyes. A knowing gaze can be the sexiest part of all. That's how you really get a target to blush."

In a trap that I walked right into, he matched my stare eye to eye, before just barely shifting his focus to scan the features of my face.

I knew exactly what he was doing—he literally just told me—and I still couldn't stop myself from reacting just like he said.

I looked away, hopefully not blushing too furiously. "Why are you playing with me? I think we established that I can see your strategy."

"Because I like you."

I scoffed.

"What? I'm not allowed to use my tricks on someone I actually like? If anything, that's when I should use them."

"You don't *like* me," I insisted, bouncing one of my feet under the table. "You just met me."

"And it was love at first sight."

"You forgot the smile that time."

This time he did grin, but a smaller, more genuine-looking one. "See, that's what I'm talking about. Maybe it's more fun when you can see the game. Maybe I like that you can appreciate just how polished my techniques are."

A tiny thrill ran through my body. The game. It was a little fun calling out his attempts to charm me, and he said he liked being called out. If I let it go on, how long could we both play and never get bored? Weeks? Months? Years?

You know, hypothetically.

Accidental or not, his knee brushed mine under the table. My tummy did a silly little wobble, and it sobered me up, ironically. Letting me know that he liked that I could see through him or whatever didn't change anything. Falling for that, allowing him to make me feel this way because I thought we were playing a mutual game was . . . dangerous. How long before I forgot to call him out? How long before I just liked it, just trusted him?

Ross Quest is not here to play games with handsome con artists. Ross Quest is here to save her kidnapped mother.

I could almost feel myself hardening. My shoulders, my face, my heart. The machinery was settling back where it was supposed to be.

Devroe's expression fell. He sighed.

"You must be playing the Gambit for something serious, if you can lock up that fast at the prospect of getting distracted for two seconds."

My head snapped back to him. He had his hands in his lap,

just examining me. There was no playfulness anymore; he was serious.

"It's—" I stopped myself. Telling him about Mom, anyone really, was not a good move. Especially when I'd just established that no one was to be trusted, him included. "Everyone has their reasons for being here. Mine are important to me, just like I'm sure yours are important to you."

Devroe's jaw twitched. He straightened his tie clip. Call me a hypocrite, but I found myself wanting desperately to know what he was in the Gambit for at that moment. Not that I would, or could, ask.

"My father." He watched the countryside roll by out the window. "He was in this . . . line of work when he was about my age. He was invited to the Gambit, but wasn't in any condition to enter by that point. That's why I'm playing. I want to win . . . for him."

There was quiet between us. The hum of the car. The jostle. I wanted to know and he just . . . told me? There was a sheen building in his eyes. He blinked it away and brushed some nonexistent lint off his tie. He'd done that before, when he was uncomfortable. Adjusted something about his appearance.

He was telling me the truth.

"Did you ever get to meet him? Your dad?" I found myself asking.

He let out a wry chuckle. "I just missed him. He died a month before I was born." Now he was straightening one of his cuffs, not meeting my eye. "He left me a letter, which is . . . something, I suppose. Mum said she tried to get him to do a video or something instead, but by then, he was already so self-conscious about how he looked and how his voice had deteriorated.

Letters were more his style, anyway, according to Mum. He was a modern-age gentleman, and what's more debonaire than a handwritten letter?"

"You must get it from him."

That earned me a little smile.

That struck a chord in me. Some people don't get it, how you can miss someone you've never met. But if anything, that makes you long for them even more.

"My dad died ten months before I was born," I said.

Devroe gave me a quizzical look.

"He wasn't really my dad," I sputtered. "I mean, he was, but not. My mom went the whole sperm donor route. He was just some guy she picked out of a catalog. At least, that's who he was to her. But to me . . ." I flexed my hand, taking a good look at the ridges, the bones. I had Mom's rich skin tone, her lips, other things. But my build was so different, my jaw way more slender, and my hair coarser. All of that, half my blood, I got from a man who was really no one to her, and who she probably thought would be no one to me too.

"Sometimes I look at myself in the mirror and think about him. Wonder about, is more like it. I have his medical information and a personality test, but that's it. In an ideal world, I'd be able to hunt him down once I turned eighteen, but just my luck, my mom had to pick the guy who wrapped his car around a streetlight a week after donating. She didn't know that, but—" I dropped my hand limp on the table. "Sucks, I guess. You're lucky to have a letter."

I resisted the urge to bite my finger. A tightness squeezed my chest. I'd never really told anyone about my dad. There'd never been anyone to listen, except for Auntie, maybe. But she didn't really get it. He wouldn't have been a part of my life anyway—that seemed to be the consensus in the family. Why would I miss something I never would have had?

Maybe that's what Devroe was thinking too. My situation was hardly the same as his.

He covered my hand with his, giving it a squeeze. "I'm sorry for your loss. You're right, I am lucky I have that. And I'm so, so sorry you don't."

My breath caught. Why did it feel like I'd been waiting my whole life to hear that?

I squeezed his hand back, and we both sat there, in this beautiful, understanding silence.

A buzzing in my pocket tore me away from the moment. We locked eyes before even looking at our phones. Simultaneous texts. This wasn't good.

> There's a special passenger somewhere on your train. Paris official Gabriel Raines. We're interested in the information on his cell phone. Get it for us? The team that fails this challenge will face a one-day penalty.

> Your train arrives at the station in 28 minutes.

> Good luck. ☺

A clock, counting down from twenty-eight minutes, dropped into the corner of my screen, already ticking away.

TWENTY

MYLO AND KYUNG-SOON were at our table in an instant. Team Noelia was already on their feet. We didn't need to say anything to each other; one look and you knew. The truce was dead.

Suddenly, it seemed like everyone was fumbling for the safety pamphlets. Where were the private cars? Where was first class? Had no one else cared enough to look before?

"Private cars are at the front of the train, first class right after," I whispered.

"Awesome." Mylo slapped the table and jumped up, Kyung-soon followed right after him. They were out of the cabin in seconds. Team Noelia was rushing as well.

Devroe started to stand, but I pulled him back down. He looked at me like I was delusional.

"Wait," was all I said. Noelia, Adra, and Lucus passed by, with

Noelia giving me a taunting keep-up look along the way. I forced myself to stay still until they were gone.

"Are you expecting Mylo and Kyung-soon to do everything?" Devroe asked.

I nudged him up. "They're going the wrong way."

"You just said first class and private cars—"

"I know." I slipped past him and led the way toward the adjoining car opposite the one most of the competition had just filtered out through. I could hear Devroe a step behind me.

"All models of this train built after 1990 have a detachable caboose in case of hijacking. Hijackers tend to start at the front because they need to take the controls. In an emergency, the last car can be cut from the rest of the train with a code all the staff have. If I were an uber-important public official worried about being taken hostage via hijacking—"

"Then mingling with the commoners in the back might just be worth it." Devroe reached past me to open the door into the next cabin. He just loved being a gentleman, didn't he? "How did you know? That wasn't on the information packet, I'm guessing."

"I looked up the specs on the train."

Devroe gave me a nod; it almost felt like he was proud of me for a second. "You get a kick out of studying maps and plotting escapes, don't you?"

My face burned, so I covered with a shrug. "I just like to know where I am."

I led the way to the back of the train. Though I was sure the person we were looking for would be in that last car, I made sure to stay sharp on the way. As we neared the door to the caboose, Devroe tried to give me a crash course in spotting government officials.

"We're looking for—"

"Flag pin lapels, stressed assistants, gaggles of overly in-shape bodyguards doing a really poor job of blending in as civilians. Yeah, I know. They're probably seated next to an exit, even if they are in the last car."

The second-to-last car was fairly empty. Only a family, all on their electronics, from the parents to the toddlers, and a couple of backpacker types dozing. Devroe and I paused near the door connecting to the last car. I risked a quick peek through the glass, but the jostle between our car and the next distorted the view. Still, it was good enough to see that there were way more people in that last car.

And then I caught a brief glimpse of some awfully perfect hair.

"It's Taiyō," I whispered. "What, did he power walk here?"

Devroe frowned. "He probably came this way as a preemptive measure."

Preemptive. I'm one step ahead of the rest and still behind because of preemptive measures.

"You stay here. If Taiyō comes out ahead of me, trip him and pocket the phone."

Devroe hesitated for a split second. Did he not like the plan? Reluctantly, he nodded. "Good luck."

With that, I pulled open the adjoining doors and slipped into the final car.

One step inside, and I knew I was right. At least twenty people had to be seated in the last car. A few of them looked like normal passengers in jeans and sweaters, but most of them were obviously a part of a political entourage. Men and women in crisp suits and button-downs, tapping away on laptops or flipping through papers bristling with dozens of neon sticky notes. Toward the very back of the car was the official. Even without the lapel pin I was hoping for, his striped satin tie and interview-ready hair and clean shave were enough to peg him. He was dozing.

Across the aisle from him sat a woman with a tight military-grade bun and a pensive stare. So there was the security detail...

She eyed me the second I entered. I gave her an awkward smile—that's what normal people do when someone stares at them—then slid into a seat across from Taiyō.

"Go away."

"What's your plan? It's gonna be pretty hard for either of us to get that phone without tipping off GI Jane over there."

He hesitated. "I shouldn't be talking to you."

"Come on, do you think it's admirable thief behavior to walk away with nothing?"

Taiyō squirmed, thrumming his fingers over the tabletop. I imagined he was regretting telling me about his flawless thief ambitions.

"Consider it a field test." I leaned forward, feeling like I'd gained an in with Taiyō. "Everyone else is searching through private cars on the other side of the train; it's just me and you. Think of the lesson you could add to your curriculum. *Knowing when to work with adversaries to accomplish your objective.* Pertinent information, right?" He pushed up his glasses. Did he only do that when he was thinking, or when he was annoyed?

I sighed. "You can take the phone too."

"Why would you let me do that?"

"We've got . . ." I glanced at the timer. "Sixteen minutes left. I'll figure out a way to get it back before we get to zero. What do you say? Wanna help a girl out?"

He straightened up, seeming to think for a second before giving me a smug smile. "You handle the woman. I need a minute at least."

"What's your plan?" I couldn't help but ask. "The official's gonna notice his phone's gone right after you swipe it."

"It won't be gone." Taiyō didn't give me any more of an explanation. He made his way right over to our target. "Excuse me, Mr. Raines? So sorry to bother you." His French was almost accentless. Now that I was thinking about it, his English was too. I wondered if that was another thing he'd learned from the greats.

The official, Gabriel, looked a tad annoyed. Being awoken from a nap by a random teenager was probably making him wish they'd risked the hijacking and gone with the private cabin anyway.

Taiyō recovered quickly. "I saw your last public speech. So impassioned. If you don't mind, how did you become such a talented speaker?"

At that, Gabriel was wide awake. He did have the look of someone who loves to talk about themselves. He was a politician after all.

Gabriel waved him to sit down and started rambling on about himself. Meanwhile, GI Jane watched this new threat closely. Any stranger within close proximity of her man was bound to be a topic of interest. And I needed to get her attention off Taiyō for sixty seconds.

I took a short breath and ambled through the aisle toward GI Jane's nook. The closer I got, the harder her jaw seemed to clench. What was I going to say to get this woman off her game for a whole minute?

What would get *me* to freak out, even just a little?

Instead of sitting in the seat across from her, I knelt in the aisle beside her and put on my best secondhand embarrassment face.

"What?" she asked. Super blunt. I was sure she'd slap me away like a fly if she could.

I whispered, "I just wanted to let you know I saw a red spot while you were walking by earlier . . . I would want someone to tell me, so . . ."

Her eyes widened, and that formerly hard-as-steel expression melted into a flustered mess. "I . . . um." She glanced at Taiyō, who was nodding along like a puppy at Gabriel's every word. "Excuse me," she mumbled, then pushed past me toward the car doors.

While I returned to my seat, I caught a quick glance at Taiyō's hand near where Gabriel's phone had been plugged in earlier. Only, rather than unplugging a phone, Taiyō was plugging one back in. A decoy? Gabriel would notice eventually, but not right away. Pretty damn smooth, Taiyō.

As instantly as he'd started the conversation, Taiyō wrapped it up, insisting he was going to be at Gabriel's next campaign fundraiser. I got up and headed back toward the exit a few steps behind him.

"Didn't know you were so interested in politics," I whispered as Taiyō opened the adjoining door.

"It's good to know people," he said, but the emphasis he put on *know* hit different. I think Taiyō liked to know people the way I like to know all the turns and exits in a building.

I almost sighed in the split second before Taiyō opened the door back into the adjoining car. "Wish you'd sat at our table instead," I said. "No hard feelings."

Taiyō barely had time to tense before Devroe, now in a green corduroy jacket, tripped into him. Equally "clumsy," I yelped and pretended to almost fall too, conveniently grabbing Taiyō's arms for "balance."

Devroe darted off, leaving Taiyō and me in a jumble on the floor. A kind woman rushed to help us up. As she pulled me to my feet, I snatched Taiyō's glasses and tossed them between two seats. He scowled and mumbled something in Japanese that I was sure I didn't want translated.

Another passenger, a man in a pin-striped suit, had jumped up to check on the scene by now too.

In a rush, I brushed past him and the woman. "Sorry, I'm fine. Thank you." I twisted between them.

Trying not to run, I moved quickly back through the train cars. Some of the other passengers eyed me with interest as I passed, making me slow down. Maybe I was looking more anxious than I thought.

Finally, I reached our car. It was bizarrely quiet compared to the other cars, which were buzzing with conversations, snoring, people tapping away on electronics. Not that strange, I guess, seeing how our car, along with all its seats and tables, was nearly empty. There was only Devroe, seated in a front-facing chair in the middle of the car, and a new guy I hadn't seen before. He flipped through a newspaper across the aisle from Devroe.

I clicked the door closed behind me, and Devroe glanced back over his shoulder. He nodded slightly toward the new passenger and rolled his eyes. No more thief talk while this rando was around. But what did that matter? He had the phone. We could all just shut up and mind our own business for another ten minutes.

I slid into a front-facing seat at the back, giving me a full view of the car. A second later, Adra and Lucus slipped back inside, coming from their wasted trip to the front of the car. I was sure Taiyō had texted them with an update by now.

With the same idea as me, Adra took a back-facing seat on the other side of the car. Lucus, however, sat right across from that stranger with the newspaper, putting himself directly on the other side of the aisle from Devroe. "You have the sports section?" he asked in French. The man happily handed him that subsection. Lucus planted one foot in the aisle while he pretended to read. Suddenly, I was pretty grateful for this random new passenger. We might be in a brawl for that phone if not for him.

Taiyō returned next. A little bead of guilt swelled in me as he boldly took the seat across the aisle from me in the back. "You scratched my glasses," he said, tapping the bottom corner of his frames. "I won't forget that."

"Bill me," I said.

The door from the front opened once again. This time, Mylo and Kyung-soon entered. Mylo surveyed the car before sliding into a seat across the aisle from Adra on the other end. Kyung-soon took the seat next to him. It was like we were pairing off. Kyung-soon and Mylo across from Adra, Devroe across from Lucus, and me back here with Taiyō. The only person missing was . . .

The front door swept open. But instead of just Noelia, there was a uniformed man with her. He was white and walked authoritatively with his hands on his belt. Behind him, Noelia looked uncharacteristically frantic. Uneasy. She whispered to the man in soft French, punctuating her words with delicate nervous gestures. The glint of a badge over his breast caught my eye. One of the train guards?

The train guard nodded and stepped past her. His eyes swept over the car, connecting with mine for only a second before falling squarely on Devroe.

Crap.

TWENTY-ONE

THERE'S A FEELING you get when you just know something is about to go down, but you don't know how to stop it, so you just have to sit tight and watch things fall apart.

This was one of those moments, and that feeling was strangling me.

The guard, with Noelia right behind him, approached Devroe. "Pardon me," the guard said. "Did you bump into this young lady earlier?"

I couldn't quite see Devroe's expression, but there was an irritated hitch in his voice. "No, I don't think so."

"Are you *sure*?"

Noelia's voice was like a mouse. "I know I had my phone before. Then I bumped into a man with a dark complexion, and it was gone."

My blood was so hot it was nearly evaporating. No freaking way was she trying to get the phone like this. Even Adra was giving Noelia a dirty look, like she wasn't on board with it going down like this either.

The guard sighed. "Perhaps we can wait until we make it to the station. We'll—"

Noelia gave him the kind of I'll-have-your-job look white people always seem to be able to floor service workers with.

Floor.

I had an idea.

As fast as I could, I shot a text into the group chat. **Mylo— back row. Floor.**

I glanced down at the area under the seats. Like seats on a bus or a plane, there was space underneath all of them. More than enough space for a phone to slide through.

Hopefully Devroe got the message.

Devroe shifted in his seat. I hoped he was dropping the phone onto the carpet and kicking it right to Mylo's combat boots.

I held my breath.

Mylo met my gaze and winked.

If it wasn't totally uncool and wouldn't have given anything away, I would have fist-bumped the air.

"Look, feel free to pat me down," Devroe offered. "But I want an apology when you don't find anything."

Worry flashed across Noelia's face, but she quickly schooled her features.

The guard turned to her, like she was the deciding factor in if this was happening or not, and she nodded.

Just as Devroe was rising from his seat for a pat-down, a

voice chimed over the car's speakers, reminding everyone that we were ten minutes out from the Paris station. The guard tilted his head, apparently listening to an earpiece.

"Copy that. Yes, I'm in car seventeen." He straightened before raising his voice so everyone in the car could hear. "I'm afraid a very important passenger has lost his phone as well. Security has been asked to search everyone on this train, starting with the car we're in. You may decline if you like, but anyone who does will need to stay behind and talk with the Paris police officials."

Police? No thank you. Damn—Gabriel would have an entire train searched and call in the police just for a stolen phone?

What exactly was on that device?

The older gentleman snorted.

"Ridiculous . . ." Lucus hummed in agreement. Apparently, he and the guy were paper buddies now.

Devroe spread his arms, seemingly content as ever to be patted down. "Glad I'm not the only one getting special treatment."

The train guard searched him with all the thoroughness of an airport security agent. From his sleeves to his chest to his pants. Noelia watched intently, though I could tell she was starting to sweat now. It was one thing to say she was looking for her own phone. But now, if the guard found the target's phone on Devroe, there was no way she could claim it was hers. It would be going right back to Mr. Gabriel.

Once he was done searching Devroe, finding nothing but his own phone and at least three emergency tie clips in his vest pocket, the guard felt between the seats, in the seatback pockets, and even scanned the floor. Satisfied, he straightened up and motioned to Devroe's seat. "You can sit now, sir. You're good."

"So they tell me."

The guard turned to Noelia. A text from Devroe dropped into the group text. **Back to me.**

Devroe had already been searched. If Mylo slid it back to him, it'd be safe.

Noelia seemed to realize this, too.

She plopped into a seat right in front of Devroe, blocking the path between him and Mylo.

"Miss." The train guard gestured for her to stand back up.

Noelia scoffed. "Me? You can't be serious. I'm the victim here. I've had my phone stolen, and now you want to search *me*? I think these are grounds for a lawsuit!"

"You'll have to take that up with someone else—"

"Whatever." She cut him off with a flick of her hand. "I'll wait for the authorities."

The guard took down her name, which she said was Lyla, on a notepad and started searching for his next target.

Mylo's hand punched the air. "Me next, please." He shoved Kyung-soon's shoulder, and she jumped out of the seat and took another across the aisle, putting herself between Lucus and Adra. She didn't need to send a text for me to know that she now had the phone.

"I've never been searched before," Mylo rattled on as the guard searched him, the American accent coloring his French. "It's on my bucket list. Somewhere between meeting the president and bungee-jumping the Grand Canyon."

Mylo kept his gaze unblinkingly on Kyung-soon while the guard patted down his pants. He wanted her to send the phone back to him after his search was done.

So of course, to prevent this, Adra stepped straight into the aisle between them. "Just so you know, this tunic and scarf are custom, and if you stain them, you *will* be paying for them." She flipped her ponytail and held out her arms.

Mylo peered past them and nodded for Kyung-soon to send it anyway. Was he delusional? The odds of her getting the phone past Adra and the guard had to be something like ninety-nine to one.

And still, he looked like he was about to start twitching in excitement. He was dying to take the risk. Thank god Kyung-soon wasn't as down for the dice roll as he was.

A second before the guard finished with Adra, Kyung-soon dropped it and kicked it in my direction. I was about to pounce, but Lucus effortlessly intercepted. He clapped his boot over the phone and drew it back between his feet without even looking at it. He might have played phone soccer his entire life.

And Mom didn't think sports would've helped me be a better thief.

Now it was Lucus, looking over the top of his newspaper, winking at me. I gritted my teeth.

As the guard finished up with Kyung-soon, Lucus dribbled the phone lightly between his feet. He was trying to feint me. Keep me guessing where he was going to send it next.

With precision only a seasoned soccer player could have, he sent the phone sliding straight under Taiyō's seat. Taiyō scooped it up and turned his back to me. Was he typing? What was he doing?

Lucus made small talk with the guard about the World Cup, which I was pretty sure was his subtle way of messing with me, while he was patted down, but my attention stayed on Taiyō. He would probably try to send the phone back to Lucus in a moment.

Taiyō straightened around, but then he screwed up.

The train juddered on the track, and the phone slipped out of his hand, landing squarely in the aisle between us. I dove. He grabbed me by the jacket, trying to shove me away, but it was no use. I swiped the phone before he had a chance.

The guard frowned as we both leaned back into our seats. Taiyō put a hand up as the guard approached him. "I'll wait for the police."

The brakes outside began to squeal. The train was slowing.

The guard took a moment to jot down Taiyō's fake name, Alex. My heart pounded up my throat. Devroe shot me a look over his seat. *Do it,* he seemed to silently say.

It was a clear path from me to him. Easy. As easy as it would have been for Taiyō to send the phone back to Lucus if he hadn't dropped it.

What were the odds that Taiyō would've developed butter fingers right when it was most convenient for me?

Something didn't feel right, but there was no time for overanalyzing.

I dropped the phone and kicked it Devroe's way. Pretending to relace my kicks, I watched it slide right under his heel. No one else attempted to stop it. More sus.

I held my breath as the guard patted me down, waiting for something else to happen. Something dramatic. But nothing did.

The train pulled into the station, and simultaneously, the timer ran down.

Devroe sent me, and me alone, a smiley face. The game was over, we won.

So why did it feel like we lost?

TWENTY-TWO

THE THOUGHT THAT I was missing something nagged at me all the way from the train station in Paris to when our flight landed in Cairo.

They had to have done something to the phone, which Count conveniently told us to hang on to. Taiyō was too precise to have screwed up. But after two hours of in-flight fiddling, Kyung-soon declared the phone "probably" bug-free. Not exactly reassuring.

As soon as we landed, I bought an armful of water bottles. I chugged the first one down in only a minute, then started on another.

Devroe laughed at me as Kyung-soon and Mylo waited at the edge of the airport pick-up/drop-off point for our rideshare.

"You should've taken the water the flight attendants were offering," he said.

I wondered if Devroe had picked his outfit specifically because we were in Egypt. His vest was a sandy color, and he had on tight khaki-colored pants that shouldn't have worked but somehow did. I tried not to let myself be distracted by the way they made his eyes seem even chocolatey-er.

"I think I have PTSD from the last time a flight attendant offered me water."

"First, she didn't trust people, and now she doesn't trust water. By god, she's getting worse."

"Shut up." After downing half the second bottle, I capped it and slipped it into my backpack. The flight hadn't exactly been unpleasant, but it was nothing like the cozy experience I was used to with Paolo's six-seater either. Something about all the other people walking about the cabin and buckling and unbuckling seat belts made me feel like I was about to live out some plane-crash-and-stranded-on-a-desert-island scenario.

"I'm not used to flying commercial . . ." I murmured.

"How do you usually travel? Don't you live on an island?"

"We have a private pilot." I'd never said that out loud before; it made me sound pretty bougie . . .

Devroe ignored my comment. "Well, you should be grateful we got on the plane at all. We could've still been back in Paris on a one-day penalty like the other team."

I squeezed the strap of my backpack, shifting my weight. "Maybe taking the L with the penalty would've been better than falling for whatever they're planning."

"Will you relax? We'll lock up the phone as soon as we get to the hotel. No danger at all, all right?"

"I guess . . ." That didn't quite scratch the itch of not knowing exactly what their plan was, but you can't have everything.

Our rideshare arrived. Kyung-soon, who'd been sitting on her suitcase behind us with her headphones on, jumped up and began rolling the pink case toward the SUV. The four of us piled in and headed for our hotel.

Cairo was a gorgeous city. A sea of golds and browns. Buildings with arches and domed tops and spiraling turrets juxtaposed with glittering glass skyscrapers and the sparkling Nile cutting through it all. It was like a storybook with pages taken from a dozen different eras all sewn into the same book. Too bad we weren't here just to visit.

"I adore Egypt." Kyung-soon sighed as she peered out the window. "If only we had time to see the Sphinx and the pyramids. I didn't get to see them the last time I was here with my mentor."

"This isn't a vacation, it's a business trip," I reminded her, even though I'd just been thinking the same thing. But we couldn't both be catching the wanderlust.

Our driver, apparently as fluent in English as he was in Arabic, cast me a curious glance via the rearview. What kind of business trip could four teens be on? But I guess he wanted a tip enough not to butt into our conversation.

Devroe, in the back row next to me, leaned closer. "That doesn't mean we can't play a little bit."

I looked out the window to hide my grin. Damn him for being such an expert at drawing those out.

As the car turned, our destination revealed itself. My fingers grazed the window. The Pyramid Hotel—which to Mylo's disappointment did not take after the Luxor and was *not* shaped like an actual pyramid—glowed ahead of us. Its glass sides were tinted in gold, reflecting the sun in gilded shades. I squinted to see where the gold glare met the sky. It wasn't the tallest building, not clawing for the clouds, but boy, was it big. I let my gaze dip to the bottom floors and the cream steps leading to the ornate front doors.

"Here," our driver said, slowing as he pulled up and probably wondering what our parents did to afford for us to stay in such a posh hotel.

As we ascended the handful of steps leading to the main entrance—passing a woman in a blush-pink sun hat so stylish it made me do a double take—movement caught my eye. A small group of protesters with matching white shirts were marching on the sidewalk and waving signs. There were only about six of them, but what they lacked in numbers, they made up for with enthusiasm.

I homed in on one of their signs. Scrawled in sharp red Arabic lettering was KEEP EGYPT'S TREASURES HERE! They even had a life-sized replica—a really good one—of the sarcophagus we were targeting, propped on a dolly and glinting in the sunlight. A foam sign was taped to its mouth, reading STOP THE LOOTING! Guess not everyone was excited about this auction.

Devroe and Kyung-soon hit up the reception counter, and I kept watching the protesters and their replica sarcophagus. An idea was beginning to take shape.

I turned to tell Mylo I might have a plan, but he was now on the other side of the lobby, lounging by a marble pillar. He was being subtle, but his sights were set on a woman in a purple silk sari, who was rocking a pair of the most gauche twin tennis bracelets I'd seen in a hot minute.

She was also rocking two very obvious bodyguards, trailing a yard behind her.

Master of sleight of hand or not, anyone with two logic cells would know trying to swipe those bracelets was impossible. Those were the types of pieces you check your wrists every thirty seconds to admire. And those guards were going into high alert the second anyone even got within a ten-foot radius of their boss.

Stealing those bracelets would have been the wildest, most outrageous, most doomed to fail thing any thief could have tried.

And the way Mylo's leg was bopping, the same way it'd been on the train when he was practically begging Kyung-soon to send the phone his way, even though it was a ninety-nine-to-one-against situation . . . He was going to try it.

I speed-walked toward him, probably looking suspicious as hell myself. But it didn't matter. Mylo getting arrested would screw all of us. Didn't he get that?

I broke into a jog. Mylo started walking and was just a couple of steps away from his target when I caught him by the arm.

"Mylo!" I jerked him back. The woman, inches away from a collision, slowed and frowned at us. Her guards moved in closer.

Mylo gave her an awkward grin.

"Sorry, wasn't paying attention," he blubbered. She accepted his apology with a huff and went on her way, bodyguards included. I dragged Mylo all the way back to the front windows and away from any more possible drama. Only then did I drop his arm and give him my most sincere what-the-hell look.

"Yeah, yeah, I know." He rubbed the back of his neck. "I just wanted to see if I could do it."

"Just wanted to see? This isn't a game, Mylo."

"Technically it is."

"You know what I mean!" I groaned, slapping my cheeks. I thought I'd ended up with the better of the two teams, but that didn't matter if one of us was a gambling adrenaline junkie who was going to make reckless decisions and ruin everything. "You can't do something like that again. Not during this phase."

He put his hands up. "I know, I'm sorry. I just . . . I needed to *do* something." He fiddled for his back pocket, reaching for his phone again. Like all the other times, his face went sour looking at the home screen.

"Why do you keep doing that?" I asked.

"Doing what?"

"Obsessing over your phone."

Mylo blew out and leaned back against a pillar dividing two of the windows. He mulled over what he wanted to say for so long, I was about to think he was ignoring me. "Do you ever, like, want someone to call, but then they don't? But that makes you want them to hit you up even more? Then you're checking your phone all the time, and soon it's all you can think about every second every day?" He hit his head with the palm of his hand, jaw clenching. "But when the thing is really stuck in your head, the only real way to get it off your mind is to put yourself in a situation where you *have* to think about something else. And the best distraction? Adrenaline, a gamble, or just good old-fashioned—"

"Danger."

It was a feeling I was all too familiar with. The single-mindedness of peril. It's enthralling, its own type of high. All you can think about is *this* second, *this* heist, how am I going to get out of *this* situation.

I knew that feeling, but I'd never needed to get myself there to forget about something else. If I did, I guess that's when it would stop being a thrill and start being an addiction.

I opened my mouth, wanting to ask what—or who—exactly it was Mylo was so desperate to distract himself from, but I pivoted at the last second. It was probably weird to dig into someone's life like that. He'd think I was being pushy, and he looked embarrassed.

I turned back to the protesters outside, who'd combined their efforts into a coordinated chant, much to the annoyance of the hotel security stationed in front of them. I nodded their way. "Doesn't that replica look just about life-sized to you?"

Mylo squinted that way. "I guess so." He grinned. "Do I smell a plan coming together, Ms. Quest?"

"Maybe, or maybe a fail-safe."

"Should we wait for the rest of the crew to discuss?" He gestured Devroe and Kyung-soon's way. They were chatting about something while the receptionist entered data on her computer. Kyung-soon laughed and poked his shoulder.

Joking and friendly already. Was this a skill everyone but me had?

"Let's keep it between us for now. I wanna refine it some more," I said.

Two seconds later, Devroe and Kyung-soon were making their way to us with a bellhop in tow, wheeling Kyung-soon's pink suitcase behind him with one hand and hefting Devroe's weather-beaten leather travel bag and Kyung-soon's purple backpack with the other.

Kyung-soon waved a fan of room keys in her now free hand. "Fifteenth floor," she said. "Not quite the penthouse, and we're all stuck in the same room, but . . ."

"The security deposit alone might as well have been for the penthouse." Devroe glared at her, telling me that she hadn't contributed a penny to said deposit. "I'm disappointed that our *friends* who booked the room didn't cover that part."

I noticed something else in Kyung-soon's fan of room cards.

"What are those?" I held my hand out for one.

"Oh yeah." She tossed the little stick to me and then passed one to each of the others. "These were waiting for us at the front desk."

Mylo twirled the flash drive in his fingers. "There wasn't a note or anything?"

"Afraid not." Devroe tucked his into his vest pocket. "I'm sure we'll find out later."

The bellhop kept his face straight while he shifted behind Devroe and Kyung-soon. "Come on." I swiped one of the keys from Kyung-soon. "Let's head up before we break this poor guy's shoulders."

TWENTY-THREE

OUR ROOM WAS luxurious. Packed with plush furniture and a fridge with drinks more expensive than most meals I've had. But it was admittedly small. There was only the sitting room and one bedroom with a bathroom. Devroe and Mylo were nice enough to give Kyung-soon and me the bedroom, or at least to not object when we dropped our things in there without asking.

I wondered, did the organizers put us in the same small room because they thought it would be more entertaining?

The safe's metal bolts clicked into place. As Devroe promised, we were keeping the cell phone smothered and locked behind three inches of steel alloy. In the event someone was trying to use it to listen in, it wouldn't be picking up any sound through all that.

Afternoon light filtered through the window. It warmed my

shoulders, reminding me of home. I always preferred jobs in sunny climates. On my phone I drew lines to exit routes via the digital hotel schematics Kyung-soon was kind enough to dig up from some back alley of the internet.

Mylo took up most of a nearby sofa, while Kyung-soon dug through the mini fridge.

Devroe stood at the floor-to-ceiling window, staring out at the city with a pensive look scrawled across his face. It was almost cute to watch.

"Sucks those protesters are going to lose their sarcophagus either way." Kyung-soon skimmed the label of a bottle from the fridge before shaking her head and putting it back inside. "Even if we weren't here, it still wouldn't go to them. Some rich and probably white person is going to get it." She waved back to Mylo. "No offense."

"None taken." Mylo scrolled through an article. "Did you guys know the sarcophagus has been completely disassembled and put back together, like, three times? The archeologists who found it cut it into pieces when it wouldn't fit through the tunnel from the tomb. You can still see some of the welding lines." He put his phone down and looked at us like this was totally wild. "Kinda disrespectful, huh . . ."

A little twinge of guilt tugged at my heart. We might be keeping the sarcophagus out of the hands of these auction-goers, but we were still delivering it to the organizers, who probably weren't much better. I'd spent an awful lot of my life delivering things to people who probably shouldn't have them. But what could I do about it? If not me, then it would be someone else.

I cleared my mind and went on. "We have a one-day head start on Team Noelia. Let's not waste it."

"The preview for the auction starts at eight," Devroe said. "That's where we'll begin. The pharaoh's sarcophagus is being held by auction security. It's safe to assume we have no chance at all of getting our hands on it now, so we'll have to wait until it's sold."

Kyung-soon peeked over the door of the fridge. "We could always just pool our money and buy it ourselves," she joked.

"Oh yeah," Mylo said. "Between the four of us, if we can snag it at the opening bid, it should be only about five million apiece."

"I doubt the organizers will give us brownie points for just buying it. That defeats the purpose of the Gambit," I said.

Devroe nodded, barely seeming to have heard Mylo and Kyung-soon at all. "We don't have time to wait until the sarcophagus is delivered to its new home. Our best option is during transport. According to the auction organizer, whom I just had a most productive call with."

"Whom you were flirting with," I drawled.

Devroe soldiered on. "She said each item is transferred from auction security to the custody of the winning bidder immediately after the auction."

"The auction house doesn't provide transport?" I asked.

"Right."

I squeezed my fingers under my chin and leaned forward. "Well, that makes things easier . . . but also a bit more complex."

Devroe nodded.

Mylo looked between the two of us. "I don't follow."

I answered: "If the auction doesn't provide transport, then that means the buyers will have to provide it themselves. Each buyer has their own private transportation and security. It's complicated because we won't know whose security team we'll be stealing from until *after* the item is bought."

"Oh, crap." Mylo fell back into the sofa with a huff. "That makes it impossible to infiltrate the transport team ahead of time."

Kyung-soon, holding a small bottle of something definitely alcoholic, padded back to us. She took a sip and her face scrunched up. "So what are we going to do, then?"

The room was quiet for a moment, except for Mylo tapping his foot and Kyung-soon clinking her bottle with her nail. There was no other way to get this thing except for during transport, not without going complete *Point Break*, my mom's favorite old movie, and staging a masked holdup. The four of us versus an entire security team were not odds I'd put my money—or life—on.

I rubbed my forehead and looked back down at my phone. I'd been tracing little lines on zoomed-in blueprints for the hotel's main floor. Different routes to exits. Blue for easier routes, red for harder ones. Mindless work, really, but it's always good to know the best way out.

I frowned at the screen. A scribbled web of janky blue and red overlapping lines. An indecipherable mess, looking at them all together. But at the end of the day, you're only taking one route. The easiest route.

"No, this is good for us," I said. "Multiple security teams are good for us! It looks complicated, but it's not." My pulse picked up.

Mylo shared a glance with Kyung-soon, scratching his head. "You do know what the word *complicated* actually means, right?"

I jumped up, feeling like I was giving the TED Talk of my life, holding my phone for them to see. "When you're mapping exits for a job, it seems overwhelming when you look at all of them, but in reality, you're only going to take that *one* exit. The simplest one to get out of. Not all routes are equal. We're freaking out over the security teams because we're thinking about over a dozen of them, but at the end of the night, the sarcophagus is only leaving with one of them. And out of dozens of teams, not all of them can be equally competent. At least a handful of them have to be easier to deal with than the rest."

Devroe grinned. I may not have had Mylo and Kyung-soon yet, but he saw where I was going.

I went on. "We may not be able to do in-depth reconnaissance on all the security teams ahead of time, but we can give them a quick once-over. Or at least get a sense for which are impossible to penetrate, and which are the weakest. If we can identify the weakest teams and formulate decent plans for hijacking those, then it would just be a matter of—"

"Of making sure the sarcophagus is bought by the buyer with the weakest team," Kyung-soon finished. She let the thought sit before erupting into nervous chuckles. "You're making that last little detail sound simpler than it is."

"Kyung-soon's right," Mylo said. "The sarcophagus is the most expensive item at the auction. Half the bidders might not even be rich enough to bid on it. What are the odds that the person with the weakest security team will end up being the person rich enough to purchase it?"

"Most of the bidders will *have* the money," Devroe insisted. "It's twenty-five thousand euros just to purchase a ticket to the auction. People don't come to things like this without millions to spend." He straightened his vest from the bottom. I was beginning to identify that as a thinking tic of his. "But you're correct, many bidders may not want the sarcophagus. And if the bidding gets truly out of hand, a few might be pinched for funds."

"That still doesn't address the odds of the biggest bidders happening to have the worst security," Mylo added.

"We'll create a ranking system for the security teams and for the bidders." I tapped my foot on the carpet, like I was tapping out my thoughts in Morse code. "Before the auction begins, we'll conduct an analysis of the bidders and their security. We need to figure out who has enough money to bid on the sarcophagus and who's intending to. Once we have that information, we can determine who amongst those bidders has the weakest security. They'll be our target."

Devroe smiled. I could read on his face that he'd been imagining the same thing. There was something delicious in that. A warm feeling washed over me.

"Not a horrible plan." Kyung-soon took another sip. "But how are we going to make sure our target actually buys the sarcophagus?"

"Leave that to me," Devroe said. "Persuasion is one of my many talents."

"You're not *that* persuasive," Mylo said.

"First, don't be so sure about that. Second, don't worry. With some . . . special tools, I think I'll be able to work something out."

"Yeah, just one more thing," Kyung-soon said. "We've got a head start on the enemy, but that's not going to matter on the actual auction day. They'll be here. That could shift everything. Are we just going to . . . improvise?"

I sighed and leaned against the window, watching some of the protesters being pressed back by police. Or were those members of the hotel security? How did the hotel stop the protesters from just waltzing into the lobby, pretending to be guests?

"Wait—" I was talking before I even knew fully what I was thinking. I looked to Mylo. "We'll need to get our hands on the guest list for the auction, right?"

Mylo nodded.

"So . . . I wonder if there are any people banned from the auction, or the hotel? I'd be pretty surprised if there weren't."

Devroe laughed. "You're absolutely malicious, Ross."

I tried not to smile. "Can we do it?"

Mylo rubbed his chin. "Kyung-soon, you're our computer chick?"

"Don't call me 'computer chick' *ever* again," she said. "But sure. I can probably get into their intranet and do it. Consider Team Archenemy already banned from the premises." Kyung-soon toasted me, her eyes sparkling with mischief.

And just like that, everything settled into place. It wasn't a detailed plan, but it was the bones of something that could become great. *If* nothing went wrong.

"It shouldn't be too hard to find the transport teams if we can get into the auction's database somehow. But the auction preview starts in what . . . five hours?" Mylo looked to Devroe. "I assume you'll want to hit up the preview so you can start scouting your prey, huh?"

"Exactly," Devroe said with a wolfish smile.

"Then we should divide up." Kyung-soon left her unfinished bottle on an end table. "Two people should explore the transport teams, and Devroe plus someone else should go to the auction preview. Who's doing what?"

Recon on a few security teams or attend an expensive party with Devroe? From the way Kyung-soon and Mylo both looked at me, I already knew where I was going to end up.

"I guess I'll go change into my investigative clothes," Kyung-soon said. I gave her a *really?* look. She shrugged an apology. "I don't like parties."

"Ditto," Mylo said as he started toward the door. "Black tie meet-and-greets aren't really my scene." He glanced at Kyung-soon, who, judging by the slow steps she was taking into our room, wasn't in a rush to get prepped for any scouting.

Mylo slipped into the hall, hopefully not to get into anything too precarious in the meantime. I made a note to warn Kyung-soon about making sure Mylo didn't do anything risky on the job.

"Just you and me for the auction preview, then." Devroe dropped his hands into his pockets and smiled down at me. "Looks like we'll finally have our date."

I stood. "Is it fun, always getting what you want?"

"I rarely get what I want." His eyes seemed to darken. "That makes this even more special. But now that I think about it, candlelit dinners are too dull for people like us. It wouldn't be a proper date if there wasn't a little mischief involved."

I didn't want to smile, but I couldn't help it. Perhaps I was going to enjoy this more than I thought.

TWENTY-FOUR

I DIDN'T THINK I'd ever worn an evening gown before. Scratch that—I knew I hadn't.

The dress hanging on the back of the bathroom door was a brilliant scarlet, its fabric smooth and thick, clearly expensive, but understated in its style—a snug top that descended into slender waves below. Appropriate for the occasion but not too flashy. Perfect for blending into the jungle of treasures and wealth we were about to enter.

Taking the dress off the hanger, I dropped my towel and slipped into it. I held the bodice to my chest and tried to straighten the off-the-shoulder sleeves that dangled over my upper arms. Without heels, the fabric slumped a couple inches onto the floor. I didn't want to wear heels at all, but Devroe and

Kyung-soon had been the ones out shopping, and the dress they'd brought back for me would only work with heels.

"Wear your kicks if you want. I'm sure that won't raise any alarms," he'd said, rolling his eyes.

Just looking at the dress, I could tell the sizing was on point. Was it Devroe or Kyung-soon who had guessed my measurements?

An ungodly number of little buttons ran up the back from just below my hips to my shoulder blades. I was flexible enough to reach them, but they seemed to slip through my fingers every time I tried to do them up. Was I more nervous about tonight than I thought?

Why did they make women's clothes like this? It was like the dress was designed to need help getting on and off. I didn't have time for this, and of course, with Mylo and Kyung-soon out doing recon, the only other person left was Devroe. Unless I hit up room service . . .

What was I thinking? They were just some buttons.

I opened the bathroom door and swiped the pair of red heels from their box and slipped them on. The height lifted the dress from the floor. Something about that small change made me feel completely different from before. Not like I was a girl playing dress-up, but a woman going out for the night.

"Devroe?" I called through the bedroom door. Since he was without his own bedroom to change in, it was closed so he could get ready. "Help with this dress, please?"

I went back to the bathroom mirror and waited. A few moments later, he appeared in the reflection behind me. My breath caught, and I tried not to let my expression change.

He'd finished dressing . . . and damn, did he look good.

His tux was a smooth, flawless suede black. The velvety texture of his jacket screamed at me to run my fingers over it. His bow tie wasn't a millimeter out of place. The brilliant white of the shirt against the beautiful shade of his brown skin contrasted gorgeously. Everything about him looked sharper than before. The lines of his jaw. The little strokes that were his eyelashes. The slight waves in his hair. He always dressed to impress, but tonight he was a daydream come to life.

He was on fire, and I felt dangerously close to melting next to him.

I broke out of my trance just in time to see that Devroe had frozen too. His eyes were stuck on me in the reflection. The look in them made me do a double take of myself. From the dress and the curves that weren't fully realized under the unbuttoned dress, to the arm that was protectively holding it up over my chest, to my braids, which I'd spent an hour YouTubing how to pull up into a wide twisted bun with little golden beads. What was he thinking? Was he thinking anything at all, or just trying to make me think that he was?

"Button me, please?" I asked. "Before this whole thing falls down."

Devroe shook himself and gave me a devilish smile. "Well, we wouldn't want that, now, would we?"

I rolled my eyes, but then had to bite my lip as his fingers began moving up the buttons one by one. His touch was a whisper brushing over my spine.

"Ever been to something like this before?" he asked.

"My mom is usually the one who does the incognito work.

And we specialize more in grab-and-go assignments than those that require charming information out of people."

He finished the last button but seemed to hesitate before letting it go. "You're missing all the fun." He matched my gaze in the mirror. "The rush of swiping something when no one is looking is intoxicating, sure. But it's nothing quite like finessing someone to tell you the code to their bank account without even knowing it. Or drawing them into mentioning exactly where in their summer home they keep their prized Fabergé egg collection, even though they've only known you for a few hours." His eyes glowed with the lust of the hunt as he spoke. That lust for the game. Was that the look we'd shared earlier, when our thoughts aligned?

Had I had that look too?

"You enjoy playing with your food. Dangerous."

"Everything worth doing is dangerous." He was staring straight at me, and I felt my breath catch again.

I had to stop this. For all I knew, I was his next meal.

"So what's the trick to this?" I turned from the mirror and strode past him toward my backpack on the opposite side of the bed.

Devroe followed me out of the bathroom. "It's easy. Start up a few calculated conversations, get to know people, gauge how much money they have. Simple stuff."

I rummaged through my backpack, feeling around until I found familiar metal links. "Should I bring a pen and paper for notes?"

"Don't be funny. Or nervous. I promise it won't be as hard as you think."

I started to wrap my bracelet around my wrist, but Devroe swooped around the foot of the bed and grabbed my arm, stopping me.

My eyes snapped up to meet his.

He shook his head in an awfully condescending way. "No, not tonight."

"Why, because I'm not allowed to bring weapons on our date?"

"Because the links are all discolored and grungy. It looks like you stole it off a bike rack. The key is to blend in, remember? This draws attention."

I hated it, but he was right. We were just scouting people tonight anyway, and at the end of the day, I don't need a weapon to fight. I am the weapon. Plus, if I kicked off my shoes, the heels would make pretty good blunt blades too.

"Fine, whatever." At that, he let me snatch my arm away. I tossed the bracelet back into my open backpack. "But I'm wearing it tomorrow. Even if I have to have to wear a cartoony fur coat to cover it."

"Perhaps we can have it colored gold by tomorrow. That color is . . . good on you." His eyes traced the glimmering gold beads I had mixed in with my braids. So he had noticed them.

"Enough sweet nothings," I said. "We should head down. The preview will be starting soon. Unless you're planning on us being fashionably late?"

"With you on my arm, I'd be showing up fashionably at any time."

"Am I going to have to put up with these lines all night?" I asked, heading toward the door. I bet Kyung-soon and Mylo were enjoying a nice, quiet evening of recon and tailing security teams while I was spending the whole night trying not to be seduced myself.

Devroe faked offense. "You don't like them? Guess I'll have to try harder, then. If I want to earn a second date."

I scoffed as I opened the door. "Maybe. If you successfully help me pass another phase."

TWENTY-FIVE

IF THERE'S ONE universal truth about almost all obscenely rich people, it's this: They're a lot more punchable than the average person.

I resisted the urge to uppercut the man in the fifty-thousand-dollar tux in front of me, while he continued his story about how he'd not only fired his last three landscapers but hadn't paid any of them either because their work was "less than perfect" and obviously his lawyers were superior to theirs and what were they going to do, sue him?

This somehow managed to draw hearty laughter from everyone in the vicinity.

Instead of an uppercut, I settled for swiping one of his extravagant ruby cuff links before I abandoned the group.

Sighing, I took a quick breather by the ballroom bar. The

preview was absolutely sprawling. Here in the main room, rows and rows of pedestaled treasures were divided off with velvet ropes. Crowds of the most elegantly dressed, self-entitled guests ogled them in between conversations like the one I'd just left. Two hours we'd been here so far, chatting it up and collecting data. I thought it'd be hard poking around to find out how much money people had and if it was enough to make them a serious contender for the sarcophagus, but to my surprise, most were eager to give, at the very least, strong hints as to how big their fortune was. If you've got it, flaunt it. Especially at a place like this.

I looked toward the centerpiece of the room. At the very front, behind its own square of velvet ropes and flanked by two sharply dressed security members, was our target.

The perfectly carved face, youthful and flawless, stared blankly at me from across the room. He was dazzlingly beautiful. A trickle of sadness touched me. At the end of the day, this was just a coffin I was looking at. Where was the person who was laid to rest in it? The mummy wasn't being auctioned along with the sarcophagus. Was anyone else thinking about him too? What were the odds he'd ever get to be at peace in his own resting place again?

Pushing aside any sentiment that might make me question stealing it myself, I took a breath and got ready to go out for another round.

But as I scanned to find a new target, something interesting caught my attention. A man was approaching the sarcophagus. White, middle-aged. He should have blended in with everyone else. But even from a distance, I could tell his tux was leagues below par compared to the rest of the partygoers. There was a flat expression on his face. He was unenthused to be here.

That was something I hadn't seen yet. A cheap suit and a sour attitude. What was he doing up near my target?

I headed that way.

While I was weaving through the other guests, the man was saying something to one of the guards. They'd been keeping other guests from touching and poking the treasure all night. The entitlement of some of these people to do something like that was unbelievable.

But to my surprise, after what looked like a short conversation and a flash of a card from the man's wallet, the guard unclipped the velvet rope, letting the man step closer.

Now, that was odd.

My steps slowed as I neared. The man had some sort of instrument in his hand, the size of his palm, black. He held the end to the chin of the pharaoh's face.

"Is that a Geiger counter?" I asked.

The man didn't look at me. "No."

"Oh, then what is it?" Maybe there were more charisma-injected ways to get this information, but this was something I hadn't been briefed for tonight.

"No," he reiterated, still not sparing me the slightest glance. He bent, scanning his device slower. Numbers that meant nothing to me blinked on a digital screen. "I have no interest in talking with you. Go away."

My face burned. Was he onto me or just being a prick in general?

"Excuse me, what's going on here?" A woman in a glittery black gown glared at the guards. "I thought the rule was no touching, no pictures? Why has an exception been made?" She gently tapped the man's shoulder. "Sir, how much did you offer them?"

The device in his palm beeped. He slipped it back into his inner jacket pocket and, just as fast, shook her grasp off and power walked back through the ballroom without so much as an apology.

"The audacity!" the woman scoffed. The guards clipped the rope back in place, much to her annoyance. My gaze was frozen on the strange man.

There was something weird going on here, and if it had to do with my sarcophagus, I couldn't just not investigate.

Making sure I remained unremarked, I headed after him. Considering how fast he was walking, I thought he might have been eager to get the hell out of this gala he clearly didn't want to be at. But to my surprise, and maybe his chagrin, he instead turned into the second, smaller ballroom. Here the ceiling was lower, the bar was twice the size, and the vibe was much more like a cool supper club. A proper band played instead of a quartet, and the middle of the room had been turned into a makeshift dance floor. But, you know, for more like waltzes and promenades instead of anything fun, like line dances.

Devroe was doing his thing here, laughing with a pair of older women like they'd been familiar forever.

I ignored him, keeping my focus on the target, trying not to let him notice me.

The man checked his smartwatch, then sighed and took a seat at the farthest stool at the bar. The bartender approached him, but before she could get a word out, the man shut her down with his favorite word.

"No."

She bit back a grimace and retreated. He looked around the space, and so I turned quickly away. When I glanced back, a young woman was slipping into the seat next to him. She was in a cocktail dress, just barely meeting the black-tie requirement.

Another less-than-exquisite guest. What were these people doing here?

She smiled at him, giving him the sort of look someone would give their grumpy uncle when trying to get them to smile.

He didn't look amused.

The waltz shifted into a cover of "As the World Caves In," and a lot more couples cheerfully joined the floor.

I used the opportunity to slip through the mass of people to the back of the room, hopefully with a better angle to listen in on this guy's conversation.

This had to be the most paranoid target I'd ever tried to tail. The second I got within an eight-foot radius, he stopped talking and his eyes slashed toward me.

I averted my eyes and made a beeline for Devroe.

"Love." I grabbed his arm, startling him just a tad.

"Talia. These are my new friends," he said. "Ladies, this is my stunning fiancée."

The women both forced smiles. "How do you do?" the one on the left said, a lot less friendly than she'd been with Devroe just a second ago.

"Good. Do you mind if I steal him? Thanks."

Before Devroe could protest, I pulled him onto the edge of the dance floor. "What the hell is going on?" he whispered. "I wasn't done with them."

"Shut up," I said. "Dance with me."

He obeyed, and if I hadn't been in heist mode, I might have melted completely at the warmth of his hands settling on my hips. "Do you see that man at the edge of the bar?"

"Next to the embarrassingly underdressed woman? Yes, I'm not oblivious."

"What are they saying?"

The first chorus hit, and the violins and piano went all in, drowning out most other sounds. "Easier said than done," he said.

"You can read lips, can't you?"

He narrowed his eyes at me, and I cocked a brow, splaying one hand over his chest and letting my other curl around his neck. He pulled tighter on my waist, drawing us closer so my head rested on his shoulder, and he was looking over mine.

He still smelled so delicious. Not that that was the focus right now.

"Genuine," Devroe said. "Sar-sarcophagus. He's confirmed that the sarcophagus is genuine. He's saying . . ." Devroe paused. His fingers flexed on my hips. I fought the urge to squirm. "Something about the dating being correct. Now she's talking."

He was silent, watching for a moment, and there was nothing for me to do but listen to the music and feel his chest rising and falling. I was surprised I couldn't feel his heart, being this close.

Could he feel mine, thumping contentedly?

"Museum, she said she's got the go-ahead from the museum. If it's real, they want it."

The music built, the violins synchronizing.

"What? The British Museum?" He'd had an English accent, the No-man.

"I think . . ." Devroe drifted, focusing. My mind raced. The British history museum? They had a history of acquiring these sorts of things for their exhibits, but if the protesters outside were any sign, people weren't really vibing with the idea of

Europeans whisking away their treasures anymore. No way they could just show up and bid on something like this.

Unless they did it under a little cloak-and-dagger. Made it look like a third party was bidding, then maybe that third party anonymously donated the exhibit to the museum?

Devroe tensed. I could feel it like it was my own body. I lifted my head. "What?"

"Two hundred million. That's how much they've allocated." He looked down at me. "That means . . ."

"They're going to win."

TWENTY-SIX

THIS **MIGHT ALL** be pointless." I started pacing the moment we were back in our room. "You read two hundred million, but who's to say they won't go even higher than that if push comes to shove? Two fifty? Three hundred?" I kicked my heels off, letting them skid across the carpet.

"Whatever the number, it'll be something the other guests won't be able to meet. Or at least won't *want* to meet. Coupled with the fact that security connected to the British Museum is unlikely to be the weakest." He rubbed his jaw. "Yes, it does complicate things. But no more than before."

No more than before? We were dabbling with geopolitics now. Didn't that throw up any red flags?

"How does this not change anything?" I blurted out. "The plan was to isolate whoever had the weakest security and ensure they won the sarcophagus. But who has enough money to beat the Brits? *And* what do you bet their security is top-tier too?"

"I know, all of that's true," Devroe said. He wasn't looking at me, but past me. "That means that to make sure the person we want wins the sarcophagus, we'll have to somehow get the museum's buyers to back out before they jack the price so high that our person can't beat it."

A knock sounded on the suite door. No way it was Mylo and Kyung-soon yet. They likely wouldn't be done scoping out all the security teams from the list Kyung-soon had ripped off the hotel's intranet until after midnight, and it was barely ten thirty now. But Devroe didn't seem surprised. He opened it as a room service waiter complete with a little burgundy jacket and white gloves rolled in a cart carrying a bottle of champagne in an ice bucket and champagne glasses. A single rose sat in a small vase in the center. I tensed. *Really? Now, Devroe?*

Devroe directed the man to leave the cart in the middle of the room. He gave him a tip nice enough to make his eyes pop, then shut the door behind him.

"Our 'date' is over, Devroe," I said as he pulled the bottle out of the ice. "Can we get back to talking about the job we're here to do? Besides, I don't drink."

Devroe popped the cork, like he hadn't heard anything I said.

"Always jumping to conclusions," he said. "I'm counting this entire job as our first date, just so you know. But I didn't order this to get you tipsy." He poured the champagne into one of the glasses, filling it halfway, though its bubbles climbed to the brim of the glass. "This relates to the job." He poured another glass as well. "How are we going to keep the Brits from bidding too high on the sarcophagus, you ask? Simple. We just have to make sure they're too out of their senses to keep bidding."

Devroe left the glasses on the cart and made his way over to his travel bag. After rummaging around for a minute, he found a suede box and opened it to reveal a gold watch. He swapped out the one he'd been wearing—a much nicer Omega—for the new one.

"I liked the old one better."

"You're not the only one." He snapped it into place. "But that one didn't have as many features as this one."

With the new watch on, he picked up one of the glasses and swirled it between us. "Hold this."

I reluctantly took the glass. "I told you I don't drink." I went to set it back down, but a change in the champagne made me pause. The bubbles in my glass were dancing in shades of blue now.

I lifted the glass and stared through the translucent teal. "You're a magician too? How does it work?"

With the glass still hovering inches from my nose, he swiftly ran his wrist, the one with the watch, over the top of my glass. He jerked the watch only little. So slightly that I wouldn't have noticed if it weren't literally in front of my eyes. A tiny latch opened under his watch. Little specks that looked like dust sprinkled into the champagne, dissolving the instant they hit.

"Slick. The blue is a little off-putting, though."

"That's just a leftover from another job. I needed to inspire someone not to drink something. People tend to send their drinks back after they spontaneously change color."

"Where'd you get it? The watch, I mean," I asked.

"Trade secret, love. I don't reveal for free. I do share on occasion, though."

He put the glass down and went back to the box, snaking out a string of diamonds in a silver tennis bracelet. It was the perfect mirror to his watch. Simple but elegant. Formal enough that it wouldn't be out of place at an event like the auction but understated enough that it wouldn't draw too much attention if worn at a coffee shop or bookstore. Wonderfully versatile.

He gently lifted my wrist, putting the bracelet around it. "It won't just be sugar tomorrow night. The chemical I'm planning on using, when given in the correct dosage, should make the target disoriented. They won't be able to remember to blink, let alone bid on something. They'll also be so pliable that a passing stranger should be able to convince them to buy an artifact they had no intention of buying. I thought we'd only need to do the latter, but now that there are two guests who'll need influencing—"

"You want me to do some of the sleight of hand as well." I twisted my wrist and the new piece of jewelry on it, watching it glimmer under the room's light. "Should I ask why you just so happen to have a women's bracelet ready to go for a situation like this?"

He smiled lightly. "You're not the first girl I've had to work with on the fly."

"Is that supposed to make me jealous?"

"Does it?"

I bit my lip. "So we're practicing, then?" I hovered my bracelet over one of the glasses. A dozen different ways I twisted and turned my wrist, but nothing came out of the bracelet.

"No, no, no." Devroe moved behind me, and in a swift and delicate move, he placed his hand over mine. "Gently," he told me. His fingers brushed my wrist lightly. A throbbing feeling shot up my arm. His touch was like feathers. And so warm.

"Pull up your wrist the tiniest bit, and then bend it a few degrees. It has to be an intimate gesture." His voice spread over me. I wanted him to keep talking. To stay right where he was. For these couple seconds to go on for the rest of the night. He was a flame again, his heat radiating.

No, get it together, Ross. I would only get burned. I had to focus on what he was saying, not on how much I liked listening to him say it.

He gently guided my wrist over the other glass's rim, angling it just a touch. It was subtle, but I felt a small pop against my skin. Devroe reached around me to the glass, taking a small sip of the champagne.

"Sweeter than candy," he said. My breath swelled. I turned around. He hadn't taken a step back, and when he lowered the glass, it felt like he'd closed a distance of a thousand miles.

The room lights were dim, but he had a glow to him that couldn't be ignored. My chest rose. His eyes didn't leave mine. Well, until they dropped a few inches to my lips.

"Do you want to taste?" he whispered.

Taste?

Did I?

My heart squeezed, aching for me to do something.

He dipped down. Or maybe I was moving up to him. Because I did want to kiss him. And that was why I couldn't. If I gave in, then he'd win. Didn't he say so on the train—he liked that I could see the game. Did he like it because that would make winning even more delicious for him? Was he in it for me, or was he in it . . . just for the win?

Someone across the ocean, Mom, was counting on me. Was

I gonna gamble that, gamble her, catching feelings for some boy who told me he was playing with me?

I wouldn't. I couldn't. My heart, and Mom's life, were too important to risk.

I jerked back, snapping the tension between us in an instant. "I need to practice." I pushed him back a step. "Give me a couple hours. I'll get the hang of it."

Devroe studied me for a moment. His face fell in a way that made my heart twist. He looked . . . defeated. "Sure." He threw off his tie and headed toward the suite door.

"Where are you going?"

"Nowhere." He straightened his cuff. Leaving again, just like he ran off on the train when the conversation started veering in a direction he didn't like. When he didn't get what he wanted.

"Wow, you're so mature, Devroe."

With the door half open, he gripped the knob so tightly I thought it might break. His eyes flared as he looked back to me. "Why are you acting like you don't like this? You're so brainwashed into thinking everyone is out to get you, you've put your own feelings on mute. You don't even trust yourself anymore."

I blanched. It felt like his words had just punched me in the stomach. But I couldn't let him see that. "Oh, boo hoo. Go ahead and wax poetic about how distraught you are that all your charm can't get the one girl you really want to kiss you, or some other cliché stuff like that. I'll give you a few minutes to get the phrasing right."

He scoffed. "I already told you, I'm used to not getting what I want. Just never been screwed over as a byproduct of someone screwing themself before. Call me if you decide to stop lying to yourself."

And then he was gone, slamming the door behind him.

My eyes stayed glued to it for at least a minute after he left. I bit my finger. What did I just do? Why did I feel like I'd just stomped a fire out when I was freezing in the tundra?

Because he was right. Foolish or not, trustworthy or not . . . I liked him.

Oh boy.

TWENTY-SEVEN

NO! NO! NO! NO! NO!

I reread Auntie's text and groaned into a pillow. After over an hour of dealing with a confusing tug-of-war of emotions about Devroe and failing to distract myself with practicing the bracelet trick, I caved and sent her a message. She would either respond by cooing about my first crush—oh gosh, was I admitting that to myself now? That he was my *crush*?—or with a very stern lecture about how now was really not the time to be getting distracted with dangerous, not-to-be-trusted boys. Which, fair. I knew that. Hence the whole tornado of feelings in the first place.

I'd started with **What if I told you I might have an ally here?**

Auntie: **What kind of ally?**

I deleted, like, ten different responses before going all in with **I almost kissed him.**

Auntie: **NO! NO! NO! NO! NO!**

From me: **He hasn't screwed me over yet . . . and I think he could've before.**

Auntie called, and because I'm a dweeb who would probably fold if I had to hear her berate me about this in real time, I declined.

Auntie: **He's a thief. He's playing you. DO NOT KISS YOUR COMPETITION.**

Auntie: **Be cautious. There's no such thing as too careful.**

With a groan I dropped my head onto the desk in the bedroom. She was right; I knew that before I texted her. But it was one thing to know something and another to have it said to you. No one, including Devroe, was to be trusted.

Still . . . I'd be lying if I said a tiny part of me hadn't been hoping she'd tell me it was safe. Just a little.

My sulking had only lasted a few minutes when I heard the suite door open again. My heart skipped. Was it Devroe? No, the chatter of two people in Korean, with voices sounding nothing like his self-assured, charismatic cadence.

My shoulders dropped, whether from relief or disappointment, who knows.

"What up?" Mylo switched to English for me, since I'd mentioned earlier that Korean wasn't a language I knew. He came in carrying a Happy Meal—nothing like post-midnight McDonald's—which he slung on the bed.

"Hey!" Kyung-soon, carrying a carton of fries, snapped and pointed at the greasy Happy Meal box. "Not on my bed."

"Uh, your bed?" Mylo tested, looking at me.

I shrugged. "I don't really care."

Kyung-soon threw a fry at me. It hit my cheek. "Hey!"

"You think you're okay with it now until you're sleeping in a bunch of crumb-infested, grease-soaked sheets." She settled belly-down on the bed, but with her fries poised off the edge.

Mylo took the L with grace and retrieved the Happy Meal. He leaned in the door frame, munching away while he gave me a quick once-over. I still hadn't changed out of my party clothes, aside from ditching the heels. "Nice look. Where's Devroe?"

"Nice look? She looks like she stepped out of *Vogue!*" Kyung-soon tossed a fry at Mylo's face. He somehow managed to catch it in his mouth.

"My bad," he corrected. "*Very* nice look."

"I don't know where Devroe is," I said, answering his earlier question. "He left after—" *After what? After we almost kissed and he called me out on having trust issues?* "After we got back. The plan's gotten more complicated."

Mylo's eyebrows jumped.

"But we've got a fix. It shouldn't affect your side of things. How did the scouting go?" I asked.

He stretched his arms. "As expected. There are some surprisingly weak transport teams."

Kyung-soon sat up. "But besides that, what did you mean by 'complicated'?"

I gave them the rundown about the British Museum buyers and Devroe's plan to keep things on track. By the time I was done, Mylo was sitting on the floor by the foot of the bed with Kyung-soon perched on its edge next to him.

"Do you know the alias name they'll be bidding under?" Mylo asked.

"We listened for a while. Devroe thinks he read the name Sandury? Sam—"

"*Sanbury?*" Mylo scrolled through what looked like an app version of spreadsheets.

Kyung-soon peered over his shoulder, and he laughed in a this-is-ridiculous sort of way. "Oh yeah. We're *not* penetrating their security," Mylo said.

She froze as she looked at the screen before looking back at me. "We ranked all the security teams on our way back. The higher the ranking, the more difficult to steal from."

"And what ranking did the Sanbury team earn?"

"They're number one."

I took a deep breath. "So now we have to make extra, extra sure that these people who have millions and millions of dollars to blow don't win, because if they do, we've wasted our one-day head start on this fruitless chase!"

I pressed a hand to my head. A stress headache started to pulse behind my skull.

"Hey." Mylo's voice beckoned me back from the pit of frustration and anxiety I was about to slip into. He gave me a calming look. "Chill out. We're gonna make it work. Like you said, Devroe's already got a plan. This phase will be a piece of cake, especially with all four of us on it." He slid off his jacket. "Now, whenever Mr. Kenzie decides to grace us with his presence, we can get to work on cross-analyzing our results and picking the lucky bidder who gets to win tomorrow night. Until then, I think I'm gonna order a milkshake from room service." With that, he left the room, closing the door behind him. Something about the nonchalant way he rephrased the situation helped my shoulders relax and my breathing steady. He was right; all we could do was plan. And if everything went according to it, we'd be cool.

Kyung-soon rolled off the bed and pressed her back against the door. She was finishing off the last of her fries now. "So . . . what went on between you and Devroe?"

I narrowed my eyes at her. She lifted an eyebrow.

"The assignment went fine."

"Just fine?" Kyung-soon twirled the end of her ponytail. "You had a night out in a gorgeous evening gown, floating around a ballroom with diamonds and money and all the things normal girls daydream about, and everything was only *fine*?"

Did she see something I didn't even know I was giving off? Was there that much to see?

"We're not normal girls, though, are we?"

"I guess not. Do you need me to unbutton you?" She grasped for me in a playful way. Consenting, I turned my back to her. "Evening gowns are so much more practical when you have a maid to dress and undress you," she continued.

"You have a maid or two back home to undress you?" I moved to catch my slacking dress. Kyung-soon was efficient.

"My mentor does. Well, usually. She specializes in long cons with cushy perks." She leaned over my shoulder and sniffed. "I saw the champagne."

"Devroe and I were using it, but for the job." The diamond bracelet weighed on my skin. Feeling silly for still wearing it, I slid it off. "I wasn't, like, getting drunk with him or anything."

"Right."

I grabbed my bag, then slipped into the bathroom to finish changing. Like we'd known each other forever and not just two days, I kept the door open slightly to keep talking.

"So," Kyung-soon went on while I slipped into my pajamas,

"he called up for champagne, you were both dressed in your finest, then he just left, and nothing at all interesting happened."

I stopped, watching myself in the mirror. Perceptive, wasn't she?

"I don't know what you mean," I said.

"Oh, come on. It's pretty obvious that he's interested in you."

"As interested as I am in learning how to pick new locks and crack new safe models, maybe." I faced her while leaning against the doorway and started peeling the gold beads out of my braids, collecting them in my hands. "He told me that himself, on the train. That he liked playing his game with me."

"Doesn't that mean he really likes you, if he let you in on that from the start? It's like he knew you were a worthy opponent and that's what set his heart on fire." Kyung-soon crossed her hands over her heart and sighed. "*So* romantic. I had a feeling he was into you, since he had us waiting around for you and Yeriel when we were leaving the museum. You guys would have been disqualified for sure. But I saw the way you and him were talking at the museum—"

"Hold on," I interrupted. "He had you *waiting* for us to leave? You didn't just happen to catch us when *you* were leaving?"

She paled. "He didn't tell you that?"

I shook my head.

"Huh. Well, like I said—he really is just that into you."

I fumbled for something to say, but my mind was swirling with questions. Devroe was a fool if he actually waited for me to leave the museum. If things went sideways, he could have been caught or ended up in the hospital too. He was smarter than that. He wouldn't have waited for someone unless he had a good reason.

Be cautious.

Auntie's words were ringing a lot truer than they had earlier. Maybe I was being played, even if I didn't know how yet.

Outside, I heard the suite door unlock, and Mylo complained that it wasn't his milkshake.

Devroe was back, and it was planning time again.

TWENTY-EIGHT

TWO HOURS AGO, I might have contemplated apologizing to Devroe after this team meeting, but now I couldn't help but wonder what his plan was, if he'd been waiting outside the museum for me . . .

Gathered around the couches, we cross-referenced our information from the night to determine the winner of our most-money, worst-security competition. The winner wasn't one of the people I'd spoken with, but rather one of the women Devroe sized up. Her name was Sadia Fazura.

"She's a socialite from Malaysia." Devroe settled back into his armchair. He was out of his jacket and tie now, with nothing more than his stark white tux shirt left. Somehow that made him look even more like a model in a cologne ad. Except instead of a smoldering gaze, tiredness was written all over him. He looked like he'd just gotten done stressing over something.

He went on, "She's in her late thirties. Her husband's a prosperous second-generation business owner. Loaded, he's got a fortune but no faithfulness. Sadia seems to frequent auctions to collect things on her husband's dime—probably to compensate for his constant cheating."

Kyung-soon's eyes widened. "You learned all that from one conversation?"

He tried not to look too prideful. "When you make people feel comfortable, they'll tell you almost anything."

"So she's got money," I said. "How much, exactly?"

"Around two hundred million in an account she shares with her husband, from what one of her friends let slip," Devroe said. "Though I assume she came to the auction with the intention of spending only a fraction of that."

"But you can make sure she ends up with the sarcophagus no matter what, right?" Mylo asked, sitting with his legs out on the floor.

"Leave it to yours truly." Devroe's gaze shifted my way. "So long as Ross can make sure the museum proxy isn't able to overbid."

All the eyes darted to me. A rush of adrenaline shot through my chest. Devroe already made a connection with this socialite target, so that left the museum proxy to me. It was the most delicate part of the heist, and it was *mine*.

"I can do it," I said. It had to be true. To fail would put us in serious danger of losing the phase. I couldn't let that happen.

"Mylo and I will set everything in motion with her security

tomorrow." Kyung-soon jumped straight into their side of the plan, like there wasn't any doubt Devroe and I would deliver.

"We'll handle the hijacking part," Mylo said, bouncing off Kyung-soon. "We already started scratching out a basic plan for the lower-tier security teams. For Ms. Fazura's transport team, we should be able to shimmy our way into her transport truck ahead of time." He checked the info on his phone again. "She's holding her winnings at a warehouse near a private airport on the other side of the city. Once we arrive, we will find a way to move the sarcophagus into a separate storage unit and drive it out." He and Kyung-soon shared a glance, as if running through an entire scenario of slipping into the transport truck together without saying any words.

I spoke up next. "Since Team Noelia is banned, it'll be harder for them to maneuver in the building. They'll probably pivot to attacking while the sarcophagus is on the move."

Devroe rubbed his chin. "They're resourceful enough to learn who's bought the sarcophagus and how it's being transported in the time that it'll take between the sale and the sarcophagus heading out. I bet they'll try to make their move then. And we'll have ensured it's the one with the weakest security for them." He sighed. "We can't leave the entire part two of our plan to just Mylo and Kyung-soon." His gaze moved back to me. "We all need to be there, prepared for when they show."

I nodded. "So . . . after the auction, you and I dip out and link up with Mylo and Kyung-soon? It would be smart if we booked our own transport truck to the warehouse. Since Mylo and Kyung-soon will be inside the target's storage unit, they can let us in from the inside."

Mylo snapped and pointed at me. "Bingo."

"Well, we won't head over right after," Devroe said. "We should probably change first. As much as I love black tie, it's not exactly subtle."

I couldn't help my giggle, along with the rush of curiosity that hit me. It'd be interesting to see him in joggers and sneakers for a change.

With the plan solidified, Mylo gestured for Devroe to toss over the bottle of champagne, which was resting in a now-melted bucket of ice. Amused, Devroe reached back to pass it to him along with an empty glass.

"Don't put anything in my drink," Mylo told him.

Devroe chuckled. "You've got nothing worth stealing."

"I'll ignore that." Mylo poured a glass. "Why am I the only one with a cup? Let's drink to a job well done."

"Too soon!" Kyung-soon said.

"Nah." He offered her the glass, which she took. "You can't mess something up after you've toasted to it. It's a law of the universe."

"Hm." Devroe grabbed an empty glass off the champagne cart and held it out. "Then let's toast to my long life and an over-flowing bank account, please."

"Fair enough." Mylo filled it up.

"Let's add a toast for me coming up with the best wish ever." Kyung-soon lifted her glass.

"And you, Ross?" Mylo asked. He looked around. "Do we have any more cups?"

"No, thank you." I lifted a phantom cup into the air. What did I want to toast to? What did I want?

Two weeks ago, I'd have known exactly what to wish for. Freedom. Something new. Other frivolous things. The only thing I should've wanted now was my mom back.

But, in a weird way, I found myself wanting to wish for more moments like this.

"I'll toast to . . . always knowing what to toast to in the future."

Devroe's shoulders slumped slightly. Was he disappointed? What did he expect me to say?

Mylo snickered. "Not bad." The three of them downed their drinks, and I sloshed my invisible one. In over-the-top fashion, Mylo drained his glass, then drank more straight from the bottle. My god, were they all used to drinking? I took a little pretend sip to try and hide a flush on my cheeks. I may have been jumping from rooftops and practicing armlocks for the past seventeen years, but my social life suddenly felt like I'd been watching cartoons at the kiddie table while everyone else was growing up.

Kyung-soon dropped down to the floor next to Mylo and held out her glass for a refill. He didn't hesitate. Okay, the two of them were definitely familiar with the drinking scene.

"Don't give yourself hangovers," Devroe warned.

"Chill out, this is light stuff, *Dad*," Mylo said.

Devroe's mouth twitched. "Don't call me that."

"First I'm not allowed to drink too much, and now I'm not allowed to call you Dad? You're a lot more of a buzzkill than I pegged you for," Mylo scoffed, and took another swig. I wondered if he would've stopped there if it weren't for the drink. "I get the no hangovers thing, but what's with the dad stuff? Do you have secret daddy issues? We're all friends here, you can tell us."

"Dude—" I started. I was sure it was harmless, but he was treading delicate territory.

Devroe interjected. "You really don't have any sense of self-control, do you? If you want to get far in this industry, you should learn when to shut the hell up."

What was left of Mylo's smile dropped. He may not have known what he was poking at before, but now Devroe was on the offense, and he wasn't going to just take it.

"*I'm* the one who doesn't have self-control?" Mylo gestured to himself. "Not the guy who stormed away on the train in a big hissy fit. Tell us, who'd you go and cry to during all that, since apparently it wasn't Daddy?"

Devroe's jaw tightened. The mood was snowballing into something horrible. Something dangerous.

I jumped in. "Maybe we should get some sleep." Rolling my lips, I made eye contact with Kyung-soon. Support. She looked like she was already on it, about to say something, but Devroe was one step ahead, and he only had words for Mylo.

"At least my parents would notice I was gone."

Just like that, the tension snapped. Mylo was pallid. Withering. Watching him was like watching a spark flicker away in my palms.

TWENTY-NINE

DEVROE DIDN'T STAY to watch the fallout. For the second time that night, he stormed out.

"Devroe—" I reached for him as he left, but barely managed to brush his pocket. Kyung-soon rushed after him, leaving me and Mylo solo.

"Mylo . . ." I took a tentative step closer to him. He didn't move, just stared at the carpet. How weird this was. Just a few minutes ago we were cheering each other. Now it was . . . this.

I hadn't put it together myself before; maybe I could've. Someone he was always waiting to hear from, but who never called. Someone, anyone, to check in on him.

"He really is good, isn't he?" Mylo didn't let out a wry chuckle, or give me a lopsided smile, or anything else I would've expected. "I'm going for a walk."

He left, and after a little deliberation, I followed, even though I wasn't invited. But he didn't tell me to go away, so I kept on, eventually coming shoulder to shoulder with him. Why? I had no idea. But the instinctual part of me said I didn't need to leave him alone, not to mention if there was any time Mylo was going to act out and do something totally wild, it would probably be now.

"You don't have to babysit me," Mylo said after we'd descended too many stairwells, gone down an elevator, and somehow found ourselves roaming the lobby. It was déjà vu from earlier. The protesters were even still on the sidewalk, camped in tents with their signs taped to the sides. "I'm not gonna try to steal the front desk or something like that."

I shrugged. "Didn't think you were. Okay, maybe I kinda did. But I don't mind just walking too. If you really wanted to be alone, I think you would've told me to go away by now."

Finally, he gave me a little chuckle. "Guess Devroe's not the only one with people-reading skills, eh?"

We stopped in a quiet section of the lobby, and it was silent between us for a second.

"Do you wanna, like, talk about it?" I asked awkwardly. I'd never really gotten to try on the concerned-acquaintance thing before.

"Not right now."

"Okay." I pursed my lips and twisted my toe into the tiles. "You wanna snoop through Devroe's phone with me, then?"

Mylo's head snapped up. I fished Devroe's phone out of my back pocket and waved it in front of him. It'd been pretty easy to swipe while he was storming out.

Mylo laughed. "For me?"

"And me. I've got my own investigating I wanted to do. But

maybe you can send middle finger emojis to all of his contacts or something?"

"Ah yes, the perfect revenge."

We settled into a leather sofa near the windows, and I dug into my other pocket. "I borrowed this from Kyung-soon's stuff." One of the cords I'd seen Kyung-soon using to connect her phone to the French politician's when she thought she could break into the phone. Hopefully it'd work on Devroe's.

"Devroe's phone. Kyung-soon's tech. Did you snag something from me too?"

"I actually did steal your eyeliner for the preview."

"I knew it!"

Biting back a smile, I used Kyung-soon's cord to connect my power port to Devroe's.

A folder-shaped app popped onto my home screen. The text underneath read iPhone (162). It was downloading.

"It's working!"

"So, what is it that you're looking for?" Mylo asked. The loading circle was up to 25 percent already. "If you're not just doing this because you're irritated with him or something?"

"Suspicious things. You know." I shrugged.

Seventy-five percent. Mylo threw his arm over the back of the sofa. "Oh, I see, you've got a crush on him."

My cheeks burned. Mylo threw a hand up. "No judgment," he said. "He's hot." But I don't really see it going anywhere if you're going to be this suspicious—"

"It's up."

I opened the file for Devroe's phone. My home screen was replaced with his, black with a quote in white lettering. *A great brigand becomes a ruler of a nation.*

"I know this!" Mylo beamed. "It's a Zhuangzi quote. 'A petty thief is put in jail. A great brigand becomes a ruler of a nation.'"

I stared at Mylo.

"I may have been reading up a bit since the museum. Maybe Devroe has too. He's a man of class." He rolled his eyes. "Go ahead, let's snoop."

"Messages." I tapped the speech bubble icon. Devroe's messages, as of an hour ago. There were dozens of names, dozens of people. Unread messages about clients and orders and a few feminine names ending with winky emojis.

Our group chat was at the top. But under it were a few private threads, several in languages with characters I wasn't familiar with.

"Can you read any of these?" I asked, scrolling down. The Mandarin I could read, but the rest . . .

"I speak a lot of languages, but I can only read ones with the English alphabet."

"Bummer," I mumbled.

I kept fishing through Devroe's phone. The less I found, the more I felt myself crumbling.

What was I doing? Searching through the phone of a guy I sort of had a crush on because . . . what? Because he waited outside a museum to help me? Because my aunt told me not to trust him?

"This was pointless." I offered the phone to Mylo, wanting it out of my hands. "Here, send your middle finger emojis if you want."

Mylo frowned. "Mum." He didn't take the phone, just tapped the screen and pushed it back to me. "You can always tell the truth about a man by how he treats his mom, right?"

Mylo had opened a thread, and because I'd already gone shamefully far, I looked. The chat there took me back for a second. It was nothing like what I was expecting. My chat with Mom and Auntie was full of silly little messages and requests to go pick things up from the store, come into the living room because they didn't want to walk up and see me. *G'night*s and *love-you*s speckled in between. What I saw here was . . . odd.

Most of the messages were from Devroe. Every night, he sent one with only one word: **Alive**. Read tags were on for Mum. Occasionally, she texted back, every few days, sometimes a week in between. But they weren't messages, weren't even words. Just numbers. Short strings of them.

"Okay, that's cryptic," Mylo said. "And I thought my parents were taciturn."

Taciturn. He really had been hitting the books since the museum.

I closed out Devroe's text messages. "It's probably a code," I said.

"Why would the only correspondence between Devroe and Mummy be coded?" Mylo pondered.

Now, that was interesting.

Feeling a little calmer but strangely reinvigorated, I opened up Devroe's photo gallery. Maybe there'd be a key somewhere in his phone, and I could decode whatever he and Mum were talking about.

The gallery was disappointingly bare. Like, unusually bare. There were only two pictures inside. I tapped. The first was an upload of a picture. In the frame was a young light-skinned boy with fluffy, dense hair in an adorable button-down shirt and shorts. He smiled wide, and even though he couldn't have been more than nine or ten, you could tell from his silky lashes and the shape of his smile that he was going to grow up to be handsome as everything.

Devroe. Little Devroe.

Behind him, sitting with an almost angelic elegance on a stone bench, was a woman. She was darker than Devroe, several shades darker, with pressed hair that fell down her back. Her smile was less . . . electric than little Devroe's. Much more of a Mona Lisa smile, if even that. Common sense, and the matching silky lashes, told me that I was looking at his elusive mum.

"Hey, is it just me, or does it look like they're in a graveyard?" Mylo double tapped a corner of the background. Being an uploaded image from an old camera, it wasn't exactly crystal clear. But there was an obvious field of grass and some kind of large stones behind them.

I fought a shudder. Family pics in a cemetery—now, *that* was cryptic.

I swiped forward, if only to get my mind off the last picture.

The next one didn't help.

This picture was a snapshot of a lined sheet of paper. It was yellowed, old. Frail-looking. Lines of ink starting to melt into the page over time. Even so, I could tell from the picture that someone had taken excellent care of it.

I sucked in a breath, my heart skipping as I realized what it was. The letter Devroe had told me about on the train. The one his dad left for him.

I looked to Mylo, expecting him to tell me to click it off or something. But damn it, his eyes were already scanning the page. And there went the last thing that might have made me stop.

I read.

Son,

It feels strange, writing that word. Son. I never thought I'd have one of those. But now that you're on your way, I can't imagine not having one. Life's funny that way. Don't think that I'm not happy about you, though. I don't think I've been so happy in my entire life. Which is ironic, given everything else. The best things you get in life are usually things you weren't expecting. Remember that.

I'd call you by your name, but I don't really know what it'll be yet. Diane, your mum, wants me to come up with one. Don't tell your mum, but I'm really stressing about it. Names are important, sometimes they're your first impression before you even meet someone. I'll keep that in mind and try to come up with something good.

How you dress is important too. Your clothes tell people how you think of yourself, so you should always dress to impress. Let people know that you're something valuable. (Don't ever let your mum catch you wearing a clip-on tie, she'll give you her sour face for a week. Trust me, I know.)

What else is important? Don't be stubborn, unless it's important, then don't be stubborn, be unwavering. Be a gentleman, always. Charm will get you farther than cruelty. If you fall in love someday—and it's okay if you don't—whoever they are, make sure it's with someone you can be your whole self with. It's dangerous to love half of a person. And I guess it wouldn't hurt to find

*someone like your mum too. Not to brag, but I
kinda aced it with that one.*

*Speaking of your mum. She needs you. Always
listen to her.*

*I'll try to write again if I can. I hope we get to
meet, if not in this life, then after.*

—Dad

Swallowing, I put the phone facedown. My eyes were stinging.

"You good?" Mylo touched my hand, startling me.

Clearing my throat, I nodded. "Yeah fine, just . . ." It just hit a little too close to home.

I really wanted to be angry at Devroe. But after reading that, it wasn't in my heart anymore. He was a kid dealing with drama of his own.

Just like me.

THIRTY

THE NEXT DAY, the hours were ticking down until the start of the auction, and I couldn't find my meteor bracelet.

Mylo left to pick up a special project after we had a long chitchat with some of the protesters. The organizer of the movement was more than happy to talk our ears off about her innovative theory of franchising museums to contain all the same exhibitions and artifacts, using replicas to show off treasures from foreign countries—i.e., the replica sarcophagus she and her group had. Lack of funding kept the project from taking off just yet. Mylo and I took pamphlets and made a hefty donation to the cause.

After that, I'd memorized, then rememorized all the hotel's exits, and there was only so much pacing I could do to avoid thinking about the letter on Devroe's phone and a gnawing sense of guilt for snooping so thoroughly into his life. The more I thought about it, the more I felt like I hadn't just used the playbook *How to Invade Someone's Privacy in Unforgivable Ways*, but also rewrote it with bonus chapters.

Now I tore apart the room looking for my weapon. My security blanket.

Nothing.

I huffed and threw down my backpack after I emptied the pockets for the third time. I know it is super ironic coming from me, but having something you need stolen is one of the most frustrating things in the world. Double frustrating when you're pretty sure you know who took it but can't do anything about it.

I texted Devroe. Mylo had slipped Devroe's phone back into his pocket while offering a slightly genuine apology for poking at him last night. He didn't seem to notice we'd borrowed it.

Where are you? Where's my bracelet?

No response, but I saw that he read it.

I could've screamed into a pillow. Since I was alone, I did.

I was waiting in the living room with my arms crossed when Devroe finally decided to return, with a garment bag over his shoulder and at least three gift bags with different colored tissue paper in the other. I tried not to think of that picture of little Devroe when I looked at him.

He shut the door. "Waiting for me? Don't worry, I'm right here."

"Not *you*." I wriggled my wrist. "I know you took it. I told you I wanted it back tonight."

"And I told you it didn't match."

He strode past me toward the bathroom.

I followed him through the bedroom and leaned on the

doorway of the bathroom while he hung his garment bag on a free hook. I took a breath. "Are you doing this because—" Did he know what I'd done? *I should tell him, be honest.*

He looked at me through the mirror and started to unbutton his vest. "Because . . . ?"

I caved. It was just a little lie, it didn't matter. "Nothing." I shut the door.

TONIGHT'S DRESS WAS my favorite of the two Devroe had picked. Last night's was a seductive red, but this one was a stunning rose gold. The fabric, though hip-hugging, moved gently with my body. Wearing it, even with the painful gold heels, made me feel like a lick of golden fire dancing in the night. And thanks to the side zipper on this dress, I didn't even have to ask for Devroe's help getting it on. Maybe it was unnecessary—actually, I knew it was—but I sent Auntie a pic. She sent back a string of heart eyes, followed up by a recovery text reminding me to not get distracted, be careful, yada yada. It made me smile. Even she'd gotten distracted by the glitz for a second.

When Devroe came out in his tux, I did my best to ignore the electricity jumping between us. Our eyes connecting, I could read the hunger in him just as I felt it in myself. I told myself it was just excitement for the hunt.

I swallowed, needing to get back on target. "Okay, it's time. Where's my meteor bracelet?"

Devroe deflated a touch, like he'd been hoping I'd say something else. He drew a thin silver box, tied with a shiny gold bow from his tux jacket. He wrapped it? Talk about dramatic.

"I told you I'd give it back," he said.

I snatched the box and ripped the ribbon off. "You know it's not a gift when it was already mine."

I popped open the box. When I saw what was inside, I went still. It was so familiar, yet different. More beautiful.

What used to be a grungy aged silver was now rose gold. It looked like a piece from an edgy Tiffany collection. Something that would be totally overpriced but sold out in minutes.

I drew it link by link from the box, marveling at the way it sparkled under the light. Devroe took my wrist and helped me wrap it on.

"I told you it would need to be camouflaged if you wanted to wear it tonight." I soaked in the warmth of his fingertips as he slid on the ring and snapped the metallic ball into place on it. "Now you can wear it anywhere. Without looking like you just left a biker club."

A little flutter swept through my heart. It was just a weapon— but it was more than that. He took something I'd had my whole life solely for practicality and made it stunning.

I fumbled for words. How did he know I'd like this? It was the best gift anyone had ever given me.

Maybe it was impulsive and cringey, but I couldn't help it. I threw myself into his chest, wrapping my arms around him. He tensed for a moment, and I was going to pull back. But before I could, he melted into a laugh and returned my embrace. His arms were warm and strong and soft under the velvety fabric of his jacket. He smelled like spice and cinnamon, and I didn't hide the way I breathed it in. As intimate as the moment was, it felt as if we'd done it a million times.

"You don't owe me for this one," he said.

I rolled my eyes and stepped back. He had something of a

lopsided grin on while he straightened his collar. "About last night. I shouldn't have lost my temper. A friend once told me that gifts are the best apologies, so consider this one." He looked like he was holding his breath. For me?

"You didn't do anything to me." If anything, it was Mylo who deserved the apology. Even so, after everything I found in his phone, I really couldn't hold it against him for getting so emotional about bringing up his dad.

"Not that," he clarified. "I shouldn't have snapped at you after we got back. Trust has to be earned, I know that. You were right, maybe I'm not used to having to try so hard to win something, but I am going to keep trying, unless you really, really do want me to stop."

I ran my fingers over the links of the chain. This should've been perfect, and I could see in his eyes that he meant it. He was going to stop flirting with me, playing our little game if I said it this time. A given out. A smarter version of myself would have taken it.

"I stole your phone last night," I sputtered instead. "I stole your phone and I used Kyung-soon's tech to hack into it and I looked through all your stuff because I thought you were suspicious and . . . yeah. I'm sorry."

I held my breath.

Devroe just blinked at me. "You hacked into my phone . . . and found?"

I looked away, rubbing my arm nervously. "Honestly, a lot of languages I can't read and some other stuff. But that's not the point. The point is, I'm sorry. I'm starting to get that I have a lot of stuff I need to work through with myself, and if I'm being honest, I still don't really trust you even if I might *maybe* want to. You should know that before you decide to keep holding out any serious hope for this."

Devroe rubbed his chin and turned away for a moment.

The moment turned into a minute.

"You hate me now." I knew I shouldn't have said anything. When did being a stand-up person ever work out for someone like me?

"I . . . feel like I should be angrier than I am," he finally said.

"So . . . you *are* angry?"

He chuckled lightly and turned back to me. "It's hard for you not to look for the worst in people, isn't it?"

"I'm working on that."

Devroe sighed. "Well, I did say I liked playing games with you. I can't really say I didn't know what I was getting into. And I did steal something from you."

I rubbed my revamped meteor bracelet. When he put it like that, it made it sound like I hadn't totally crossed a line.

He offered his arm to me. "Even?"

It wasn't the same, but he was accepting my apology.

I took his arm. "Even."

THIRTY-ONE

THE BALLROOM WAS flooded with people, power, and oh so much money.

Two steps in, and I was reminded just how large the Pyramid Hotel's ballroom was. Tonight, even with the stage and rows of politely spaced chairs and tables, it seemed like it was twice the size it had been last night. But maybe that was because I had someone to look for.

Once we passed through the entrance point, I reluctantly slid my arm out of Devroe's. As fun as it might be to waltz around with him all night—who thought I'd be admitting that to myself?—he had his heiress to charm, and I had some phony antiquity dealers to drug.

Maybe for show, he pressed a soft kiss to my cheek before he left. "Have fun, queen."

Queen. Why did that word sound so warm and smooth coming from him? It slid all over me.

I prayed my cheeks didn't actually look as heated as they felt and tried not to look like I was totally melting inside as he paced away, leaving me to my own work.

Lingering near the ballroom doors for a moment, I checked our group chat. Mylo and Kyung-soon were on their way to the spot where we would intercept poor Ms. Fazura's security once she'd purchased the sarcophagus.

I slipped the phone back into my clutch, then went to work pretending to adjust my braids with a little compact mirror as I searched the room for people I recognized from the previous night. All the while, my ears stayed perked toward the check-in until I heard the words I wanted to hear.

"Sanbury," the person said to the agent checking them in. They were here.

I used my compact to look at my target for the first time. She certainly stood out. A striking woman dressed in all black. She wasn't wearing an evening gown like 99 percent of the women at the event. Instead, she wore a plain black pantsuit with practical kitten heels to match. Her gray-streaked brown hair was pulled back with a simple claw clip. It was much more day-at-the-office than black-tie attire. But I suppose this *was* business for her—just as much as it was for me. A briefcase hung at her side. Something twisted in my stomach watching her pass through the entrance as casually as if she were going to lunch meeting. Didn't she feel bad at all?

Well, who was I to say what someone should feel bad doing or not? It was different for me, though. I was doing it for Mom, not to help grow some uber-rich museum's profits.

I watched her approach through my peripheral, a determined look on her face as she entered the ballroom. I followed at a distance. Which table would she choose? She was early; there were still plenty of empty seats to pick from.

Not stopping to talk to anyone, she weaved through the room to one of the tables directly in front of center stage. Of course, she'd want to be right by the action. Without hesitation, she laid her slender briefcase by the side of her chair and slipped out her phone to type a brief message. Letting her employers know she was here?

She was skimming the auction program as I approached. "Good evening," I said with a smile. Her eyes skipped up to me. "Is this seat taken?"

She looked like she was about to wave no, or something like that, but before she could, something behind me distracted her.

"Yes, actually. But I don't mind moving one seat over."

I froze. That voice. No freaking way.

I turned around in disbelief.

Noelia, in a shimmering white-and-silver evening gown with a pinched waist and skirt that looked too angelic princess for the devil I knew, approached the table. Her face, framed by loose curls, didn't give anything away. Well, except for those icy eyes. She'd wanted to shake me, and she'd succeeded.

"What are you doing here?" I said without thinking.

She took the seat on the opposite side of the proxy museum bidder, and I reluctantly settled into my own seat. My heart thundered. Where was Devroe? Had he seen her too? Was the rest of her team here? I did a quick scan of the ballroom but found nothing.

"I'm here to bid." Her tone . . . it was like we were old friends.

Something that pressed my buttons in all the wrong ways. "Well, maybe just watch. I don't think I'll be spending nine figures on anything." She tipped her head toward my target for a moment.

Why did she do that? Did she know about the British Museum buyers? But how would she have figured that out? They had to have some sort of plan, but . . . what?

Stop panicking, Ross. Figure it out.

I couldn't make a scene. I nodded politely, dropping my hand under my chin. "Where are your friends? Are they coming too?"

Noelia frowned. "I don't know who you mean."

Hm.

"Little Miss Boschert." A tall European man with a French accent smiled widely as he made his way toward us. A woman at least a decade and a half his junior clung to his arm.

Noelia looked like she wanted to groan, but only for the edge of a second, before a delighted smile swept across her face. "Mr. Lusk!" She hopped up from her seat and pressed a delicate kiss to the side of his cheek.

"We didn't see you come in, dear," the woman said.

"How are you here, anyway?" Lusk gave Noelia a curious look. "I thought this auction was drinking age and up."

Noelia pressed a finger to her lips. "Don't tattle on me, okay?"

The woman laughed lightly.

The man, however, remained serious, watching her in almost a fatherly sort of way. His voice dropped a few decibels, but it was still clear as day to me when he said, "Is that how you got on that ban list? You shouldn't be sneaking into events, Noelia."

His companion hit his arm. "Honey, leave her alone. We did worse when we were her age, right?"

"Thanks for fixing that for me," Noelia said softly. "I promise, it was just a misunderstanding."

She shifted on her heels. Was she uncomfortable talking to these people or talking to them in front of me and the museum proxy? She had to know I was mentally recording everything. Noelia must have been pretty desperate to stoop to using her actual connections to get back in the game.

The man gave her a reluctant nod. "Do you want to sit with us? We have a private table toward the back."

"No, I want to be up front. But thanks, though. For everything, truly."

"Are you going to visit the boys next month? It's open house at Hauser. The boys tell us that Nicholi misses you so much—"

"I might be," she interrupted. "We'll have to see." Noelia smiled brightly, obviously trying to end the conversation. It worked. They exchanged kisses once again, then the pair set off toward their private table across the increasingly crowded ballroom.

With a small sigh, Noelia sat back down, biting back a grimace.

"Know people everywhere, huh?" I cut my eyes back to the couple drifting away. Maybe I could use that. "You should go sit with your friends. Do you know them through business or something else?"

She read the threat behind my words. *Maybe if you don't back off, I'll go tattle about how they're probably being conned by your family somehow.* Was it a hollow threat? Maybe a little. For all I knew, they'd actually been clients of the Boscherts at some point, but based on how typical-teenager she was playing with them, I'd have bet that wasn't the case.

I would've thought Noelia was totally unaffected by my threat, if not for the tiniest twitch of her lips. She was an expert at hiding what she was really feeling. "Who are you here with?" She flipped her hair back and glanced behind her shoulder.

I swiped my clutch off the table, then rose, turning to my target. "Will you hold my seat, please?"

The woman seemed to debate with herself for a moment. She was here to work, not to get distracted shooing people away from the seat next to her, but she relented. "Sure."

Noelia waved as I headed toward an unoccupied corner of the ballroom, somewhere Noelia couldn't snoop on my phone's screen, but still close enough for me to keep sight of her. I hit up our group chat.

!! Noelia is here!!

Where was Devroe?

Far across the room, chatting it up with his target, I finally spotted him checking his phone.

Kyung-soon: **Wait, all of them? Just her?**

Mylo: **We banned them . . . are they incognito?**

I typed fast. **Just see her. Probably more here.**

I couldn't help but chance another hasty scan of the whole room, looking for anyone even vaguely reminiscent of Taiyō, Adra, or Lucus. Surely if Lucus were here I would've felt a shiver down my spine or something, but I found nothing.

Devroe: **Where?**

Front table, third from east wall. I hit send, then frantically typed again. **What're you doing?**

Devroe's typing dots danced before I finally got a response: **Sitting close. We'll keep close.**

Devroe and his companion were making their way toward

my table at the front. Noelia was chatting with another guest.

Where was the rest of her team? The ballroom was filling up fast, creating a sea of soft laughter, clinking glasses, and satin and tuxes that would have been difficult to find anyone in, let alone people trained to not stand out.

I hated this. Not knowing all the variables. Knowing that someone was actively working against me. I guessed that was what the organizers wanted. Excitement, unpredictability. But more than that, probably, to see how we worked under pressure.

So naturally, they had to add some more fuel to the flames.

My phone buzzed again.

It wasn't Devroe. It wasn't our group chat at all. A message blinked over the screen from a number I was becoming all too familiar with.

> Penalty game! Remember when we played on the train? We're not letting you know the penalty beforehand this time. Rooms 2410 and 2310—there are digital folders we'd like to access. You've got 30 minutes.

> Make sure you don't get caught. ☺

As if things weren't already complicated. Now we had thirty minutes for a rewardless, punishment-driven side quest.

My gaze shot to Devroe. Trapped in a conversation, he wasn't going to be of much help.

He was stuck with Ms. Fazura. Penalty or not, making sure she purchased the sarcophagus was essential to our plan. And one of us needed to stay and keep up with the auction, since Team Noelia was here. From his one glance, I knew he wasn't going.

That left me.

Noelia was making her move, too, texting someone. She'd one-upped me at the museum. I one-upped her on the train. We were one to one, and I was ready to finally take the lead.

Thirty minutes until the auction started. If I won, surely this penalty, whatever it was, would put us at an advantage in phase three.

I rushed as casually as I could out of the ballroom. I could win this penalty game. Even if I had to do it on my own.

THIRTY-TWO

What're you doing?

Do we need to come back?

Mylo and Kyung-soon were blowing up the chat. I responded:
No, keep to the plan. I've got this.

I used my clutch to press the button to the twenty-third floor, then the close door button at least a half dozen times. Noelia had been following me, I was sure about that, but I couldn't see her.

Great. So now I didn't have a clue where she or the rest of her team was. That was worrying me more than anything else.

The elevator stopped on the twelfth floor. An older Egyptian woman in a conservative gown with a fur shawl took her time settling inside. She appraised her eyeliner in a gilded compact for a few moments before dropping it in her purselet. I didn't know this woman, but there was something familiar about her. Where had I seen her before? When she got off on the fifteenth floor, I bumped into her. She was so nice about it, I might have felt a twinge of guilt for pocketing the mirror—if I hadn't had other things to worry about.

The elevator stopped one more time on the twenty-second floor, and a little girl with brown skin and dark brown curls got in, yawning as she hit the roof button. There was a foam dart tangled behind her ear.

Ignoring her, I flipped up the top of the compact and leaned against the side of the elevator. My heartbeat sped up as the doors opened on the twenty-third floor. I'd only have a few seconds.

Staying in the elevator, I angled the mirror out to get a view of the floor. Even without being able to see the room numbers, I could tell which room was 2310. The door was flanked with a pair of security guards, looking bored but not inattentive. We couldn't catch a break with security lately.

"Isn't this your floor?" the little girl asked as the doors started to close.

"My bad. I meant to hit twenty-four. Will you press the button for me?" She gave me a suspicious look before pressing it, so I informed her about the dart in her hair, and her attention shifted to fishing it out.

I used the compact mirror again on the next floor, and same as before, the door was guarded. I huffed and snapped the mirror closed. Maybe I should have taken up Mylo and Kyung-soon's offer to come back. But even if they did, which, being real, was not a bright idea, what was going to happen? Mylo would distract them with card tricks while Kyung-soon and I tiptoed inside, Pink Panther style?

There was a smarter way to get into 2410 and 2310. It wouldn't be a task if it was impossible.

The numbers pinballed in my head: 2410 and 2310. Even without the blueprints I'd memorized, I knew 2410 was right above 2310.

That was it. We weren't supposed to be going in through the front doors.

The elevator's doors were just starting to close when the bell to the adjacent elevator chimed. Noelia stepped out, flicking a key card in her hand, as if she were just heading for a suite, but stopped when she glanced back and saw me. I dove to press the close door button, but she stuck her hand between the doors to keep them open.

"Where are you going?" She made it sound like we were casual friends, just running into each other. "Isn't this your floor, too?"

Was she trying to play with me? I looked past her shoulder to the guards for room 2410. Maybe she was trying to get the guards to clock me.

"No, it's not," I said through gritted teeth.

She cocked her head. "Oh, sorry." Noelia noticed the little girl, who was still plucking away at her hair. "Hope you have better luck this game," she whispered, then released the door.

I scoffed. "You mean 'again'?"

"Sure." The doors closed between us, and I let out a breath before hitting the twenty-fifth floor button with my clutch. The little girl didn't say anything about my indecision about what floor I wanted to go to this time.

When the door opened again, the floor was deserted and room 2510 refreshingly unguarded. Giving the hall a quick once-over, and after an unanswered knock, I found one of my credit cards and got to work on the door. Magnetic locks were most definitely not my favorite kind, and it took an eternal half minute of sliding, jamming, and pushing until that satisfying click finally sounded. I slipped inside and pressed the door closed behind me, locking the deadbolt.

A cozy living room flanked by at least two tidy bedrooms and a small bar area spread out in front of me. Two bedrooms, huh? Would've been nice if we had a room with two bedrooms, but I guess wishes don't come true until you earn them.

I headed to the balcony. A toxic mix of adrenaline and nerves choked me as I looked over the edge. The breeze felt like it wanted to suck me down into a one-way crash course with the earth.

Right below me, though, only ten or so feet away, was room 2410, and below that must be 2310.

The lights were off. Hopefully that meant no one was home.

I gave myself a mental pep talk as I slipped off my shoes. *It's really just a ten-foot jump, and I could land that in my sleep. Might as well pretend the extra five hundred or so feet aren't even there.*

I went back inside. There was a decorative flower arrangement on an end table, with clear marbles holding the stems in place. I fished one of the little balls out and sent it clattering onto 2410's balcony. Anyone in the room would have heard it. If they came out, then it *wouldn't* be in my best interest to jump.

No lights turned on.

I had to do it. For Mom.

My hands were uncharacteristically sweaty as I tossed my

heels onto the lower balcony, then bit down hard on my clutch. I had to haul my dress up to my thighs to get over the edge of the railing. At least this was the side of the hotel facing the desert. If I fell, I could fall in privacy, which was maybe a plus?

Somewhere in the back of my head, I could picture Mom doing something just like this. Only she wouldn't have hesitated.

Following Mom's lead, I jumped.

I landed on the balcony with a light slap. A few braids slipped out of my updo. I barely managed to keep the clutch from falling out of my mouth. A rush of pride washed over me. I knew I could do it.

Room 2410 was identical to 2510. Same bedrooms, same plush furniture, same mini bar. But "tidy" was not how I would describe this one. Clothes were piled over the backs of chairs and tables. Dirty plates were stacked in the corners; peeking into one of the bedrooms, I saw a whole mountain of used towels climbing up the wall by the bathroom. Housekeeping clearly hadn't made a visit in days.

Whoever was staying here didn't want anyone coming in.

Running up to the suite door, I peered through the peephole. The guards outside hadn't moved an inch.

Twenty-one minutes left.

Computer. I needed to find a computer. Count had been helpful enough to specify *digital* folders.

A quick scan of the living room didn't turn up any sort of laptop or tablet, but someone who had guards in front of their suite and wasn't letting housekeeping in probably wasn't leaving their valuables out in the open. People seem to be particularly worried about their belongings being stolen in hotels; that's why they have safes.

I slipped into the master bedroom, remembering how the safe in our room was behind a small mirrored cabinet near the bathroom.

Got it.

I knelt down, putting myself eye to eye with a large black-and-silver safe about half as tall as me. A green-numbered keypad glowed in the center of the door.

After the Gambit, I was going to make my subspecialty hacking keypads.

I examined the numbers. Some were more faded than others, specifically the zero and one, but this was a hotel safe, not a home safe. The numbers were worn from general use, not from the same code being used over and over again.

I sat back for a second, propping myself up on my hands. My fingers nipped the edge of a dirty plate. A splatter of ketchup smeared my fingertips.

"Ugh." I jumped up and hopped into the bathroom, running water over my fingers.

Sticky fingers. Hmm ...

I scanned the bathroom counter. Hotels like the Pyramid always have way too many complimentary items. What were the odds they'd have—

I swiped a small bottle of baby powder from the back of the toiletry basket and returned to the safe.

Let's hope this messy guest doesn't keep his hands as clean as he should.

I held my palm open in front of the keypad and blew. A small cloud of white kicked up, tickling the keypad and dulling the green glow. I slapped the rest of the powder off my hand, then leaned closer to the keypad and blew lightly over it. Some of the powder flew off the keys, but on four of the numbers, little fingerprints held it in place.

A rush of glee raced through me.

0, 1, 2, 4. There were twenty-four different four-digit combinations with four numbers. I could try them all, or . . .

2410.

The green lights flashed, the deadbolts snapped back, and the door clicked open.

Real clever, my guy.

Two shelves waited inside. At least ten racks of Egyptian cash, and a laptop, tucked into the bottom.

The body of the laptop was matte black, but vibrant silver, like frozen liquid mercury, trimmed the edges. Very high-tech. My fingers itched. This was making me want a new laptop. Maybe *this* laptop.

There was a password screen, black with green text, waiting for another, probably longer and harder-to-identify code. I bit my finger. Now seemed like a good time to FaceTime Kyung-soon. But when I opened my clutch, I spotted the flash drive we'd all been given when we checked in. My heart pounded. This had to be why we had it, right?

I plugged it in, the password box filled with a dozen dots, and the desktop blinked to life. A task bar slid into the corner.

DELETE HARD DRIVE?

YES

NO

Delete? Obviously, the answer was yes. Why else would this be the pop-up?

What did they want me to delete?

I moved the delete pop-up aside and tried to tap the file icon. The screen flickered, and the mouse turned into an X. I tried the start button. Same result. Apparently, this easy-delete break-in flash drive was also here to make sure I wasn't able to access anything on the computer. Bummer.

I was about to tap *yes* on the "Delete?" pop-up when I froze.

I grabbed my clutch and dug to the bottom, quickly finding the hack cord I'd stolen from Kyung-soon. She'd walked in on me trying to slip it back into her stuff earlier, and so I'd stuffed it back into my clutch before I got caught.

If I was lucky, this laptop would have a . . .

A c-port, dusty with disuse, dug into the back. I attached my phone to the laptop.

HD 401 uploaded in under sixty seconds. I checked the timer. **17 minutes.** The auction was going to start soon. Detaching my phone, I hit yes on the pop-up. A loading bar appeared.

```
Deleting 15%
```

In the meantime . . .

I tapped the new folder icon on my phone. At least twenty folders, all in alphabetical order were inside. Some of the titles were mundane—*Accounts, Associates, Bookings*—but others were stranger. *Safe Houses, Black Boxes.* I tapped open that last one. A string of email addresses pulled up, most a hodgepodge of numbers and letters.

Was my family's black box address here?

I scrolled until I found it. To anyone else, it would have been a random string of characters and numbers, but I had it memorized.

Who the hell's laptop was this?

What else was the organization trying to delete?

My eyes frantically jumped from folder to folder, until one stuck out unlike any of the others.

Big Tam.

Gambit.

I couldn't have tapped faster. Eleven names appeared. Boschert, Noelia. Kenzie, Devroe. Quest, Rosalyn. Shin, Kyung-soon. Michaelson, Mylo. Laghari, Adra. Itō, Taiyō. Taylor, Lucus. Antuñez, Yeriel. There were two more I didn't recognize, both in red, along with Yeriel's.

Was this guest investigating the organization? A rogue member, maybe?

I tapped the first name on the list, Noelia's. It led to a new page, with an address and a name. *Boschert, Nicholi.* A European address, Switzerland. I scrolled down. There was a picture. A young man with blond hair who looked to be around the same age as Noelia. The picture was grainy, taken from afar. He was walking somewhere, not looking at the camera. Completely unaware of whoever had taken this picture.

A cold chill ran over me. Nicholi. Noelia's brother? It was the same name that couple downstairs used. Why did the organizers have his picture? And an address?

I went back to my own file. Quest.

My breath caught. The Quest folder had far more pictures than the Boschert one. Pics of Mom, Granny, Papa, Auntie,

Great-Aunt Sara, even a couple of me. I recognized the hair Mom had just last month, captured in a snapshot of her leaving Paolo's plane. My heart sputtered.

Mom's name was clickable. Obviously, I had to see where the link led.

I was redirected to a new folder.

PAST GAMBITS (2002)

No way.

Frantically, my gaze devoured the list. Only seven names on this one. Abara, Chen, Schäfer. But there, in the middle of the list, was **Quest, Rhiannon: Winner.**

What the actual hell.

Mom didn't just know about the Gambit, she'd competed. And she hadn't just competed, she'd won. How did this never come up? Not just from her, but anyone in the family. Did no one know? Why wouldn't she mention it?

What did she wish for?

I skimmed the names again. Boschert was there too. *Boschert, Noah.* Noelia's dad? It was the only other name I recognized. Mom always did seem to have beef with the Boscherts, but I'd thought it was just a territorial thing. Maybe the roots of that went all the way back here too.

All this history. Mom never mentioned . . .

I wanted to call Auntie. She had to know something. And damn, I wanted an explanation.

The loading bar on the laptop swelled, covering the entire screen.

HARD DRIVE DELETED

Without warning, the screen went black.

Kissing my teeth, I ripped out the memory stick and closed the laptop. Count's timer gave me fifteen minutes.

For now, I needed to move on.

THIRTY-THREE

CURIOUSLY, **WHEN PLUGGED** into the computer in 2310, the flash drive asked if I wanted to copy the hard drive. I tapped yes, but since this laptop didn't have a c-port, I didn't get to snoop on what I was copying. I spent the loading time digging through the file from the 2410 laptop some more on my phone.

I scrolled through links like *Clients, Contacts, Numbers,* and *Master List.* I found myself opening the phone number one, and up popped a spreadsheet with a whopping five thousand entries. Only a hundred lines down, I was finding names with addenda like *(vice president)* and *(CEO)* behind them. Using the search box, I typed in *Quest.* My name and cell number, along with Mom's and Auntie's, were there. Thankfully, there wasn't anything like *(thief)* behind ours. They were incriminatingly italicized, though, so maybe it was implied.

I tapped my chin for a few seconds before typing in another number. All of Count's texts about penalty games had made me forcibly memorize it. Lo and behold, there was a result. *Aurélie Dubois.*

So she did have a real name, a very French real name. Interesting.

I exported it all into my fam's black box. Surely Count was going to pop up and tell me to stop?

She didn't. I deleted the original file from my home screen undetected.

With the actual flash drive done loading, I returned the laptop to its safe and got ready to make the jump down to 2210. No lights came on when I dropped the marble again, so after tossing my heels, I bit down on my clutch for a third time and made the last swing onto the balcony.

Landing in a crouch, I flipped my braids back. My updo was a mess by now. Ten minutes left on the countdown. This was going to be tight.

I scooped up my shoes, about to slip them back on and high-tail it out, but the curtain by the balcony door rustled, as if there were a breeze.

Only the curtains were behind the glass, and the door was shut. Someone was inside, waiting with the lights off. I had a feeling I knew who it was.

I rushed to throw my heels down to the next floor and slip over the railing as the door flew open. Taiyō was like lightning. I unsnapped the weight on my meteor bracelet, but with a twenty-story drop right behind me, I had no space to maneuver. I landed one blow to his jaw before he grabbed my arm, twisted it behind my back, and slammed me to the ground.

I kicked against his hold, but he twisted my arm tighter and dug his knee into my back.

With my face pressed against the cold concrete, I did my best to glare up at him. "Payback for scratching your specs? You wouldn't, like, let me Venmo you the difference and forget about all this, would you?"

He might have smiled, but it was gone before I could be sure. "Don't worry about it. I think this makes us even."

"Taiyō's actually pretty petty, who'd have guessed." Noelia's silver heels halted a few inches from my face. I strained to look up at her. She fished the flash drive out of my clutch.

"How did you know I'd be in here?" I asked. "Tailing me this whole time?"

"No need. I know you better than you think. Eight years later, and you're still swinging in through windows."

My breath caught. She remembered that? Nine-year-old me had been overly eager to show off to Noelia about how I could scale the walls into any room at the school. Well, any room up to the second floor, at the time. She'd told me it was the coolest thing she'd ever seen.

How much else did she remember about me?

Whatever. It didn't matter now anyway.

Switching to Japanese, Noelia said something and tossed Taiyō a pair of cuffs from her own purselet.

I chuckled, but maybe that was my own frustration bubbling out of me. "You know I can get out of those in twenty seconds, right?"

"We'll see about that."

Taiyō jerked me up. I tried to use the opportunity to step on his foot, hook his leg, or something. But he was prepared, twisting my arm into a painful lock the second I was on my feet.

I swallowed an agonized groan, not wanting to give them the satisfaction of a full scream. Taiyō calmly started walking me the handful of steps toward the ledge.

My heart was thundering in my chest. "Hold up—" I tried to plant my feet. With my hands twisted behind my back, I grasped as tight as I could at the fabric of Taiyō's shirt. If he thought he was throwing me over the edge without getting pulled off himself, he was in for a hell of a last-minute surprise.

He shoved me against the railing. I nearly tripped from that force alone. This time, I couldn't hold back my scream.

"Wait, wait, wait!" Oh god, they were really going to do it. They were going to kill me.

I was over the railing. My heels scrambled to balance on the sliver of balcony between the railing bars. But it wasn't enough. I was facing a free fall.

"Calm down." At the last second before my collision course began, a pair of pale arms wrapped under mine, pulling me back. The ground, a merciless drop, was all I could see as my heart pounded in my throat.

Until I felt the cuffs. They clicked around my wrists, locking my hands behind me to one of the railing bars.

I was stuck, facing the plummet, and despite my skill as a contortionist, there was no way I was getting the bobby pins nestled in my braids anywhere near my hands without risking losing my balance. Falling with my wrists pinned behind me would mean dislocating both shoulders and likely snapping both of my wrists too.

Maybe the force would crush all the bones in my hand. They'd slip right through the cuffs and . . .

Oh god.

Fingers brushed my wrist. I thought Noelia was going for my weapon, but instead she unclipped Devroe's diamond bracelet.

I tried to jerk my wrist away, but the motion only threatened my balance. I had to keep still, doing my best to hold on to the railing behind me with my cuffed hands.

"What, you've gotta take my jewelry too?" I twisted my neck to get a look behind me.

Noelia clipped the bracelet onto her own wrist, admiring its shimmer under the night lights. "I'm much more interested in what's inside." She patted my shoulder. "Don't worry, I'll keep our museum bidder company for you, all right?"

How did she know about that in the first place? How did she know about the dose in my bracelet?

Straining to look past her, I realized Taiyō wasn't wearing proper black tie. In fact, that vest. Was he dressed as a waiter?

It hit me like lightning. "Are you ... stealing our plan?"

Noelia smiled.

Oh my god, they were.

I sputtered. "But how? We stashed the phone in a lockbox. No way you heard anything." I wanted to rip my hands out of the cuffs and throttle her. Both of them. We knew they were going to try to spy on us with the phone, and we stopped them.

Noelia said something, and Taiyō chuckled. It was the first time I'd seen him laugh at anything. "I don't hold a grudge toward you for tackling me on the train," he said. "It gave me a perfect opportunity to slip our real bug inside your jacket."

My jacket, the one that was sitting on the back of a chair in the suite.

From adding them to the ban list, to the auction preview, to the dosing and security transportation derailing.

Everything that happened between Devroe and me . . .

If Taiyō and Noelia were hijacking our roles at the auction, then I was positive I knew where Adra and Lucus were. Waiting at the point we were supposed to link up with Mylo and Kyung-soon, probably ready to jump them the second they pulled up.

On the train, he never did anything to the phone. It was just . . . misdirection. And we fell for it.

"Devroe's not just going to let you slide in on his target. He's going to notice when I don't come back."

"Are you sure?" She shifted the tennis bracelet. Did she really think they could get Devroe with his own trick?

Could they?

Noelia's clutch buzzed.

"Game's over," Taiyō said. "We should go back down."

Noelia nodded. "I don't know how you'll explain this when the guests get back, but try not to slip until then."

I heard her heels moving away and couldn't help but call out one last time. "Why did you turn me in back at the ski school? Was it because your dad lost to my mom and you hate me because of it? Always been out to impress Daddy, or has the double-cross, fake-friend act always been a Noelia original?"

Her steps slowed. "You—" She was still for a second, and for some reason, I imagined that look she had staring at Yeriel in the museum, before Adra dragged her away. "I do what I'm told, and I fake for a lot of people, but I never had to fake it for you."

With that, she left me. Again.

THIRTY-FOUR

I **TWISTED MY** wrists, groaning as the cuffs dug into my skin. Taiyō hadn't given me much slack. The metal was starting to cut off my circulation. A thief's nightmare.

Why didn't I let Auntie dislocate my thumbs when I had the chance?

I scraped and scraped the cuffs against the bars behind me, testing the unlikely possibility that there was a weak spot in the links I could manipulate, but had to freeze whenever my balance got shaky. How long had it been since Noelia and Taiyō left? Probably just a few minutes. But minutes were everything right now.

I closed my eyes. *You need to pick the lock, Ross. Just pretend you're not, like, two hundred feet up.* Maybe if I crouched just right, I could tilt my head between the rails and dig one of the pins out of my hair.

Taking calming breaths, as calm as breaths can be twenty stories in the air, I tried to lower myself down, but the farther my knees bent, the more my weight shifted forward. I could feel my feet sliding off the ledge.

I straightened back up. Defeated.

For all I knew, Devroe was about to be drugged, and Mylo and Kyung-soon were heading into a trap.

What were the odds this room's guests would come back soon? Even if I had Devroe's charisma, I didn't think I could spin any sort of logical explanation for this.

Minutes passed. Endless, sour, agonizing minutes. The breeze was picking up, taunting me, moving freely, and snapping the hem of my dress. The sand stretching out in the distance looked more and more like the sand back home, just before it slipped under the waves. Only here, instead of meeting the water, it stretched until it met the sky. My heart darkened as I looked at it. After this, I didn't think I'd ever get to go home. At least, it wouldn't really be home. Mom was my home, and she was gone.

I choked back a sob. How long without contact would it take for her captors to realize that I wasn't gonna be able to deliver? How long before they stopped answering? How long before her body was sinking away into the ocean somewhere? The last thing she'd ever know was that I failed. I got her into this, and now I'd failed this last-ditch effort to get her out of it. Auntie would know it too, the whole family I'd been so eager to get away from. The family I'd thought wasn't enough. Maybe I wouldn't have to go home at all. Maybe they wouldn't want to see me anymore. I'd go down as the Quest who got another Quest killed.

My last few days had been littered with mistakes. I wished

I'd been clever enough to realize what they did with the bug. I wished I'd been fast enough to keep Yeriel from being shot. I wished I hadn't tried to run away from Mom.

I wished . . . I'd kissed Devroe.

My eyes started to sting.

"What are you doing?"

I startled but kept my footing.

The little girl from the elevator, now in polka-dot pajamas, watched me curiously from the next balcony over. A younger boy with the same dark hair peeked out from their ajar balcony door.

"I'm . . ." I fumbled, then shook the cuffs behind me. "I have mean friends."

The little boy whispered something to her. She nodded. "We don't think they're your friends."

In spite of everything, I actually laughed. "You're telling me."

The girl said something to her brother, but the wind carried it away. She pointed into their suite. "We're going to call security to help you."

"No!" I yelled. She and the boy, who hadn't made it back inside yet, froze. I could already see the disaster of explaining to security how I'd ended up cuffed to a balcony in a room that wasn't mine.

I cleared my throat. "That'll take too long. You think you can toss me a bobby pin?"

They whispered again. "We can't throw that far," she said, tucking a few wind-whipped strands of hair behind her ear.

"But you have a dart gun."

They lit up, rushing into their room. A minute later they were back, the boy with a bright orange gun in both hands and the girl with a little pool of foam bullets carried in her shirt.

She jammed a bobby pin into each of the three darts, and her brother pressed them into the barrel. The kiddos looked like little soldiers.

The boy took aim. I stretched my palm to give him the widest target. He shot, but the wind blew the dart off course. He tried again, but it bounced off the side of the building. Another three times, and he just kept missing.

"Let me try!" The girl swiped the toy gun from her brother, who whined and crossed his arms.

Like a true expert, she dropped to a knee and closed one eye as she took her aim. Slowly, she adjusted for the wind, waited a few seconds, then shot.

The dart hit my palm dead center.

Yes.

"You got lucky." I barely heard their argument while I unclicked the cuffs. The second they were off, I rolled back over the railing onto the balcony. Safe, solid ground had never felt so nice against my feet.

I saluted my new friends, grabbed my heels and clutch, and sprinted back into the suite.

There was already a text waiting for me. From Count, received twenty-five minutes ago:

> You lost the penalty game. All digital communication between your team will be unavailable for the next 60 minutes. ☺

It took all my power not to hurl my phone onto the floor and stomp on it. Fine, if I couldn't give my team the heads-up via text, then I'd have to go on foot.

When I slipped into the elevator, I bumped into a slender man in a navy-blue suit exiting.

"Excuse me," I mumbled in Arabic, patting the man in apology. Hardly bothered, he waved back at me as I pressed the close door button. As soon as the doors shut, I brought out the phone I'd palmed from him. My phone couldn't contact the others, but someone else's . . .

I dialed Devroe's number.

It didn't even ring once before I got the this-call-can't-be-connected chime.

My phone buzzed. From Count:

Nice try. ☺

I glared at the little black security camera up in the corner of the elevator watching me—it and god knew how many people.

I flipped them the finger.

The elevator was on a painfully slow descent. It felt like each second was piling onto the mountain of time I'd already lost. By now, the main auction had to be well underway. Or at least, the sarcophagus, which was scheduled to go up closer to the beginning of the event, had to have been sold by now. So much had already been decided while I was balancing on a balcony.

Mylo and Kyung-soon still had no idea of the mess they were about to walk into.

The elevator finally hit the lobby, just as I finished straightening myself into something presentable. I squeezed out the moment my body could fit through the doors, flying toward the ballroom. It took a few minutes to get past security again, but once I was back in, I followed the auctioneer's voice like it was the path to salvation itself.

Item 77 was now making its way toward the stage.

Item 77 . . . The sarcophagus had been 39. It was long gone.

My gaze dropped to the tables that had been mine and Devroe's. A single seat was empty at my table, flanked by two swaying figures. Well, one was swaying, the other bouncing with giggles. The bidder from the British Museum and Devroe's target. They were both totally out of it. It looked like Noelia and Taiyō had succeeded in hijacking our plan. They'd aced it down to the last letter . . . so far.

My heart trembled. Where was Devroe?

Each moment I spent looking for him was a precious second lost. I needed to be on my way to the warehouse to help Mylo and Kyung-soon. If all four of Team Noelia were on their way there, they might not get out of the fight unharmed.

Hate it as much as I did, I was about to say screw it and move on when I spotted a figure across the room fiddling obsessively with his jacket sleeves. Then his collar. Then his tie. He was frowning while he looked down at himself, like he couldn't understand why he couldn't get every single crease and seam exactly where he wanted it to be.

Even out of it, Devroe was still somehow totally himself.

I weaved through the crowd to reach him. By the time I did, he was slumped over the bar, babbling to the bartender about how he swiped these cuff links from some bloke in the lobby. The bartender hardly seemed to be paying attention, thankfully, and kept his attention on a glass he was polishing.

"Dear!" I called.

He picked up his head, then smiled at me. Not the collected, charm-your-pants-off, infuriatingly perfect smile I was used to by now. This time his eyes were sparkling. It was a smile like he'd just come back from war and I was the girl he'd been dreaming about ever since he left.

"Ross! Where have you been?" His expression dropped as I took his arm and ushered him away as fast as I could. "We're supposed to be on a job, you ca-can't slack off like that."

"I'll remind you that you said that later."

As we made it out into the lobby, he leaned over to take a whiff of my braids. "Your hair smells like coconuts."

"Excuse me." I called over a bellhop who was just leaving the elevator. "Will you take my fiancé up to our room, 1530? He's had a little too much to drink." Without waiting for an answer, I transferred Devroe to the bellhop's hands, then dug in my clutch for a bill to give him.

Devroe protested. "What . . . no, you're not coming with me? I want to stay—"

"I'll be up later." I slapped a small wad of Egyptian two-hundred-pound notes in the bellhop's gloved hand. He lit up in an instant, giving me an eager nod.

"Yes, will do, miss. Come along, sir." The bellhop tried to tug him away, but Devroe reached for my hand.

"Promise you'll come back?" His lip trembled, as if he was truly worried that I might not.

I gave him my surest look. When I was running through all of my biggest mistakes on the balcony, not kissing Devroe had been on that list. That was something I couldn't ignore, but I could compartmentalize it. "Yes, later. Promise."

He relaxed and reluctantly let go.

I immediately missed the warmth of his touch. A part of me wanted to call him back, to make sure he made it to the room okay.

The stronger part knew I had a job to do.

I cracked my neck, shook out my hands, and headed outside to find a car to hot-wire.

THIRTY-FIVE

I DITCHED THE Lexus I "borrowed" a block from the airport warehouse. One of the armored trucks transporting winnings from the auction was en route just ahead of me. That was my ticket past security and into the warehouse.

After speeding ahead of the truck and abandoning my car—and heels—I waited in an alley near the last stoplight before the warehouse. My breath caught in my throat as I eyed the light. This truck was my ride in. If it didn't hit a red light, well, my chances of sneaking flawlessly under a truck moving thirty miles per hour were not good.

The universe must have owed me some luck after everything else tonight, because the light flicked to red just before the truck rolled up. I managed to slip into position—not the easiest in this dress—and get a grip on the undercarriage just before the wheels started rolling again.

The metal under the car was almost hot enough to burn. My wrists were still stinging from the cuffs, but I tightened my hold with every jostle. I was only a foot and a half away from having my skin scraped off at fifty miles per hour.

I made myself count the turns I'd memorized from the route to the warehouse, until I was sure we were about to enter the lot.

The truck slowed and hit a bump. The security spikes.

With a reserve of adrenaline I didn't even know I had, I hauled myself up even further. My arms screamed. The metal claws brushed against my back. I shuddered. Any closer, and they would've broken my skin.

Ripped gown, mess of braids, bruised wrists, and skin covered in sweat and dirt and oil from hiding underneath a truck. And I'd thought I was going to a high-class auction tonight.

The truck backed into an open loading bay. I rolled out before they made a full stop and crept around crates and boxes to a metal door in the back of the unit. Judging by the turns the truck took, I was somewhere on the west side of the warehouse. The private unit Ms. Fazura's team would be delivering the sarcophagus to was in the same area. That's where Team Noelia would be.

I crept through crates and makeshift hallways, following the schematics in my head. My blood was pulsing in my ears by the time I picked the lock and slipped into Ms. Fazura's private unit. Voices, but I didn't hear Mylo or Kyung-soon. Were they hurt? Did we fail?

From between two shelves, I spied into the back of the room. Taiyō and Lucus were tightening the last straps around a large crate loaded into a truck. The truck that Mylo and Kyung-soon were supposed to load the sarcophagus into if everything had gone according to plan.

"Ow." Mylo's voice.

Relief flooded over me. Mylo and Kyung-soon were sitting back-to-back, hands tied together, next to a row of crates. Adra had found a little pile of pebbles, which she flicked teasingly into Mylo's and Kyung-soon's faces.

Kyung-soon's face scrunched up whenever one of the pebbles hit her. Her cheeks were so red and her glare so heavy, she looked angry enough to snap out of the ties and strangle Adra.

"Ow!" Mylo said again. Adra'd landed a shot on his forehead. She laughed.

"Leave them alone." Noelia was leaning against the side of the truck. She'd had time to change into tights and a sweater with her hair pulled back into a ponytail. One of her heels was kicked up, and I could make out some sort of red-pink design under her boot, but not specifically what.

"Chill out, I'm not hurting them." Adra flicked another rock at Mylo. "But they're losers. Losers get flicked. Look what they're wearing too. Raven black layered with charcoal and onyx? I've been wanting to slap some sense into these faux pas since Marseille." Adra made a gagging gesture. To be fair, in her black jumpsuit and knee-high suede boots, she still managed to look more chic than anyone has the right to look mid-heist.

"At least I didn't try to *shoot* them like someone else." Adra took aim in Lucus's direction, but stopped, seemingly thinking better of it.

I held my breath. The crate they were loading—was it the sarcophagus? Did they really figure out everything about our plan?

What was I going to do about it? Fight all four of them?

I was just about to unsnap the weight off my bracelet. It'd be one last attempt, probably a failing attempt, but I would scrap to the end against anyone who tried to keep me from getting my mom back.

At the last second, Mylo caught my gaze. He winked.

I let out a relieved breath so heavy, I forgot to pay attention to my bracelet. The links of the chain clattered against the metal shelf.

The other team froze. Lucus jumped down from the truck with a gun out. He held it with two hands. Carefully. Precisely. "All right, Quest, come out slowly. Or come out fast, I'd love a reason to shoot."

A shudder ran down my spine. There wasn't a hint of a joke in his voice.

Raising my hands, I stepped out of the shadows.

"And I thought I'd already seen the worst fashion had to offer tonight." Adra looked back to Taiyō and Noelia. "I thought you pushed her off a balcony or something?"

"You realize you have to listen to all the words in a sentence to understand what someone's trying to tell you?" Taiyō went back to making sure their crate was secure.

"Yo." Mylo waved with the hand tied behind his back.

Kyung-soon blew some wayward strands of hair. "No cavalry?"

"Sorry to disappoint," I said. Kyung-soon sighed.

Noelia cocked her head at me. "How did you get out?"

I gave her my brightest smile. "Trade secret."

Lucus used the gun to prod me back toward Mylo and Kyung-soon. Adra, who apparently kept zip ties in her bra, shoved me down next to them and tied me into her bouquet of captured enemies.

"Rough night, huh?" Mylo said, nudging my shoulder.

"You have no idea."

"We should put them somewhere else." Taiyō crossed his arms. "Count will make contact soon. They'll probably escape those ties once we're gone."

"Or we could bench them permanently." Lucus hadn't reholstered his weapon.

I felt Mylo and Kyung-soon stiffen. He said it so casually.

"Still on offense . . ." I twisted my wrists in the zip ties. "How's that been working out for you?"

"I dunno, how's defense been working out for you?" He started to raise the gun again.

"Enough." Taiyō shot Lucus a hard glare. "Robberies that turn into homicides increase the solve rate of the cases by over two hundred percent. We're going to do this as clean as possible. Think before you act, Lucus."

Lucus's eye twitched.

"Yeah, chill, Lucus," Noelia added. "They won't make it far trying to follow us, anyway. Plus, no one else is getting shot."

Else. She was talking about Yeriel.

Outnumbered, Lucus reluctantly holstered his gun.

The team prepared to leave. Adra blew us kisses before Lucus slammed the truck's back door shut. Taiyō gave us one last pitying glance before moving to the driver's side.

"Say hey to Count for us, all right?" Mylo called.

"I hope you crash," Kyung-soon added. She didn't sound nearly as joking as Mylo did.

I stared down the truck as it pulled away, and we were left in silence.

Minutes passed. Five, ten, fifteen. The three of us sat in the quiet. Waiting, until we were sure they weren't coming back.

Kyung-soon's shoulders jumped. Mylo began to chuckle. A giggle bubbled up in my chest, too.

"What the hell happened to you?" Mylo said.

"Did they actually leave you hanging from one of the top floors?" Kyung-soon asked.

I shimmied my way down to try and find one of the sharper pins I kept in my hair. After the balcony, it felt beyond good to know I could reach them.

"I will tell you every detail later. But for now—" I finally slid back far enough to swipe a bobby out of my braids. "I've been tied up enough for tonight, I think." I wiggled the head of the pin into the opening between the zip tie and the tail of the plastic, then wrenched it up and up until I was able to drag the tail back into the loop a few inches. I dropped the pin and slipped one of my hands out.

"Are you guys going to tell me why I just found out about this plan on the ride here?" Kyung-soon asked.

The zip tie loosened, Mylo brought his hands back around to his front, hopping up and rubbing his wrists before offering a hand to Kyung-soon.

"Ross figured the less people who knew about the switch-eroo, the better. Guess she was right."

Kyung-soon adjusted her black crocheted beanie. Very thief-chic. "Whatever."

I scanned the boxes around the room. "Which . . . ?"

"Here!" Mylo kicked a box near the port door. One of many

boxes that Ms. Fazura's team deposited when they were unloading her winnings from the auction.

From her back pocket, Kyung-soon whipped out a pink switchblade. Like she did this every day, she hopped down and got to work prying up the edges of the crate. The corners eased up one by one until the top popped off completely.

All three of us leaned over to peer inside. There, peeking out between shredded crate packing, sat a flawless, glimmering golden face. Ruby eyes lined with teal.

I couldn't help but take a breath. It wasn't the whole sarcophagus, just the head, but damn, I could still feel the magic radiating off this piece.

Kyung-soon and Mylo skirted off in different directions, each prying up the tops of boxes left in the room.

"Did you have any trouble finding the lines from the last deconstruction?"

Kyung-soon laughed. "Ha! It was a lot harder putting that fake together in the moving truck. Where did you get it?"

"The protesters outside the hotel. They had a pretty convincing replica, remember?"

"Ross was generous enough to donate to the cause," Mylo said. "In exchange for one of their replicas."

"Clever." Kyung-soon heaved the pharaoh's face from the crate.

If only Mom could see this. My Jigsaw Job made hers with the vase back in Kenya look like baby's first heist. She'd lose her mind, in all the best ways, if I got to tell her about this.

When I told her about this.

"How do you think Count's going to react when they turn in our version?" Kyung-soon asked.

"Now, that's something I actually hope they get on camera." A rush of delight raced through me.

"Oh!" Kyung-soon hopped over to another box. "Where's Devroe, by the way? Wasn't he supposed to meet us here too?"

Oh, Devroe. I snickered. Without the stress of the situation overwhelming me, it was almost funny, the way I left him. "He's . . . wasted. I should probably get back to him, actually. You guys got it from here?"

Mylo twirled his strange metal welding and cutting pen in his hand. "I took it apart, and I can put it back together. Don't worry, we'll get this thing loaded up and sent to our safe house in no time."

Kyung-soon nodded.

Maybe it was screwy to leave like this, but I mean, what did I know about welding? Even if I did know anything, the way my hands were shaking as the residual adrenaline pumped through my veins was not going to let me be of much help right now. I'd just gotten off the most exhilarating roller coaster, my heart still drumming and my legs wobbling.

Devroe wasn't here for it. Everything in me wanted to tell him all about it. He needed to be updated—that's why I told myself I wanted to see him. It had nothing to do with the smile he gave me.

So I left my teammates to it and headed back out into the night.

THIRTY-SIX

YOU CAME BACK!"

Devroe pulled me into an embrace the second I stepped into the hotel room. He breathed in my hair. His voice was still shaky—almost as unstable as my breath. How long until this dose wore off? I'd hurried here to make sure he hadn't stumbled and busted his head on the tub or something while we were gone, and I'd hoped he'd be more himself by now.

He sniffled. Had he been crying? "I thought you wouldn't come back. That you . . ." He trailed off, and I found myself wildly curious to know what the end of that sentence would've been.

"Devroe . . ." I shifted out of his embrace. He sighed but let me go. "You know you drank something you weren't supposed to, right? That's why you're acting like this."

"I did?" He blinked a few too many times, drawing my gaze to his silky lashes. "I feel . . . fine."

"Okay." I took his hand and led him back toward the sofa. But I had a feeling he'd follow me on his own.

"Tell me, then." I motioned him down so he sat on the couch, then lowered myself next to him. "The drug you used to dose the drinks earlier. How long do the effects last?"

His face scrunched up. "Um . . ."

"You *want* to tell me," I said, looking straight into his eyes.

He smiled. "You're so beautiful." He raised his hand and brushed my cheek. I almost leaned into it but caught myself and pushed it back down.

"Devroe, how long?"

"I don't know. Four . . . four hours? But I'm . . . Can I kiss you?"

Heat ran up my body. Devroe was leaning toward me. His eyes, through the haze, dilated with longing.

"I don't care about the Gambit. I don't want to be in it, any-ways," he said. "I just want to kiss you."

A shudder ripped through my chest. Maybe he hadn't been playing with me all this time. He really wanted to kiss me.

And I wanted to kiss him too.

But not like this.

"No." With all the restraint left in me, I pressed my palms into his shoulders and pushed him back.

He frowned like a little boy. It was actually quite adorable. "Please?"

"No, not now."

"Why not?"

"Ask me tomorrow. All right?" If he even remembered. Would there be another moment tomorrow?

Devroe groaned but nodded, accepting the disappointment. I sighed. *Get your breath back, girl.*

"You should go to sleep." I thought about leaving him on the sofa, but imagining that he'd have a better chance of falling asleep in a real bed, I took him there instead and gently tucked him in. "You'll feel better in a couple hours."

"I'm . . . I don't feel bad now. Do I?"

"No, but still. Just until Mylo and Kyung-soon get back."

He smiled dreamily. "I like them." He loosened his tie and unbuttoned the top of his shirt. "I hate that they're going to lose."

My hands stilled on the covers. Devroe's mind, for better or worse, was an open safe right now. I could reach in and grab whatever answers I wanted. Irresistible.

What did I want to know?

"Devroe," I began. He looked at me. Or maybe he'd never stopped looking. "Do you really think you're going to beat me?"

I held my breath, half expecting him to snap back to sobriety and storm off again.

"I have to. For Mum."

I stiffened, and pushed him to go on. "I thought . . . on the train you told me you were playing for your dad."

He rubbed his head and groaned. "I don't wanna talk about them. I'm tired of talking about them. She never stops talking about him."

My heart throbbed in my throat, and the same type of guilt I'd felt reading that very private letter in his phone overwhelmed me. I would've hated if someone pushed me on this topic while I was . . . incapacitated. Actually, I would've hated being probed at all in this situation, but I'd already crossed the Rubicon here.

"Shh, it's okay. We don't have to talk about it." I rubbed his shoulders, frantically trying to get him to relax again. What the hell was wrong with me? I should've left it alone.

Maybe there was another route of questioning here.

But Devroe was fading. His eyelids looked heavy. I wasn't going to get much more out of him. "Devroe . . . can I trust you?"

He wiped a tear away. "I dunno. That's up to you."

My breath caught. The words reverberated around me. Up to me, huh? No one had ever put it that way.

Looking down, I fiddled with my nail for a second. "Are you just saying that because, I dunno, you're planning on playing me?"

"Ross." He took my hands in his, moving faster than I thought he could in this state. He searched my eyes, like he was looking for permission to keep going. "I don't want to hurt you. I've never had a proper girlfriend before. None of them were real. They never knew me. You feel real."

It was probably a whole different kind of foolish to take the words of an out-of-his-wits boy as gospel, but I still found myself sniffling with relief. I wanted to believe him. After all, the whole point of this was that he didn't have any reason to lie now.

Devroe hesitated. "Will you lie down with me? I hate sleeping by myself."

My throat tightened.

I looked to the door, then back to him. He was already making room for me. And he looked so desperate.

"Uh, sure, just . . . gimme a minute. You probably can't tell, but I kinda look like a Black Barbie that got run over by a semi right now."

He chuckled. Real, genuine, boyish chuckles. That more than anything made me want to get back to him as soon as possible.

It took a few minutes, but I rinsed off in the shower and

slipped on a PJ shorts and shirt set. With a jolt of remembrance, I patted my jacket down until I found Taiyō's bug—cleverly placed under my collar behind my neck—crushed it between my fingers, then chucked my whole jacket into the hall just to be safe. When I slipped back into the bedroom, Devroe was already snuggled on his side, face buried in a pillow.

I slid in next to him. He lifted his arm like he was going to pull me against his chest but stopped just before.

"It's okay, you can." I put his hand on my waist, letting him pull me close. He hummed in delight.

I could feel his heartbeat under my palms. His light breath just barely tickled my own lips. He was adorable like this. Yet so handsome. And his hand, the way it weighed over my waist. I really could fall asleep like this. Tonight, and any night.

"Devroe," I said softly.

"Hm?"

I ran my hands across his chest, eliciting a soothing hum from him.

"Why were you so angry when I didn't kiss you? Last night?"

Still, he didn't open his eyes. "Because . . . you weren't giving me a chance. It's not fair . . . I don't want to be the bad guy."

I was only going to stay for a while. Just a little while. But something told me to stay longer. To give it a chance.

And before I knew it, my eyes were closing too.

I WOKE IN a warm cocoon of blankets and sunlight. Everything was snuggly and soft and beautifully bright.

And spacious. I was the only one in the bed. Where was Devroe?

"She's awake!" Mylo peeked in through the open door of the bedroom. In the living area, I saw a white-clothed table that must have been brought in while I was asleep. Shaking the sleep away, I stumbled out of the bedroom. In one of the four chairs at the table, Kyung-soon sat with her legs folded under her. No Devroe in sight. There was a K-pop song I didn't recognize playing. Kyung-soon bopped her head in time. With her back to me, she must not have known I could see her silently collecting all the silverware from the room-service table and stashing it up her sweater sleeve.

I snickered.

"Oh, morning!" She pressed a finger to her mouth. I gave her a nod as Mylo sat back down next to her.

"The sarcophagus is safe?" I asked. "Did Count send you a location?"

"Reassembled and delivered to a private plane at the airport just a couple hours after you left," Mylo said with a proud smile of his own.

Relaxing, I fell into one of the open chairs. The sweet aroma of fruit, syrup, and bready things wafted up from the table.

"Have you checked your email? Apparently, we've got a flight out of town." Kyung-soon popped a strawberry in her mouth and waved her phone at me, an e-ticket on the screen. "We leave in five hours."

Mylo had covered his plate with pancakes and waffles—the complete opposite of Kyung-soon's fruit plate—and now patted around the table. "Oh, come on!" He dropped his head on the table. "You're bleeding me dry."

"Like you bled all of us dry with your little card game on the train?" I teased.

He groaned into the table, dug out his wallet, and pressed a twenty into Kyung-soon's open hand. She graciously anointed him with a fork and knife.

This was already a great breakfast.

"So." Mylo bounced back quick. "What ended up happening with Devroe? He looked pretty out of it when he left this morning."

It was obvious by now that he wasn't in the suite—not a lot of places to hide. We'd fallen asleep together, and now he was gone. Had Mylo and Kyung-soon seen that?

"He may have gotten a dose of his own medicine."

Mylo and Kyung-soon paused for a second before realizing what I meant. "Wait . . ." Kyung-soon laughed. "You mean?"

I reached for a pitcher of iced coffee—I didn't even know you could order it in pitchers—and we began sharing stories of the night. Everything from my being cuffed to a twenty-story balcony, to dragging Devroe out of the auction, to sneaking into the warehouse via the undercarriage of a transport truck. I skimmed over the part about how I ended up in bed with Devroe.

"I guess that's why he disappeared," Kyung-soon said. "He doesn't do well with embarrassment."

Embarrassed . . . Maybe. Or was he avoiding me? How much did he remember? If he did remember, was he regretting what he'd told me?

This was so much easier when I was pretending I didn't like him.

"Well, I'm glad you got to see him a little out of it," Kyung-soon continued. "So, did he confess his secret love for you while he was unable to compose himself? Because that's totally what would happen on TV."

Mylo leaned back in his chair. "Ah yes, the old drunken confession trope. My favorite, followed by the one where one lover steals the other's phone because they think their S.O. is up to something." He waggled his eyebrows.

"Eat your pancakes, Mylo." I raised a hand to him. Kyung-soon frowned, not getting the reference.

She tapped her fingers against the side of her glass before sighing dramatically. "Okay, I have a confession . . . So, Devroe may have hired me for a side gig during the first phase."

Mylo and I exchanged a curious look.

"For?" I asked.

She squirmed. "Well, he asked me to kind of put in a good word for him . . . with Ross."

That . . . wasn't what I was expecting. "What kind of good word?

"Nothing weird!" she insisted. "More like, I don't know, you have a crush on someone, so you ask their best friend to kinda push them your way?" Her cheeks flushed lightly. Then, without warning, she disappeared under the table.

Mylo straightened up. We shared a startled frown. "Uh, Kyung-soon, whatever you're doing, I don't think Ross and I are consenting . . ."

"Shut up, Mylo." Kyung-soon reemerged. She dropped a large round box with silver trim in front of me.

"When did you even put that down there?" Mylo muttered, but my focus was on the cylindrical box. Kyung-soon gestured for me to open it, as if that wasn't obvious.

I popped the top off, just accepting this bizarre pivot in the conversation. A little smile swept across my face. It was a hatbox. Inside was a gorgeous blush-pink sun hat sitting atop crinkling gift paper. My eyes widened as I lifted it out. I'd seen this hat before, when we arrived at the hotel. A tiny designer's tag was sewn inside. Valentino Garavani.

"I saw you ogling it when we got here, but I didn't steal this one!" She fished a handwritten receipt from the box and handed it over. Mylo, peeking too, whistled at the price. Two grand for a hat was something else. "It's around the same amount Devroe paid me for my services or whatever. I felt bad, since we're actually friends now. My mentor used to say that apologies without recompense are just excuses, so this is my real apology."

She shrugged, looking away, doing that thing where she tried to act like she wasn't really paying attention, which made the fact that I knew she did care how I reacted even more sweet.

I petted the hat for what felt like too long. Too many thoughts were fighting for my attention. Devroe paid Kyung-soon to be his wingwoman. It was a deception, but kind of a charming one. I guess this was how Devroe felt when I admitted to stealing his phone. Maybe I should have been irritated, but I wasn't. And now this silly, beautiful little apology hat. Then the last thing Kyung-soon said. She felt bad . . . since we were actually friends now.

Were we?

"I really don't like being manipulated," I said. "But I also really like this hat."

"Then let's call it even for now," Kyung-soon offered. "From now on, all honesty, all the time, okay?"

She said *honesty*, but did I really believe it? Can you trust any thief?

Maybe, just for now. Just for a second, it wouldn't hurt to.

I hid a smile. "Okay."

THIRTY-SEVEN

At the terminal. He here yet?

Taking a breath, I replied to Kyung-soon's text. **Don't see him.**
She responded with an eye-roll emoji.

I rubbed a knot in my neck while I scanned the buzzing
airport. Only half an hour until our flight left, and Devroe was
MIA. We knew he was reading our texts; his read tags were on.

The murmur of the airport felt like a tornado swirling
around me. Massive Cairo International was making me feel
even smaller than it should have, swarmed with passengers
even on the unpopular flying day of Thursday. Was Devroe
going to show up at all? No way he'd quit over embarrassment
about last night.

I squeezed my backpack strap and paced down the wide corridor of the airport. Why was I spending so much mental capital

on him, anyway? My focus should be on the Gambit. On Mom.

Peeking out from between the rows of shopfronts, a sleek silver-and-black sign read SKY-GLIDERS CLUB LOUNGE in both Arabic and English.

Lucky me, I caught a tall man in a business suit just as he was leaving. We brushed into each other, mumbled apologies, and went on our ways.

In his wallet, the silver-and-black Sky-gliders card was easy to find. The door sang a welcoming tune after I swiped the card across the scanner.

The lighting was dimmer inside. The bustle of the airport dulled, replaced with soft, calming music.

A sitting room with only three people lounging in it stretched out before me. A map on the wall showed more sitting rooms, a bar, and even private sleep quarters.

As I passed the front desk, I slid the wallet to the attendant. "Found this by the door." Maybe the man would come back to look for his wallet. Maybe not.

Inside, early afternoon light burned through a champagne-tinted window, adding a golden glow. I fell into one of the cushy black leather sofas off to the side and opened my thread with Auntie. This morning I'd given her a general I'm-safe, moving-on update via FaceTime, and even though it'd only been a couple of hours, I kinda wanted to call again.

Or maybe . . . Mom? The second phase was nearly wrapped. I'd been holding off, but it wouldn't hurt to call with good news, right? Hell, I was sure even her snarky-ass kidnapper would be happy to know that I was progressing decently.

I was just about to hit dial when someone else slipped into the room. Someone in a vest and jeans.

"Devroe." I sat up, pressing my hands into the sofa's cushion. "Were you following me?"

He seemed to be at a loss for words, looking like he wanted to run away. "Not for very long." He perched on the leather armchair across from me. "Who are you calling? I didn't mean to interrupt . . ."

"Uh, just my aunt." I put the phone facedown. We sat there while awkward silence stretched between us. Was I supposed to talk about last night? What Kyung-soon told me? Would he—

"I'm sorry." A veil of shame covered his features. He shifted his weight. "What happened last night . . ."

I tried not to lean forward. *Yeah?*

"At the auction. It was amateurish to let them get me. I should have been more careful. But I wasn't, and instead I made myself totally useless, yet somehow you managed to succeed anyway." He ran a hand over his hair.

My shoulders relaxed. "You're not used to apologizing, are you?"

"Well, I'm not usually wrong about things." Already, this was a horrible apology. So much less poised than his usual game. Genuine. He owned it and kept going. "But when I am, I *always* say sorry. You should know I only ever say it when I really mean it." His eyes went all around the room—everywhere except mine—before he forced himself to meet my gaze. "Which is why I'm also saying sorry . . . if I said anything unsettling last night."

My heart sunk. "You don't remember?"

"A little?" he said. "It feels sort of like a dream, like that space in between being asleep and being awake. I don't know if my memory is accurate or not." He was still again. "Did I do or say anything . . . noteworthy?"

Where to start. "You said . . . that I could trust you."

His face went pale. "I did?"

"You're acting like it's not true."

He adjusted his vest. "No, I'm just . . . surprised that I would say that." He looked away, breaking the eye contact he was so talented at for a second.

"You said you wanted to win the Gambit for your mom. Is she, like, pressuring you to win or something?"

"Hardly." He tugged on his sleeve. "She won't tell me where she is, just sends coded messages about how she thinks people are following her. I haven't seen her in months. Her mental state goes up and down, and I'm worried she's not in a good one right now. I thought if I won the Gambit, I could use my wish to find her." He shrugged in a defensive, boyish sort of way, face flushing. My next question would have been why he didn't just say that in the first place, but I was hiding my own secret about my mom being in danger. They were different situations, but still, I understood wanting to keep something like that close to the chest.

I cleared my throat. "You also told me I 'felt real.' Whatever that means."

For the first time since I'd met him, Devroe was fidgeting, and not with his clothes. His leg bounced. What was he debating within himself? Seeing him like this made me want to push further. I wanted him to feel real too.

"Also," I went on. "You said you'd never had a proper girlfriend." I laughed. "I'm ninety-nine percent sure *that's* not true."

His leg stilled. Whatever he'd been debating within himself had been decided.

"I've never liked anyone before," he said.

"Yeah, right. You've never liked anyone, everyone else was just a game, and I'm the special—"

"I'm serious," he snapped. He was looking dead at me now. "This is real. I mean, I've had flings before, and I've had friends before, but . . ." His jaw tensed, and then he released it. "None of them knew the real me. They never knew where I came from, what I did for money, what I was really thinking. It was all just a show. Just another job. I was never my whole self with them, and they weren't ever real to me. How could I have actually cared about people in counterfeit relationships?"

His gaze softened on me. "But you . . . you feel genuine. Like an actual, real person that I could know. And I really, really like you for it."

My breath thinned, but I forced myself to speak anyway. "So that's the only reason? You only asked to kiss me because I felt . . . tangible to you?"

"No, of course not. I wouldn't have asked to kiss you unless I desperately, undeniably wanted to." The way his accent flew over *desperately* and *undeniably* sent shudders through my stomach. "I suppose I've never really wanted to kiss someone before, and I'm trying to understand why you're the first. Perhaps it's because you're real. Or maybe it's because you're real *and* resourceful. Real *and* strong. Real *and* determined." His voice turned into velvet. "Real *and* beautiful."

His words wrapped around me, safe and cozy. But also tight and binding. Like the sticky strands of a spider's web.

Devroe rubbed his neck, going a tinge red for a second. "Confession? I may have hired Kyung-soon to sort of shift you my way too. Though with the way this is going, I'm beginning to want a refund."

No, no way. Did he just tell me that, without being prompted, with no reason to, out of nowhere?

I jolted up and started pacing, biting my finger.

Oh my god, what if . . .

"Ross?" Devroe jumped up too, looking a little frantic. "Are—are you okay? What's wrong?"

Tears were starting to prickle my eyes. I shook my head. Devroe was in front of me in a second, placing his hands on my shoulders. Poor thing, here I was on the verge of something I didn't even fully understand, feeling like I was about to start sobbing, and he was probably confused as hell.

I took a shaky breath, wiped the edges of the would-be tears away, and looked up at him. "You're—you're really not, like, out to get me?"

He gave a little laugh. "How many times do I have say that?"

"Every time. If we do this, you say it *every* time I ask."

"Then no, Ross Quest, I'm not out to get you. Believe it or not, most people aren't." He tucked some braids behind my ear, and I shuddered.

I rested my forehead on his shoulder. "I think . . . I've wasted a lot of my life. Mom told me that I couldn't trust anyone, and it made me feel—" My voice broke off in a sob. "So alone." I wrapped my arms around Devroe and just breathed him in. He felt like a buoy in the ocean. I'd been drowning, and he was there the whole time.

Devroe hugged me back. His chin rested on my head. He was warm, so warm. I never wanted to let go. He whispered, "Lucky you, I think you've got a lot more life to make up for that."

I pulled back from him. Devroe swiped the newest tears off my cheeks. I rolled my eyes but didn't fight the little grin. When he was done, he dragged his finger under my jaw and tipped my head up.

"*Now* can I kiss you?"

I cupped his face and pulled him in myself.

His lips were soft at first and then they moved over mine with a feeling of undeniable want. I snaked my hands around his neck to pull him closer. Oh my god, he tasted perfect. Like trying my favorite candy for the first time.

I could have stayed there forever. I wanted to. When he deepened the kiss, I couldn't help but moan, desire pooling in my belly.

His kiss was a riptide threatening to pull me out to sea.

A buzz from his vest pocket cut the moment short.

Devroe groaned.

My back pocket vibrated as well.

"What a bummer," I mumbled.

From Kyung-soon: **Flight is boarding.**

"Ditto." Devroe slipped his phone back into his vest, then pulled me snug to his chest again. I giggled.

"Back to work," he said. But his smile faded as he said so.

"What's wrong?" I asked.

Devroe shook his head and his eyes cleared.

"Nothing." He brushed his fingers over my braids. "Nothing at all."

THIRTY-EIGHT

OF ALL COUNT'S rendezvous places, this was the outlier. When I saw that our tickets were to the British Virgin Islands, I expected to be confined to another back room or secret underground wine cellar, not for our driver to drop us off at the gates of a private resort. Sunlight drenched everything, including the sand stretching out from the patio we were sitting on now and the ocean beyond. The smell, salt water and sea foam, and the constant white noise of lapping waves reminded me of home. But I couldn't get too comfortable. Just because you feel at home doesn't mean you're home free.

"Do you think they're going to show?" Kyung-soon asked, checking the time on her phone. Count said to be here by noon. We'd been chillin' here for an hour and hadn't seen a hint of

Team Noelia, who hadn't technically been eliminated yet. Five more minutes, and they'd be past the deadline.

"If not, they are missing out." Mylo crossed his arms behind his head, leaning back to soak in the sun.

A server, clad in a bright pink shirt, arrived with Kyung-soon's drink. It was something cute and red with a candied rim and little umbrella not unlike the real umbrella angled over our table.

"We should come back to the Virgin Islands sometime." I pinched the curve of my brand-new sun hat and looked out over a pair of wind surfers gliding over the water. Yeah, it was a little out of place wearing a hat this glam, and it didn't match my outfit at all, but I wanted to wear it. "In the fall. Trust me, no one schedules their beach vacations for October—we'd have everything to ourselves."

"Um . . . maybe not." Kyung-soon played with the umbrella in her drink. A rush of nerves shot through me. Was I being pushy? "I . . . don't really like water," she admitted.

"Don't tell us you can't swim." Mylo nudged her.

She shrugged. "I can swim, I just prefer snow to beaches. I vote five-star ski resort."

I snorted. "Skiing isn't really my thing . . ."

"Devroe, what do you think? Snow or sand?" Mylo asked.

Devroe ran his thumb over his tie clip, his gaze a thousand miles away. "Before we start planning vacations, I'm still upset Kyung-soon and I were left out of your secret Jigsaw plan."

That had made for an interesting in-flight conversation.

Kyung-soon jumped in. "Relax, Devroe," she said, playing with her hair. "You know how it goes. The less people who know something like that, the better. And it all worked out, right?" She smirked. "Well, for us."

"Still." Devroe rubbed his temple. "I don't like being left out of the loop."

"The next time I'm planning inner-mission twists, you'll be the first to know," I promised.

"What do you think the last heist is going to be?" Mylo folded his arms over the table. "A museum, then an auction. Whaddya think the odds are we'll get to rip off Caesars Palace for the last phase? Go full-on Ocean's Eleven?"

"You *would* like that." Kyung-soon smiled sadly as she took a sip.

The unspoken truth was, we couldn't be a team in phase three.

Footsteps. A server guided in the latest arrivals. Noelia, Taiyō, Lucus, and Adra. They were in the same clothes that we'd last seen them in. And for once, Taiyō's perfectly parted hair was mussed.

I bit back a grin. There was nothing to be said.

They claimed a table on the opposite side of the patio, trying very hard not to look our way.

Count swept in. It'd been a few days since we'd seen her, but her tablet still rested like a baby in her arm. Today she was wearing a burgundy pantsuit.

"Congratulations on completing phase two." Her eyes slashed toward Team Noelia. "Well, some. It was most entertaining to watch. I hope our organizers don't mind me saying that this has been one of our most talked-about sessions in years. Exactly what we were hoping for, considering who we have playing this year."

I gripped the back of my chair. Yes, what a grand old time they must be having watching us from the spectators' seats.

"Naturally," she continued, "half of you didn't quite make the cut this time around."

"Yeah, yeah, let's get on with it," Mylo said, waving her words away in total confidence. "Let's go ahead and cut the deadweight so we can move on."

Count smiled, but in a forced sort of way. "If you insist. Ms. Quest, Ms. Boschert. You'll both be moving on."

We all snapped to attention. My heart squeezed. I was moving on to the next phase. That was good . . . but Noelia?

Kyung-soon scoffed. "But they lost!"

Devroe shifted uncomfortably in his chair. At the other table, Taiyō grumbled.

"I made it clear from the beginning that this is not a pass-fail test," Count said. "We evaluate individual performance and can eliminate whoever we like. Ms. Boschert, we greatly admired your idea to appropriate your competitors' plan with your teammates' help, and showcasing existing connections to get past your ban from the hotel. Therefore, you get to move on." Count turned her attention to me. "We admired it almost as much as we appreciated your plan, Ms. Quest, to switch the sarcophagus with the one Ms. Boschert's team ended up bringing us. Therefore, you also get to progress."

I couldn't bear to look back at my table. If Noelia and I were safe and half of us were getting eliminated, then at least one—maybe more—of them were out. It was only a matter of who.

Devroe balled his fist over the table. Mylo remained deathly quiet. Kyung-soon chewed her nails.

"Well, our organizers have decided to be generous," Count said, clearly relishing drawing out the suspense. "They're curious to see how this next development will turn out."

The air was so tight there was barely any room to breathe.

"Ms. Quest, Ms. Boschert. We're going to let you choose one person each who continues with you to the next phase."

THIRTY-NINE

I **WAS FROZEN.** Noelia, not so much.

"Taiyō can move on." She crossed her legs and folded her hands over her lap, not even looking back at the rest of her team.

"The hell?" Adra jolted up. Lucus looked like he was ready to punch Noelia, decency be damned.

Noelia shrugged. "Sorry."

Taiyō relaxed a little in his chair.

"I—" Adra twisted the hand with all her rings, looking like she was dead set on not going down without a fight. But Count was quick to step in.

"Ms. Laghari, Mr. Taylor. It's time for you to leave." As she spoke, two servers circled out from behind the bar. But they weren't holding trays this time. They lifted their Hawaiian shirts up, revealing that Lucus wasn't the only one packing. "If you don't mind."

Lucus's fingers twitched, starting to reach for his belt. I didn't move. Was this about to erupt into a gunfight?

The servers watched him closely. Lucus scoffed. "There's only two of you."

As if on cue, about six other servers filed in from the back, lining up behind Count like soldiers behind a general. Count cocked a brow, as if to say, *Seriously?*

At this, Lucus backed down. Adra hesitated, her eyes jumping over the goons behind Count. If Lucus and his gun didn't have a chance, she sure as hell didn't.

"What made him better than us?" she growled.

Noelia looked completely placid, more like a preprogrammed robot than a girl. "Nothing. I just think the chances of anyone being stabbed or shot are dramatically lessened without either of you around. Also, I didn't appreciate you trash-talking my shoes when you thought I couldn't hear you."

"You—"

Count cleared her throat, cutting off whatever else Adra wanted to say.

Lucus, about to burst a vein, brushed past Count. "For your sake, I hope we don't meet again."

Reluctantly, Adra moved toward the exit.

Noelia didn't bat an eye.

With them gone, Count raised an eyebrow at me. "Ms. Quest?"

"I can't." Devroe, Mylo, Kyung-soon. If I picked one, what would happen with the other two? They'd hate me. *I'd* hate me. "No way, I can't choose. I won't."

"Yes, you will."

"No, I *won't.*"

"You'll pick someone, or you won't move on."

These people. They were sadists.

My hands clenched into fists. "They're gossiping about this too, aren't they? Eager to see who I'm going to save."

Count's lips quirked. "Does that matter?" Her tablet buzzed, and she gazed down at it before bringing her head back up. "We'll give you one minute. Or you're out too."

I burst out of my chair. Count took a step back and raised an eyebrow. Why had I jumped up? I wasn't going to attack her. I couldn't. So with a shaky breath, I turned back around to my table. They were staring at me, silently screaming at me. All of them.

Kyung-soon dropped her gaze. "Do what you have to do," she said.

Mylo laughed in a nervous fit. "Yeah." He cleared his throat and rubbed the back of his neck. "No hard feelings if it isn't me. Right, Devroe?"

He nervously slapped Devroe's back, but Devroe didn't move. Of the three of them, his gaze was the only one that wasn't anxious or sad. It was pleading. Scratching and clawing and pleading.

What would the next phase be? I had to be picking a partner, right? Why else would they set it up like this?

"Thirty seconds," Count said.

My breath hitched.

"Twenty seconds."

What gave me the right to choose?

"Ten seconds."

"Ross," he implored.

"Five seconds."

"Devroe," I whispered. "Devroe moves on."

Kyung-soon crumpled into herself. Mylo let out a single sad chuckle. "Unlucky odds, huh?"

"Fair choice," Count said. "Ms. Shin, Mr. Michaelson. Thank you for playing. You can leave now."

I swallowed hard, not moving. "Guys . . ." What was I going to say? There was nothing to say.

"Don't sweat it, Ross." Mylo clapped my shoulder. "It's not cool to hate someone for listening to their heart. Right, Kyung-soon?"

Kyung-soon gathered herself and stood. "What he said."

I was breathless. They weren't angry. I didn't deserve this. Didn't deserve them.

And I didn't deserve what came next.

Kyung-soon threw her arms around me, so hard I almost tripped and took both of us to the ground. "I hope you win," she whispered. "Hit me up if you need anything." She pulled back and winked at me, then looked down at Devroe, who was avoiding eye contact with any of us.

"Wait." My designer hat. I suddenly felt naïve and silly for wearing it at all. I slid it off. She deserved it back.

Kyung-soon stopped me with a hand on mine. "No," she said. She was more serious than I'd ever seen her. "No, it's still yours."

Count cleared her throat, reminding us that they were supposed to be dipping out now.

"Come on, Kyung-soon," Mylo urged. "Let's go get a real drink, huh? I know a killer place in Miami."

And then they were gone. Out of the Gambit.

"On to the final phase," Count said.

I collapsed into my chair. Sadness and relief swirled around me. A really confusing combination. I looked to Devroe—what was he feeling?

He didn't return my gaze. Instead, he was pinching one of his cuffs furiously, his jaw clenching.

"You're on your own now," Count said. Our own? I bit my lip hard enough to bleed. So we hadn't been picking partners. That clarification might have changed my choice, which was probably why they didn't give it.

My phone vibrated. "I think you'll find it's a little different from the previous phases," Count continued.

Feeling exhausted already, I pulled my phone out of my back pocket.

What I saw made my stomach churn. It was a picture . . . of a person. No other explanation, no more info. Count let the silence stretch, and it said more than she could.

The person was the target. Even worse, I recognized who I saw. I'd seen him in the files I stole back in Cairo.

Nicholi Boschert.

It took all my self-control not to look at Noelia.

"Please tell me this is a joke," Devroe sputtered. Whose picture was he looking at?

"They don't joke," Noelia said. For once, there wasn't a hint of sarcasm in her voice. She glanced at me, something worrisome written in her eyes, but she hardened them a moment later and dropped her phone on the table.

Taiyō took a screenshot, then tucked his away.

"May we inquire," Taiyō asked calmly, eyes on Noelia's

screen, "about your intentions for these targets? I see there are multiple."

Noelia flipped her phone facedown, hiding whatever, *whoever*, Taiyō had seen.

"More than anything, we're interested in testing your skills and resolve. Do you have the stomach?"

"That wasn't an answer." I tried not to scream. "No way you only want to see if we'll kidnap them just because you told us to."

Count's tablet buzzed again. "Somebody watching thinks you're very cynical, Ms. Quest." She went on. "We have no intentions of *killing* them, if that's what you're worried about. As a matter of fact, it is imperative that you bring your target to us alive. Beyond that, what we do with them isn't your concern."

The edges of my vision blackened. I was going to be sick.

"No killing," Noelia said. "But what about other types of force?"

"Permitted," Count said. "But don't expect to be commended for bringing in a target half dead."

My legs felt shaky. If I had been standing, surely I would have collapsed by now. A person. A kid.

This wasn't right.

"I . . ." My voice was so weak even *I* barely heard it. "I don't want to do this . . ."

"What was that, Ms. Quest?"

"She's fine," Devroe answered for me. Somehow he'd changed seats so he was close enough to grip my shoulder. *Fine?* Was he fine with this? Was everyone else?

Where was the line?

Was I willing to cross it to get my mom back?

"How much time do we have?" Devroe asked.

"Three days," Count said. "We'll send you individual drop locations when the job is done. You may begin . . . now."

Noelia and Taiyō wasted no time. They hopped up and split off in separate directions, no goodbye. I stayed put. My body felt as inanimate as the chair I was in.

My eyes bored into Count's. The unconcerned expression on her face made my blood boil.

"*Aurélie Dubois.*" Count went pale. "That's your name, isn't it? What part of France are you from? Paris or Marseille? France isn't that big. Does your family still live there?"

She swallowed. I stood and moved closer to her.

"Help me get my mom back," I whispered. "Please. I'll owe you for the rest of my life, Ms. Dubois." I was teetering on the line between pleading and threatening, but the quiver in Count's gaze told me it was working.

A furious string of buzzes from her tablet drew her attention away.

"They like you," she whispered, looking at the screen. "I'm sorry, I can't help you." A blaring alarm sounded from Count's tablet. "Good luck, Rosalyn." She gave me a little nod, then one to Devroe. "Mr. Kenzie." Then she left us with our task.

FORTY

THERE WERE FOUR exits in the cabana. I'd scouted them all out under the pretense of looking for the bathroom when we first got here. Know your exits, pick the best one. That was my thing, wasn't it? Always knowing the best way out.

There had always been an escape plan. Always another exit. But maybe today was the day I finally hit a dead end.

"What are we going to do?" I murmured, more to myself than Devroe. "I don't see a way out of this ... There's always another way out." I pressed my palms against my forehead, trying to wring out some loophole in what Count might have said. Something implying that there was another way to win this phase. Something like the secret exit at the museum. Something that would click and tell me that I didn't really have to kidnap someone.

But there was nothing. Complete the phase or lose.

I couldn't lose.

"I guess . . . we're going to do what they asked."

I snapped around to look at Devroe. "Just do it? You're cool with that?"

"No, I'm not cool with it, but if this is what it is, what's the alternative?"

He was saying what I was thinking, but hearing it out loud, in Devroe's voice, made it even more sickening. "These are *people*, Devroe." I felt my lips quiver. "Real people. Lives—"

"So are we." He grabbed my shoulders, steadying me. "You've been playing for something important. I could see it in your eyes since the first phase. You haven't told me what it is, and that's okay. But it is something important, isn't it?"

I squeezed one of the hands on my shoulders. Even after I took the leap of trusting him, old habits died hard. "My mom. She's been kidnapped. Her ransom is a billion dollars. I couldn't get that fast enough, the best thief in the world couldn't."

"So you entered the Gambit." Devroe's jaw shifted. "I was right, then. You have to keep playing."

"But . . . this isn't a game anymore! No phases, no targets. Just *kidnapping*, Devroe."

He straightened his vest, hands free now that I'd jerked out of his embrace without even realizing it. "I don't like this either, but there are bigger stakes. Maybe you should call your aunt. Aren't you worried about her too?"

"Why are you worried about my aunt?" I flexed my hands. "Who's *your* target, Devroe?"

It was crawling back up my spine. Suspicion, distrust.

Devroe's face fell. "You're regressing, Ross."

"Give me your phone." I held out my hand.

His jaw clenched, but he tossed it to me anyway. I kept my eye on him for a second before looking down. It was a picture of a young Japanese man, maybe a couple years older than us. "Taiyō's brother," he filled in.

Immediately I regretted making him do this. I rubbed the bridge of my nose. "I'm sorry," I said softly.

"Whatever. It's fine. You're stressed." I felt like it wasn't fine, but now wasn't the time. I'd really have to work on my trust issues later. If there was a later after something like this.

I turned away from him, biting my finger, hand shaking.

Devroe rubbed my shoulders. "It's okay," he promised. "Or maybe it's not. But this is the situation. What would your mom do if she were here?"

What would she do?

I could ask her.

In a flash I had my phone out and was dialing the number. It wasn't on speaker, but Devroe was close enough that he could hear too.

"Little Quest, always finding the least opportune moments to call, aren't we—"

"Put my mother on the phone. Now." My tone left no room for quips. The captor grumbled. There was some rustling, but then . . .

"Baby girl?"

"Mom!" Hearing her was like a sigh of relief. "I don't know what to do."

"Did you make it to the last phase?"

I nodded, even though she couldn't see it. Devroe was quiet, eyes fixed on the phone. "Yeah, but . . . I don't know what to do next."

"Win."

"It's a kidnapping, Mom." I squeezed the phone, probably leaving indentions in my case. "He's a kid. A fourteen-year-old. I can't do that, and now I don't know what to do. I'm sorry, I'm so, so sorry . . ."

The other end was quiet for a second. I thought I could hear Mom tapping her nails on something. Was this her realizing how impossible the situation was too? How hopeless we were?

Was this her realizing that if I couldn't do this, we might be on one of our last calls ever?

"It's not that difficult to steal a person."

My blood ran cold. I whispered, "What?"

"You could do it. If you really needed to, baby girl. I have faith in you."

The room was spinning. I could feel my face contorting. *My mama isn't saying this. She's not saying this, and she's not saying this so . . . coldly.*

"Why are you okay with this?" My voice shook. "You're supposed to tell me not to do it. You're—"

The Gambit twenty years ago. Mom had played. Mom had won.

Was the third phase the same back then?

"Oh my god," I said. "You did this. You kidnapped someone during your Gambit."

She didn't acknowledge the fact that I apparently knew about her having been in the Gambit, though Devroe's eyes went wide with a dozen questions.

"They were related to one of your competitors—"

"No," Mom insisted. "They were a stranger. Irrelevant."

Then this part was new. Guess the organization likes to keep things fresh.

"Does it matter who it is? It's the only way, Ross," Mom said. "It's this or let me go."

A sound like a metal door opening cut through the call. "They're coming back. Make the right choice, Ross. I love—"

The call cut off.

Something tightened in my throat. Mom wanted me to play. She wanted me to win. She expected me to do it how she did it.

My whole life I'd been doing things how she would do them. *Stop wondering what Mom would do. What* wouldn't *Mom do?*

From the dead end in my mind, a new exit opened up. Small, slender, risky. But it was there, and it was mine.

I pulled back from Devroe. He peered down at me, confused. "Ross . . ."

I took off. It'd only been a couple of minutes since Noelia and Taiyō left. Sprinting the way she'd gone, I found her outside, hailing an SUV at the curved drive. Taiyō was nowhere to be seen.

A valet opened the door for Noelia, who was too distracted by a frantic call to do so herself.

I threw myself into the back seat after her. Noelia startled, which was fair, seeing as I'd come a few inches short of landing right on top of her.

"What the hell are you doing?" She was so flustered, she spoke in French.

I shot a glare at the driver. "Give us a minute."

"No, *you* get out!" Noelia tried to kick me out, literally, but I held firm.

"It's about Nicholi." She froze. "Can't get through to him, can you?" Her call was still dialing out. No one had picked up. "You know it's not a coincidence."

Noelia swallowed, her face pale and her grip on her phone loosening. She spoke, this time to the driver. "There's a ten-euro tip for each minute you give us."

That was enough to have him hustling out of the car. While Noelia was distracted, I snatched her phone from her, with fairly little resistance, then tossed it, and my own cell, outside.

"You said you wanted to talk about Nicholi, not steal my electronics," she said, despite not having fought that hard to keep it.

"No phones. They could be using them to keep tabs on us."

"Who cares!" she snapped. "I don't care about this damn game anymore. Only about—"

"Nicholi." She used to ramble about how annoying he was all the time. I guess that's sibling code for *I love him.* "He's my target."

Noelia tensed. Her fingers flexed like she wanted to hit me, but hitting me wasn't going to make it not true.

"They would give him to you," she murmured. "If you came here to get me to beg . . . I'd rather not do that."

"I came for your help."

She eyed me cautiously. "Don't screw with me."

"Does it seem like screwing with you is my top priority right now?" I rubbed my temples. "I'm not going to take your brother."

Noelia scoffed, like that was the most unbelievable thing she'd ever heard. "You're forfeiting the Gambit?"

"I'm reassessing. I have a plan, but I think I might need you."

Noelia shifted uncomfortably in her seat. She crossed her arms and tilted her chin up. A burst of déjà vu hit me. For a second, nine-year-old Noelia was sitting across from me, doing the exact same thing. People really don't change.

"Don't be a diva, Lia." I didn't even realize I'd called her Lia until her attention snapped back to me. Two weeks after we met, she'd granted me the privilege. *Only people I like can call me Lia, so you can now too.*

Noelia's crossed arms relaxed. Her leg bounced. "How . . . how do I know I can trust you again?"

She was asking *me* that? Even now she couldn't help messing with me.

I watched for a crack in her act. A hint of humor or sick glee. There was nothing. Instead, the corner of her lip twitched. She was nervous . . . She meant this. She really thought I was the one who couldn't be trusted here.

"Because—" I fumbled. How do I really make someone with so much history trust me?

You have to trust them.

"Who's your target?" I asked quietly. If mine was someone Noelia cared about, and Devroe's was someone Taiyō cared about, then the odds were . . .

"Someone with the last name Quest. A woman, looks like she's in her early thirties."

Auntie. Even though it was expected, it still made my breath catch.

"I assumed she was your cousin or something," Noelia finished.

"Or something." I took a long breath. What I was about to do was probably as far away from what Mom would do as I could ever get. "Love Hill, Andros, Bahamas. The north part of the island. That's where she is."

Noelia gawked. "Why would you tell me that? Are you out of your mind?"

"I know your brother is at a boarding school called Hauser in Switzerland. I know where he is, and now you know where my aunt is. I'll even write it down for you. I'm trusting you. So please, Noelia, even if it's just this once, trust *me*."

Everything was on the line now. I was risking Auntie, and maybe my mom, for what? The chance to do things differently?

A chance to do things a better way. My way.

Noelia sighed. "What's your plan?"

FORTY-ONE

AFTER OUR CHAT, I felt a little bad shoving Noelia out of the SUV. She screamed as she hit the gravel, hair disheveled and looking absolutely pissed.

"Leave me *alone*," I snapped, before waving a very confused rideshare driver back in. Noelia mumbled something about how it was fine. Through the opposite window, I spotted Devroe. I'd sprinted away like a maniac. No telling what he thought had gotten into me.

"Devroe!" I called him over to the vehicle. While the door was open, I swiped my phone from where I'd dropped it. Noelia brushed past him, slapping dirt off her skirt and huffing back inside to wait for another rideshare. Devroe glanced from me to Noelia, totally perplexed.

"You ran off to get into a goodbye brawl?" Devroe slid in next to me.

"Something like that. Excuse me, sir, do you have a pen and paper?" The driver tossed me a little lined notebook with bent edges and a mechanical pencil from the glove compartment. I sent him in the direction of the airport, then started writing.

"My aunt is her target," I said. "I had to tell her to back off."

I showed the paper to Devroe.

Be cool. Noelia's with us now. Org listening.

Devroe didn't even flinch as he read it. Instead he took the pencil and wrote under my line, with the notebook still in my lap. "So you came back around on . . . your assignment?"

Plan??

"I'll do whatever I have to do," I said. "If that means taking orders I don't like, then it is what it is."

Playing our own game. Are you in?

The driver watched us through the rearview. *If* he was just a driver.

Devroe hesitated for a barely noticeable second before scribbling again.

Always, with you.

PRETENDING I DIDN'T notice Noelia tailing us was more difficult than I thought, but we couldn't have the organizers thinking we were scheming together, so if I had to let myself look a little careless to do that, then whatever.

Devroe and I blew upward of eight thousand American dollars on a last-minute charter jet to Switzerland. For any listening ears, I insisted it was faster than flying commercial. But really, it would give us privacy. I had a feeling any scheduled flight to Zurich would be littered with bugs.

This whole competition was turning me into a hypervigilant superthief.

Less than two hours after the start of the third phase, I was watching us rise into the clouds. Only four people were on the small eight-seater: me, Devroe, the "flight attendant," and the pilot.

"You should get some sleep," Devroe said once we'd reached cruising altitude. I tossed him my phone, and the flight attendant handed hers over as well.

"Wake me up in a few hours," I said.

He stashed the phones at the very back of the plane, where the engine hummed the loudest, stuffed inside a drink cart and smothered in my jacket just to be sure.

"In Cairo you were sure the phone was bugged, and you were wrong." Devroe just had to remind me about that as he settled back into the wide white leather seat across from me.

"I was only wrong about how they were doing it."

I pursed my lips at the flight attendant, who plopped into the seat in front of me and swiveled around to face us. She tugged off her dark brown wig and dropped a pair of glasses into her lap. "Don't look at me, that part was Taiyō's plan. He was pretty pissed about everything on the train. I think you hurt his feelings."

"Where *is* Taiyō?" I asked.

Noelia hummed inquisitively. "If you and I are targeting each other's families, and Devroe has Taiyō's brother, then . . ."

We both looked to Devroe. "You think your mom will be

okay?" I asked. It felt weird bringing up the only alive member of his family he'd told me about with Noelia sitting so close.

Devroe straightened his cuff, looking a bit peeved at the question. "She'll be fine."

God, how I wanted to pry some more, but now was so not the time.

"You didn't mention that *he* would be involved." Noelia gestured toward Devroe without really turning his way.

Devroe scoffed. "You know, Taiyō's not the only one who's still pissed about the way things went on the train."

I guess I couldn't blame him for still being sore about that, even if he hadn't mentioned it since.

I expected a tongue click or something, but to my surprise, Noelia's lips drew into a straight line while she studied her lap for a too-long second. "Sorry, that wasn't cool. It's just . . . I'm sorry. Or whatever."

Not a perfect apology, but still, wow.

I cleared my throat to break an increasingly uncomfortable silence. "Your brother," I started. "Why does the organization want him?"

Noelia shrugged. "Um, to screw with me? Pit me against my rival? Add a little personal drama?"

"All of the above," Devroe added.

"Doesn't add up," I decided. "Everything we've stolen so far has had real value, political or monetary. One of the reasons my auntie doesn't work as much anymore is because her cover was blown by one too many of the wrong people. People who I'm sure would pay to get their own slice of revenge. She has *monetary* value."

"My brother is fourteen," Noelia said, with an eye roll. "He doesn't have a whole rogues' gallery who'd pay to beat some revenge out of him." She shivered at that last thought.

"You're sure?"

She looked at me like I'd asked if she was sure her name was Noelia. *"Yes."*

I leaned back, tapping my fingers over the arms of the seat. "What about Hauser?"

Noelia recrossed her legs and squirmed, confirming I was onto something.

"It's an all-boys boarding school," she said. "Obviously I didn't attend myself."

"What's he doing there?"

"Learning."

"Learning what?" Devroe asked. "People like us don't go to school for college prep."

Noelia huffed. "He's on assignment. It's family business. I'm not really supposed to talk about it . . ."

"Uh-huh." I waited for her to go on. We were past the point of what we were supposed to do.

She relented. "There's a prime minister's son who goes to school there. Somebody wants to destroy his dad or something. Nicki's supposed to be befriending him, finding something to ruin his papa with."

I just blinked at her for a second. "Is the whole befriend-and-then-betray thing just standard practice in the Boschert family?"

She didn't answer that. I probably didn't want her to.

"Your family is trusting an assignment like that to a fourteen-year-old?" Devroe asked.

"It's a long con. He doesn't need to find anything damning

until before the next election," Noelia said. "You'd be surprised what kind of information gets around at these schools. There's a reason so many dramas take place in boarding schools for rich kids. It's like a petri dish for secrets and pent-up family trauma."

A whole petri dish of secrets . . . from one of the most elite schools in the world.

I think I was starting to put together exactly where Noelia's brother's value was, and why the organization might have wanted him.

And it was something we could leverage.

I leaned forward. "Who else goes to this school?"

BELIEVE IT OR not, but you can only discuss the details of threatening a major underground society for about three or so hours max before you run out of things to say. Four hours into our ten-hour flight, we'd flown right into the night. Devroe was reclined in a seat, head lolled to the side and snoring lightly. I alternated between watching him and scanning Google Maps in ten-minute stints, dissecting all the routes in and out of the town before restashing my phone with the rest.

Noelia flipped through a complimentary magazine for the third time.

"Why is it always the handsome ones who snore?" she said after at least half an hour of silence. It took me a second to realize that she was talking about Devroe. Something in me fluttered at hearing someone else call him handsome.

"I dunno. He didn't snore the last time."

Noelia lowered her magazine, cocking a brow at me. "Last time?"

My face was suddenly on fire. "No, I mean the last time we were . . ." Noelia bit back a smile, and I found myself holding in a chuckle myself. "Whatever."

She closed the magazine, dropping it on a polished pull-out tray. "Do you remember that girl who stayed in the suite next to us? The one from Canada? You could hear her two doors over, I swear to god."

I did remember her, just barely. A Black girl with thick 4C hair. Couldn't remember her name, though. What else did I remember?

"I . . . I stole some hair lotion out of her room after mine ran out." I laughed, despite myself, the memory suddenly flooding back to me.

"Yeah, which you clogged up my hair with and I couldn't wash out for a week."

I remembered that too! Braiding Noelia's hair . . . or trying to, before it went wrong.

"I'd never had a white friend before!" I said. "How would I know that you shouldn't put oily hair lotion in white people's hair?"

It'd been horrifying at the time, but looking back, it was pretty funny. Both of us frantically trying to wash all of the gunk out of Noelia's clumping hair. Just thinking about it made me laugh hard enough to make my stomach hurt. Noelia was trying to look like she was still irritated about it, but she gave in to a fit of giggles too.

"Thanks for talking me out of just cutting it off," she said when we started to die down. "My papa might literally have killed me for cutting it without his permission."

I was silent for a second. "He's hard on you, your dad?"

Noelia looked away and gave a slanted shrug. "Nothing I can't handle."

Why did that sound like the worst answer she could've given? I squirmed, not really knowing how to go forward with this sort of inquiry, but not wanting to just glaze over it either. "You know, my mom can push me pretty hard sometimes too. I mean, I know she does everything for my best interest, but she's never, like, hit me or anything, if that's something you wanna, like, um, talk about—"

"My god, it's nothing like that." Noelia rubbed her temples. "Please don't ever trade in the thief lifestyle for a career in therapy."

Yeah, I probably could've addressed that so much better.

Noelia bit her lip, shifting in her seat herself. "Papa is just . . . He never hesitates to tell you when you've disappointed him, or how thoroughly. And it's like, sometimes even when he's not telling you to do something and he's just suggesting, it's not really a suggestion, it's a test to see if you'll do it." For a second her eyes were away, like she was thinking back to a very specific memory.

I followed her gaze down to her shoes. Another pair of boots with a subtle design on the soles. I remembered something she mentioned back at the hotel. She had a pair of shoes like mine before, and her papa made her throw them out.

One of his little tests, then?

"What's so important about passing his tests, though?" I asked. "Can't you just say, I dunno, screw that?"

I winced. That same reasoning was what got Mom in her

situation when I did it. But at the time, it'd felt right, even if the result proved that it wasn't. Maybe this was the right answer for her, even if not for me.

Noelia scoffed. "*I dunno, screw that?*" she repeated my words in a mocking tone, and in French too. Seemed like she was a lot better at venting her feelings in her native tongue. "I can't be the next head of the family if I don't impress him."

"Head?"

"There are a lot more Boscherts than just me, Nicki, and Papa, you know. Aunts and uncles and cousins and grand-parents. Someone has to lead them all; it's a chain-of-command thing. Papa is the current head, so he gets to pick the next one. It's usually your oldest child, so everyone in the family thinks it's going to be me. It should be me . . . but . . ." She wrung her hands. "I've been beginning to wonder. It seems like whenever I slip up on something, he mentions how exceptional Cousin Freare is, or how much Cousin Anna has matured recently." Noelia was so tense she looked like she might pop at the slightest touch. She looked genuinely scared, and it made me angry for her. Her father had had her walking on eggshells for years probably, dan-gling her future over her head.

In another universe, it might have been funny in an ironic sort of way. Me on the one side of the world desperate to get away from my family and her panicking, trying to stay at the top of hers.

I didn't want to tell Noelia some crap about how she should tell her papa to piss off, or that doing what her family wanted didn't matter, or anything like that. One conversation in a plane wasn't going to change a lifetime's worth of conditioning. I'd only just managed to start breaking out of mine. And if she really did want to be the head of her family or whatever, screwing the rules completely probably wasn't the best advice.

I didn't have an answer for her. I barely had answers for myself.

I reached out and kicked the edge of Noelia's boot. She startled, and I gave her a smile. "I'm sorry you have to be perfect Noelia for your family. It's their loss, not getting to see what's under your hood and everything. But . . . the world is bigger than your family. I might be an enemy or whatever, but for what it's worth, I like the Noelia with the weird kicks a lot better. If she wanted to send me some links to some neat stores sometime, I would maybe check them out." I shrugged, wanting to keep it cool and not too cringe.

Noelia just watched me for a second, expressionless. Then she gave me a little nod before flipping some hair behind her shoulder in a move I thought was much more not-friendly Noelia, but I relaxed when she smirked at me. "As if I would ever let Ross Quest steal my shoe styles. I'll send you pics after, purely for bragging purposes."

"Just don't be surprised if some pairs go missing after that."

"Hm, we'll see."

We snickered again, and somehow I ended up in the seat next to her, scrolling through my Etsy shoe-shopping cart. It would've been a pretty charming night, until I backtracked to my home screen to get to my Pinterest app next.

Noelia grabbed my wrist. She was pale, and her eyes were frozen on my phone. Not in the curious, fun way they'd been before.

"Her." Noelia tapped my screen, right between two apps.

"My app store?"

"The woman!"

I frowned at my screen. Right, my home screen was me and Mom, her face smushed against mine. "Yeah, I know. Having my mom as my home screen is kinda cringe, but—"

"That's not your mother." Noelia said it like if anyone was sure, it was her.

"Gonna have to disagree . . ." I said slowly.

Noelia looked up to me, her brows knitted together. "Ross . . . that's *her*. From the ski camp."

She just had to bring that up. We were having such a good time. "You never met her. Mom didn't come get me until after you ditched."

"She was there!" Noelia insisted. "She was a staff member or something. She was the one who gave me your note."

I could feel a little piece of me starting to put it together, but my brain wouldn't. Not yet. "I didn't leave you a note. You did. It said to rendezvous under the staircase in the foyer instead. I went there, and one of the instructors was waiting for me. She caught me with everything."

"I never sent that," Noelia said. "Your note said to meet in the guesthouse. I didn't *ditch*. I waited for hours, and you never showed up."

Mom had come to get me so fast; a few hours later, I was gone. Gone and heartbroken about my best friend betraying me.

How would Mom have gotten there so fast? Unless she was already at the school.

Oh my god.

"Ross?" Noelia's voice sounded far away. My whole philosophy on trusting thieves, on friendship, she'd rigged it from the start.

My eyes stung. Silently, I leaned my head on Noelia's shoulder. She didn't say anything, just took my hand.

I was going to save Mom's life, but after that, I was going to get an explanation.

FORTY-TWO

ARE YOU SURE this is going to work?"

I flicked the corner of the folded note Noelia had given me. You'd think leaving the note in Nicholi's room would be enough, but Noelia insisted I give it to him in person. Something about someone in the past being tricked by forged handwriting. That, and I guess getting a handwritten note that was supposedly from his sister instead of a text, email, or anything people in this century actually do was probably pretty sus. If somebody left a note under my door with a time and date, I might go, but not to be friendly.

Noelia huffed over the com in my ear. To make sure no one was overhearing us, we were using analog coms, totally old-school. Devroe just so happened to know a place nearby to get some. One day I'd have to ask him to map out his web of international connections for me.

"I'm sorry, but whose brother are we rendezvousing with? If I said this is going to work, then it will. Noelia Boschert doesn't concoct losing plans." Another scratchy sound rustled over the feed, letting me imagine she was mumbling to herself about how ridiculous I was to question her or whatever. It would've been petty to remind her how it was my planning that screwed over her team during the last phase, but I wanted to.

Fighting the urge to scowl, I gripped my backpack—new, plaid, mostly empty. It was just for looks, something to match the pleated skirt and blazer. To anyone watching, I looked just like any other student from the sister school a twenty-minute walk away. Several gaggles of girls made their way to Hauser in the afternoon to link up with friends or boyfriends. None of the guards at the school's gate batted an eye at me.

The campus was ridiculously massive. Like someone took a slice of Central Park, dropped a few stately buildings inside, and wrapped an iron gate around it for safekeeping. The map I'd studied on the way didn't do it justice. I might have gotten lost if I hadn't had a little voice in my ear guiding me.

"The dormitory is that redbrick building with the arched windows."

With a quick scan, I found the one Noelia was talking about. A steady stream of students were trickling from another campus building toward it, and most of the visiting girls were migrating that way too.

"Does he usually come back to the dorms after class?" What was I going to do if Nicholi decided not to come back until sundown?

"Stop overthinking it," Noelia said. "Just . . . vibe until he gets there."

"I told you I should have gone," Devroe said, his first words over the feed.

"Ross, do me a favor. Look around and count how many Black boys you see."

She was right about that. I was almost at the dorms now and hadn't seen any. "To be fair," I whispered, "there aren't exactly a lot of Black girls either." I'd seen two, maybe three others.

"You're not at the girls' school, you're at the boys'. I promise you one of the guards would have noticed that Devroe wasn't one of the four Black boys who go to school at Hauser."

"You're very attentive to how race adjusts the situations around you, Noelia," Devroe noted, absolutely stuffed with salt.

Noelia paused. "Use your advantages, even if you don't deserve them. It's something my papa always says."

Thankfully, I reached the dormitory before either Devroe or I had time to unpack that.

Inside, I found a crowded entrance hall adjacent to an open space for study tables with library lamps and reading chairs. A rush of students were dumping bookbags and settling into tables or racing up the sweeping staircase into the upper floors.

Again, a lot less boarding school and a lot more something like a grand hotel or private university. I almost wished I was the one getting to go undercover here.

"Nicki's room is on the third floor," Noelia said, her voice bringing me out of the daydream I might have been slipping into. "I . . . don't know which one specifically."

"Wonderful," I muttered, catching a judgmental frown from

a redheaded girl coming down the stairs. Talking to yourself is not a good look.

I made my way up the main staircase. Wide hallways were speckled with doors spaced far enough apart that even if I hadn't studied the building's specs ahead of time, I still would've been able to guess just how ridiculously spacious the rooms inside were.

Trying to look like I was waiting for someone, I watched for Nicholi. Though I'd never met him in person, I'd spent at least two hours studying pictures of him, including the one Count gave me and some Noelia had. I could pick him out of a police lineup by now. Noelia also mentioned his tendency to always be walking with one hand in his pocket, so blond hair, blue eyes, white, male, fourteen, hand in pocket. Dozens of students made their way in and out of the hall, but still no Nicholi.

"Have you seen him?" Noelia finally asked after ten minutes of silence.

"She would have mentioned if she did," Devroe said.

"He might have passed you by. Are you paying close enough attention?"

Did she think I was a total amateur?

I thwacked the com in my ear, sending a loud crackle into the feed. Hopefully that got my point across.

"Very mature, Ross," Noelia said. I bit back a smile.

Another group of students hopped up the steps. A cluster of boys, all of them with dark hair, so not who I was looking for. I would have immediately averted my attention, but something about one of them was distracting. His features were half-hidden behind the other kids, but I could tell he was

Asian, had glasses, and not a strand of his hair was out of place.

I jolted up. Another group of students were climbing the stairs too, blocking my view.

The boy disappeared.

I rushed toward the stairs, sidestepping everyone in my way. When I got to the top of the steps, the boy was trotting down the last few.

"Taiyō," I said softly.

"*Our* Taiyō?" Noelia asked. "Why would he be here?"

"That doesn't sound right to me," Devroe said, hella doubtful. "My mum could be anywhere, but I don't think she's in a European boarding school."

"Maybe he's not going after your mom."

Taiyō, if it was him, was making a beeline for the exit. If I wanted to know for sure and catch up to him, I'd have to leave now.

But that was when I spotted him: Nicholi Boschert.

If I hadn't recognized his face and hair, that hand in his pocket, bouncing as he climbed the steps, would have been enough. Two other boys flanked him, one with his blazer thrown over a shoulder, rambling about something, and the other yawning into his hand.

Taiyō, or his body double, was slipping away, but Nicholi and his companions were drawing closer.

"Great," I mumbled.

"What's happening? Are you going after Taiyō? Don't! You're supposed to wait for Nicki—"

I ripped out my com, took a small breath, and trotted down the steps, smiling as I put myself right in front of Nicholi.

"Nicki, right?" I cut off whatever story Nicholi's blazer-less friend was spinning. Perhaps this was the target he'd been befriending for the last few months?

The friend laughed. "Nicki? Are people calling you *Nicki* now?"

Nicholi's face tinged red. "My name is Nicholi."

"Oh, Noelia said it was Nicki." He froze. Now that I'd name-dropped his sis, I had his attention.

"She said to tell you hi if I saw you." I pretended to peel a piece of fuzz off his blazer, dropping Noelia's note into the pocket at the same time. The way he tensed told me he knew exactly what I was doing, even if he wasn't sure if I was dropping a threat or a message just yet—until I capped it all with my next line. "She said Marlow misses you too."

Nicholi straightened. *Marlow*, their code word, according to Noelia. He gave me a little nod. I was on his side.

With a wave, I headed down the stairs. One of his friends spoke up. "Didn't know you had a sister. Is she hot?"

"See, this is why I didn't tell you I had a sister," Nicholi said. The rest of their conversation faded away as they continued on.

I weaved the other way, through the entire foyer, until I was right back at the front doors, staring out into the yard. Pointless. If Taiyō had been here, he was long gone by now.

FORTY-THREE

KNOW I saw him."

At least, I thought I did. But the more Devroe questioned me, the more I wanted to double down on it.

Devroe stood behind the sofa—a very uncomfortable wicker couch with only a woven quilt for a cushion, all standard for this boho chic house rental—watching me work through my thoughts as I paced over the patchwork carpet.

"Maybe you saw someone who looked like Taiyō." Devroe pinched his nose, making me stop and glare at him. What, was *I* stressing *him*? "Let's just take a second to think about why he would be here. Did he show up for the sole purpose of messing with you?"

I fumbled. "I dunno! Maybe he's not going after his target.

Maybe he's . . ." I sighed and flopped into a very tight and itchy wicker chair. "I dunno. But he was there." *I think.*

Now I was the one feeling stressed. This wasn't the exhilarating kind of stress that Mylo was addicted to. Something about this felt dangerous. Like, able-to-shatter-everything-if-I-didn't-keep-an-eye-on-it dangerous. "I thought we were going to trust each other," I whispered.

"We are."

"Really? 'Cause I had an easier time trusting Noelia with my address than you seem to be with me right now."

I barely saw his sad smile before he schooled himself back to normal. He glanced back toward the bedrooms, back to where our phones and any other buggable devices were tucked as far away as we could get them without chucking them outside. "We were playing by their rules before, but this is different now, Ross. You're walking a tightrope over a snake pit. If you get distracted, you're going to fall, and I can't bear to watch you slip."

Devroe looked like he was holding his breath, waiting to see whether I was going to give this up or not. Was he that concerned for me? A warm, fluttery feeling rippled through me. No one had ever been protective of me, no one outside of my family. It was . . . charming.

But charm wasn't enough to trump my instincts, and they were telling me I was right to be worried.

Noelia stomped back into the living room, boasting a pretty sour expression. She tossed a burner cell at Devroe's chest, which he caught with one hand. "I tried calling, but there's no answer. Then again, I don't know why Taiyō would answer a rando number that's not Count, anyway." She perched on the arm of the sofa, ankles crossed like she was on a throne or something. "Too bad I can't call from my number ..."

"You can't call anyone while we're holding you hostage," Devroe reminded her.

In shorts, barefoot, and with her hair pulled back into a loose ponytail, it was almost comical how un-hostage-like Noelia looked right now. But so long as it *sounded* like we'd pegged Noelia as our fake flight attendant and decided to keep her from causing any trouble while we were around the phones, then she could wear whatever the hell she wanted.

Noelia fiddled with her ponytail. "He probably wouldn't have answered for my number either. Everyone was a little ... irritated with me when we realized the sarcophagus wasn't authentic."

For Noelia's sake, and since we were being at the very least cordial now, I didn't let myself smile.

"It doesn't matter," Devroe said. "It probably wasn't him, anyway."

Noelia scoffed. "If Ross said she saw him, then she saw him, *Kenzie*."

I froze. Noelia standing up for me was not what I would've predicted a week ago. Devroe's jaw clenched, but Noelia just cocked an eyebrow at him, daring him to say something else. "Even if she wasn't sure about it, which she said she is, we're not risking my brother's safety on a 'maybe it was just a boy who looked like him.' We need to take preemptive action. Preventative medicine is the best medicine."

"Is that another quote from your stellar, elitist father?" Devroe asked.

Noelia ignored that. I shot Devroe a glare. He could really cool it with the animosity.

"I'm with Noelia." Saying that aloud still felt weird. "Maybe we could adjust our plan for tonight. Noelia has to stay here, but it wouldn't hurt if you could tail Nicholi and make sure nothing happens."

"You want me to play bodyguard for him?"

"If Taiyō's here to snatch him, he'll have an easier time doing it off school property. Can't you follow him while he's off campus to meet me and make sure nothing happens?"

I wasn't sounding unreasonable; I knew I wasn't. So why the hell was Devroe looking at me like I was 100 percent killing his vibe right now?

He stood, straightened the bottom of his vest, and gave me a tight smile. "It's your plan. Whatever you want, Ross." He crossed the room and kissed my cheek, drawing an eye roll from Noelia. He left for the porch outside.

Noelia waited for the back door to click shut to speak again. "He's difficult. You should be careful with him, Ross."

"Are you trying to give me friendly dating advice?"

She shook her head slowly, still looking at the porch door. "No, this is professional advice."

With that, she returned to the other side of the house. A small part of me wanted to follow her and ask more about what the hell that meant, but I stopped myself before I made it two steps.

Sunset was looming outside. I had my own rendezvous to prepare for, and an assignment I couldn't mess up.

FORTY-FOUR

*J**UST MAKE SURE** he's fine, okay?*

Noelia's last words to me before I set out echoed in my mind. So did my reply.

I promise.

This had to have been the most chaotic week of my life. I'd gone from hating Noelia on a Monday to making promises to protect her family on a Friday. Now here I was, at a café two blocks down from a pub frequented by rich teenagers, waiting for her little brother, a white-collar thief in training, to link up with me.

While I waited for nine o'clock to come, I thought about that promise and, surprisingly, how important it was to keep it. Especially after learning the truth about Mom, I wasn't going to betray Noelia.

The café, scented with coffee beans and syrup, sat in total silence. No jazz music, no students tip-tapping away on laptops. I'd broken in a couple hours after closing and disabled the alarm system, so it was just me, a bunch of empty tables, and a switched-off open sign.

My leg was bopping furiously by the time my freshly bought laptop's time read nine. Like clockwork—no, like he was very well trained—Nicholi slipped inside on the dot. He made it look casual, with that one hand in his coat pocket, even as he was entering an empty café.

He glanced over his shoulder as he sat across from me at the two-person table. "I'm pretty sure someone was tailing me from the school."

"It's cool, he's with me."

"And you're with Noelia?" Nicholi gave me a side-eye very reminiscent of his sister.

"Shockingly." He snickered at that. "Do you have it?"

Nicholi scanned the inside like he hadn't been sure that it was empty before, then dug a black thumb drive out of his pocket. "This took me all day to work into a spreadsheet. Ditched studying for my trig exam to do this."

"Something tells me your future doesn't hinge on acing a trig exam." I plugged the drive in. A chat box at the bottom of the screen pinged. There were only two other participants in the chat, K and N.

From N: **It's 9. Update?**

I typed.

R: **He's here. K, I'm sending you the spreadsheet.**

K: (👍

Nicholi peeked at the screen. He scooted his chair over and

gestured for the keyboard. I pursed my lips and tried to turn the laptop away from him. "This isn't a for-kicks group chat."

"Yeah, sure, whatever." Nicholi shrugged me off, slapping my hands away and getting his on the keys.

R: **Got into a mess, Lia???? Need little brother to help you fix it???**

I watched the typing dots dance, waiting for Noelia to snap something back about how Nicki was the one who owed her, on account of jumping through all these hoops to keep him from being literally snatched. Nicholi didn't know exactly how much danger he'd been in. I mean, I hadn't exactly told him.

But instead of something like that, she just sent back an eye-roll emoji. Classic.

K: **Spreadsheet received. I'm cross-referencing** ☺

My breath hitched. This was the moment everything came together or fell apart. Did I really have the leverage I thought I did?

Nicholi thrummed his fingers on the tabletop, having the audacity to look bored while my world was possibly about to fall apart.

If it doesn't work, at least Plan B is right next to you . . . and he trusts you now.

I shoved that voice as far back in my mind as I could.

"So . . ." Nicholi hummed. "What exactly is this for? When Lia's note asked me to type up everything I've dredged up over the last year, I sort of assumed this would be a drop-and-go type of thing. But now I can tell there's something else going on here."

He had no idea.

"I have my own spreadsheet of people who've . . . kinda pissed me off," I said. "So as long as you spelled all the last names right, my friend is going to merge them."

"Ah, and you're hoping the people on your hit list overlap with the people on my dirt list. Fun."

A direct email from Kyung-soon just to me. There was an attachment.

K: **Whoa.**

I double-clicked the little paper clip. The new spreadsheet was so large, it took a few seconds to load. But once it did, rows and rows of names and numbers and addresses unfurled on the screen. Every few rows there was a highlighted name. I tapped the first one I saw.

Dean Pratt, Chief Operating Officer of Pierce Pharmaceuticals Global. Has two illegitimate children, currently living with his mistress in Barcelona. Address . . .

Nicholi nodded at the screen. "My suitemate Louis's papa."

"How did you get the address?" I asked.

"He and his half siblings do a pen-pal thing. I jotted it down one day."

I kept scrolling, finding another highlighted annotation. Felcia Kowalski. Member of the Polish Supreme Court. Casual heroin addict. Attached was a picture, fuzzy, but clear enough, of a woman obviously prepping to shoot up, slapping her arm and everything.

"Henri invited me home with him over a three-day break. His mother was really nice when she wasn't . . . you know," Nicholi explained.

I stopped, seeing a very familiar name. Dubois.

Count.

"This one." I circled it with the mouse and looked at Nicholi.

"Oh, Gerry! His moms got divorced two years ago. He said he wanted to go with his other mom, but this one paid off the judge to get full custody. Kinda screwed up, seeing as she leaves him at Hauser ten months out of the year and never lets him see his favorite mom." There was an attached sound bite, which I'm sure went into much deeper detail. Maybe enough detail that, in front of a real judge, would be enough to lose someone custody.

I kept skimming through, finding one incriminating thing after another. There might not have been something for everyone on this massive spreadsheet, not even close. Only forty or so entries. But looking through, I knew it was more than enough.

No wonder they'd wanted Nicholi out of the game. His dad had sent him to Hauser to take down one guy, but he'd vacuumed up enough dirt to ruin at least a dozen political careers and plummet just as many stocks. The kid was a walking, talking tommy gun with all the ammunition I needed.

"Knowledge is power, huh," I said.

Nicholi's lips drew into a straight line. "Knowledge is control." I had a feeling that was another quote from Daddy Boschert.

In the chat:

R: **We've got it. Thank you, both of you.**

K: ♥

Nothing from N, but no time to dwell on that. This wasn't done just yet.

Using my black box account, already opened up, I started to compose an email, attaching the world's most incriminating spreadsheet.

"No, no, no, you're trying to threaten someone, right?" Nicholi nodded at the screen. "Only send them a snippet of the spreadsheet."

Let them guess how much I really had. He really was good at this, wasn't he? When someone has to imagine their own worst-case scenario, it'll always be worse than reality.

I copied out a snippet of the spreadsheet, a portion that had Count's dirt in it. Just a taste.

After, I checked on another composed email I had waiting. An email with so many recipients, Kyung-soon had to help me put it together. Every single email on the spreadsheet from the hotel—and there were thousands of them—was in that recipient box. To that email, I attached the full dirt spreadsheet.

I had my pieces in order. It was time for my move.

"Give me your phone."

Nicholi frowned but dipped inside his coat for it anyway. "You have a fresh-out-of-the-box laptop but no cell?"

"I left it in my car."

Dialing Count's number, I held the phone to my ear. Nicholi leaned in, intent to hear whatever was going on himself. I swallowed, hoping he wouldn't freak out if he heard anything about what I was supposed to be doing with him.

Count, as expected, picked up after only one ring.

I spoke first. "Hello, Aurélie."

I could almost see Count bristle. "I assume you're calling from this number because you've acquired your target? May I ask what happened to your cell phone? You've been—"

"Quiet lately? Yeah, I've been busy. Look, I need to email you something. You got an address for me?"

Everything was quiet for a second. Still. Nothing but the darkness, Nicholi's shoulder pressed against mine, the coffee bean aroma, and the thunder of my own heart against my rib cage.

"What is this about?" Count said slowly. There was a hitch of apprehension in her voice. Unease.

"An email address," I said.

To my surprise, Count actually huffed. There was some rustling before a notification showed up. A string of numbers, letters, and symbols connected with an @ sign. I didn't waste a second sending my taste-test email.

"I'll give you a minute to look things over," I offered. Count took that minute, and a few other people did as well. A handful of distant voices slowly built behind her.

My leg jumped under the table while I waited for her to come back.

"What is this?" Was Count actually yelling? People really lose their composure when things get personal.

"This is me winning." I leaned into the table. "I'm done with your rules, so now we're going to play by mine. Here's how this is going to go, Aurélie. I have a very valuable spreadsheet with the contact information of very, very important people. I don't know which ones are a part of your organization and which ones aren't, but what I do know is I also have a lot of incriminating information on several of them, and unless you do exactly what I tell you, I'm going to send all of that juicy information to every single email I've got. Understand?"

Count scoffed. "Don't overestimate yourself. We've made emails disappear before."

A counterthreat. Animals always try to bulk themselves up when they know they're in danger. Her mistake.

"Oh, I'm sure you can make them disappear . . . eventually.

But can you make a thousand disappear? Five thousand? Ten thousand? All before anyone sees it?" I narrowed my eyes. "Can you hack my computer and delete the file faster than I can hit send?"

I wished Mylo was here. A gamble like this would've set his heart on fire.

"What . . . do you want?" Count asked.

My threat had worked.

"A billion dollars." The words rushed out of me, startlingly different from that collected swagger I had just a few sentences ago. But who gave a damn about what Count or the rest of them thought about me anymore. "I want it wired to an offshore account. Immediately. I'll send you the details."

I held my breath. It sounded like Count was discussing something with whoever else was with her.

"A hefty sum, Ms. Quest. Is that all?" Count asked.

Was that all? I had these people at my mercy . . . for now. It probably wouldn't be long until they figured out a way to permanently negate my blackmail plan. Hours, at the soonest. But for now, I was in control.

Don't push your luck, Ross.

"That's it," I said. Everything else I wanted in life, I could get myself. Most of it . . . I already had.

"We'll push the transfer through. It might take a while—"

"I think we both know you can get a rush job. You've got ten minutes."

"Fine," Count said, sounding a bit resigned. "It's a shame you didn't just play to win, Ms. Quest. We would've loved to have you for a year."

FORTY-FIVE

"THAT WAS BADASS." Nicholi clapped my back as I loaded up my laptop. He had all the energy of someone just walking out of a pretty awesome spy movie. Not gonna lie, I was a bit pumped up on those vibes too. Not to mention the euphoric relief of knowing my mom was about to be safe. I didn't have to kidnap anyone, and I was officially done with the Gambit.

I may not have won, but I freaking *won*.

"You should come with me back to the house rental," I said, pulling open the café door and walking out into the fresh night air. "I was trying to keep my partnership with Noelia on the DL from . . . those people before, but now I'm sure she'd want to see you. She's worried."

At that, Nicholi's pale face flushed pink. I guess being close with your big sis isn't cool. "Nah, you can send her my way, though. My friends are probably wondering where the hell I went." He turned back toward the pub down the street.

I cocked a brow. *"Friends?"*

"Friends. Targets. It all gets screwy, you know?"

Yeah, I actually did kinda know.

"Thanks for the free entertainment." He waved back to me. "Tell Lia she owes me, big-time."

He dropped one hand in his pocket and started down the sidewalk. I made my way toward my car, a hot-wired Hyundai, feeling pretty great as I flopped into the driver's seat. I almost didn't know who I wanted to call first. Noelia, to tell her everything was good with her little bro? Kyung-soon, for an in-real-time thanks? Devroe? No, it was probably safest to let him keep his attention on Nicholi until he got back to his dorm—just in case.

Auntie. How hadn't I decided to call her immediately? She was probably losing her mind worrying about me. And Mom. Now I'd get to tell her to take a deep breath and kick her feet up. Mom was coming home . . . and me? Could anyone in the fam really fault me if I took a few international freelance assignments with my new crew?

No, with my new friends.

I leaned my head against the driver's side window, feeling content as a kitten while I rehearsed how I wanted to tell Auntie what had happened, how I got Mom back, and why I wasn't coming home without telling her exactly where I was going. Hell, I didn't even know where I was going next, but it felt like I was headed somewhere awesome.

While I was organizing my thoughts, I watched Nicholi strolling down the sidewalk. His head was tilted, probably thinking about everything that just happened. He was distracted.

Maybe that was why he didn't see it coming.

A figure swooped out of an alley. He locked Nicholi into a choke hold and was clearly pressing something over his mouth.

It was Taiyō.

Nicholi struggled, but his squirming died down fast. For one weak second, I froze. Nicholi was supposed to have a tail. In a moment, Devroe was going to pounce on Taiyō. That was his job.

So where the hell was Devroe?

After two seconds, I knew. He wasn't here.

"Damn it!" I revved the ignition and hit the gas. Without thinking, I flicked the headlights on first, though. Taiyō saw me coming and quickly shoved a wobbly Nicholi into the back seat of a black sedan on the curb. He skidded into action just ahead of me . . . with Nicki in tow.

One hand on the wheel, I fumbled with the analog com still in my pocket.

The line was total static. Someone had shut off the feed.

I threw the com into the floorboard.

Taiyō was headed north. I'd mapped all the fastest routes to the nearest airports and train stations. Either Count had given him a drop-off spot or Taiyō was smartly putting his money on Count's rendezvous location being a secluded airport instead of a train station buzzing with witnesses.

He was taking the fastest route to the hangar a few kilometers outside of the city, but I had the faster car.

With one hand on the wheel, I tore open the glove compartment. The taillights of Taiyō's sedan burned ahead. Someone screamed as I blew through a crosswalk.

There was a pen in the compartment. One hand on the wheel, I ripped a page from the car manual, scribbling over a paragraph about the perks of Hyundai's high-strength steel.

Two flashes, then jump!

I wrapped the paper around a full water bottle and clipped it on with the elastic from my ponytail.

Please, please, god, let this kid still be conscious, and double please, let him have the same edge as his sister. Hopefully diving out of a moving car would be less daunting than the thought of being kidnapped.

I was approaching Taiyō's tail. He jerked from side to side, like this was Mario Kart and he wasn't going to let me take the lead.

The sight of a one-lane bridge up ahead seemed to calm him down. No way was I going to edge around him there. And he was right. But I didn't want to pass.

My engine revved. I pushed the car to its limits and pulled up to the side of Taiyō's car.

The lanes were tightening into one.

The bridge's concrete railing was ahead. I needed to merge.

I had seconds before I was going to collide head-on with the railing.

Using my bracelet, I smashed the back window and threw the bottle in, then slammed the brakes into screaming. The steering wheel shook violently as I swerved back into the single lane. My chest dug into my seat belt. The smell of burnt rubber clogged my nose. Taiyō continued across the bridge at full throttle.

I'd missed the railing by inches, if that. Through the rearview, I saw a few pedestrians running my way. I whipped into a U-turn and skidded away before they could slow me down with their concern.

I knew the path Taiyō was going and that there was a faster

route; as long as I sped like my life depended on it, I could get to that sharp turn outside the city limits before him.

Wind shrieked through my open window, blowing back my braids. My tires screeched around every turn. The wheel juddered, like the car too was running on adrenaline instead of gasoline. It was a miracle I didn't run into any police.

The buildings started to dwindle. Soon fields and farmhouses took their place. I looked to the side, where I knew a lonely road toward the hangar was waiting. I couldn't see any headlights or taillights through the grass.

I flicked off my own lights, trusting moonlight and memory to guide me as I drove. Halfway to the intersection between my path and Taiyō's, the shimmer of headlights flickered in the distance.

I was ahead of him.

I skidded across the intersection. Dust kicked up around me as I jerked to a stop. The curve in the road sat maybe twenty yards ahead, and past that, the outline of a far-off hangar.

My breath came slow and shaky while Taiyō's headlights sped nearer. This had to be timed perfectly.

The rush of Taiyō's tires over the pavement swelled into a roar. Seconds before his SUV ripped past me, right before he slowed around the curve, I flashed my lights twice.

Come on, don't cave, Nicki.

One of the back doors flipped open. Nicki dove out of the car, rolling into the dirt. Taiyō's brake lights blared. I flipped my lights on. Nicholi stumbled up, huffing and gripping his shoulder. Taiyō was rushing into a U-turn.

I sped to a stop next to Nicholi and flung the passenger door open.

"I thought you said he was with you!" He jumped in. Dozens of bleeding cuts littered his forehead.

"Different guy."

"Where the hell is your guy?"

That was a really good question.

I sped back down the road Taiyō had come from. A few seconds later, and he was back on my tail. I hit the gas, intending to easily outpace him, but we weren't picking up speed.

A light dinged on the dash. Low tire pressure. Something on the side of the road must have punctured the tread.

How long until we were really losing speed?

"Put your seat belt on."

Nicholi, hands bleeding, fumbled to click it in place.

Taiyō was gaining ground behind us.

"You have your phone?" I asked. He patted his pockets and shook his head.

"No, I think he took it. Right before he . . ."

I tossed mine into his lap. "The passcode's 0928. Google the make of that car back there."

He didn't waste time, only obeyed. "Um, it was a . . ."

"Looks like a Tesla S60. Search what type of body it has."

His thumbs flew over my screen. A few seconds later, an answer: "Um . . . 'the 2020 S60 model boasts a sleek aluminum body'—why? How does that help us?"

Taiyō was on our tail now. The speedometer dropped under sixty. He'd be able to pass us soon. It had to be now.

My throat tightened.

"Because this car has a steel body," I answered. Then, without giving myself time to think about it, I slammed the brakes.

Taiyō's car couldn't avoid smashing into us from behind.

My body rammed into the seat belt.

The collision felt like thunder.

Sounds of twisting metal and shattering glass roared around us.

I gripped the wheel through all of it; then, only seconds after everything stopped, I moved my foot back from the brakes to the gas.

Steel beats aluminum.

Our engine hadn't been touched, and we were able to drive away, though metal scraped the ground behind us.

My gaze shot to the rearview. The front of Taiyō's car was totally crushed. All I could see was crumpled metal and shattered glass.

My chest throbbed. I had to put my eyes back on the road. Was Taiyō . . . ?

I swiped my phone back from Nicholi, who looked as shell-shocked as I felt, then dialed the number for Swiss emergency services.

"I need an ambulance," I said as we drove away from the scene.

FORTY-SIX

IT TOOK ALL of five seconds being out of danger for Nicholi to get his senses back.

"Holy crap." He slapped the color back into his cheeks, then punched my shoulder.

"Hey!"

"What the hell? You never mentioned someone was going to try and snatch me!"

I took a shaky breath. "Sorry. I thought I had someone watching you. But he's . . . I don't know where he is."

"Why'd you call the medics for that dude?" Nicholi's question pulled me back to reality before I had the chance to tailspin into a panic attack.

I just looked at him, then peered behind us to watch Taiyō's wreckage getting smaller behind us. "Because he needed one."

Nicholi scoffed. "My papa would say to let him die."

"No offense, but your papa sounds like a prick." Sparks dragged behind us. The car was starting to sway on its flattening tire. This whole thing was a mess. "Try to call Noelia."

Nicholi nodded, shook some glass out of his hair, and dialed. He had her number memorized.

"She's not answering."

Panic. Even more panic, I hate to admit, than when I saw Nicholi being shoved into a car clouded my head. Noelia wasn't answering. Devroe was missing. There was a big-time disaster here; I just couldn't see it clearly yet.

"What now?" Nicholi asked.

"We're going to see Lia."

I PRACTICALLY KICKED open the door of my rented apartment. All the lights were off. Nicholi fumbled to flick them on.

"Noelia! Devroe?" I called. The living room was empty, though Noelia's laptop was still awake on the coffee table.

"You sure this is the right place?" Nicholi questioned.

He shut up when a muffled moan echoed through the adjacent hallway. We followed the voice to the small bathroom door. Locked. This time, it was Nicholi who kicked it in.

Noelia was triple cuffed to the sink's pipes. Her mouth duct taped, and her eyes red and tired.

"Holy crap!" Nicholi pushed past me, kneeling by her. He patted himself down for a pin or something. I quickly tossed him a bobby from my braids.

While he worked to open the cuffs, I ripped the duct tape off her lips and let her spit out the rags stuffed in her mouth.

"What happened? Where's Devroe?"

"He's—" A fit of coughs cut her off.

"Yeah, take your time. I'm sure you're not on a timetable or anything," Nicholi said, unhelpfully, unlocking the last set of cuffs.

"Shut . . . up . . . Nicki . . ." Noelia rubbed her raw wrists. The coughing drew out a couple tears.

"Noelia," I said. *"Devroe."*

"Who do you think did this to me?" she snapped but collected herself a second later. "He came back early. And he . . . he took the address you gave me."

No. No way. This was not happening.

"You're lying." Even as I said it, I didn't believe it.

"I'm sorry." Her voice cracked, and more tears, different tears fell. "I didn't just give it to him without a fight. How did he know I had it?"

A pathetic sob escaped me. My eyes stung. "I told him." I sniffled and blinked them back. There was no space for shattering yet.

I pulled out my phone screen. For a fractured second, I just looked at Devroe's contact, as if that would tell me where he was, what was going on. I opened the copy I'd downloaded from his phone, like it would automatically update with airport itineraries I could follow. No luck, obviously.

Crouching, I started digging through again. What had I missed the first time? I went back to the text thread of him and his mum. The same mum he said he had to win the Gambit to find. Her texts back to him were just random strings of numbers. Devroe said she was sending him coded messages.

Why were they all the same number of digits?

I opened his contacts, just a bunch of unnamed saved numbers. With shaking hands, I tapped one. The contact had a location saved under it. So did the next number, and the next. Going back and forth between his messages and the contacts, I cross-referenced the numbers.

They were the same numbers in his contacts. She wasn't sending him phone numbers to call. She was sending him locations. He knew where his mum was this whole time. That meant he lied to me about his wish.

If he wasn't wishing to find his mum, what was he wishing for?

A lone text dropped onto my screen. From Devroe:

I didn't have a choice.

I'm sorry.

"I . . . I have to get to my aunt." I stumbled out of the bathroom, still feeling like I'd just gotten off the world's cruelest merry-go-round.

Devroe knew where I lived. Where Auntie was. She must have been his real target. But he had a fake picture cued up and ready to show me. Had he known this was the final phase the entire time?

Outside, I dialed Auntie's number.

No connection.

I tried the home number. Again, no connection.

Finally, I dialed the red phone.

It rang.

Auntie picked up. "Ross?"

"You need to leave—"

"What?" The call went scratchy. "Where . . . you . . . ?"

"Get off the island!" I screamed, but it was no use. She

couldn't hear me. The call cut off. I dialed again, and this time, like with the other numbers, it didn't connect at all.

Panicking, I called Count for the second time tonight. But now it felt like I was the one who didn't know what she was walking into. "I'm getting rather tired of seeing your number, Ms. Quest."

"Connect me to my aunt!"

More aggravating murmurs in the background. "Why would I do that?" Count finally asked.

"Because I'll wreck your world with that spreadsheet if you don't."

"Oh, really?" Count scoffed. "That was over an hour ago. Check your computer. You might have a hard time finding what you're looking for."

My hands were sweating. Everything was sweating. My life was slipping through my fingers.

"Look, you played your hand, Rosalyn," Count said. "It was impressive. Because we're an organization of our word, we're still working on the wire transfer. However, you don't get complimentary favors without some quid pro quo."

"Fine. What do you want?"

Count paused. "We're not sure yet. Hold tight."

I opened my mouth, but the call disconnected. When I called again, the number was unavailable.

These. People.

Mom. I needed her. I needed her to tell me what to do.

So I called. But when the phone connected, it went straight to Mom this time. She started talking before I could. "Ross, I didn't know it was her. I didn't know he was—"

Just like the call before, the call went scratchy, then died.

I screamed. What was happening? Everything was falling apart, and I didn't even understand why.

If there was one thing I wasn't about to do, it was hold tight. I needed to get on a plane home. But even if I left right now, Devroe still had the lead. I was too far to get to Auntie before him. But . . . my friends weren't.

Mylo had said they were going for drinks at a killer place in Miami. Florida was only an hour's flight from the Bahamas. Maybe they were still there.

I didn't have many contacts to search through.

"Hey . . ." Kyung-soon drew out. "I hope you're not calling for another copy of that spreadsheet, because it's literally, like, disappeared from all my devices. I've never seen hacking this good, it's kinda freaking me out—"

"Don't worry about that," I said. "Is Mylo still there?"

"If by 'there' you mean downstairs trying to rig one of the slot machines, then yeah."

"Good." I took a breath. "Look, I know you guys don't owe me anything else and you've already helped me once today, but . . . I need your help again."

"Anything," she said. "As long as it's interesting, I'm sure Mylo will be down too."

I needed their help. There wasn't another way. "Book a flight to Andros, Bahamas. I need you to save my aunt."

FORTY-SEVEN

AFTER **AN AGONIZING** ten-hour flight, I touched down in Nassau, one airport transfer and charter away from home. But while I had connection, I wasn't going to waste the opportunity to see where they were and what was happening.

I dialed Mylo first. No answer. I tried Kyung-soon as I pushed my way out to the jet bridge. By the time the phone connected, I was sprinting into the terminal.

"Kyung-soon! Where is she? What happened?"

"Unfortunately, their plane has been rerouted. Their plane is being held on the tarmac in the Florida Keys."

Count.

She continued. "Didn't I tell you to hold tight?"

"I think we both knew that wasn't going to happen."

"True." Why did it sound like she was grinning on the other end?

If I ever got the chance to punch Count in the face, no consequences, I was going to do it.

I rushed past baggage claim and sputtered to a stop outside the arrivals area, waving down the first free taxi I could see. "What do you want? Either you've got an update on the bank transfer or you've figured out what the price for getting my aunt back is."

"Both, actually. It's fortuitous that you didn't listen to me. Since you're in town, how about we all meet and discuss the . . . new situation."

My phone vibrated. An address on Nassau. I recognized the area. The only piece of major real estate on that corner of the island was an unfinished hotel. How very *them*. "We're excited to see you."

THE BAHAMA-MAR HOTEL had been under construction for years. I remembered driving by as a kid with Mom, peering at the ever-present plastic rimming the windows. From the outside, it looked like a resort, but inside, tarps and scaffolds hung over everything. The smell of paint and cement smothered the air.

A text from Count:

I darted through the halls trying to find it. Without signs, I was fumbling through a labyrinth. But the farther I went, the more put-together the hotel's interior began to be. Carpeting appeared under my checkerboard sneakers. Gray walls faded into color. Finally, I found myself in the fully finished lobby, where a plaque with an arrow pointed me to the Coral Ballroom. I ran to the massive double doors at the end of the hall. Pulling one open, I lunged inside.

Lit with a spotlight in the middle of the ballroom was a figure standing in wait.

Devroe.

Just a few hours ago, I was wrapped in his arms. I'd naïvely let myself fall for him. I'd done the unforgivable: I'd trusted him.

The rose gold bracelet he'd given me was still around my wrist. Did he take pride in that? I unclipped my meteor bracelet, fully prepared to use it.

"You've been playing me this whole time?"

Before I got to him, and before he could say something I probably didn't want to hear, the lights came up just enough to reveal a shadowy sea of onlookers. Their roar of applause made me skid to a stop. The figures watched from a balcony a floor up. Backlit, I could only see their silhouettes. No faces. Just shapes. Until my eyes adjusted. Then they were an audience of evening gowns and tuxedos and sparkling jewels and tasteful haircuts, clapping and whispering amongst themselves like they'd just seen a grand show. I shook with fury.

As my sight adjusted to the darkness, some of the silhouettes became clearer. More than that, familiar.

The man in the pin-striped suit. I'd seen him on the train to Paris. An older woman clapped approvingly, her large brooch recognizable from when I'd run into her in the museum. I turned slowly, spotting another man from the hotel in Cairo. I'd swiped his phone when he was leaving the elevator. Yet another older gentleman, now sipping from a champagne glass, had pretended to read a newspaper in our train car.

The pieces clicked into place around me. Throughout this entire competition, the organizers hadn't just been watching us over cameras. They'd been there, in person. Manipulating it, *us*.

"Congratulations, Mr. Kenzie," a familiar voice said over the applause. Count stepped forward. She wore a glittery red cocktail dress but still held her tablet like a talisman. "You've officially won this year's Gambit. And, Ms. Quest, well, you've made quite the mark. This year was one of our most interesting yet." She looked up to the onlookers. "But now it's time to really wrap things up. You have a wish, Mr. Kenzie, and I think I know what you're going to wish for." Her tablet screen glowed with something I couldn't see.

I groaned. "I don't give a damn about his wish. You can work that out after we talk about my aunt. Where is she?"

Count rolled her eyes, still looking at her tablet and not at me. "Things are more . . . connected than you realize." She turned her tablet around. On it . . . was Mom.

"Mom!" I raced up to the screen, trying to take it from Count, but she jerked it back, keeping it in her grip. All over, everyone watching from above seemed to be using their own screens, phones, and tablets, and I had a feeling they were watching the same feed as me.

Mom swallowed. She was sitting; there were goons standing behind her. I couldn't see their faces, but a shadow and the way she glanced in front of her told me that there were way more than just what I was seeing on-screen too.

Snarling, I looked to Count, who was annoyingly placid

about all of this. "You were supposed to send the money." Why was she still being held captive?

"Oh, we sent the money. All one billion wired to an account registered to another account, and then another that led back to an account in the Bahamas."

Wait . . . the Bahamas?

I knew the Bahamas was a tax haven for lots of people, but the way Count said it . . . What were the odds . . .

Mom started to speak. "Ross, I—" She reached for her screen, like she could touch me.

Count cut in, projecting her voice like this was a stage for her audience. "These aren't the captors who were holding your mother. It's hard to be imaginary people. They're ours."

She was talking, but my brain was frozen on the quick snapshot I'd gotten of Mom's hand. Her fingers, her nails. When I last saw them, they were all perfect and glossy. Now two of them were scuffed and chipped, as I'd expect from someone who'd been held captive in some brig for the last couple of weeks. But the other three nails were perfect, flawless. It was as if . . .

As if she'd been scuffing them herself, and someone interrupted her.

I felt sick. The room started to tilt. My hands were shaking. I didn't want to believe it. I didn't I didn't I didn't. But as soon as I realized it, I knew it was true. As true as I knew it was that she'd set up the whole situation with Noelia all those years ago.

She'd conned me.

"Oh my god . . ." Tears prickled my eyes. Angry tears, devastated tears. "You were never kidnapped."

The room was silent, everyone watching, eating up this reveal as it ate away at me.

Mom's mouth fell open; for once in my life, I genuinely believed she didn't know what to say to me. "You ... weren't supposed to know."

And there it was. If there was any chance of it being not true, of me being wrong, it snapped away right then.

"WHAT IS WRONG WITH YOU?" I was screaming. I was crying. I could feel a piece of my heart rotting away. My voice barely cut through the sobs. I shook my head, over and over. "I almost died! I thought you were gonna die! I hated myself for lying to you, and I hated myself even more for trying to leave—"

I cut myself off with a particularly powerful sob, then wiped my eyes on my sleeve. Oh my god, that was why she did it. She'd probably seen the invite in the black box long before I had, and she used it to put this nightmare together.

"I wasn't trying to hurt you," Mom insisted, putting her hands up. "And I never put you in any danger I knew you couldn't handle. You're fine, aren't you?"

Fine? Was this what she called fine? My sanity, my emotions. Those were both dangerously close to being permanently dented. "You knew before," I said slowly. "That I wanted to leave, that I was going to leave. And because you're unstable, you couldn't have it." I could see it with cruel clarity; it'd been my reality for the last few weeks. How could I ever leave her after I'd been the cause for her almost being murdered, of her being held hostage for weeks? I'd wanted her so desperately every second she was gone. Anything to get my mama back, anything to be with my mama again. I would've stayed with her for years, and if I ever even entertained the notion of leaving, all she'd have to do was mention that one time I tried to leave and got her kidnapped. She'd use that to scare me away from leaving the way she'd reminded me of Noelia's "betrayal" for years. And when that wore off, she'd find a new way to keep me with her.

My hands balled at my sides. "You're evil," I said.

"I was just trying to steer you in the right direction," Mom insisted.

"What about Auntie? You got her kidnapped! Did you know?"

Mom just pursed her lips.

Clearing her throat, Count stepped in, looking eager to drop more bombshells. "The senior Ms. Quest reached out before the start of this year's competition enquiring about what this year's phases would entail. We usually would be tight-lipped about this, but she explained her intentions and assured us if you did enter, you wouldn't have any advance knowledge. So, yes, I informed her of this year's exciting twist in the final phase."

She knew Auntie was on the target list this year.

Count went on. "She proposed an arrangement. In the event of her sister's capture, five hundred million for her return."

Five hundred million . . . out of the one billion she had me transfer for her supposed freedom.

"So not only would you get me stuck to your side for a few more years, but you'd get to walk away with a cool five hundred mil." I let out a chuckle, because it was just so ridiculous. "Who cares about the trauma Auntie would suffer. Hard to believe your crap about wanting to keep your family together when you're getting that much secret money out of it."

Mom looked down. If this woman decided to cry, I was gonna really lose my mind.

"We would've been willing to honor her arrangement had you won the traditional way, like the senior Ms. Quest insisted you would, but things didn't take that turn, and now there are other factors to consider." Count looked over my shoulder, prompting me to turn too. Devroe was still there, watching, glowering. I'd almost forgotten about him in the middle of this chaos. There was too much going on. Too much pain for me to process it all.

Count continued. "As I said, Mr. Kenzie, you have a wish. And if I know Ms. Abara as well as I think, I know what she's expecting her son to wish for."

Abara. I knew that name. Where?

The flash drive. Past Gambits. My mom's Gambit. Abara was one of the competitor's names.

"Your mom played against mine," I said softly. Devroe tugged on the bottom of his vest. So I was right.

I laughed. "I can't believe I bought all that noise about playing for your dad. You were really just here to beat me as salty revenge for your mom's loss?" I didn't want it to sound like it stung, but it did sting. Everything stung. All the teases and kisses and moments, just part of his own long con. I saw it coming, and chose to take a chance anyway.

I wouldn't ever make that mistake again.

Devroe's jaw clenched. "My dad did want to play the Gambit. But when he got too sick to play, Mum went instead. She was so close to winning, and wishing for the organization to do everything in their power to save him." His gaze shifted to Count and the tablet behind him. "And then someone beat her, and stole the wish, even though she knew what Mum was playing for." Devroe stormed forward. There was a deep pain in his eyes. He glared at Mom through the camera. "What did you wish for? What was more important than saving a man's life?"

Mom stared through the screen at him for a long moment.

I wanted to know too. I needed to know that she hadn't always been as vicious as I was just starting to understand.

But even with a question like that in front of her, Mom had the audacity to flick her wrist at Devroe and glance away. Like he was nothing and she really couldn't have cared less.

The pain on Devroe's face was almost unbearable.

"Heartless as always, Rhiannon," Count said, amusement in her voice. "At least you will go out being your truest self." From out of the frame, one of the goons behind Mom raised a gun to her head. She sucked in a quick breath as the barrel hit the side of her head. I would have yelped, but the feel of a barrel pressing against the back of my own head stopped me in my tracks. I froze.

"We've got a man on Jaya Quest in the back room too," Count informed the room. "And we can have a team take care of the rest of them before the end of the day. What would you like, Mr. Kenzie? We can kill Rhiannon Quest, or even destroy the entire family. It's a pity for the industry, but so be it. Just say the words, and it's done."

My breath was coming in quivers. Mom, Auntie, Granny, Papa, even my great-aunt. All of them dead.

And me too. My life could be over in seconds. Even if I tried to fight off whoever was pressing the barrel to my head behind me, there were more of them. I knew that.

It was the perfect revenge.

What was he waiting for?

Devroe had taken a few steps back. The room was paralyzed with delicious tension. Delicious for the people watching from above.

And Devroe was just standing there. He was trembling. But whether it was from anxiety, or anger, or something else, I didn't know. His gaze was on the ground. "My dad, he told me to listen to her."

Always listen to her. I remembered that line from his letter.

"She's probably watching, you know," Count said, egging this on. "Are you going to disappoint your mother?"

"Devroe," I whimpered. And to my surprise, he looked up at me. He was still glowering, and still couldn't quite meet my eye, but it was something. *"Please."*

His glare cracked for just a second. He turned his back to me. "I wish . . . to save my wish for later."

The room erupted in whispers and gasps. "Are you sure?" Count pressed.

"That's my wish."

Count sighed. The barrel pressing into my skull disappeared. I fell to my knees with relief, pressing a hand to my mouth. Looking up at Count's tablet, I caught a glimpse of Mom, eyes closed, letting out her own held breath before Count turned the tablet back to herself. "Let her go for now."

I heard the chime of a call ending. Mom was free. As much as my feelings toward her had decayed, I relaxed knowing she wasn't still in their grip. But Auntie . . .

"My aunt." I stumbled up, my heart rate picking back up to the frantic pace it'd just fallen from. "I need her back. I'll do anything." Whether or not they were still honoring Mom's prior arrangement, or if everything had been blown to hell with all of this drama, I needed to know.

Count read something off her tablet. "Yes, we've decided to

amend our agreement about that. We'll accept the payment for her, but with a caveat—you accept your own year-long contract with us." Count hid a delighted smirk.

A year. A year with Devroe?

I shook my head. "What if . . . Devroe decides to use his wish?" I shuddered, the sensation of the barrel still in my head.

"Then we'll cross that bridge when we get to it. But in the meantime, we'd relish your employment. You've both proven quite impressive . . . and surprising, in your own ways."

Maybe this was for the best. A year with Devroe—perhaps I could keep an eye on him. Someone had to.

"I accept."

"Delightful." Count beamed, and the crowd murmured a pleased consensus, except for some who still seemed miffed that they hadn't gotten to see an entire family wiped off the board in seconds. But I suppose getting to watch me and my new archnemesis be forced to work together for a year, with an atomic bomb hanging between us, would be gossip-worthy entertainment enough.

And for all they knew, Devroe would use that wish, eventually. It wasn't judgment day averted—just put on hold.

Count tapped her tablet. "You both should get ready to leave. Your year together starts now."

Devroe and I locked eyes, and a million unsaid things stretched between us.

A year working with my enemy, trying not to get killed.

Luckily, I had a new rule number one: Trust no one.

ACKNOWLEDGMENTS

OH MY GOD THIS IS A REAL BOOK! AND YOU'RE READING IT??!!!

Three years ago, after one of the most fortuitous dreams of my life, I opened up Google Docs, titled my new project *thieves' gambit?*, and started typing. One mentorship program and too many revisions later, and here we are.

Not gonna lie, I'm pretty awful at acknowledgments. Trying to thank every person who deserves it is like trying to thank every star that lights up the night. I couldn't do it properly in a hundred pages, let alone a couple, but bear with me as I do my best. *Clears throat.*

First off, I need a round of applause for the bestest agent out there: Chelsea Eberly! There have been a lot of dazzling, heart-pounding moments over the course of this book's production, but no moment has yet to surpass the exhilaration I got when I saw that first email from you. The day you offered to rep me is still one of the best days of my life—even if I crashed my car two hours after. (Did I ever tell you about that?)

Thank you to the YA goddess herself, Nic Stone. I was going to shelve this book before you picked me as your 2021 Author Mentor Match mentee. Thank you for seeing the potential first.

Similarly, to everyone at Author Mentor Match—thank you for existing! In an industry that's built on connections and networking, it can be hard for reclusive authors like me—especially authors of color—to get a foot in the door. I genuinely believe *Thieves' Gambit* would be buried at the bottom of my Google Docs right now if not for this program.

To my baller Penguin team! All of you, just . . . wow. Stacey Barney, I don't think it's possible to be more in step with an editor. Are you sure we're not the same person living out a Jekyll-and-Hyde scenario? (Also, sorry I mailed you a potato that one time. It seemed like a good idea at 2:00 a.m.) Caitlin Tutterow, I'm so grateful I got the chance to work with you too! What did I do in my past life to deserve getting to work with not one, but *two* of the sharpest, cleverest editors in the industry?

Thank you to the rest of my abundant Penguin team, to publicists extraordinaire Olivia Russo and Lizzie Goodell, the marketing wizards, Theresa Evangelista for my cover, Suki Boynton for the interior design, my copyeditors Ana Deboo and Cindy Howle, and the numerous people who have put so much into this book who I don't know half as well as I should. Thank you especially for loving this book behind the scenes.

Thank you a kazillion times to the phenomenal Simon and Schuster UK team, including but not limited to Lucy Pearse, Dani

Wilson, Sarah Macmillan, Nina Douglas, and Emma Finnerty. (I just met some of you for the first time a day before writing this, but I've felt your enthusiasm for this project for months!) Also, all my thanks to Charlotte Bodman for introducing my book to the S&S UK team and so many other publishers across the globe. You've made this book even more international than the cast itself.

Shout-out to all the glamorous Hollywood folks on the *Thieves' Gambit* movie team! Thank you to my film/TV agents, Dana Spector and Berni Barta. What a powerhouse team. Never in my life could I have predicted the bidding-war frenzy that the film rights for this book would turn into, but if anyone could drum up that kind of Hollywood magic, it's you two. (I still dream about the French toast at Lumière's; please take me back there when we meet again.)

All my love to my amazing producers and execs at Temple Hill and Hodson Exports, my director Steven Caple Jr., and the executives at Lionsgate, who all seem to love this book even more than I do. (And believe me, I love it A LOT.) I'm looking forward to all the best things in the future.

Since you'll never forgive me if I don't put your name in here too, thank you to my baby brother, Keithen, for all the semi-helpful brainstorming sessions. Every now and then you have a damn good idea. And yes, okay, thanks for sort of, kind of, *maybe* coming up with one of the twists for me. (Eye roll.)

Thank you to my friends, who let me drag them through the ups and downs of this process with me. The ones who indulged me while I rambled about the adventures I wanted to have way back when we were teenagers, and who drop everything to join me on real-life ones these days: Ilyanna, Tanesha,

Kerrigan, Jasmine, Victoria, and Paulina (even if I don't see you enough these days). Ross found her crew, and you guys are mine.

Bianca, I suspect you're more like a final boss than a crew member. But if one of my friends has to become my mortal enemy, I want it to be you. (Don't actually betray me, though—I will destroy you.) Oh, and hi, Faye! Keep an eye on her for me, won't you?

All my love to my library family at Main and North Shreve (Ranee, Pam, Geoffrey, Lynn, Kathy, Regina, Chris, Molly, and Helen). The library was my rock during the strange years between leaving high school and becoming a full-time writer. Some of the best memories of my life are with you guys. A special shout-out to Pam and Geoffrey for listening to me babble about books I was writing for three years straight and never once complaining, and for not tattling on me when I'd drift into the YA section for too long just to stare longingly at the spot where I knew my book would be. I miss you guys the most.

Jessica McCart, I owe you a lot. It's hard to look back on your life and see exactly where the trail of dominoes that led you from one event to the next began, but I believe that you tipped the first one that started me on the path to my life now. I don't know why you picked me—a bushy-eyebrowed sixteen-year-old who called her interviewer the wrong name and had *just* got her license—to work in your library, but in doing so, you set the trajectory of my future. Words you said to me during our last week working together have become the anthem of my life: "Don't ever let being afraid stop you from doing something you really want to do." I remembered those words when I committed to becoming an author, I remembered them when going on submission with this book, I remember them when I get nervous about traveling alone to new places, and I remember them every time I want to write something so ambitious that I'm scared I won't be able to pull it off. I wouldn't be who I am today without you, and this book wouldn't exist without you either.

Finally, and most importantly, thank you, reader. You're the reason books exist. Free time is becoming more and more of a commodity these days, so I thank you for choosing to spend some of yours in my over-the-top, melodramatic thieving world. Hopefully you'll visit again soon.